BERNICE L. McFADDEN

Bernice L. McFadden is the aut...

van, *Nowhere is a Place*, *The* ... *Gathering of Waters* and *Glorious*. She is a three-time Hurston/Wright Legacy Award finalist, as well as the recipient of three awards from the BCALA. McFadden lives between Brooklyn, New York and New Orleans.

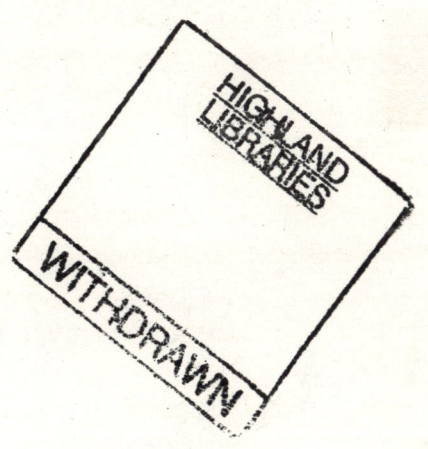

ALSO BY BERNICE L. McFADDEN

Praise Song for the Butterflies
The Book of Harlan
Gathering of Waters
Glorious
Nowhere is a Place
Camilla's Roses
Loving Donovan
This Bitter Earth
The Warmest December

As Geneva Holliday

Groove
Fever
Heat
Seduction
Lover Man

BERNICE L. McFADDEN

Sugar

HIGH LIFE **HIGHLAND**	
3800 21 0014117 7	
Askews & Holts	24-Nov-2021
AF	£8.99

VINTAGE

3 5 7 9 10 8 6 4

Vintage Classics is part of the Penguin Random House
group of companies whose addresses can be found at
global.penguinrandomhouse.com

Penguin
Random House
UK

First published in the US by Pulme in 2000
First published in Great Britain by Vintage Classics in 2021

penguin.co.uk/vintage-classics

A CIP catalogue record for this book is available from the
British Library

ISBN 9781784877316

Typeset in 12/14.75 pt Bembo
by Integra Software Services Pvt. Ltd, Pondicherry

Printed and bound in Great Britain by Clays Ltd, Elcograf S.p.A.

The authorised representative in the EEA is Penguin Random House
Ireland, Morrison Chambers, 32 Nassau Street, Dublin D02 YH68.

Penguin Random House is committed to a sustainable future for our
business, our readers and our planet. This book is made from Forest
Stewardship Council® certified paper.

For Mommy & Daddy

Acknowledgments

I ask God for so many things on a daily basis, I must acknowledge him first and foremost, because if not for him where would I be?

Thank you, God, for supplying me with the strength, wisdom and creativity to begin, continue and complete this book.

My mother and father, Robert and Vivian McFadden, for coming together and giving me life and love. My daughter, R'yane Azsa Waterton, my greatest, most beautiful work of art. My grandparents, those living and those who watch over me from the great beyond: Thelma and Wilfred Nettles, Gwendolyn and Harold McFadden. My siblings, Reggie, Misty and Kris. My niece, Shania Simon, nephew, Myles McFadden, and sister-in-law, Maritza Barzey-McFadden.

My Sister-Friends & Soul Brothers, for their consistent encouragement, love and support, Robyn Roundtree, Quovardis Banks-Lawrence, Pascale Villate-Jacques, Cicely Peace-Edouard, Wanda Toney, Charlette CeCe Jimbes,

Elizabeth Warren, Sonia Rillera, Lionel Crichlow, Dean Henry and J. R. McNeil.

My creative writing teacher, Professor Margaret Lamb of Fordham University, for teaching me the art of story-telling and encouraging me to push forward.

My agent, James Vines, for recognizing my talent and sharing my vision. My editor, Laurie Chittenden, who also shared my vision and worked tirelessly on this project to make it a dream come true. Anita Diggs of Warner Books, for recognizing the possibilities and guiding me to the rainbow.

To family and friends, who are special to me and let me know that they care and are concerned about my well being, Dolly Green, Diana Crichlow, Anita Miles, Kathleen and Laura Taylor, James Griffin, Cheryl Bernard, Margaret Bernard, Fay Nurse, Bentley "Rooney" Green, Carlo Law-rence, Laura Smiley, Anthony Lloyd, Stephanie Pearson, Lisa Ford, Sheridan Abraham, Estela Olivier, Eustace Thomas, Errol Ellis, Ian Chandler, Piercson Fenty, Wayne Alleyne, Richard Small—where are u now?—and Tonya Bodison.

To the women writers who paved the way, Nella Larson, Zora Neale Hurston, Maya Angelou, Toni Morrison and Alice Walker. A special Thanks to J. California Cooper, who took the time to verbally respond! *Thank you.*

Aretha Franklin and Nina Simone, thank you for pro-viding my background music.

The ones who made my life extraordinary and remain with me in spirit, Rebecca Hopkins, Ruby Nelson, Virginia Cummings, Richard May, Rose Tyler, Peggy Ann Williams, Menyon "Minnie" Nettles.

And finally a special thanks to the new people in my life who added additional support and encouragement through the final part of this particular journey, Dawn Nedd, Sophia Black, Donna Trotman, Jackie Quidort, Marsha Cox, Marie Rosemond and Elton Andrews.

God Bless Us All.

"There's a little bit of hooker in every woman. A little bit of hooker and a little bit of God."

—Sarah Miles

BEFORE

Spring 1940

Jude was dead.

On a day when the air held a promise of summer and people laughed aloud, putting aside for a brief moment their condition, color and where they ranked among humanity, Jude, dangling on the end of childhood and reaching out toward womanhood, should have been giggling with others her age among the sassafras or dipping her bare feet in Hodges Lake and shivering against the winter chill it still clutched. Instead she was dead.

She'd been taken down by the sharp blade of jealousy, and her womanhood—so soft, pink and virginal—was sliced from her and laid to rest on the side of the road near her body. Her pigtails, thick dark ropes of hair, lay splayed out above her head, mixed in with the pine needles and road dust. Her dress, white and yellow, her favorite colors, was pulled up to her neck, revealing the small bosom that had developed over the winter.

The murder had *white man* written all over it. (That was only a half truth.) But no one would say it above a whisper. It was 1940. It was Bigelow, Arkansas. It was a black child. Need any more be said?

No one cared except the people who carried the same skin color. No one cared except the parents who had nursed her, stayed up all night soothing and rocking her when she was colicky. Applauded her when she took her first steps and cried when the babbling, gurgling sounds that came from her sweet mouth finally formed the words Mamma and then later, Papa.

They cared. The parents of sweet, sweet Jude, who would never hurt a fly, no less a human being. Look at what they did to her!

Word first came via the Edelson boy. He'd run all the way and was breathless when he arrived. Black John, the blacksmith, had found her about a mile down the road and covered her body with a Crocker sack while he put himself in the right frame of mind to start coming. He had to pop the boy upside the head, twice, this just to get him moving instead of gawking.

Black John remained behind, gathering the broken child into his arms and placing her gently in his wagon among the bags and crates of field provisions. He stood looking at the beaten body of this almost woman. In life, she was a tall child, strapping, like her father, but in death, she seemed so small. Perhaps it was because of her broken bones and the way her skin sank in the places between the breaks that made her look so tiny and uneven.

He shook his head in pity and looked up into the heavens for an answer. An arrow of blackbirds blinded the sun and then moved on. If that was clarification of why and what lay ahead, Black John never said, but he would think back on this day again in fifteen years' time.

His wife had helped birth this child, as she had most of the Bigelow children. She would take it hard, like she'd lost one of her own. He looked back at the child again and a heavy sigh escaped him. "No rest for the weary," he muttered and then couldn't think of why that would come to mind at all.

He was procrastinating. Standing there behind his wagon of potatoes, turnips, cabbage, yam and Jude, he was stretching the space between his arrival and the scene that would follow. Crying eyes and screaming mouths. He'd seen plenty of grief in his life. But grief let loose from a woman who lost a child—that was the worst type of grief of all. If you could, you'd try to avoid that sort. Because grief that comes from loss of child just took a piece of you away each time you met up with it.

And if you found yourself among it too often for too long, you'd certainly die way before your time.

No, Black John was in no hurry to go.

The sun sat watching curiously on its perch, delaying its descent into late afternoon. It was long past three and Black John's shadow stood stout before him, watching and waiting. He removed his straw hat, the one that belonged to his daddy before him. The one that he inherited when his uncle handed it to him with a quiet word. Black John could never remember the exact word that was spoken, but it left an emptiness in him. The strawberry-colored stain stiffening the center part of the hat's hump confused him more than scared him because his daddy hated strawberries.

Black John fingered the stain and looked back at the dead child, her dress blotched with her own strawberry stains. "Well," he muttered in resignation, as he pulled his handkerchief from his pocket and wiped the sweat from his brow and the back of his neck.

He moved to the cab of the truck and removed a second empty Crocker sack from the floor. Returning to Jude he looked her over once again and shook his head in pity and then tucked the Crocker sacks around her body and went to the left of the wagon. That's when he saw it. Glistening in the sun. His shadow stepped forward and shaded the glare. Black John knew immediately what it was, although he had never seen one without a woman's support, protection and guidance behind it; something like that, once seen, always known. He leaned down and with the sweat-soiled handkerchief retrieved Jude's womanhood. He would later recount (and he often did) how it quivered in the palm of his hand.

His mule closed the distance in a slow saunter that barely disturbed the road dust. Black John looked over and his shadow looked back at him. Ahead he could see the small pond of black faces, eyes big with wanting to know, eyes big with wanting to see. Black John rode right into the middle and when he stepped down from his wagon he was six years old again, his father's straw hat, with the strawberry stain stiff and dry on its hump, in his hands. He pushed through the worn and patched sea of skirts, fought through the tree-long legs of men and bit down hard on a hand that tried to cover his too-young-for-death eyes. When he made it to the clearing there was his father. Beaten so hard and for so long that his skin had bubbled up purple. The top of his head was open and there he saw precious memories and somehow-someday dreams wrapped in I Love You colors spilled out for all of Bigelow to see. Then came the wail and Black John lost a little bit of his time on earth.

That's what scared him now. The silence. The absence of that mournful homage that broke your heart, stole time from Black John and pushed the most pious to question God.

Pearl's mouth hung open, but no sound came. Her heart had broken into tiny pieces that rose up, plugging her throat, allowing only breath to pass.

She tried again when Black John laid Jude's battered body to rest at her feet, the beaten, brutalized, eyeless body of her baby girl; but all she could do was claw at her own eyes and scratch at her throat, drawing blood instead of sound.

Pearl was fighting. Fighting with the reality that there would be no more candy sweet kisses and hugs that could magically erase a problem, worry or fear. In the halls of their home, who would skip, dance and sing so loud that the dogwoods raised their branches in delight?

Who would call her "Mamma honey baby" in that teasing, innocent voice that only Jude possessed?

And there would no longer be a reason for her to answer: "Jude baby doll."

These thoughts ran through her mind until her head ached with grief. Searing hot tears fell heavy from her eyes and landed on her bosom, soaking through the black cotton dress and white brassiere, stinging her skin and scorching her heart. The pain. The pain!

Later, she turned her face toward the heavens, unable to bear the sight of the sorrow-faced men as they covered her baby's coffin with brandy brown dirt. She had prepared herself to be taken from the earth at the very moment she heard the muffled sound of the first shovelful hit the top of the small wooden box. She had asked the Lord to release her from this life and allow her to walk beside her sweet Jude as she entered the Kingdom of Heaven.

But with each shovelful of earth, the sound that marked where Jude lay, quieted, and with the last sprinkling Pearl swayed suddenly and was aware of being lifted from the ground. She smiled, believing the Lord had answered her prayers. She quickly opened her eyes to take in, for what she thought to be the last time, the faces of her husband and two sons.

And they were there, faces pinched with concern and grief, as they hoisted her up and carried her limp body away from the graveside.

She lay in bed for nearly thirty days, taking in very little food or water. Calling for Jude and crying when her call was not answered and still, as she wallowed in grief and anguish, the sorrowful wail that was reserved for mothers who've lost their only daughters, remained locked in her throat.

Pearl eventually returned to her life. Now absent of Jude. People stopped talking about it and allowed the matter to slip into the space in their minds reserved for horrors like those. She attempted to do the same, putting her pain not behind her, but beside her, where her sweet

Jude should have been, and prayed not for redemption, but for salvation.

No, the Lord would not answer her prayers on that day. Not as she had wished. She did not die. Not physically. Her soul and spirit had departed our world the moment she touched the cold, bruised brow of her child. But God would keep her walking and breathing for quite a few more years to come. He had work for her to do.

Spring 1955

Chapter One

Twenty-five days of freezing rain and thirty days of below-zero temperatures found most of the population of Bigelow bedded down with fevers and pneumonia. Five babies died that year. Their bodies were stored in the basement of the small church until the ground thawed enough to bury them. Plenty of tears fell that winter.

The people swore blind it was the beginning of the end, and those who hadn't seen the inside of a church for more than twenty years flocked in bright and early every Sunday.

Minnie Grayson warned the people of Bigelow, told them her head had itched something awful the previous summer. An itching head always meant death, destruction or devastation.

Her words came to pass when Bigelow lost the five small infants. The deaths of the "Bigelow Five," as they would be known, more than convinced the people to heed her words.

"Somethin' comin', time to save your souls 'for it's too late." People paid attention and grabbed worn (or brand-new) Bibles and asked the Lord for his mercy and forgiveness.

Come April the temperature soared. It felt like August in an oven. The lake dried up. Women refused to sleep with their men. Dogs ceased barking. The tulips that encircled the statue erected to the founder of Bigelow bloomed and died all in one day.

Everybody complained that it was hotter than hell. But only one could say for sure and he was miles away. His reason for coming back to Bigelow was only just arriving.

Minnie Grayson started scratching again, and warned everyone she came across that "God's vengeance against their town wasn't near to being done."

Clair Bell sat on her porch, feet stuck in a tub of soothing hot water, soaking her bunions. This sealed what Minnie predicted. Clair Bell only suffered with her feet when something was near to going wrong, which usually meant a storm, drought or disease. Bigelow held its breath and waited.

They watched the sky for black billowing clouds. Licked the tips of their fingers and tested the air for a shift of wind. Waited for the first flash of light and thunderous bass.

They boiled roots and leaves and drank tall simmering glasses of murky, stinking liquids to cleanse their bodies and protect them from any maladies that could bed them and in time, kill them.

They cured meat, canned fruit and pickled pork, packing their sheds full, anticipating crops lost and animal deaths.

They waited.

A storm blew in. It wasn't what they expected, but some would say later that it was just as deadly as any twister or hurricane they had ever experienced.

The storm walked into their small town on two legs in spiked, red patent leather heels. She waltzed right through the main square, blond wig bouncing to the rhythm of her walk, a leopard print pocketbook slung over one shoulder, matching suitcases in each hand. Her eyes were covered with cat's-eye-shaped, white-rimmed glasses, mirrors to her soul, unavailable for view. A Lucky Strike hung from her red-painted lips.

She was tall, taller than any man in that town, except for Joe Taylor. Tall and black as the day was long. She walked with a confidence most people in Bigelow had never known. She swaggered along like a cat in heat, leaving swirling curtains of dust in her wake.

People named her right there and then. Named her without an introduction, without two words ever passing between them. Called her things they had only whispered under their breath, or in their bedrooms when the doors were closed tight and passion drove them into saying it. Words no self-respecting, God-fearing man or woman would ever use in public. But now they publicly stated it, because they had a right and reason to.

Slut. Whore. Bitch.

She made her way down the main road past the white-washed homes with their large wrap-around porches and picket fences. Past magnolia gardens and sweeping peach trees where young boys hung precariously from knotted limbs, watching her with large dark eyes.

She walked with purpose past the general store where the white man called Abraham gave out credit and charged a 2 percent interest if you didn't settle your bill with him by the first Friday of every month.

She came down Pleasant Way, where Anna Lee (said to be the illegitimate offspring of the general store owner) swept at the dirt that always seemed to need sweeping when word came that something interesting was happening outside the perimeters of her home. Anna Lee watched the woman with an even eye and stopped her lazy sweeping, not to tilt her head in greeting but to concentrate on the vision before her. When their eyes met, Anna Lee's did not smile or blink with shame; they stretched wide and shouted: Unacceptable! Unwanted! Get out!

Sugar turned the corner that held Bigelow's only schoolhouse. It was small, white and unassuming.

She stopped short, dead in front of Fayline's House of Beauty, and peeked in at the women whose hair was in the process of being washed, dyed, teased, conked or pressed into the latest styles from New York, Detroit and Washington, D.C.

No one said hello, welcome or even invited her in for a Coke. No, they just sat, openly watching her, their arms folded defiantly across their breasts, hands resting in resistance on their hips, as she examined the chipped blue paint on the dusty store front glass that separated them from her. The paint that used to be a brilliant blue and would have in the past screamed FAYLINE'S HOUSE OF BEAUTY, but years of winter wind and summer sun had faded the letters so that they barely whispered to you what and whose establishment you stood in front of.

She moved on, aware of the pandemonium that was brewing around her.

Sugar walked slowly down a narrow dirt road, sycamores on either side giving an eerie shaded feel to the walkway. The homes that lined the street were identical in every way except color. Small, neat, board-and-shingle houses, painted white, light gray or a watery sort of blue. Two floors, two windows to each of the five rooms. Fenced-in yards that held sleeping dogs or guileful cats and mulberry bushes that sat beneath open windows shading blooming azaleas.

A sign, rusted and bent nearly in half by a passing twister or unruly adolescent, swung around and around on the lone post, stopping briefly as the breeze that guided its frantic spin lulled.

GROVE STREET.

Sugar stopped, set her bags down and pulled a damp, folded piece of brown paper from her bosom. The address, written in black ink, was now smudged, causing the 10 and Grove Street that were written there to blend into each other, becoming nearly indecipherable.

She looked from the paper to the sign post and back to the paper. Satisfied she was in the right place, she retrieved her suitcases and walked toward her new home and new life.

Behind her the people of Bigelow buzzed like flies around shit. The heat forgotten, all thoughts were on the woman that had just strutted her way right through the main square in front of their children, and more important, in front of their men.

They hated her immediately, not knowing of her childhood or the life that, after only one day of living it, would have had them calling out to the Lord for help.

They hated her and did not know that she had never loved in *that* way. *That* way—when a man and woman come together and the cost involved is one that no bank could ever lend out, no national mint could ever print, reprint or discontinue.

They hated her because it was clear that she had been one of them at some point, but had left before she would mature into a woman that tied her hair up in worn cloth at sunset and pushed her sleeves up around her elbows to begin an evening of toil after having toiled all day for the Man. Baking bread and churning sweet butter, growing butter beans and collard greens in the yard behind the small house that would (during her entire life time) belong to the bank even though she had a thirty-year mortgage that should have been paid off five years ago, but somehow the bank keeps telling her about interest that was miscalculated back in '46. And so now she owes for a few more years, but they can't say how many for sure, and she won't demand an exact count, because she's colored and they're not and this is the South, 1955.

At night she would kiss her children (never less than four offspring) good-night. If she was lucky and owned a radio, she could sit on her porch or in the tiny living room and listen to a radio show and chuckle at the humor, because a day of picking cotton, chopping wood or canning fish leaves you with little strength to out-and-out laugh. You save your laughter for real good time evenings, when the boss man is an extra day away. Blessings may shower her and that hot talent Ella Fitzgerald may come across singing "A-Tisket A-Tasket" and get her foot to tapping and maybe even humming along, but not too hard because she's darning a holey sock as she listens to this song about the basket, or hemming hand-me-down pants, and working with a needle by candlelight can be tedious. She's got drawers soaking in a bucket behind the house that have to be scrubbed and hung to dry in the night air, but her husband has bathed tonight and splashed a little of that drug store aftershave on his cheeks; that means he wants to do more than just lay beside her, he wants to lay up on her and inside her. So she leaves the drawers to soak for another hour or so, while she does her duty as Mrs and pleases her man, because she can function on three hours of sleep. Keeping her man well fed and fucked are number one priorities that she can't slack on because you can never know when a woman dressed to the nines with a blond wig, long legs and a high fat ass that should have been equal to you in almost every way may decide to hop on the first southbound Greyhound and end up looking at you through whispering letters on a dusty storefront window.

Chapter Two

The phone blared out and startled Pearl, causing her heart to skip a beat. She still had not grown used to the sound of it. The black speaking and hearing contraption that she had waited patiently nearly two years for while Ma Bell decided whether it was cost effective to put up telephone lines in a town full of coloreds with low-paying jobs was ringing for the first time all day. Pearl had picked up the phone at least twice that day and listened to the clicking sounds that traveled through the long snake-like cord that exited the bottom and disappeared into her wall. And now after watching it and tip-toeing around waiting for it to ring, it does just that and startles her breathless.

"Lord have mercy." Pearl jumped at the shrill sound of the phone and then moved quickly into the living room where the phone sat on its own table for easy viewing. Pearl was short and stout and her walk was more like a waddle than a stride. Her arms were thick and visibly strong from years of lifting heavy household objects and pushing a scrub brush back and forth over countless wooden and tiled floors. She was sixty, but her face was still very youthful. Her husband called her Bit, a nickname that carried over from the days when Pearl was short and petite. Pearl is still short, but *petite* is a word and a proportion long forgotten.

"Hello?" Pearl answered the phone in a labored voice.

"I think she here! She ain't too long passed my house … girl, she is a sight!" Shirley Brown was rattling a mile a minute. "She coming in your direction."

"Shirley, who you talking about—"

"The one the Reverend told you about. The one you suppose to welcome and all. She a sight. If that's her she a sight, Pearl!"

Pearl listened to Shirley ramble on excitedly as she vaguely recalled the conversation she'd had with Reverend Foster just two weeks ago.

"Pearl, you have been a faithful member of this congregation for years." Reverend Foster moved in close to her as they stood in front of Bigelow's First Baptist Church. He lowered his voice so that the congregation that was leaving Sunday service would not hear what he was relaying to Sister Pearl. He took her lightly by the elbow and guided her away from the crowd.

"Don't tell no one, but you are one of my favorite followers." He smiled at her and Pearl lowered her eyes away from his handsome face and soft eyes. He smelled like the air after a good rain. Him being so close to her made her feel light-headed.

"I hear we gonna have a new resident in our small town. A woman coming in from over in Short Junction, taking over the house next door to you."

"Hmmm," Pearl said and nodded her head.

"So I figure since you are such a dedicated member, and my favorite, you would be the perfect person to welcome her to our little community and eventually bring her into the fold."

Pearl looked up from his shiny shoes, which seemed a little too fine for a Reverend in a town made up of sharecroppers and factory workers. But she pushed the thought away and tried to concentrate on his words.

"Would you do that for Reverend Foster, Sister Pearl?" His voice was pleading.

"Of course, Reverend. When we expecting Mrs ... Mrs?"

"Oh, it's Mizz Lacey, a niece, I believe, of some people over in Short Junction," Reverend Foster said, lowering his voice another notch and looking over his shoulder as he did. "We expecting her any day, I suppose, Sister Pearl."

"All right then, Reverend, I'll be looking out for her then." Pearl smiled and walked slowly toward her husband who was patiently waiting.

Now Pearl watched from her window as the woman walked up to and stopped right out in front of her house. "She's here," is all Pearl managed to say before she placed the phone back in its cradle, cutting off Shirley's rambling.

Was this the woman the Reverend spoke of? The woman Pearl had been asked to guide and help and eventually lead into the flock? Was this her? This woman didn't look as if she'd ever spent a second in a house of worship, much less knew what one was. But there was something else too. A slither of something familiar that Pearl was yet to put her finger on.

Pearl stood there in the shadows, half of her body in the living room, half in the hall. The woman leaned back on one leg, dropped her cigarette to the ground and smiled a knowing smile. Pearl held her breath. Did the woman see her spying?

A crack of a bat and the roar of the crowd from the second hand radio sent Pearl scurrying into the kitchen like a frightened mouse.

The stranger laughed a low bitter sort of a laugh and walked the less than fifteen feet to #10 Grove Street. She walked slowly up the front steps, stooped and retrieved the key from beneath a worn mat that said: GOD BLESS THIS HOME.

Pearl held her breath as the woman unlocked the door and disappeared into the house, allowing the screen door to slam loudly behind her.

Afternoon moved to evening and the sun set slowly over Bigelow, leaving purple-orange streaks across the Arkansas sky. Pearl had settled herself at the kitchen table, taking up a silent vigil by the open window, hoping to catch sight of the woman in #10 with the familiar face.

"Bit? What you doing, daydreaming again, girl?" Joe, Pearl's husband, stood in the kitchen entrance. He was a towering man of sixty-two. Amazingly, the gray had just started to creep into the blackness of his temples. "I been calling you for dang near ten minutes, ain't you hear me call you, Bit?" Pearl met his questioning eyes. She'd been sitting there at the kitchen table, attempting to separate the peas from their pods, her attention totally consumed with the woman inside #10 Grove Street.

"Bit?" Joe was still waiting for an answer from his wife. Instead what he got was a dubious look topped with guilt.

"Aw, baby, I just been in here popping these peas," Pearl said timidly. They both looked down at the two lone pods that lay on the wooden table. "Well, I guess I was sorta daydreaming too," Pearl added shyly.

Joe's gaze moved from the pods to the open window that looked directly onto the closed living room window of #10 Grove Street. He knew from pure instinct (and from being with the same woman for more than 30 years) that she wasn't telling the whole truth.

"Oh really?" was all he said, and turned to move back into the living room. Pearl immediately felt bad. She was caught and too silly to admit it. She walked into the living room and realized that the light that stretched along the wooden floor for most of the day had disappeared. The heat had subsided enough for Joe to have turned off the fan. A cool breeze came in on the tail of the blanketing dusk.

"Joe, how's 'bout we go on down to the Rib Shack. It's Saturday, don't feel much like cooking. 'Sides, the heat done drained me dry."

Joe just smiled.

"C'mon, baby, what you say?" Pearl pushed. Joe got up from the couch and walked over to his wife, lightly tweaked her nose and shook his finger. "Let me get my shirt," was his reply.

Joe was a simple man, enjoying simple pleasures. A hearty card game with his friends, evening meeting with his

Mason brothers or fishing alone on the edge of Hodges Lake. These are the things that pleased him and brought him quiet joy.

God-fearing and soft-spoken, all that mattered to Joe was his wife, family and leading a life worthy of entering Heaven. Nobody could ever accuse this man of raising his hand or his voice in anger. He understood things about life and women that other men just couldn't.

Joe was a tall man standing nearly six feet, three inches, with skin the color of amber. He had a strong presence about him, the kind that made people move two inches more than necessary out of his path. People felt most comfortable addressing him with a slightly bowed head, avoiding the eyes that seemed to see straight through to your soul.

Pearl had gazed into those very same eyes long ago and fell in love. She knew the first time he took her small hands into his own that this would be the man she would give herself over to until death parted them.

They met after the war. That's when Bigelow came alive again. Men returned home to their wives and sons returned to their mothers. The cannery, a main source of employment before the war, reopened. Word of this traveled far south and people that once held jobs there received it like a cool breeze to a heated brow. Men and women dropped their gunny sacks filled with cotton, oranges or watermelon, and stood tall for the first time in years. The sound of machetes cutting through the air could be heard for miles as they were flung high above the tobacco and wheat fields. And like an Old Testament exodus, hundreds of people left Jackson, Clearwater, Salem and Charleston on foot, by cart and donkey and if possible by train headed for Ashton. Headed for home.

Joe Taylor was one of those who came home; a soldier boy who'd fought alongside white men who wouldn't share the same toilet with him or drink from the same well back home, but in the end, before the last breath left their dying bodies, did not hesitate for one moment to turn pleading eyes on him.

And so Joe put aside his memories of an uncle, naked, beaten, burnt and lynched, left to die hanging from a branch of a pecan tree. He shook the vision of his mother slapped so hard by a white woman that she permanently lost the sight in her right eye. He erased from his mind the words: "coon," "monkey" and "nigger"—words a soldier had used hundreds of times during his lifetime and just moments earlier on Joe before the shell ripped through his body.

Now this white soldier lay clinging to the last threads of life, his insides scattered around him, war sounds echoing in his ears and turns to Joe. "Please," he utters, because he's scared of death and does not want to die alone among bombs and bullets. It no longer matters to the soldier that Joe is Negro or colored. All that matters is that he is there.

Joe has read the Bible and the Good Book says: Forgive and forget and love thy neighbor. With these words in mind, Joe lays his gun down and takes the dying man in his arms. Carefully, tenderly like a fragile newborn he rocks and shushes the man as the soldier whimpers at the sight of his blood running from his open wounds and seeping into the earth. Joe lulls the man into the afterlife, places his head gently on the ground, closes the lids over his empty eyes, retrieves his gun and continues to fight for a freedom he would never be fully entitled to.

It was back in the evenings, when Pearl made her way home from washing, ironing and cleaning all that wasn't hers and would never be hers, she'd stop and stand for hours as close to the men as possible to listen in on their talk.

They gathered in small bunches outside the Rib Shack, spitting distance from the hat shop where Pearl stood, pretending to admire the hats in the window, while eavesdropping on their conversation.

Pearl had listened to Bigelow's young men tell their stories of war and love. She smiled as they imitated the *oui ouis* and *Bonjours* of the pale thin-lipped French women who would do what the colored women wouldn't.

She listened, while her stomach twisted and turned as Mickey Johnson described how they sawed off his ravaged leg while he watched, a block of wood clenched between his teeth.

Izzy Cox told of a man who fought for two days, his intestines hanging from his stomach like snakes. "How the hell did that boy fight like that, Izzy?" a doubtful voice from the crowd asked.

"That nigga put his guts in a bowl, took the nylons he was gonna bring back home to his woman, and bound it tight around his waist." No one said a word. "That boy had some Indian in 'im," Izzy added, and used his finger to make a swirling motion near his temple. The crowd of men nodded knowingly. A man was bound to do anything once he had some Indian in him. Everybody knew Indians were crazy.

After that story, Pearl didn't go around them for a few days. She couldn't get the picture out of her mind and had a hard time eating out of a bowl.

It was during one of those late afternoons that she first heard Joe Taylor speak. She'd seen him standing tall. Always quiet, maybe brooding. She did not know.

He spoke with a voice so low and deep, it reminded Pearl of rolling thunder before a late summer storm. His voice, like the thunder, caught you off guard, and before you knew it lightning bolts were dancing among the clouds and painting the blackened sky with streaks of bluish gold. That's how Pearl remembered it. His voice shook her and she unfixed her gaze on a wide-brimmed black hat with white imitation ostrich feathers. She tilted her head slightly to the side and snatched a quick look at the man that caused her soul to quake.

"Yup, that sure was some pretty countryside. Rolling hills and all. When I was there it reminded me a little of right here. I had a mind to just keep on going after it was all done," he said while studying the palm of his massive hand.

"Black men ain't never been nothing but chattel to these here white folks. Always been that way, always will be that way." The men fell quiet around him, lost in the thoughts brought about by Joe's statement.

Joe continued, "I can't say that I was proud to fight for my country, not say it and be truthful 'bout it. But I can say I felt proud when I looked around and saw the white men fall, bleed and die just like the colored."

One of the men, Benny Parks, who'd lost an eye in the war, cocked his head sideways so he could take all of

Joe in with that one good eye, and asked in total bewilderment, "Now why would that make you feel proud, Joe? How death gonna make you feel proud?" The rest of the men kind of leaned in closer in anticipation of his answer.

Joe started off in the slow easy manner he was accustomed to. "I felt proud because there was the proof right there on the battlefield that we was men just like them. Not monkeys or some ornery creature that hid its tail in its pants. But men that bled the same red blood." The men milled Joe's words around in their minds for a bit, digesting each syllable and allowing it to restructure itself within them. Each of these men would repeat these words in separate company, claiming them for their own.

"I guess that is something to be proud of, Joe. Yup, hadn't thought of it that way," Benny Parks said.

Their stories propelled her to approach the group. She knew most of the men. "How ya'll doing this afternoon? Benny. Charlie. Gibson." She called off the names she knew and nodded a greeting to those she didn't. When she got to Joe, she nodded and fixed her eyes on his for what seemed like an eternity. Gibson spoke first. He was a scrawny man, smallest one of the group. Only action he caught during the war was the hard sole of a soldier's boot making contact with his jaw as he bent to remove a slop bucket full of shit and piss.

"Why, Miss Pearl, 'bout time you stopped staring at them hats and come over and say hello. How's your mamma and daddy doing?" Gibson asked, taking in Pearl's Coca-Cola bottle figure.

"Oh they just fine," Pearl said, glancing back at Joe. A wry, knowing smile briefly surfaced on Gibson's lips.

"Pearl, you remember Joe Taylor, don't you? This Mike and Cora Taylor's boy from down round Hancock way … near Jessie's farm." Gibson turned to Joe and continued, "This here is Henry and Belle Mason's girl."

Joe squinted at Pearl. "Yup, sure do remember you. Your daddy drive for the McHenrys, don't he?" He continued, answering his own question, "Yup, I seen him in that shiny fancy car, carting them look-alike girls through here to wherever." His attention turned back to the palm of his hand. Just as Pearl was about to agree with him, Joe looked up to meet her gaze. "Yup, you the one usta come to church with all them pretty dresses on. I sure did think you all was rich. You and them fine dresses."

Pearl gushed with sweet embarrassment. "Oh, yeah. I mean, naw we ain't rich. But you remember that?" She sure didn't remember him.

"Yup, I remember when we was leaving, me and my family, going down to Florida, you know, for work and all. I remember you was standing down underneath that old maple tree that usta be near Boones Ridge. Whatever happened to the tree? Anyway, we was on our way out, and you was standing there trying to keep from getting wet, the rain was just starting to fall. Pink bows. Pink shoes. You sure was small. My mamma saw you, pointed you out to the rest of us. I remember she called to Papa, told him to look at that pretty little bit of a girl dressed in pink under that maple tree."

Soft chuckles floated up from the group of men like small butterflies. Joe just said whatever came to mind, didn't care who heard it or their thoughts or opinions on it.

"Uh-huh, I remember that day like it was yesterday." Finished, he turned back to examining his palm. Pearl was speechless for a minute or two. She could not even recall that day. She couldn't have been more than four or five years old. She could feel red warmth climb from her bosom up to her neck and then spread across her face. "Well," she said in a voice that sounded a bit too high. "I best be going. It was nice talking with ya'll," she said as she hastened to depart the company of the man that seemed to say all the right things.

"I believe you best be going." Joe agreed and looked up into the darkening sky. "Sun is dipping pretty low. I think it best if 'n I escort you home."

He didn't ask, he just said it and there was no trying to talk him out of it. And Pearl didn't want to. He moved to her side and fell into step.

That was the first of many walks home. Joe claimed her. Claimed her petite build and brown skin. Full bosom and long lashes. The crease behind her knees and the scar under her chin. They all belonged to him. He didn't have to say it aloud. Everyone knew she was his and respected it.

He came to her one day with a bouquet of wildflowers, and handed it to her on their fourth walk home. He told her it was time for him to meet her parents and explain his intentions.

Joe took a job with the railroad to supplement the money he was making at the cannery. He wanted to marry Pearl and place her in their own home as soon as possible. The extra money would enable him to do just that.

He got down on his knees, right in front of Henry and Belle Mason, and asked for Pearl's hand in marriage. He pulled a pink silk ribbon from his pocket with a tiny gold band with a wisp of a diamond tied to the end. Belle

Mason broke into tears and Henry Mason nodded his approval and with a big grin and wet eyes, he slapped Joe hard on the back.

They were married in the one-hundred-year-old Baptist church and celebrated steps away in the area where the old maple once stood that shielded Pearl from the rain and allowed Joe Taylor the first look at his future.

Chapter Three

Sugar sat still in the darkness of her living room and looked through the window at the approaching dawn. She hadn't been able to sleep a whole night since she arrived in Bigelow, and for the past eight mornings she had sat smoking and watching the sun slip up and over the horizon and settle itself snugly into the sheltering sky. She would remain there long after noon, her mind wandering through a jungle of memories until sleep finally took her.

She shifted and lit another cigarette. The smoke danced in the thin stream of light that filtered through the window and Sugar felt self-pity slip into her soul as she reminisced on her life so far.

It seemed to her that getting ahead was something reserved for people that already had their feet placed one in front of the other. Sugar, well, she guessed she was just born with both feet turned backward, 'cause every step she took placed her one step closer to where she'd been instead of where she was trying to get.

Her mother gave her up before the cord had stiffened and fallen off.

She was born just thirty miles down the road, in Short Junction. A town not unlike Bigelow; tract houses, and a general store that carried everything you wanted and some things you didn't. A bank that was barely open twice a week since colored folk deposited their money in jars, buried it in their yards or stuffed it in their mattresses. They hid their money in a shoe or hat box and placed it on the top shelf of their closets, behind the box that held the family mementos. Most often, though, they placed it between the pages of their Bibles, believing God would watch over it. No, wasn't much need for a bank in Short Junction, but it was there anyway.

There was a church that doubled as a school during the week. Sugar never went there to learn or pray. But it was there just the same.

People in Short Junction grew their own vegetables and slaughtered their own hogs and chickens. They washed their clothes by hand in large tin tubs, scrubbing them clean with lye soap that ate at your skin long after your hands were through using it. People hung their clothes out on ropes that ran from their houses to the buckeye trees that could be found in everyone's backyards. The noonday sun bleached their whites and nurtured the spinach, tomato and potatoes that grew in their gardens.

Short Junction's residents traveled ten, fifteen and sometimes twenty miles a day to work. They worked in nearby Sunflower, Beacon and Jamison counties, cleaning white folks' homes and raising their kids. And at night they'd travel back to Short Junction to clean their own homes and raise their own children.

On Sundays, there was church service and a lot of whooping and hollering in the name of Jesus Christ and after service they would gather on the lawn in front of the church and devour fried chicken, macaroni pie, baked sweet potatoes and potato salad until the sun went down.

I guess you would say Short Junction was a family town, filled with people that cared about one another, but Sugar was never a part of that family.

Three sisters, the Lacey women (as they were known), took Sugar in and called her their own. Their history became her history.

They owned a big house that sat right outside the city limits of Short Junction. This house was willed to them by their mother, Gwen Lacey. Gwen was a half-breed, the product of her slave mother, Abbey, and slave master, John Lacey.

It was said that John Lacey purchased Abbey for eight hundred dollars, outbidding two others who also wanted the strong backed, ebony beauty. John Lacey had stood before Abbey, pretending to examine her teeth for decay and her gums for disease, but his eyes never once left hers. He was smitten immediately and his knees went weak at the closeness of her. His hands trembled as he passed them over her long, strong arms and down the sides of her thighs. To him, her skin felt like silk and her scent was like newly turned earth. His heart beat hard in his chest and his manhood, dormant for so many years, strained against his fine wool slacks.

He did not intend to fall in love with a Negroid woman; he had tried to find love in the simple smiles of the lily white virgins of Short Junction and the other surrounding towns. Tried until he could no longer stomach the gardenia perfume that rose like smoke from their cleavage. He feebly campaigned against other bachelors that matched his wealth and status (it was required, otherwise he might have been labeled a queer) for the arched wrists and dainty hands of blond-haired, blue-blood maidens whose mouths promised eternal love. But John knew their love would run gone if he could no longer provide the gold, silk and jewelry these women claimed were necessary for their survival.

He loved Abbey as a man should love a woman, no matter the color. He gave her his name, his seed and the left side of his bed for twenty years. And when he died, he left her and their daughter everything he'd ever owned.

Gwen Lacey was nearly grown when John Lacey died, and his relatives came and pillaged what they could. Fine linens, furniture and jewelry. They cussed Abbey and spit in Gwen's face as they tore the fine velvet curtains down from the windows and removed the silverware from the kitchen drawers.

They wanted the house too, but the will was legal and binding and they could do nothing about that.

I, John Lacey, give and bequeath to Abbey, a woman of color, formerly my slave but since emancipated and with whom I have had one daughter called Gwen, the sole and exclusive right to the house and property it sits on as well as the horses, cattle and all the monies of which I die possessed.

John Lacey 1858

"Mark my words ... that nigga better enjoy this while she can, 'cause she and that beast she calls a child won't be here for long!" a cousin of John Lacey screamed after a lengthy and heated argument with Samuel Gittens, John Lacey's lawyer and confidant. The cousin stormed out of the house, but not before grabbing the silver candlesticks from their place over the fireplace.

Abbey Lacey was not illiterate; John Lacey had made sure of that. She in turn taught their daughter, Gwen. Gwen Lacey, who was high in color, with long tight curls that hung about her face giving her a wild, seductive look, was a rebellious child and remained the same way into adulthood. Gwen was courted by many men, black and white, but in the end chose a man named Isaac Thorpe who was half Chickasaw and half black.

Isaac was a gambler and a hustler. He was a smooth-talking, handsome man that wooed Gwen into allowing him to move into her home. Abbey was completely against it, warning her daughter that this man she thought she loved was something less than genuine in his claims of love for her. Gwen fought her tooth and nail, reminding her mother that this was her house too and she had all rights to place under the roof any person or persons she chose.

Abbey and Gwen argued even as Isaac Thorpe's heavy, muddy boots announced his arrival.

Isaac turned the seven-bedroom house into a brothel, convincing Gwen that this was good business by adorning her with beautiful dresses and jewelry bought with the money he made from the misuse of flesh. In return, over time, Gwen gave Isaac three beautiful, bright-eyed baby girls.

As the years passed, he brought in Creole women from Louisiana and Seminoles from Florida to work. "Add a bit of variety for the customers," he said aloud. And for himself. But he kept that thought secret.

The first time Gwen caught Isaac with one of the women, he explained to her that it was necessary for him to test each and every woman he employed. "Gwen, I need to make sure these here women are doing all the right things to keep the mens 'round here coming back for more."

Gwen dug her nails deep into her palms in order to control the anger that was growing within her.

"It don't mean nothing to me, baby. You know you the one I love," he said and then asked her very nicely to leave the room while he finished handling his business.

She did, her eyes full of hurt and tears.

"What kinda women you is? You gonna let a man lay up on another woman in your own house and not do nothing about it?" At first she thought her mind was talking to her, but then she caught a blurred shape moving past.

"It ain't none of your business," Gwen yelled at Abbey before storming away.

Time is something that changes all things and it is true in Gwen Lacey's case. Gwen had been sent to the edge of madness, but she did not step off into it. She let it mold her and clear the fog she thought was love from her mind. She warned him, as she had before, but her voice carried something other than pain this time. Had he listened, he may have lived his life to the end God had set for him, but he ignored it.

"Isaac, if you lay down with one more woman in my house I'll kill you dead!" Gwen screamed outside the bedroom Isaac was holed up in with whatever woman he had chosen for the evening.

Gwen took her three daughters and placed them in the barn with the horses. Kissed them all tenderly on their heads and told them to stay put and stay quiet and no matter what they heard, not to move from the barn until she came for them.

The house was full. Men coming and going. Satisfied that they had found some release, some companionship, someone to listen and agree. Gwen walked into her home, her beautiful home, and for the first time in her whole life asked God for forgiveness. She moved slowly up the large staircase, smiling at the men and women that passed her on their descent. She traced the smooth polished oak banister with the tips of her fingers and savored the coolness of the wood. She walked to the end of the hall, past Abbey's room, stopping to peek in to see her mother sound asleep. Abbey still slept on the left side of the bed, a habit she could not break even though John Lacey had been dead and gone for nearly twenty-four years.

Gwen quietly entered the room, walked over to the side of the bed, went down to her knees and pulled the shotgun from beneath it. Abbey stirred and moaned in her sleep.

Once back in the hall Gwen moved on, stopping only to press her ear against each bedroom door and listen for Isaac's sounds.

She entered her own bedroom, the one she had conceived and birthed her children in, hoping to find him straddled atop one of the Creole women; this would surely justify her blowing his head off as well as assist in quelling the guilt that was building within her with every step she took.

When she opened the door she found Isaac Thorpe, the father of her children, alone, his throat cut from ear to ear. Gwen looked on, fully understanding and quite disappointed that Abbey had beaten her to killing him.

So the story goes.

Long after Gwen passed away, her children, May, Sara and Ruby Lacey, raised Sugar.

They told her that her mamma just dropped her off one day on her way to some other place with some man that she thought would make her happy.

They said that she was in such a hurry that she didn't even have time to name her.

"Ya'll go on and call her anything you want! She belong to ya'll now!" She was said to say as she jumped into his fancy automobile and waved good-bye.

Only a wisp of truth lay in that story.

Sugar spent fifteen years in Short Junction. Her friends were the wind, sun and trees; her playhouse, the woods and the river that flowed through it.

Her memories, the ones she allowed to remain, often wondered on a day when she and Sara went to town to pick up a few things from the general store. Sara gave her a peppermint stick and told her to wait outside until she was done. Sugar did as she was told and amused herself by watching the comings and goings of the people that lived in Short Junction.

The women smiled sweetly at her as they passed in and out the store, the men ignored her. She knew most of the men of Short Junction; they visited the Lacey home and the Lacey women quite often. Sugar had a jar full of shiny pennies to prove it. The men always gave her pennies. Their way of buying her silence.

On that day, just as the wind was beginning to kick up the dust in the road and a horse brayed loudly in a nearby stable, another little girl joined Sugar outside the store.

She sucked contentedly on her own peppermint stick, watching Sugar shyly from the corner of her eye. Sugar had never been this close to another child, and at the age of five, this nearness caused her heart to clamor with excitement inside her chest.

"What's your name?" the little girl finally asked, in the way only a little girl can.

Sugar considered her. Her worn dress, bare dirty feet and uncombed hair.

"Sugar," she said and waited for her reaction.

"Hmmm," the little girl uttered and looked thoughtfully at her peppermint stick. "That your mamma in there?" she said, pointing in the store. There were only two women in there, Sara and the woman who'd come with the little girl, and neither one of them was Sugar's mamma. In fact, at that tender age, Sugar had no real sense of what a mamma was. She'd heard the word used in conversation, but its meaning was foreign to her.

She shook her head no.

"Where's your mamma at?" the little girl asked, her eyebrows raised in surprise.

Sugar shrugged her shoulders.

"She dead?" she asked and her eyes widened.

Again, Sugar just shrugged her shoulders.

The little girl looked into the store again and then back at Sugar.

"Ain't you got a mamma?" she said with shocked disbelief.

Sugar just stared blankly at her. She had a May, a Sara and a Ruby. She didn't have a "mamma."

"What's a mamma?" she asked, hoping the little girl would shed some light on this thing that seemed so important.

The girl returned the same blank stare.

"Don't be talking to the likes of her, Caroline." The little girl's mother came out and dragged her by the collar away from Sugar. Her bare feet skidded across the dirt, leaving squiggly lines behind. "She a Lacey and we don't fraternize with those type of people."

"Those type of people," Sugar muttered to herself and moved to reach for another cigarette. Her face was wet with tears, but she did not notice. She tried to distract her mind and focus on the dust that swirled in the thin stream of light that filtered through the window. But like a storm, there was no stopping these memories, no matter how painful they were. Sugar leaned back, inhaled, and let them come back to her.

They lived in a big yellow and green house surrounded by willow trees and wildflowers. Sugar spent hours out and about the flowers and trees, trying to block out the heavy breathing and moaning that sailed down to her on the evening breeze.

Friday and Saturday nights found men and women from all over the county sitting in and around the Lacey home, where the good times rolled as long as you had the money to keep it going.

They came for the conversation, corn liquor, catfish and Lacey pussy.

The Lacey women sold themselves a sliver at a time. Leaving some back to fill the years when there would be no lean hard body to press against theirs and whisper sweet syrupy lies into the swell of a breast.

Time stopped and stepped aside to allow Sugar to walk away from the trees, leave behind her wreath of wildflowers and put away the sweet songs she sang aloud to the meadow. Time made way and Sugar strolled right into womanhood.

You see, no one ever told her to keep her legs closed and crossed at the ankles. No one ever said: "Save it for the one you love" or "Good girls say no."

They'd been watching her for some time. The men. Watching the way her ass grew out and moved up and onto her back. The way her legs lengthened and the muscles strained hard against her skin when she walked. The tight knobs that once struggled against her blouse had suddenly blossomed to something full and buoyant, ready to be held, kissed and caressed.

Her scent told them she was ready.

She went with him into the empty room. Some name-less, faceless him. They went to the same room that saw Isaac die.

She did not get kind words or gentle kisses. What she got was callused hands and boots that were worn thin at the sole. A man who, after he was done riding her, sat on the edge of the bed, his face in his hands, and wept out his guilt.

Guilty—'cause he was laying with someone else besides his wife.

Guilty—'cause he was paying out money he was supposed to use to buy food for his family.

Guilty—'cause the smell of Sugar reminded him of his own twelve-year-old daughter.

It was done and over. Tears mean nothing in the Lacey home. Just the two dollars on the dresser.

A door slammed in the distance and jerked Sugar away from her memories. She looked at her wristwatch; it was ten past six. "He's running late today," she mumbled to herself. She got up and walked over to the window, parted the curtains enough to see the tall, dark man bound down the stairs and then turn on his heel and bound back up to place a quick forgotten kiss on the cheek of his wife. Seconds later he was gunning the engine to his old pick-up and was off down the road.

Pearl stood out on the porch, her thin robe pulled tight around her against the morning chill, until the truck faded in the distance. She then turned her attention to Sugar's house. She stood there for quite some time, straining her neck this way and that way, trying to see whatever it is she thought she would see. Sugar smiled in spite of herself.

Nosy people irritated Sugar, so she began to keep the curtains drawn. Little it did, they still kept coming.

The town women were the worst. A few had ventured over to #10 Grove Street on more than one occasion, sometimes with their children in tow, always with food; knocking at the door and peering in the windows, hollering hello. Sugar would just sit there listening and waiting for them to leave. She did not need nor did she want to be friends with anyone in Bigelow.

Nevertheless, they kept coming. The women of Bigelow in their dainty dresses and light makeup. Some even wore white gloves on their hands and veiled hats usually reserved for Sunday church, weddings, baptisms and christenings. Some even jiggled the doorknob. Pearl watched all of this from her kitchen window and waited to see if the mystery woman would appear, and if she did what would she say?

But she never did and the women would clear their throats, look around, set their baked goods wrapped in shiny tin foil down in the rocking chair, or tuck them back under their arms and walk swiftly away. Some would stop at Pearl's house, pretending they'd come all that way to see her in the first place. They'd sit and smile, speaking on small things. Family mostly, inquiring about Pearl's two sons. "How Joe Jr and Seth getting on up North?" Pearl knew better and accepted their Corning Ware filled with peach cobbler or stewed pears, served them coffee or tea and told them her boys were doing just fine. The women really only wanted to know one thing, and that was if Pearl had met her yet. But they behaved like the Bigelow women they were raised to be and engaged Pearl in light conversation that involved everything and everyone except her neighbor.

"Oh, by the way ..." they'd say as Pearl showed them to the door and thanked them again for the visit, "have you met your new neighbor yet?" They'd say it with such an air of mock disinterest that it made Pearl want to laugh, call them phonies and point an accusing finger at them.

Instead, she bit the inside of her cheek, shook her head and said, "No, I haven't had the pleasure."

The women would transform then; their eyes would go wild and they'd have to fight to control the froth that formed at the corners of their mouths. "Oh, I seen her in town. She look like a harlot if there ever was one. What she gotta dress that way for? And all that makeup! She wear wigs that them white women wear, long, blond or red! I tell you, Pearl, not in all my years have I seen a sight like her. Umph!" Their words would run in a fast stream that made Pearl's head hurt.

Pearl would just raise her eyebrows. "Really," she'd say with exasperation.

"Yes, really. You better watch yourself living so close to her and all. Best you keep away from her, she don't look like she mean nobody no good. Coming through town without even a hello. Umph! Who does she think she is?"

Pearl would close her door to their backs and their two-faced attitudes. She didn't much like people like that, and didn't care to eat food made by people with such wicked hearts, so the pie, bread or cake would end up in the garbage.

Chapter Four

Pearl blushed mauve with embarrassment as she ascended the steps. They creaked loudly under her weight and announced her arrival to everyone in and around the house. She'd been reduced to following the example of the gossiping women that came to this very same door with the intention of weeding out this foul seed that was now living among them. Befriend her, find out who she was and what she was about and then run her off when they find that she did not meet with their requirements. She being the color of crude oil and maintaining its qualities, Sugar would not and could not mix. That was their only interest. Pearl's intentions were different.

From the first day Sugar arrived and Pearl laid eyes on her from the shadows of her hallway, she was struck by the familiarity of her face. Her heart had skipped an entire beat when the woman stopped in front of her house. It wasn't because of how she looked or the way she was dressed that threw Pearl for a turn, it was her profile that caused her to catch her breath and grab her chest. For a split second Sugar looked everything like her Jude. Sweet, sweet Jude, spending the rest of eternity in a pine box, six feet underground.

For a quick instant Pearl thought Sugar was Jude and had to control the impulse to run out through the front door and grab the woman in her arms. But then Sugar turned toward her and smiled and Jude's face melted away like lard left out in the hot sun.

Pearl had to, needed to see her without the annoyance of shadows. She wanted to make sure her mind wasn't playing tricks on her again.

For the first year after Jude died she seemed to see her face everywhere. In her dreams, looking up at her from a dish that rested in the sink waiting to be cleaned, in her own reflection in the mirror and peeking at her from behind the living room drapes. Sometimes she would call to her, "Jude? Jude, baby, is that you?" And walk over to where she thought she saw her daughter's almond eyes. Joe, if he was there, would grab her firmly by the shoulders and guide her back to bed or the couch. "She gone, baby," he'd say and sit and rock her until the tears and weeping were done.

It was the hardest time in her life and after fifteen years it was still hard.

The worst incident had come when she and Joe went to Short Junction to meet the train. Joe's nephew and his wife were coming in from Jackson to spend some time with them. It wasn't too long after Jude's death. Colored papers were still hot with the story. No one had been picked up as a suspect and the police had all but given up on their halfhearted efforts at finding the killer.

The wife of the nephew was a nurse in Jackson and Joe had felt it would be a good idea to have her around. Pearl didn't seem to be getting any better; he thought he would lose her to grief.

Pearl stood beside him, lifeless, shoulders slumped, giving her a hunchbacked appearance. Her dress hung slack from her body, which was growing thinner by the day. Her straw hat sat limp on her head and stiff gray strands of hair poked out from beneath it like wild weeds. Her eyes were small dull black stones that held vast emptiness. She was nothing more than a dead tree trunk in the middle of all the hustle and bustle of the station.

Joe was holding her hand and looking toward the train that had just pulled in. Joe Jr and Seth stood restlessly behind them, tugging at their shirt collars. People rushed to the train, waiting anxiously for loved ones to appear. Children chased each other around and between the legs of grown folks, and porters moved like sleek, black wildcats to and fro, moving large steamer trunks through the buzz of people like rats through an intricate maze.

"Here they come, Pearl," Joe whispered to her and squeezed her lifeless hand. He was waving at them as they approached. Pearl lifted her head slightly and tried to offer a weak smile, but none would come. Jude had taken her smile with her. And then her head bounced. She caught sight of a girl, just the same age as Jude, dressed in a dress that was too mature for her. Her face was painted, hiding the last threads of innocence. She turned to say something to the man that was with her, excitement swirling all over her face. Pearl saw her. Saw Jude. And began to walk toward her, slow at first, pulling Joe along with her. He followed, believing she was walking to greet his nephew, but she blew straight past them, her speed increasing to a run, leaving them standing, mouths agape, in shock. "Pearl?" Joe had yelled above the throng of the people. "Wha—" and then he saw what Pearl was rushing toward. He saw the girl that looked so much like his dead daughter and his heart thumped hard in his chest. He gripped Pearl's hand and jerked her sharply backward; she slammed into his chest and then turned eyes on him that reflected such savagery it made him shudder and he smelled his own sudden fear break out on his body in tiny beads of sweat.

She spoke to him between clenched teeth and quivering lips. Pearl looked like a trapped animal. "Turn me loose, Joe Taylor." And he did, without thinking of the consequences, he turned her loose and with the agility of a child, Pearl raced through the station toward the young woman and she screamed her dead daughter's name as she went, "Jude! Juuuudeeee!!!!"

Thank goodness it was too late. The girl had boarded the train. "All aboard!" was yelled one final time and the whistle was sounded. Steam bellowed out from beneath the cars and then the train started its steady movement as it pulled slowly out of the station. Pearl was running alongside it, her hands reaching out to touch the steel cars that were now swiftly whisking past her. She called Jude's name one last time and collapsed onto the platform.

A year passed before Pearl smiled. Another year before her laugh, high and gay, was heard again.

Not a day went by without her thinking of her daughter, but she kept the vision of her mutilated body buried deep in a section of her mind reserved for horrible things that scared and frightened her.

Pearl reconstructed her life, bit by tiny painful bit and now a woman, just the profile of her Jude, was slowly fragmenting what she had spent fifteen years putting back together.

Pearl balanced the sweet potato pie in one hand and knocked on the chipped and peeling screen door with the other. The window to the right was open and the curtains pulled aside revealing the misty gray-black within. She resisted the urge to tilt her head to peer inside. That's what someone else would do, she told herself. She waited and then knocked again, the sound of her knuckles making rapid contact with the wood echoing loudly up and down the street.

She shifted on her feet and looked at the rocking chair that moved gently back and forth in the warm spring breeze. Small clay pots filled with mint and jasmine lined the base of the partition that encircled the porch area. The plants were in full bloom and enveloped the house with their fragrant soothing aromas.

Ivy crept silently along the side of the house and stretched over to run the length of the banister. Pearl was amused; she'd never noticed the ivy before. Not even when Old Mrs Wilks was living there.

Pearl knocked again. Still no answer. She sat down in the rocking chair and rested the warm pie on her lap. "I'll just rest a bit," she lied to herself. She was actually lying in wait. She rocked slowly back and forth, the yielding sounds of the chair and the smells of mint and jasmine easing away any apprehensions she may have arrived with.

The previous owner, Beulah Wilks, had been dead and gone for more than ten years. She'd been a nice old woman, pint-sized and frail with dull brown eyes and hair like snow, soft and white. Pearl and Beulah had made small talk over the years; neighborly chit chat that unfolded their lives to each other.

Beulah Wilks moved to Bigelow from Waco, Texas, with her husband and infant son. The husband died not too long after they settled in and she raised her son alone, supported by her deceased husband's war pension and her tailoring skills. She never remarried and never mentioned to Pearl any desire to marry. "Men are like children. They need too much time and attention. I ain't had the patience to go back to mothering two men instead of one, so's I stayed alone and liked it." Pearl was taken aback by the old woman's candor—talk like that was nearly alien coming from a woman who was raised in a time when they believed a woman needed a man to survive and the man made the woman complete.

Beulah watched Pearl's sons, Joe Jr and Seth, move from boys to men and then North. She was there when Jude was found, and sent casseroles of food over daily for three months.

During that time Pearl had never met the son Beulah spoke constantly about. She glowed with delight whenever she said or heard his name mentioned: "Clemon."

He was her pride and joy and although she didn't see him often, he faithfully sent her a letter with money the first of every month. "Had a little trouble 'round these parts some time ago," Beulah confided. "He don't feel safe comin' 'round here no more." The old woman never mentioned what type of trouble and Pearl didn't ask.

The one and only time Pearl had laid eyes on him was about ten years ago when Beulah passed away, fell down dead among the beloved flowers, fruits and vegetables she spent all her time tending.

Pearl remembered he was a slight man, built like his mother, so small that a strong wind could come by and lift him from the ground and carry him up into the tree-tops. Pearl addressed him as "Mr Wilks."

She held his small hand in hers and stared solemnly at the bald spot on his head that so perfectly reflected the sun, and said her condolences: "She was a mighty fine woman, your mother was." Joe squeezed his shoulder and nodded in agreement. She had approached him after the funeral as he was preparing to leave. His mother's body lay waiting inside her coffin on a wagon. He was taking her body back to Texas for burial.

"Thank you," he said without looking at them and walked away.

The house had stood empty for all those years, no FOR SALE sign in the front yard, the fruits, flowers and vegetables dying from lack of love and attention.

Pearl rose from the rocking chair, her eyes wet with the memory of loss, and turned to knock one last time. The pie was cold now and her heart had cooled along with it. A tall dark woman stood in the doorway staring directly at Pearl, an off-white towel wrapped loosely around her head and short blue robe cinched tight around her long body. Her thighs glistened wet with water.

She looked annoyed, her face was twisted to one side with irritation and she watched Pearl through her slanted eyes.

Pearl was startled and stumbled back, her behind hitting sharply against the banister, causing her to cry out with pain and surprise.

"Yes?" Sugar said as she eyed the woman and at the same time reached into the breast pocket of her robe, pulling out a crumpled pack of Lucky Strikes and a book of matches. Pearl could not respond; she was staring intently at the woman's face. She wanted to reach out and touch it, scrape away the features that weren't Jude's, leaving behind the ones that were.

Sugar lit the cigarette and it dangled loosely from the corner of her mouth. She squinted her eyes against the rising smoke. "Yes?" she said, louder now, more intense.

"I—I ..." was all that Pearl could issue. She was stunned stupid and had forgotten her very reason for being there.

Sugar stood back on her long mahogany legs and adjusted the towel around her head. "You just come by to use my rocker?" Sugar said. It was more an accusation than a question. She inhaled deeply on her cigarette and let the smoke out in tiny puffs of white.

Pearl found her voice. She opened her mouth and allowed the words to spill out in a senseless jumble, hoping at the end they would combine and become something intelligent. "I'm s-sorry for rocking in your chair. I just came by to introduce myself—I mean, welcome you to Bigelow." Pearl looked again at the glistening thighs and then down to the small puddle that was forming beneath Sugar.

"Did I—I come at a bad time?" she said a bit too loudly. She jerked a bit at the volume of her voice and then halted her babbling, breathlessly awaiting a response.

Sugar smirked at the short, wide woman in her starched blue dress and stiff white collar. So much perfection in one place was unsettling to her. "Yes, yes you did," she said, her voice chilled and stiff.

"Shoot, I sure am sorry, Miss," Pearl uttered and shifted her eyes away from Sugar. She wanted so much to stare into her face, but pulled her eyes away from those familiar features and concentrated instead on the staircase just behind her. As an afterthought and after a short period of silent awkwardness, she shoved the pie out before her. The movement was hard and fast and it slammed into the half open door that Sugar held ajar with one hand. The impact startled Pearl and she released the plate; it went crashing to the floor, sending bits of crust and sweet potatoes across the porch.

They stood there looking stupidly at the mess that had been made. Pearl went down effortlessly to one swollen knee, picked up the pan and began gathering up the broken pie bits, apologizing as she did.

Sugar did not move, but continued to draw on her cigarette as she watched the old woman's head bob up and down and listened to her *Lord have mercys* and *For goodness' sakes.*

Sugar shook her head in surrender. "C'mon in 'for I catch cold. Leave it be, the ants will take care of it," Sugar said and walked into the house, leaving Pearl to catch the closing door before it slammed and bounced back on its rusty hinges.

She followed Sugar into the gray darkness of the foyer and then the living room. Pearl was uncomfortable with the dim lighting and the heavy smell of stale cigarette smoke. The room needed sunlight and a good airing out, but she sat down without comment where Sugar had indicated she should sit.

Sugar took a seat directly in front of her. An old wooden coffee table, its polish long gone, separated the two women.

Pearl recognized the furniture. It had belonged to Mrs Wilks. A battered green sofa, its cushions not looking as if they could withstand another heavy dust beating, and two wingback chairs made of the same material of putrid green.

Nothing much had changed, except the cross that once hung directly over the fireplace was gone, although a clean imprint of it remained. It seemed to glow in the gloom of the room.

"Will you replace it?" Pearl asked, knowing full well she'd started the conversation off ineptly.

"Replace what?" Sugar asked, bewildered.

"The cross," Pearl said and pointed to the empty space on the wall.

Sugar looked in the direction of Pearl's pointing finger and stared at the space for a while. She hadn't noticed it before. "No, I don't think so," she said as she smashed the finished cigarette into an ashtray that held what looked to Pearl like hundreds of butts. She glanced again at the space and then absently pulled another cigarette out of the pack and lit it. She turned her attention back to Pearl just as the yellow and blue flame from the match illuminated her face. Pearl caught sight of Sugar's almond-shaped eyes, high cheekbones and smooth dark skin. Her heart leaped from her chest and to her throat.

My God, she looks like Jude in so many ways, she thought to herself as she fought to retain her composure.

"Well," Sugar said in a long drawn-out exhale of breath and smoke. The "well" came as an interlude to a lulling conversation, but there had been no real conversation so far.

Pearl shifted uncomfortably in her seat. "I'm real sorry 'bout that mess. I really wish you would let me clean it up." Her voice was uneven and she wanted to leave that dark, cigarette-choked room and return to the sunshine and clean fresh air outside. She wanted to move away from the face that looked so much like her Jude's.

"Ain't nothing," Sugar replied in a long lazy drawl, and then she took another long drag on her cigarette.

"Well it sure is nice to finally meet you. I been trying to get over here for a while, but you know how it is, you get caught up doing one thing or another and before you know it, it's bedtime." Pearl laughed at the end of her sentence, a small girlish giggle that she hadn't heard herself use since her youth.

No, Sugar didn't know. But she shook her head yes anyway.

"Well I best be going, I done taken up too much of your time already." Pearl stood abruptly and pushed her hand out toward Sugar. "Nice meeting you," she said without looking directly at her.

Sugar stared at the hand that was extended before her. She didn't offer her own. "You didn't tell me your name," Sugar said quietly and drew again on her cigarette.

"What?" Pearl said stupidly, her hand beginning to ache from its suspended position.

"Your name?" Sugar said, making sure each word came out crisp.

"My name?" Pearl was confused. Hadn't she given her name? She tossed it around in her mind. She realized she did not know the woman's name and evidently had not given her name either. Or had she?

"Oh dear! I'm Pearl. Pearl Taylor," she said all flustered and took a step closer to Sugar, her hand still extended, now in greeting instead of good-bye.

"Sugar. Sugar Lacey," Sugar responded and lightly took the old woman's hand in her own.

There was electricity when one hand enfolded the other. It caused both of them to jump and they snatched their hands apart.

"Damn static electricity," Sugar mumbled and wiped at the palm of her hand. She pointed down to the old faded section rug that at some point had been a bright rose, but now had been walked on and spilled on so many times it was more like a ragged maroon.

"Sugar? Well, that's an interesting name. Is it a nickname?" Pearl asked, finding a conversational tone now. The shock had done something to her insides, jump-started her voice and quelled her nervousness. She could look into the woman's face for longer moments, and although she still saw fragmented pieces of Jude hiding there, it seemed not to upset her as much now.

"No, that's my Christian name. Why? Don't you know sugar is brown first? White folks couldn't stand the fact that something so sweet shared the same color as the people who cut the cane, slopped the hogs and picked the cotton. So they bleached it to resemble them, and now they done gone and fooled everybody. You included," Sugar said with a laugh. May Lacey was famous for telling that little story, and now here Sugar was repeating it.

"Oh," Pearl said, blushing at Sugar's chiding.

Another thick awkward silence hung between them.

"So uh, you family to Mrs Wilks?" Pearl asked.

"Who's that?" Sugar asked, getting up from her chair. Sugar was quite familiar with the name but preferred to play dumb. This woman was asking too many questions and Sugar had no intention of giving up as many answers. The robe slid open a bit and revealed a corner of her thick, bushy triangle. Pearl saw this and turned her eyes toward the bright cross space on the wall. "The woman who used to live here, she been dead for some time now. You her granddaughter, maybe?"

Sugar pulled her robe close around her again and removed the towel from her head to reveal a short snatch of thick black hair. It held tight to her scalp and looked as if it would resist even the hottest straightening comb. "I don't think so," Sugar replied with no real interest in the subject.

Pearl was confused. Since there had never been a FOR SALE sign on the house, the only logical conclusion would be that it was willed to a family member, most likely her son. But here was this woman saying "she didn't think so," which made no kind of sense to Pearl. Either you know who your grandmother is or you don't know.

"Your daddy wasn't Clemon, Mrs Wilks's son?" Pearl pressed.

"Miss Pearl, I don't know who my daddy is or was," Sugar said and walked out of the living room and to the front door. She swung it open and waited for Pearl to appear. Pearl pushed her head out from the living room into the hall and realized that her visit had come to an end.

Pearl cleared her throat and smoothed her dress; she lifted her head up a bit and started toward the door. She stepped over the threshold and turned to face Sugar. "I'm sorry 'bout everything and excuse me if I offended you with my questions. It's just that Bigelow is a small place and we all like to know who our neighbors are. You understand, don't you?" Sincerity was gleaming in Pearl's eyes.

"Sure do," Sugar said sarcastically and firmly closed the door in Pearl's face.

Pearl stood there looking at the closed door that was only inches from her face. She'd never experienced in her whole lifetime the humiliation she had encountered in this one day.

She looked down at the drying bits of pie and sure enough, the ants were hauling tiny loads of it away.

Chapter Five

"So you went in there ... what it look like ... what she look like ... I only seen her once from afar ... she look black, though, black like tar. What she sound like ... she use all them big city words ... what she got ... more coming or just her one?"

Shirley was talking so fast it sounded like one long, bad soprano note. Shirley and the heat was not a good combination, not at all.

Shirley Brown was older than Pearl, probably by about a good twenty years. She wore a wig that seemed to defeat the purpose of wearing a wig. It was a stiff, bluish gray mass of horse hair that looked more like tangled piano string. It should have been discarded a long time ago, but Shirley loved it to death, preferring it to her head of soft gliding gray that resembled spun silk. Shirley wasn't frail, although she appeared that way. Time had bent her over a bit and life had kicked her in the behind on more than one occasion, so she walked tilted forward, looking as if she would tumble over at any moment. She was medium built and walnut colored. All in all, she was a comical-looking woman; her face was long and thin and she wore large black-framed glasses that magnified her eyes to ten times their normal size. You couldn't look dead at Shirley without wanting to laugh. So just to keep the peace, you didn't look dead at Shirley.

Shirley had been married three times, buried two husbands and was now alienating her third with her rumor-mongering ways.

Shirley Brown had been Shirley Brown twice in her life. At birth she was born into the name, and then she gave it up at twenty and became Shirley Jenkins. Twelve years after that she became Shirley Atkins. The name Brown was re-installed when she married her third husband, Parker Brown.

Pearl and Shirley were friends by association. Shirley worked alongside Pearl's mother, Belle, in the McHenry house for more than thirty years, so Pearl had known her her whole life. Shirley moved to Bigelow with her second husband and had been there ever since.

And now there she sat spilling out word after word, sounding like a squealing pig going to slaughter.

"What were you doing 'round here anyways?" Pearl asked for the umpteenth time. Shirley was exemplary at picking and prying, but she was also the queen of evasion.

"Oh ... I was coming over here to see you." Shirley was lying, Pearl could see it in her big magnified eyes. Shirley didn't have a car, and neither did Parker. They begged for rides to town. Pearl lived on the opposite side of Bigelow, a good twenty minutes' walk for a person still holding on to his youth; more than an hour for an old body with one foot slipping into the afterlife.

"Shirley Brown, you would not walk all this way to see me," Pearl said as she placed the kettle on the stove to heat.

"Sure I would, honey," Shirley said without looking at Pearl. Her eyes drifted to the open kitchen window. "So, her hair really blond?" Shirley asked, trying hard to keep the eagerness out of her voice.

Pearl gave a little laugh and shook her head in surrender. She sat down across from Shirley and folded her hands loosely on the table. "No. Her hair is short, black and nappy like the rest o' us."

"Uh-huh," Shirley grunted and dug deep into her oversized, overused black pocketbook, pulling out a bag of peanuts. Without being asked, Pearl got up and retrieved a plate from the cabinet. Shirley was a peanut fiend. She ate them the way people smoked cigarettes and she put them in her Pepsi and drank them. Pearl set the plate down in front of Shirley and turned to remove the kettle from the flame. At that moment a flutter of red and yellow moved quickly past Sugar's open window. They both saw it and each reacted in her own way. Pearl stood motionless, the kettle in hand, suspended in mid-air. Shirley stood up from her chair, so slowly it was comical. She moved as if at a baseball game, watching in amazement as the winning ball went sailing over the heads of onlookers and out of the stadium.

They stood there, frozen, holding their breaths, waiting for her to pass again. Waiting for the bright yellow and red to dance briefly in the window once more.

Nothing.

Shirley sat down. Pearl poured the hot water into the waiting teacups. They sipped in silence, both watching the window.

The first thing Pearl heard after she saw the smooth dark chocolate skin was the shattering sound of bone china as it made quick and unexpected contact with the kitchen floor. The second sound was Shirley's quick intake of breath, and the last and final sound was her own voice whispering, "Sweet Jesus." It was said not in prayer, but in total and complete disbelief.

"Oh, my God, she's stark naked?"

Pearl was sure that Shirley wanted her words to form a statement, but it came out as gauche as the situation at hand.

Sugar had returned to the room and now she was sitting, as naked as the day she was born, in front of her window. One leg swung lazily over the arm of the chair and the other stretched out before her. A magazine rested on her lap and she flipped idly through the pages with one hand while the other languidly moved her cigarette to and from her mouth.

Curtains, white and transparent—nothing like the heavy drapes that graced the other homes of Bigelow— moved in and out like waves guided by a soft summer gale. They did not hide her, or Sugar's dark triangle of pubic hair.

Pearl stared at Sugar's pussy. But she did not see it as it was, she saw a memory of a day when a man came to her, head bowed, and unfolded a handkerchief that held her daughter's cootie-cat. That's what Pearl called it and her mother before her and so that's what she taught Jude to call her own. Cootie-cat.

Pearl had avoided looking at her own cootie-cat for fifteen years. And Joe, well, he wished he could say that he had touched it or caressed it within all those years.

He longed to be able to say it was so, but that would be a blatant untruth. If asked, Joe would say: No, I have not seen it since spring 1940. All I have is my memory of it.

John Lee Hooker's "Burnin' Hell" quickly filled the background and replaced the fog that shrouded her whenever she was forced to remember. She heard Shirley talking fast and she lifted her head above the fog, thankfully being able to tear her eyes away from Sugar.

"I ain't never seen no mess like this in my entire life! Who the hell sits 'round butt naked for all the world to see!? Lord have mercy, Pearl, what kinda trash you got living next door to you?"

Shirley was crouched down on the floor, her dress hiked up over her knees. Pearl could see her stockings, rolled up around her varicose-ridden thighs, choking them. She spoke in a conspiratorial whisper and her eyes were like globes behind her thick glasses. Pearl just looked down at her. She was horrified at what she'd just seen and at the memory it forced on her, but seeing Shirley crouched down below the windowpane, peeking up every three seconds to snatch a look at Sugar's privates, well it was just too humorous a scene and Pearl had to bite down hard on the inside of her cheeks to keep from laughing.

The guitar and harmonica were dying, the sound of John Lee Hooker's voice faded and Sugar was gone.

Shirley stood up and her knees creaked loudly. "Can you believe this?" she said, her hand extended out toward the window. Her mouth kept opening and closing in disbelief and sweat trickled down from around her temples. A sweet, sickening musty smell rose up from her body that was nearly as suffocating as her overpowering personality. Pearl stepped back, trying to escape it and Shirley.

"I gotta go ... this ain't right and she ain't right, Pearl. You gotta husband, Pearl."

There is silence and Shirley need not say any more; her words carried heavy meaning. "That's all I'm gonna say on it."

She left, leaving peanut shells still on the plate, stepping over shattered pieces of china. The news would spread quick and fast now. Pearl considered pulling the phone from the wall.

Chapter Six

The morning came in raw. Smelling like a sea that was nowhere near Bigelow or Arkansas. The wind was blowing wrong, causing a backdraft to come off of the canning plant. It was mackerels then. It seemed every year the plant was canning something new. This year it's mackerels, and from time to time the smell of discarded fish parts traveled the few miles and settled thick as smoke in and around the towns that bordered Ashton. It didn't remind nobody of the sea. That smell reminded people of an unwashed woman.

That's all Pearl needed after what she saw yesterday. The smell of an unclean woman traveling around her nose and seeping in the cushions of her couch. Unwelcomed. That's what it was. The smell and the woman across the way.

Pearl was up early and was moving about the house doing nothing really, just waiting for the sun to come up full in the sky and then her job as wife would begin. The house was quiet except for the soft padding of her slippered feet against the wood and the linoleum-lined kitchen. There was the even breathing of her sleeping husband permeating the background. The kettle was on the stove and the water jumped and bubbled against the heat inside the tin structure. Pearl looked into her cabinet, and there were five teacups now instead of six. She reached for one and her feet carried her to the window. She hadn't meant to go there. Not right then. Not so soon in the morning. But she was there tugging once, twice and then the shade gave in suddenly and snapped up and out of her hand. Pearl jumped and dropped her teacup. There are four teacups now.

What she saw surprised her. Surprised him. The two of them; him on the outside passing between the houses, leaving his size twelve shoeprint in the wet earth, green jacket hanging over one arm and shirt half undone, revealing dark tight curls of hair on his chest. He glowed pale beneath the approaching dawn. He was smiling, thinking about what had just been done to him, over and over again. But the smile was frozen and unnatural when Pearl saw it. The crash of Pearl's teacup got him moving again, unfroze the stupid contented smile on his face. He stared hard at her, nodded his head and mouthed "Mornin'."

Pearl nodded back and pulled her thin, yellow robe around her. Looking into his eyes chilled her. A scream scrambled to the base of her throat. She threw her hand over her mouth and gagged instead.

She was at the front door before he rounded the front of the house, and she couldn't stop herself from grabbing hold of the cold metal doorknob and swinging the heavy door wide open. She stepped out on the porch and caught sight of him as he stepped into the green and white 1955 Bel Air Sports Coupe. Had Joe been witness to this, he would have whistled long and loud at the automobile. It was fine and slick.

The engine revved up just as the sky began to pale and then it was shooting past Pearl. She watched until the car blurred and then disappeared.

Something just wasn't right about a white man on Grove Street, in a fancy car, leaving a black woman's house in the early morning hours. Something just wasn't right. It was as foul as the raw air that was picking up potential with the morning sun.

There was too much activity on the normally quiet Grove Street. Cars were coming and going, filled with men, a few with women—two, three, four times—up and down the street, people hanging out the windows and pointing at #10 Grove Street, wanting to catch a glimpse of the naked woman.

Joe nodded and waved at the people as they went by. Happy to see them at first and then confused as to why they were there at all, driving past his house over and over again. He waved one man over. "What ya'll doing?" he asked, scratching his head in bewilderment. He asked his question and then looked up at a truck filled with watermelon pulling up on the opposite side of the road. Customers were already lining up.

"You don't know?" the man said with a laugh.

"Nope," Joe replied and looked back at his wife, who had followed him out on the porch.

"Ya new neighbor like to walk 'round outside her house ... naked." The man's voice thickened a bit when he said it. Joe recognized that sound and backed away from it.

"Is that right?" he said, and folded his arms across his massive chest.

The man was grinning, not paying Joe much mind now. He thought he saw movement in the front window.

Joe thanked him for the information and walked back to his porch. "You know anything 'bout all this?" he asked Pearl. Pearl did know about something, but these people couldn't possibly be here to witness what she had just yesterday. "Something 'bout the woman next door walking around outside naked?" Joe continued, looking at Pearl's forehead instead of her eyes.

"They here to see that?" Pearl said flatly. "That ain't right, Joe. She ain't no circus freak. And she wasn't outside, she was in the privacy of her own living room … the window just happened to be open, shifting the curtains a bit. Shirley was here when it happened, done blown it up to something it ain't. These people gotta go, Joe. Our home is here too. They can't be 'round here like this." She turned and walked back into the house. Her eyes never left the street when she spoke and her voice never rose.

Joe hitched his pants and lifted his head a bit higher, gathering his full six feet three inches and 250 pounds. Something was going to be done about this.

Pearl didn't know what he said, probably not much, and he only spoke to two people: the watermelon man and someone on a bike, didn't need to speak to more than that, the others would see and get the hint. The people respected Joe's words, not sure of what he was physically capable of, and not wanting to push him to test it, they moved along and away from Grove Street.

She didn't tell him where she was going, wasn't necessary. He was asleep on the sofa, the television watching him, a half-empty glass of Coke sitting on the floor, the ice melting loudly within it, a half-eaten bologna sandwich on a plate next to the glass. Sunday afternoon found him snoring in his second favorite snoozing place, after the far side of the middle pew in Bigelow's First Baptist Church, the part that was hidden by a column.

She slipped quietly out the back door, pie in hand, and walked across the thick grass that separated her house from Sugar's. The screen door was open a bit, swinging back and forth on its hinges. "Hello," Pearl yelled twice before she walked in. She could hear a man's voice, happy and chipper, coming from the living room. A commercial for soap coming from a radio she couldn't see. "Hello?" once again and then she was on the stairs moving up to the second floor of the house one step at a time. Step. Listen. Step. Listen. Nothing.

The house echoed empty, yet she kept going.

The center hall was bright; dust particles danced in the fat slants of light that came in through the window at the far end. Pearl looked down at her black shoes, spit shined by her husband; they looked more expensive than their five dollars' worth against the worn, burgundy and gold swirled carpet. She stepped forward and found herself between two rooms, the bedroom and the bathroom. Both doors half open, revealing contents and details. She turned toward the bedroom intending to push the door open, but her attention was focused toward the hall window. She stepped forward and her hand missed the feel of the oak door, as it swung open before she could make contact.

Sugar stood before her, a towel wrapped around her body. A wasted effort, the towel was too small and like the half-open doors, revealed most everything and more than nothing at all.

"What you doing in my house!" Sugar yelled and stepped forward.

"I—" Pearl was flustered mute.

"What you doing in my house?!" Sugar demanded again. Her breath, heavy with cigarettes and pork and beans, invaded Pearl's nose and she coughed.

"I—I called out, but no one answered. I just wanted to try again ... bring another pie for you since—"

Her speech was cut short. The pie was airborne and spinning above her head. Sugar's rage had overwhelmed her and triggered her hand to slap at the pie. When it landed, it landed on Pearl's head. Sweet potato and crust slid down the sides of her face and onto her dress, made a home in her hair and clung to her lashes.

Pearl didn't move, not even to wipe at the pie in order to remove it from her head and face. She just stared at Sugar. Sugar was stunned, stunned at her quick act of anger, and her face showed her surprise and growing regret.

"Sorry" tickled at her tongue but Sugar would not release it, so it moved into her eyes where Pearl interpreted it.

She laughed at the pie on her head and her stupidity. It was a full-bodied laugh, not at all as rich as a good bottle of wine, but it was a laugh nevertheless, and she had laughed so little in past years. Sugar laughed too, unsure at first and then more securely.

More than ten minutes passed before they got themselves under control. Sides aching and faces wet with tears, they knelt together to pick from the floor what had missed or left Pearl's head.

"Well, Miss Pearl, seems as if I'm never gonna actually get to taste your sweet potato pie," Sugar said as she scooped pie from the top of Pearl's head.

"Sweet potato pie your favorite?" Pearl asked.

"All-time," Sugar said.

"We'll make the next one together then," Pearl said, cementing her place in Sugar's life, using words she had used with Jude years before.

"I ain't much of a cook, no less a baker," Sugar responded.

"Don't matter, life's 'bout learning new things anyway," Pearl said.

Chapter Seven

"I don't need you!"

Sugar woke up and the words were spilling from her mouth. Loud and obnoxious. She believed she must have been screaming because the words still bounced off the walls of her bedroom.

They were bitter words, sour in her mouth where once upon a time they'd been familiar, tasteless things that were just a part of life.

I don't need you!

The words stayed with her, echoing in her mind. She closed her eyes and squeezed them shut, placing her hands over her ears to block the words out completely. That didn't help at all. They weren't outside of her, sitting in the chair across the room or even standing over her trying to poke her awake. They were inside her head, living in her soul, and now she was holding them in, trapping them there for good by holding her hands over her ears.

What had it been? A dream maybe, certainly not a memory of something that had actually happened. She'd never had to use those words in her real life. She never had to make a statement to anyone with regard to what she needed and didn't. No, she had been self-sufficient for most of her life—not counting time spent with the Laceys and Mary.

There had been no love to scrape away at her, leaving only crumbled bits of flesh where there once was a whole person—she didn't have to pretend that she didn't need him when she knew she did. No, that was someone else's life.

Mother, maybe? No, she had never had one to rebel against.

Hmmm, strange.

Perhaps it was Pearl. She was quickly becoming a part of Sugar's life. It had started slow. The baking of the pie was the maiden voyage to their friendship, and then other things. Tending the garden that they both thought was dead. Turned out that it was just dormant. "What it needed was a little love and attention," Pearl said when the first pink blossom flowered. Sugar wasn't sure if she was speaking about the garden or something else. She wasn't good at reading people without having looked into their eyes. Pearl never held hers still enough to allow that. They were always shifting here and there. Darting around like a fly, resting only for short periods, and then on the move again.

Joe was nice too, she felt an instant respect for him. Something she had never had for men. Something about his posture and slow, careful talk.

They went to town together. What a pair. Pearl always in one of her starched cotton dresses with the small, white, delicately embroidered collar and Sugar in a glaring, red, hot pink or orange dress that sat dangerously above the knee, revealing a hefty portion of thigh that was accentuated with spiked high-heeled shoes. Red, black or blond wigs stretching down her back and bouncing happily up and down on the rise of her backside. She smiled at no one when she turned her heavily powdered, blue eyelidded, crimson lipsticked face on them.

"Why do you hide yourself under all of that ... makeup?" Pearl often asked. Sugar never answered, just snorted air out her nose, sucked her teeth or lit a cigarette.

People stared blatantly. Not caring if the two women saw. They approached them from behind, making their presence known with loud, stringent greetings that were directed at Pearl. Small tiny words passed between them, dainty chitchat that was weighed down with spitefulness. They ignored Sugar, pretended that she was nothing more than air. Foul air. With noses held high and eyes boring in on Pearl, they really wanted to ask what would drive her to associate with trash?

Pearl would entertain them in conversation, uneasily, always aware of Sugar standing nearby. She tried once or twice to include her in the conversation, but the women as well as Sugar always seemed to walk away just as Pearl's words of introduction began to verge upon them.

"Don't you want to meet people?" Pearl, exasperated, would ask Sugar.

To the women, Pearl would say: "She's really very nice." The women didn't want to hear any more. They'd been hearing talk, seeing things that didn't sit right with them, things that should not be going on in Bigelow. Things that hadn't started happening until Sugar's arrival.

The men, however, were more accommodating, friendly even. They always spoke, went out of their way to do so. Came toward Sugar and Pearl with large, all-consuming grins. They tripped over themselves to get to Sugar—tipping their hats as they came, greetings rolling from their half-open mouths and a sparkle of desire in their eyes.

Very interesting.

Pearl wanted to ask Sugar where her money came from. She seemed to be available at any hour of the day. Most times. Maybe, Pearl contemplated, she was a wealthy heiress hiding out among simple folk for a spell or maybe she was a criminal doing the same.

A lot was absent from their conversations despite the friendship that was growing between them. Some things can't be broached so soon. Some things must be left unsaid for a while. Two months is not long enough to peel back the skin and reveal the truths that hide beneath it.

Sugar saw the curiosity in Pearl's eyes. It was growing more and more every day. Expanding, lengthening and maturing. Sugar was trying to avoid it. She did not want to reveal her life before Bigelow and she convinced herself that she wouldn't, no matter what. But something inside of her was weakening and she found the words of her life sitting on the tip of her tongue when she was close to Pearl and their hands brushed when planting or mixing dough for bread. Those words almost spilled out and she had to swallow quickly to keep them inside of her.

"Tell me 'bout up North. That's where you were before here, right?" Pearl asked one day as they sat at the kitchen table separating field peas. The morning was wet and by afternoon an uncomfortable gray heat had settled in Bigelow, pulling buckets of sweat from foreheads and underarms, sending the mosquitoes on a feeding frenzy. Sugar's hand slowed when the question was asked. "Oh, tell me about St Louis. One of my childhood friends moved there," Pearl continued. Sugar rolled one lone, brown pea beneath her index finger and then she raised her eyes to meet the top of Pearl's head.

"Well?" Pearl said without raising her head. Her eyes remained focused on her chore. Her fingers moved quickly as she pushed the good peas to the left of the pile and the bad, bruised, discolored peas to the right.

"Ain't nothing much to say." Sugar's mouth moved to say more, but only breath came out.

"Nothing?" Pearl's head rose and her hand movements stopped. "C'mon, got to be something. What you do when you was up there?" Pearl's tone was light on top but there was a pull beneath the words that would surely suck Sugar in if she did not step carefully.

"I—I worked for a woman," Sugar said in a low voice.

"That true, doing what?" Pearl pushed. She leaned in.

"What?" Sugar asked stupidly, already tripping over the lie she was laying down.

"Yeah, what kinda work did you do for the woman?" Pearl's voice probed.

"I, uh ... well she ran a house for uh ..." Sugar was searching for the wrong words, the words that wouldn't tell the whole truth. The right words, the true ones, dangled before her and she had to shift her eyes and close her mouth lest they jump in and spill out.

"Well?" Pearl pushed again.

Sugar scratched at the heat rising around her neck. "She ran a house for—for women. I—I cleaned up around the place." The words were out as quick as Sugar was up and out of her chair. Pearl's eyes widened, but she said nothing else. She went back to pushing her peas. She let Sugar be, for now.

Sugar swallowed but it became harder to digest the truth about her time in St Louis, Chicago and Detroit. She did not want to reveal her fifteenth year, the year she walked away from Short Junction. Small town ain't fit for a woman that ain't never had a mamma. It ain't fit for a woman that never had any friends. It ain't fit for a woman that dreamed beyond the confines and goings-on of the green and white Lacey home.

She picked up and left with the next man that said, "Sugar, girl, you somethin' else! You something special! Oohh wee! Girl, I could really get use to this type of lovin' six days a week and twice on Sunday!"

They left Short Junction on a slow-moving train to St Louis, surrounded by the sweet smells of fried chicken, sweet biscuits and by the steady buzzing of talk about the girl that was found dead in Bigelow, some twenty or so miles down the road. They said she was beaten so badly her own mamma didn't recognize her. Women covered their mouths and gasped in shock. A man called out over the sea of "I don't believe it!" and "Can you imagine?" and revealed the worst thing of all: " Her—her ... privates were cut out and laid on the ground beside her."

Sugar didn't believe the whole story, small-town folk will stretch a story until it became a tale. But she did believe that that was a sign that her departure was right on time.

St Louis was where life began picking away at her with the same slow, steady reverence of the train that brought her there.

She was awed by the buildings that stood taller than the pine trees in Arkansas, her eyes burned against the bright light of day that bounced off of the glimmering sidewalks. Sugar was completely unprepared for the fast-stepping, high-fashioned, quick-talking black people that moved around her like bees around a hive. She wanted to be one of them.

He dropped her off with a woman he called his sister. She lived in a brownstone house that looked like every other house on that street—the only distinguishable qualities about them were the variety of potted plants that graced the windowsills and the color of their doors. Mary Bedford's door was red.

Step behind the red door and you were accosted by the sweet smell of Midnight in Paris perfume. The perfume had been worn for so long by Mary and the women that worked there that it seemed to seep from the walls and move from room to room on the back of the air driven by the constantly whirling ceiling fans found in every room. Throughout the house the hardwood floors were so polished that you could look down and see what color drawers you wore.

The parlor had one small loveseat with a glass table in front of it. Other than those two items, the room was bare.

Farther down the hall was a small eggshell-colored kitchen. An ice box, stove and square white countertop table with two chairs filled the space to capacity, leaving little room for the sun's rays to settle. A bathroom, painted years before in pink and mauve, was adjacent to the kitchen. You could often find yourself sitting on the toilet and craving for the bacon that sizzled right on the other side of the wall.

The basement was for gambling. Plenty of men had nearly lost their lives over ill thrown dice or a slightly bent card, but Mary didn't play that shit, and would have you cut into unidentifiable pieces if you tried to pull a fast one.

He promised, without looking at Sugar, that he would be back in a while. Mary Bedford shoved some bills in his hand, closed the door behind him and told Sugar, "He ain't coming back, so don't look for him to do so. He's a liar, a cheat and a thief. But you've laid down with him so I suppose you know all that."

Mary Bedford was copper colored, short and stocky with breasts that resembled overripe melons. She wore a long black curly wig that touched her behind and often got caught in the spaces between chairs and sofas. Her laugh was loud and harsh and her teeth were yellow from smoking two packs of Luckys a day.

"You sure are black, gal" was the second set of words to her. And she reminded her of this fact every day after that.

"Your mamma black like you? Ah, it don't matter, they got a lot up here that like 'em like you. What's that they say? The blacker the berry the sweeter the juice?" She laughed.

Sugar was scared. Her heart beat a hundred miles an hour in her chest. The fear was plastered across her face and she fought to keep her tears from falling.

"Is your juice sweet, honey baby?" she asked her. Sugar could smell the left-behind scent of some man coming off her breath.

Sugar wanted to yell at her, hit her, but seeing she was standing in her house, she decided it was just better to leave and reached for the door.

"Gal, you don't know a soul in St Louis, so make it easy on yourself. You. Not me. So go on up to the first room on the left and take off all your clothes."

All Sugar could think was: *This woman must be funny or something.* She'd heard tales about city women doing it with one another. Sugar had experienced quite a few things in her fifteen years, but laying with a woman wasn't one of them.

"For what?" Sugar said in her most vicious Lacey voice, placing her hands on her hips.

Mary just laughed. "So's I could check your hair for lice. Can't have lice, you know. A lot of you country bumpkins got 'em."

Sugar clucked her tongue and rolled her eyes. It was obvious to her where she'd been left. A whorehouse. Same shit, different state. "Shoot, I don't need to get butt naked for you to check my hair."

Mary just flipped a wisp of hair away from her brow and said, "You do for me to check them pussy hairs of yours."

Sugar spent five years with Mary. They weren't easy years—years done on your back never are—but they were years that could have been done harder somewhere else. Mary passed along forty years of know-how to Sugar and Sugar became second in charge of the house when Mary was away.

One Sunday as they sat together in the kitchen, absorbing the street sounds and smells of summer, Mary turned to Sugar and stared at her long and hard. "You leaving soon, ain't ya?" she said matter of factly. Mary never held her girls, they were free to go when they wanted to but hardly ever did.

"Thinking about it," Sugar replied without looking up from the magazine she was lazily flipping through. Mary sighed and scratched at her head. Her face was absent of the Monday through Saturday stage makeup she wore. Her salt and pepper hair was braided in a hundred pickney braids that stood straight up in the air. She looked older than her forty-five years.

"Hmm, figured that. Lemme ask you something, Sugar. Why you act like you hate everybody? Especially men. You talk to them like they dogs in a gutter somewhere." She continued, weary of waiting for her reply, "If you hate 'em as much as you act like you do, then baby, I'm sorry to say, you in the wrong business."

Sugar had had little episodes with a few of the men that came to visit the house. She'd cuss 'em and maybe even get in a slap or two. "She a little spitfire ain't she, Mary!" they'd say, wiping their lips on their way out through Mary's red door. Then to Sugar, "I'll see you next week, you little devil, you." They always came back.

"First of all I don't hate everybody. I don't even hate anybody. Men ... well, really no need to talk to them any better than I do. 'Sides, this here is business, a business that involves very little conversation," Sugar replied.

Mary pondered that for a while.

"Still, I can't believe you get all the requests you do when you never even offer a smile or a kind word—"

"Well, it ain't hurting nothing, is it? It's obvious they like the way I talk to them. Shit, Mary, I could talk about their mammas and they'd still come back for more."

"Is it 'cause you didn't know who your daddy was? Is that why you talk to men like you do, treat them like you do? All men ain't like your daddy. All men don't walk out and leave their babies—"

Sugar viciously cut her off. "It ain't about me not having no daddy or no mamma, it ain't about nothing, I just ... I just ..." She slammed her hands down on the table in frustration, causing Mary to flinch with surprise. Something in her wanted to let go, but she didn't know how.

Mary was quiet for some time. They just sat and watched and listened to the children play and laugh below them.

"Sugar, ain't you ever had no good times?" she said with a bit of sadness in her voice.

"What you mean?" Sugar said, knowing all too well what she was talking about. Sugar had seen good times being had all around her, in the Lacey house, in Mary's house, but never had one that she could call her very own.

"It seems to me," Mary began, and then decided to get up and stretch, "Whew, seems to me that I ain't never see you look up from whatever you were doing and just smile."

"Just smile? Smile at what? At who?"

"Smile into the air, girl!" she said and waved her arm through the air.

"That's crazy … smiling into the air," Sugar said and turned her head away.

"Naw, chile, it ain't crazy, you smiling into the air 'cause a good long-time-ago thought caught you off guard. Not 'cause you crazy," Mary said, sat down and looked back out into the world.

"I guess you right, then. I ain't never had no good times."

Sugar saw the way Mary's eyes looked. Not hurt, but worried. Worried that she was sitting down with a twenty-year-old woman who had never had any good times.

"You better start, 'cause time is running and a life without good times ain't a life worth having."

Sugar left not too long after that conversation. There was something else she could do. Something that she'd been doing for years. First in the fields of Short Junction amongst the poppies and daisies and then later, alone in her bathroom, beneath the heavy sounds of the shower masking it away from the world. Or so she thought. Her voice had soothed Mary many nights as she listened to it filter through the walls of the house. Sugar could sing like an angel.

Mary hugged her tight at the bus stop. Sugar swore she saw tears swimming in her old eyes. Mary shoved a card in Sugar's hand. "He's an old friend of mine, lives in Detroit, owns a record company there. Tell him I sent you and he'll be sure to talk to you."

Sugar hugged her back hard and thanked her. For the first time she felt different. Special. Not just Sugar Lacey from Short Junction, Arkansas, but Sugar Lacey, ready for the world. Sugar daydreamed all the way to Detroit. She believed her days of working on her back were over and done with.

She arrived and called Al Schwartz as soon as she stepped off the Greyhound.

"Mr Schwartz, Ms Mary Bedford said I should call you to—"

"Who?" The whining, annoyed voice crackled back at her.

"Mary Bedford—"

"Mary Bedford," he repeated, "Mary Bedford? Listen sweetie, I don't know a Mary Be—"

"Mary Bedford of St Louis," she said, cutting him off.

There was silence for a while.

"Yes," he said. The Hollywood had left his voice.

"Well, she said I should call on you while I'm here—"

"Oh really. Did she now?"

She felt it, the sleaze. She could detect sleaze a mile away.

"Yes, Mr Schwartz. She said I should call on you and that you might be able to help me. You see, I'm a singer."

Silence.

"Okay, sweetie, if you're a friend of Mary's and she specifically asked you to look me up, well, then fine. Where are you now?"

"I'm at the bus station."

"Hop a cab and come on by."

Detroit was even bigger and busier than St Louis.

"Say, listen," Sugar said to the cab driver as she ran her fingers over the business card. "What type of name is Schwartz?"

"Jewish," he said.

She had never met a real live Jew before. Well, not that she was aware of.

She walked into a building that had marble floors and marble walls. She walked into the elevator, a bent-over old black man mumbled a hello and then asked her which floor. "Fifteen," she replied and moved to the back. The elevator crept through each floor. Sugar smoothed down her tight red dress and fluffed at her short strawberry blond wig. The old man looked over his shoulder at her once.

A large desk sat no more than five feet from the elevator doors. Behind it was a woman whiter than the whitest white person Sugar had ever laid eyes on. Her skin was the color of talcum powder and you could see tiny river veins threading through her face, neck and hands. Her red hair was swept up into a beehive; her lips were so thin they disappeared when she frowned. She looked at Sugar with her baby blue cat's-eyeshaped glasses and asked her to have a seat.

Sugar sat for nearly an hour and a half. The woman behind the desk kept looking at her like she was a piece of rotting meat. Sugar knew that look. That look slowly stole away the special feeling she'd had with her all the way from St Louis.

Wasn't that something, one look from a pale white girl with bad hair and glasses sent her reeling back to Short Junction and no good-time thoughts.

The box on the desk buzzed and some words came out.

" 'Scuse me," she said, snapping her fingers in Sugar's direction, "Mr Schwartz will see you now."

She pointed toward a door at the end of the hall.

Al Schwartz was small, balding and white. He smiled and Sugar saw that his teeth were too big for his mouth.

"Well, hello, Miss. Uh … what was it again?"

"Sugar," she said as she shook his hand. It was clammy.

"Please sit."

Sugar looked around the large office. Fancy. White thick carpet, gold records hung on the wall. Pictures of Mr Schwartz and a variety of singers Sugar knew and didn't know.

He sat behind his big shiny black desk, grinning at her with big teeth and rubbing his hands together like she was going to be his next meal.

"So, Sugar, how is ole Mary?"

"Oh, she fine," she said, trying to keep the pleasantness in her voice, trying to keep a smile on her face.

"That's good. I haven't seen her for quite some time, at least fifteen years or more," he said, kind of absently. "So, you sing, do you?"

"Yes."

"Where have you performed?" he asked, getting up and coming over to sit on the desk right in front of her. His legs were open a bit. Just a bit.

Sugar leaned back in her chair. She smelled his sweat, and it didn't smell good.

"Well ... just church," she lied.

"Church? Really," he said, closing his legs. "You're a church woman, are you?"

"No," Sugar says and his legs open up again. Wider this time. "Hmmm, interesting," he said. "So, how do you know *our* Mary?"

"Our Mary"? Mary always said she didn't belong to anyone. Maybe he hadn't heard that.

"I worked for her for a while," Sugar says. No need for her to lie about that. She hadn't realized that some lives were based on the lies people told to get by.

"Really ... interesting," he said again. Sugar supposed he liked that word a lot.

"And Mary said you should call me?" He seemed a bit surprised.

Sugar's smile was beginning to waver and she thought, *We've been down this road before. How many times does he want me to answer that question?*

She did not answer him, not verbally, she just nodded her head because she felt that if she opened her mouth she might say something that might not be too nice. Mary begged her to be nice. This is Mary's friend and Sugar wanted to be nice, but she knew he wanted her to be nicer than she had intended on.

"Nice dress," he said and those teeth were showing again. He was closer now, so they were even bigger. She made a bet with herself that he was a biter. She didn't want to fuck him, she knew he'd leave marks.

"Thank you," she said. Quiet again.

"Yes, um, red suits you well," he said and his eyes traveled over her. She could feel them; sleazy, slimy little things that felt like fingers, moving down and over her breasts, across her stomach around her behind and then down between her legs.

They sat there in silence for a while. Him smiling. Her, not smiling.

His legs were wider and his hands were playing around the zipper of his pants. She didn't even look down at what was going on there. She just kept looking at those big teeth.

"Sugar ... I want you to do one thing for me. Just one, before I hear your sweet voice." His voice was thick. She's familiar with that sound. She grew up hearing that sound.

"Just ... just ..."

He couldn't even finish. But still, she wouldn't look down. She heard the zipper of his pants come undone. She smelled his dick before she saw it.

"Just suck it?" Sugar innocently asked, still looking at his teeth. He couldn't talk, he just nodded yes, yes, yes.

"No, I don't do that anymore," Sugar said. "I'm a singer now."

His eyes flew open; and his voice became clear.

"You don't do that anymore? You don't? Oh. I'm sorry ... the rules are you suck, you fuck and anything else I want you to do, then you sing. Those are the rules."

Sugar looked at the pictures on the walls. Then down to his dick then back to the teeth.

"Did you tell Frank Sinatra that too?" Sugar said and got up to leave.

"You ain't no fucking Frank Sinatra ... you ain't even no Bessie Smith! What you are is a colored whore!"

Sugar was out the door walking past the pale woman behind the desk and hoping she didn't see the tears in her eyes. But that man, Mr Schwartz, he couldn't let her go just like that. He ran out of his big office, zipping up his pants, and he screamed:

"You ain't gonna get nowhere without me, now bring your black ass back in here and do what I tell you to do! Do what Mary sent you here to do! You don't really think I would just hear you sing just because you're—" He was stumped for a while, like he was trying to find a word that would insult her more than asking her to put his penis in her mouth.

"—you!" he finally screamed.

She wanted to turn around, to go back and slap him around for a while. He was so small it would have been easy to do. But she kept on walking and telling herself that he was a friend of Mary's and she had promised to be nice.

"I gotta tell Mary, he's a friend she don't need," she said aloud as she slammed out of the building and into the bright sunlight.

There she was, back to her beginning, but now it was worse. Now she was all alone. She traveled from city to city always trying to get someone to hear her sing, but all they wanted to do was fuck. So she gave up and gave in.

Chapter Eight

The hammer that resided in her head was banging hard today, causing Sugar to squint her eyes in pain and massage her temples. The headaches had been with her since she was a teenager. The hammer ... the bang, bang, bang just seemed to be the perpetual echo of a million headboards slamming hard against bedroom walls.

She rose from her bed and stiffly walked to the bathroom. Fragments of a dream fading in and out, trying to slip between the pain and the pounding. She couldn't bother with that now, she felt soiled, her body and hair were heavy with the left-behind smell of a john.

She sat on the toilet and let the urine fall from inside of her. She picked at the long dried rivers of cum that clung to her thighs; it flaked easily and fell weightless to the floor.

No different than the night, week, month or year before. Always the same, so why now did the sameness of her life bother her, cause her frustration and purple anger?

She wanted to slap at these men, the ones who came to find pleasure between her legs, she wanted to slap and claw at their faces when they used her roughly and wrongly, treating her as if she were a lavatory. These men who didn't stop to kiss the nape of her neck, or explore the lonely place beneath her breasts with their tongues.

She wiped herself and laughed at the comical indecency of it all, the business and the men that kept it prosperous. Who would know to look at them, Bigelow men; broad-backed, strong-chinned men that wore pride on their shoulders, spoke loving words to their wives and kissed the small foreheads of their children nightly. Who would know they laid with Sugar Monday through Saturday and asked God for forgiveness on Sunday. Same hands that cupped the soft cheek of a wife or held lightly to the elbow of an elderly grandparent, had also crossed Sugar's body and invaded her moist places. If only the Bigelow women knew, knew for sure. Right now all they heard were rumors that spelled something, but what that something was, they didn't yet know.

Sugar brushed her teeth, scouring her tongue with her toothbrush until it was pink with irritation. She worked feverishly at trying to rid her mouth of the lingering taste from the night before that otherwise found its way into every forkful of food she consumed.

She sighed and moved to the lower parts of the house, into the kitchen that held one table, two chairs, bare cupboards and a refrigerator that hummed empty. She would have to go out today, take a walk into town and shop at the small market underneath the quiet, hating eyes of the Bigelow women.

Maybe Pearl would need to go too; it would make her task so much easier. She could allow herself to be distracted by the constant sound of Pearl's voice.

Sugar moved to the living room and stretched out on the couch. She could hear the small laughter that sailed into her house from the Taylor home. Pearl. Sugar liked her, perhaps because Pearl did not question her outright. Although Sugar had caught the question in Pearl's eyes, saw it poised in the lift of her brow and slight purse of her lips. Never voiced, not yet anyway. Sugar knew it would not always be that way, the same way you knew night would not last forever and summer would follow spring.

Saturday. Bid whist night. Pearl, Shirley, Minnie and Clair Bell sat around the kitchen table, doing more talking than playing. Bid whist was just the excuse to draw them together. Tall glasses filled with lemonade sat at the wrists of card-holding hands, water moved slowly down the outside of the glasses, forming tiny puddles around their bases. It was hot enough to have all of the windows open to welcome in any small breeze that chose to come, but what the other women were hoping for, praying and wishing for, was a glimpse of Sugar—preferably naked—to appear across the way.

Shirley and her sister Minnie had fought like children over a toy about who was going to sit in the chair facing the window, until Pearl threatened to lower the shade. Shirley gave up, conceding only because she had witnessed the maiden unveiling of Sugar's privates.

"I tell you, Pearl, somethin' ain't right about that woman. And now you and her spending time together ... that don't look right at all," Shirley said, looking over her glasses at Pearl. "I say ya better keep a close eye on your belongings ... and that means Joe too!"

"Believe it, Pearl, Shirley talkin' the truth, she may be crazy but she ain't stupid!" Minnie Grayson added in a laughing voice.

Pearl moved her gaze from her cards and planted it dead center on Minnie's thin face. Minnie was Shirley's baby sister. Nearly fifteen years separated them. She was the quintessential change-of-life baby. Although they were full-blood relatives, the two women looked nothing alike. Minnie was cobalt black, short and extremely thin. Her face resembled a vulture's, long, ragged and drawn—her life was written all over it.

The only similarities connecting the two were the large wide eyes and flair for minding other people's business. They were infamous for bickering amongst themselves and insulting each other was a way of life for them.

"The Lord don't like no slack mouth," Pearl said and turned back to studying her hand of cards.

"Sure don't ... He must can't stand you at all, Shirley!" Minnie said and slapped her thigh hard with laughter.

"Hush up, woman ... I done told you once already," Shirley said between clenched teeth. She was getting riled up and her head shook in anger and exasperation against her sister. "I ain't gonna tell you again!" She shook her finger at Minnie and adjusted her blue wig.

"Aw, cool it, Shirley, you know I'm just messin' with you." Minnie waved her hand at Shirley. Pearl caught the glint of mischief in her eyes and the short tail of the smile that moved swiftly across her lips.

"Alls I know is I heard Gibson down at Motley's talkin' 'bout her." Clair Bell spoke in her scratched voice. As a young woman, the thick coarseness of her voice had been seductive, but now, pushing seventy, it came out as if from vocal cords made of steel wool; hard, brash and unappealing.

Clair Bell, the great-granddaughter of the town's first reverend, was hardly outspoken. To share the same breathing space with Clair Bell was to be alone. She behaved the exact opposite of what her physical presence presented. A large woman, a full six feet, big boned and thick skinned, Clair Bell looked as if she could beat any man in four counties. In fact she was the exact opposite. She could chop her own wood and haul a twenty pound bag of grain on her head from the general store to her front porch, but she couldn't snap the thin necks of chickens or handle the jelly-like liver of cows. She cried crocodile tears at the thin slicing pain of a splinter. Clair Bell was nothing that you would expect her to be.

And now she spoke in her small voice, the one that sounded lost in a cave deep inside her large body. Everyone was quiet, waiting for Clair Bell to tell what she'd heard. She seemed not to remember that she'd spoken at all, instead she moved her chair back from the table, raised one stockinged foot and placed it in her lap. She examined the off-color nude nylon that enclosed her foot and then began to massage her swollen protruding bunion.

The women quietly watched her for a while in disgust. All except Pearl were disgusted at the very fact that she would begin a statement of such magnitude and then forgo it to massage a bunion. Pearl, on the other hand, was disgusted that Clair was massaging her bunion right at her kitchen table.

"Well ... what they say?" Minnie asked after the quiet and the lack of information began to take hold of her neck like a suffocating grip.

"Hmmm." Clair Bell looked up from her feet. Her face and eyes always retained somnolent characteristics, and she yawned, suggesting that it was more than a look.

"Gibson. What did he say?" Shirley pushed, leaning in closer.

"Say 'bout who?" Clair Bell was truly lost.

They all exhaled loudly. Shirley sat back and crossed her arms over her sagging breasts and rolled her eyes up in the air in disgust. Minnie shook her head in dismay and turned to look at Pearl.

"What did Gibson say about the woman Sugar," Minnie said slowly, making sure she left time and space between each word so that Clair Bell could fully grasp what she was trying to say.

"Oh ..." Clair Bell stopped and tilted her head slightly upward, searching the air for the words she needed, and then very calmly she said: "He said she a whore."

There were just hearts. Hearts beating loud and excitedly, and finally they all remembered to breathe.

It was said; the damage was done. Clair Bell went back to her bunion untethered by the excitement her words caused.

"Oooh wee! Hot dang! I knew it! Right here in Bigelow ... a whore! Lawdy, Lawdy!" Shirley's eyes sparkled behind her thick lenses.

Pearl's mouth was slightly open in disbelief and Minnie was holding her stomach and laughing loudly.

"You got the whore of Babylon right next door ... and you call her friend." The word *friend* came out slick as blood. "Running 'round town with her like ya'll was cut from the same cloth. What you think about her now?" Shirley was pointing a crooked accusatory finger in Pearl's face.

"Take your finger outta my face." The words moved out of Pearl's mouth like steel pellets, her face turned to ice, her glare moved from Shirley and fell hard on Clair Bell. "That's a terrible thing to say 'bout someone. You spreading rumors, and that ain't right. How you fix your mouth to say such a thing? You don't even know her." Pearl's chest was rising and falling quickly as she struggled to take in and release air. Her heart was beating wild with anger. But her mind stepped back to a hot, heavy day when the sun refused to shine and field peas lay in waiting on the kitchen table between herself and Sugar. She remembered the questions she asked about Sugar's life and the answer she got: "*I cleaned up in a women's home.*" The words echoed false in her mind, just as they did when Sugar first uttered them aloud. Pearl ignored the warning bells that went off in her soul.

Clair Bell raised her eyes to Pearl's and smiled a little. "I ain't sayin' it, I'm repeatin' it ... there's a difference." She said this in the small childlike voice that was characteristic of Clair Bell, but the usual innocence it carried was gone. Challenge took its place.

Pearl lowered her eyes and then raised them again. She placed the cards face down on the table and got up curtly. Tears stung at her eyes as she turned her back to the women and peered out the window. "It ain't right no matter how you put it. You don't know that girl from Adam and here you are dragging her name through the mud based on hearsay. Ya oughta be ashamed!"

Who was she to protect Sugar and why should she? Didn't Jesus protect the whore by asking those who were without sin to throw the first stone? Pearl questioned herself and her actions. How much did she really know about Sugar? Not much, when you got right down to the nitty-gritty of things. Sugar hardly spoke and when she did it wasn't about anything that had to do with her directly. She spoke in circles. Pearl didn't want to prod and probe her, she could see that though Sugar had a menacing look about her, she was really very fragile. Pearl had come this far with her, had been in her home, sat with her on the porch quietly watching the sunset or listening to the sounds of life that surrounded them. Too far to let it go to waste. She was near to bringing her into the fold, presenting her to God as a saved member of the Bigelow First Baptist Church. And then there was her face. The face that reminded her so much of Jude. She couldn't turn her back and let all of that go. She wouldn't.

Confident, she turned to meet their gazes. She knew of their indiscretions. Their dirty little secrets, the ones they themselves had forgotten existed. She looked at them with eyes as black as coal.

"Maybe Gibson is confused … maybe he mean someone that look like her. Maybe someone told him about some *one time, long ago* thing that happened to her.

Something she trying to forget that done caught up with her." The women listened to the excuses as they spilled one after the other from Pearl's mouth. Their eyes shifted between each other and then back to Pearl.

"Everybody gotta past, something they ashamed of." Pearl paused and looked directly at Shirley. They held each other's eyes for one long moment, Pearl revealing, with one look, what she'd known for years. Shirley's eyes were confused and then, as if a light went on, tears of comprehension, shame and then anger filled her eyes. She turned her head sharply away and lowered her eyes.

Pearl knew the story as did everyone else in Bigelow. But Pearl was the only woman bold enough to confront Shirley with it. And she would if Shirley pushed, she'd repeat what she'd heard from her own mother's mouth, if Shirley pushed her.

It was a story that was told amongst the colored kitchen help while they cleaned up after a birthday party or the field hands as they stole sweet relief from the sun beneath the shade of a magnolia tree. They would chew tobacco or drink heavily from tin cups filled with fresh well water and lean their backs against the bark of a tree or lay themselves down on the earth and speak of small things that had happened in their lives, or others they knew. Eventually, someone would start to speak of Crazy Ciel Brown.

"Her daddy was the white man from over in Ashton. He usta own the cannery and a few other things that ain't worth mentioning because they ain't no where 'round here. I believe his name was McHenry. Had lots of money, a wife and a pair of look-a-like girls. But I guess all that wasn't enough for him. He had to have himself a colored woman too."

"How you know so much?" a doubting Thomas would ask.

"I knows 'cause my cousin on my daddy side who usta cut cane down in Florida, knew the hairdresser by the name of Rebecca, who was acquainted with one of the maids that worked there who seen it all go down—her name be Belle. Belle Mason."

That explanation was usually good enough for any disbeliever.

"Anyways, like most low-down crackers that God seen fit to give abundance to, he felt like he should be able to have anything and anyone that happened to be under his roof. 'Sides, his wife wasn't no more good to him. She couldn't meet his needs. She was a drinker."

"I can't say that I blame a man for strayin' away from a wife who put away more liquor than him. I mean, a man's got needs, you know?" The same disbeliever would interrupt, yet again.

"Will you hush and let the man tell the story?" someone would say in an irritated voice.

"Like I was saying," the storyteller would continue, "the woman of the house be passed out somewhere, while her man just be a tipping on down to the maid's quarters, pick out the one he wanted and hop up on top of her like she was one of his horses."

"What the woman name be?"

And uncomfortable silence would rise like thick smoke.

"Man, if you don't shut your mouth and let the man tell the story!" someone would hiss.

"I believes her name was Shirley Brown. Don't know where she at now, or if she even still alive. But back then she was just a young thing, barely thirteen years old from what I hear," the storyteller would say in a voice filled with innuendo.

"When Shirley got big, they say McHenry known it was his because he was the only one she had been with and he had the bloody sheet to prove it!"

A gasp would emanate as they shook their heads in loathing.

"Now ya'll don't think that the missus of the house didn't know what was going on. She knew! And ain't say one single solitary word about it!"

"A colored woman would have bust him in his head!" someone would shout out and the crowd would fall out in uproarious laughter.

"That is the truth! But ya see, she was doing her own midnight tipping down to them stables. Now whether she was laying with man or beast, ain't for me to say, 'cause I wasn't there and don't know one who was."

"Uhmph!"

"When Shirley got too big to ignore it any longer, McHenry sent her away to have that baby. His wife said she wasn't going to be shamed by what he'd done. She had to be able to go to town and them functions white people are so fond of, and hold her head up. Couldn't have people whispering behind her back.

I heard that that child, which is Ciel, was raised by an Injun couple over in Shepardsville. Well, she don't look like she got an ounce of white blood in her no how, so no one was the smarter."

"Yeah, git to the money part!"

"Well, once a month the couple would find money wrapped in cheesecloth and nailed to their door. People say McHenry was the one to send the money by way of his servants. The couple never knew where it was coming from and if they did, they didn't say.

"That man provided for Ciel good and right! And after he died, I heard that he left her a whole heap o' money!"

There would be an all consuming stillness, as the people digested the tale and drew their own conclusions from it.

No, Pearl wouldn't repeat it now, not if Shirley backed down and found her place again in Pearl's home. She wouldn't speak it but she would think it. Think it so caustically that the thoughts themselves would burn from her mind and rest like flames on Shirley's soul.

"How you all know it ain't just a downright lie," Pearl finished. Her tone challenged everyone in the room.

Clair Bell and Minnie stared mute. Shirley was afraid to raise her eyes, lest she see her past looking back at her again. Then Clair Bell spoke again.

"Well, he say he got a friend over in Hampton, who got a friend ... some high yella boy that happen to got a little money." She rubbed her thumb and forefinger together. "Don't know his name, though ... well, he asked Gibson friend if he knew one of them type of women." She tilted her head toward the open window, indicating Sugar's house. Indicating Sugar. "And Gibson friend said, that he knew one of them type of women he was looking for. Told him her face wasn't much to look at, but she made up for that in the bed."

Silence.

"She, she, she! What that mean? Who is 'she,' she ain't Sugar! She could be anyone. Could be you. Could be me!" Pearl was near to yelling, her words came out in waves of trembling emotion.

"True. He ain't call her name directly. But he did say that she was over on Grove Street," Clair Bell said.

"Grove Street run near a mile long," Pearl said, running her open hands across her moist face.

"Uh-huh, that's what the man said when he told him, but then he made it clear that he should look for her at number ten."

Clair Bell's words echoed in Pearl's head. Shirley stood and placed her hands on her hips, a triumphant smile resting comfortably on her lips, her past sins forgotten for the moment. "Told you so, Pearl," she said.

Minnie saw the darkness suddenly cover Pearl's face like a widow's veil. "C'mon ya'll, I think it's time we get going." She could see they had pushed too far. She gathered the loose cards that had been forgotten on the table. "I think it's about to storm out there," she continued, feeling an appropriate excuse was needed. "Shirley, Clair Bell, let's go."

Clair Bell shot a questioning look at Minnie. The dark sky was speckled with brilliant stars and held no threat of rain. Minnie stretched her eyes wide and nodded her head a bit. "Let's go," she said again, stern this time.

"Shirley, you know you don't want that piece of wig to get wet. It'll smell like a dog when it do and take a whole week to dry." The humor camouflaged Minnie's growing nervousness. She was uncomfortable with what had been said there tonight. The look that blanketed Pearl's face was all too familiar to her, she'd seen it roosting there for years after Jude was killed.

"Why you messin' with me all the time—" Shirley started her attack on her sister, but Pearl cut her off.

"Out, now." Pearl spoke in a low hushed voice, one that carried despair, loss and loathing. "Get out now." Her anger and disappointment could not be repressed with politeness, not this time.

The women turned, open-mouthed, on Pearl and watched her as if watching a stranger. Shirley started to speak but Minnie pinched at the thick meat that was her waistline. Shirley sucked her teeth and slapped her sister's hand away. It was now obvious that they had pushed Pearl to the edge, she was ordering them to leave her home, to get out. Not feigning a headache or claiming that she had to rise early for church. No excuses this time, they had taken her way past courteous and dropped her off somewhere near I don't give a damn!

The women left, muttering under their breath and throwing cautionary looks over their shoulders at Pearl, who sat quietly at the table, her head resting in her hands. All uttered good-byes and the sound of clicking heels was replaced one hour later by an approaching Buick in need of a new engine. Joe walked in, his steps a bit unsure, his balance slightly off and the smell of beer swimming around him. He saw his wife, kissed her wetly on her cheek before heading upstairs. He only realized that she had not greeted him, verbally or otherwise, as his head hit the down-filled pillow and sleep claimed him.

Chapter Nine

Pearl sat still, barely realizing that Joe had entered the house and kissed her. Her mind was floating above her, concentrating on things she could not quite understand. She jumped at the sound of his boot hitting the floor above her head, the creaking springs of the bed as he lay down and the cutting snore as sleep took him over.

She heard a car's engine cut off, a door open and then close, the muffled sounds of knocking and then the quick clean closure of Sugar's screen door. Pearl squeezed her head between her hands; she would not get up and spy on her neighbor. Her friend. She would not.

Morning found Pearl still seated in the chair, in the kitchen. Her eyes were swollen from lack of sleep and weeping. She'd seen. Seen Sugar passing from window to window, naked and encased in the arms of a man Pearl knew to be Carlus Harden. The moon was high and illuminated the sky so brightly, it was as if heaven had lit a bonfire. Pure black nakedness that blended and united to form living breathing darkness.

Pearl wondered if Carlus held his wife Alberta that way. If he grabbed her head and pulled it back so far that another half inch would cause her neck to snap; all this to run his tongue across her chin and down the length of her throat. Pearl shivered, and wondered if she could ever eat at the Rib Shack again knowing those hands, his fingers that cleaned and seasoned the meat, skinned and cut the potatoes and shredded the cabbage and carrots for cole slaw also probed deep inside the womb of her neighbor and handled her breasts.

In the end though, Pearl did nothing but watch until the bodies tired of spinning past the windows and fell to the floor. She saw him leave, a full satisfied look on his face. He turned once to survey the house on his way out to his car. He put the automobile in neutral, released the hand brake and let it coast to the end of Grove Street. Only then did he turn on the ignition and the headlights.

Pearl couldn't sleep after that. It was near three in the morning when Carlus left. Another man showed up less than twenty minutes later. He came on foot and wore a large brimmed straw hat. The moon was bright but not so much so to glare or burn your brow. He came across the field, head low, hands shoved deep into the pockets of his overalls. He did not knock at the front door, but moved like a snake between the houses and entered quietly through the back door. Pearl watched for the spinning bodies to appear at the windows, like performers on stage, but no one showed. The man left twenty minutes later, head still hung low.

Pearl waited for another. Maybe one would approach by bicycle or mule, drop from the sky or crawl from the earth. She wouldn't be surprised or even gasp with astonishment.

That Sunday's service was less than uplifting. The strength Pearl usually claimed from the Reverend's words and the sweet sounds of Gospel singing was absent this day. Instead, her spirit had drained from her body, her faith had been torn from her soul. She sat there barely aware of the thumping feet and the hand clapping that filled the church before butting its melodic head on the rafters. Her Bible lay closed on her lap.

Joe sat stoically beside her, one hand resting gently on her knee. His eyes, dark with concern, darted from pulpit to Pearl and lingered there on her stricken face. He'd expressed his concern, more than once, in between the "Halle" and the "lujah." A squeeze of her knee or just a searching look into those vacant eyes. He did not know what had upset her so, and she would not tell. He'd found her still seated at the kitchen table, just as she was seven hours earlier when he stumbled in from his Saturday night poker game and planted a wet, sloppy kiss on her cheek. He noted she was still dressed in her sleeveless yellow and white summer dress, the one that reminded them both so much of Jude. "You been up all night, Bit?" he said through a yawn. "Yes." Her response was insipid. "You feeling okay?" Joe's question had a casual concern about it; he knew how much Pearl hated being fussed over.

Joe said church could lose them for one Sunday, but Pearl shook her head no and moved by him like a woman twenty years her senior.

Carlus Harden took Joe's hand in his, greeting him as he did every other Sunday morning after church. They were Mason buddies and before that, childhood friends. He tipped his hat to Pearl, who would have, on a normal day, smiled and placed her hand gently on his shoulder as a gesture of kindness and warmth. Instead, Pearl averted her eyes. She wanted to point her finger and call him a fornicator, but ignored his greeting instead, preferring not to lay her icy stare on him.

If Carlus was a fornicator, what would that make Sugar? Pearl wondered.

She bit her tongue and kept her mouth shut. Her eyes fell on Alberta Harden. She was big again. This was her fourth child in five years. A young thing, she was barely eighteen when she married Carlus. A beauty, that's what people said about Alberta. The color of honey with large brown eyes, thick, long dark hair that curled like a pig's tail at the end. A vision of loveliness, but as dumb as the day was long.

It seemed the only thing she was good for was making babies. Carlus cooked all the meals, cleaned the house and sent the wash out to be done. She could barely control the three boys she had. They treated her like a doormat, and she just smiled her doltish smile while they walked all over her.

Alberta leaned back against one of the eight trees that grew around the tiny church. She needed the shade, and the rest. Her three sons, Carlus Jr, Frederick and Edward, ran circles around the tree, beating their open hands against their mouths and whooping like Indians. Pearl walked toward her, intention bitter on her tongue. Alberta smiled and slipped her hand behind her to push her weight away from the tree and to meet Pearl halfway. She wiped at her brow, "Hello, Miss Pearl, how you this fine day?" She did not speak, but sang her words. Pearl nodded. At first she seemed to have forgotten how to smile, how to bend her lips to form a happy face. "You look like you due any day now," Pearl said. Her face was expressionless and her voice flat. Alberta's perpetual smile wavered. "Sure is. Overdue, in fact," she said and shooed at Edward, who was pulling at her pocket book and whining "Want candy."

"Hmmm," Pearl said and looked over her shoulder to make sure that Carlus and Joe were still engaged in conversation. She stepped closer to Alberta, taking in her swollen belly and innocent smiling face. Her heart pained her. Did Alberta know she shared a bed with a man that shared himself with another?

Pearl's face twitched and her mouth opened to spill the baneful wisdom she had acquired overnight, but when she opened her mouth to speak, only silent words floated out, mingling with the bright morning sunshine and jasmine-kissed air.

She smiled at Alberta's waiting face posed before her, fixed with inquiry, waiting to absorb Pearl's words. "Hmmm," Pearl sounded again and laid her hand softly on Alberta's belly. "Somethin' fixing to give soon," Pearl said assuredly and turned to walk back toward her husband. Alberta fixed a quizzical look on the back of the old woman, not sure whether she referred to her impending labor or something else. "I sure hope so," she responded, not sure if her response was needed at all. She placed her hand over the moist imprint left behind by Pearl's own small hand. "Sure do."

Later that afternoon, Pearl sat quietly sipping her Coke, watching Sugar move and glide in front of her. Ass slipping out like syrup from her hot pants. Breasts, loose and swaying beneath a T-shirt that said "Memphis." Chuck Berry was singing from the transistor radio that rested at Pearl's crossed feet. "Need more ice, Miss Pearl?" Sugar called to her over her shoulder. Pearl uttered a solitary no, even though the ice had melted long ago and the heat had claimed the sweet, dark liquid making it unbearable to drink. For now though, Pearl would bear it, the act of sipping kept her from speaking her mind.

Sugar tugged at the weeds that threatened the colorful lite that Mrs Wilks had worked so hard at cultivating, the fragrant spirits she'd died among. Pearl sat quietly in the backyard on one of the two chairs Sugar had removed from the kitchen table and placed in the yard.

Pearl was seething. She wanted to kick the transistor radio over, leap from the chair and pounce on Sugar. Instead she sat quietly stewing in her own fury waiting for Sugar to say a word, one word, that would prove or disprove what she saw and what was being said about her.

"You sure is quiet today, Miss Pearl," Sugar said, still not looking at her. She had a grip on a particularly tough weed. Her words came in jerks as she fought with the weed. "The sermon must have been something else, so good it took your breath away, huh?"

Pearl said nothing.

Sugar pulled the weed free and held it up like a trophy, waving it back and forth over her head. She came and flopped down beside Pearl's feet, stretching her long brown legs out before her; they glistened beneath the sun and seemed to illuminate the grass beneath them. Sugar bent her head back to smile at Pearl. She was feeling particularly good today, elated even. She couldn't put her finger on the reason, perhaps because she only turned two tricks the previous night instead of three or maybe because the last one just wanted to caress her breasts.

She looked into Pearl's face and saw misery there, but selfishly she refused to ask what the problem was, she refused to allow this rare feeling to be condensed by Pearl's foul mood. She arched her back and raised herself up on one arm while the other reached into her back pocket and pulled out a crumpled pack of Luckys. She examined the package for a while, not wanting to look back at Pearl's disapproving eyes. Pearl let out a sigh and Sugar lit the cigarette, grateful for the calming smoke that filled her lungs and encircled her head.

"What kinda work you do?" Pearl asked. Her voice was her own but embroidered with fierce hostility. Sugar refused to react and in fact said nothing.

"Where you get your money from?" Louder now. Sugar blew large smoke circles from her mouth. The heat was tearing at her scalp, making her head feel like an inferno beneath her wig.

"What you say?" she said, daring Pearl to repeat her forbidden questions.

"I said, I wanna know what kinda work you do?"

"What kinda work *you* do?" Sugar reversed the question.

Silence.

Pearl watched Sugar cock off the smoke.

"Why you gotta dress like that for?" Pearl continued, her tone becoming more spiteful.

"Why *you* dress like that?" Sugar was mocking her now.

Pearl let out a heavy sigh. She stared at Sugar's neck, at the thick scar that healed ugly and crooked like a dead tree branch. She stared at the false hair that adorned her head, at the skimpy T-shirt and tiny shorts that molded to her body like second skin instead of cloth. Who else other than a whore would dress this way?

Sugar stood and walked away from Pearl, cigarette smoke trailing behind her like a wedding veil. "I'm tired," she said and her voice carried a lifetime of weariness in its tone.

"You can't answer a simple question?" Pearl said, standing and taking two steps toward Sugar's back.

Sugar stopped, dropped her burning cigarette to the ground and placed her hands on her hips. She turned to face Pearl. She had had enough. "Why you so suddenly interested in what I do?" She spoke through clenched teeth.

"There's been talk, talk about what you do and who you doing it with. I just wanna know what's true and what ain't."

Sugar stepped close to Pearl. Pearl could smell her stale breath and heard the pounding of her heart. She held her eyes with her own. "I seen you walking 'round your house buck naked ... windows open and all ... I ain't the only person that seen you either, half the town done seen you too," Pearl continued, her voice shaking with the adrenaline that pumped through her body.

Sugar smiled, a half smile that made her look wicked. Pearl watched as Sugar transformed back into the woman that had walked into Bigelow three months ago. She leaned back on one leg and looked Pearl over from head to foot.

"What the hell gives you the right to question me about what I do, where I do it and who I do it with? Huh? I can walk around my house naked if I want to, upside down and naked if I choose to! You know why? Because it's my goddamn house, that's why! Do I ask you about your business? Do I ask you about your life? I didn't even invite your sorry ass into my life. You pushed your-self into it, you and your damn pies!

"Just 'cause we spend some time together don't mean it give you the right to question me about my habits of living or working. You done heard some talk? Fine, people gonna talk come hell or high water. Shit, even if there ain't nothing to talk about, they gonna make shit up. They'll make shit up about me and they'll make it up about you, that's just the way people is, Miss Pearl. Ain't nobody safe from small-time bullshit talk!"

Sugar turned and stormed into the house. Pearl was dizzy—the combination of her pulse, Sugar's swirling words and the bobbing and weaving of her head as she spoke had done a job on Pearl, but her question hadn't been answered, so she followed Sugar into the house.

"You answer my question. You answer my question, Jude!"

Pearl had referred to Sugar by her dead daughter's name before during light conversation. It would just tumble out, innocently, like cotton candy, sweet and light. Sugar never commented on it, she herself had called Pearl Mary on certain occasions. Hers was a slip of her tongue. Pearl's blunders went much deeper than that.

"Jude, people saying you allowing mens to have their way with you. Have their way with you for money!" Pearl's eyes were vacant, her face wet with perspiration and she shook uncontrollably. Sugar's heart skipped a beat. Was this old woman about to have a heart attack? She wanted to go to her, move her to the coolness of the living room and lay her to rest on the couch, but her feet were like stone and would not allow it.

"I ain't raise you like that, Jude. Me and your father ain't raise you to be loose! So you tell me now, tell me if it's true. Tell me!"

Sugar made a move toward her friend. "Miss Pearl?" She spoke softly, afraid that even the slightest lift of her voice would have a traumatic effect on the already bad situation. "Miss Pearl, you need to calm down. You need—"

"I need an answer!" Pearl pumped her fists up and down in the air, spit flew from her mouth. Sugar stepped back and clutched at her heart.

"S-some of us make our living breaking our backs and some of us in this world make our livings on our backs." Sugar didn't know why she put it that way. A simple yes would have been sufficient. She supposed she needed, in some small sick way, to sting Pearl, just as she had done to Sugar with her own words.

Pearl's arms dropped down to her sides. She stared at Sugar with eyes that held years of tears. "Why?" she uttered. Pearl was not seeing Sugar, but Jude. "Why," she said again as one small tear worked its way down her cheek.

Sugar shrugged her shoulders and hugged herself. She suddenly felt vulnerable, like a child.

"She lied to me, you know, lied to me about where she was going." Pearl's body went limp and her head hung heavy on her neck. "I didn't want her to leave 'cause I knew something was going to go wrong, you know." Pearl was quiet for a long time and then she lifted her head up to look at Sugar. Sugar had never seen so much pain and sorrow in a person's face, and was surprised that the sight of it caused her own heart to ache. "J-Joe had placed the shoes on the table, just for a second while he turned to put his hat on the hook. They was new, shiny black shoes, wing tipped and all. They had just come ... we ordered them from the Sears catalogue. You know, he just wasn't thinking."

She trailed off again and looked into the dusty realm of the house. Sugar knew she was seeing it all over again. "The tablecloth had a crease in it too. I forgot, don't know why but I forgot and placed it on the table anyway. I didn't even notice it until I saw the shoes." She shivered as if a cold wind had suddenly blown through. "Those were bad signs, the two of them resting against one another. Evil coming in twofold." She shook her head and a sob escaped her. "I told her maybe tomorrow she could go to her friend's house, but she insisted."

Pearl looked behind her quickly and then back at Sugar. Her eyes were wide with grief.

"They brought her to me … her womanhood cut from her … Jude."

She whispered the last eleven words. Sugar only caught the name, Jude.

"Who was she, Miss Pearl?" Sugar was afraid to ask, but propelled to.

"She was my daughter. She was my daughter," Pearl said and quickly covered her mouth. "She was my daughter," she said again in a whisper.

The words opened up old wounds in Pearl's heart and soul and she ran from Sugar's house, pain gripping her spirit like an old familiar enemy.

Sugar leaned against the wall and slid to the floor. Something had happened here, something that she knew she did not want to become a part of but found herself somehow already deeply rooted in. It was her past resurfacing all over again.

Before Sugar knew it, twelve years had passed, and it was becoming harder and harder to survive the streets and the men of Detroit and Chicago. She was tired of slopping toilets, wiping tables and slinging hash.

She was tired of her stomach turning from eating fish and chips fried in two-day-old grease. Tired of coming home to a rat- and roach-infested room in a three-story walkup that should have been condemned years ago.

One window, thin mattress, sink and hot plate: ten dollars a week.

Johns humping and pumping on top of her. Calling her all kinds of sweet things—ain't worried 'bout how she feeling or whether it was good to her or not. They ain't give a shit, just as long as they could and make *their* worries go away. Harder! Faster! They would ride her like a prized racehorse.

Thirty minutes of that shit was like living a whole lifetime in hell.

"You gotta pull it out sometime—it can't stay in there forever, honey baby!" she would coo into their sweaty necks.

See, these johns wanna keep it in there for as long as possible. It's warm and safe. They be smilin' and talkin' all kinds of shit hoping you let 'em go on just a little bit longer. It done got real good to them and they don't want out notime soon.

But then it's over. The cold air hits and reality kicks them in the ass all at the same time. The money is on the bed or the floor, and suddenly, Sugar ain't his sweet baby no more. She ain't his fine black thang. She ain't nobody, nothing but a whore.

His fantasy is over. But for her, the nightmare continues. You see, she ain't got no place or no person to go to to make her forget. Not even for a short time.

The circles under her eyes and the constant shaking of her hands were telling her she was near to falling apart. She needed to get out. She needed to get home. But where the hell was home?

She hadn't heard from the Laceys in years. She hadn't bothered to send a postcard or a telegram since she left Mary's house in St Louis. For all Sugar knew they were dead, and if they weren't, they probably assumed she was.

A maniac john with a six-inch switchblade helped her make a quick decision as to when and where she would go. He sent her running for her life and straight to the next Greyhound bus bound for St Louis. She left that city with a bleeding gash on her neck and the blood-stained clothes on her back.

St Louis wasn't home, but it would have to do.

Sugar showed up at the stoop of what used to be the hottest colored whorehouse in town. The neighborhood had changed drastically. Twelve years ago, there were at least six different night spots in a four-block radius. Now those bars and clubs had been transformed into a butcher shop, Chinese laundry, storefront church and liquor store.

Twelve years ago you couldn't find a family on Sullivan Place, east of Macon Avenue or west of Joralemen Street. Well, not the mommy, daddy and baby kind of family. That area was comprised of hustlers, pimps and addicts. They of course called themselves singers and dancers. It was the place to live if you were colored and wanted to be thought of as somebody. Now there were children playing ball in the street and young mothers pushing carriages, smiling as they admired each other's babies.

The street still sparkled, just the way it did the first time Sugar arrived, and now she squinted her eyes against it, not needing to strain her neck to gawk at the tall buildings. She'd seen taller in the past twelve years.

A ROOMS FOR RENT sign hung pitifully in the first-floor, grime-laden window of the three-story brownstone. It replaced a sign that hung there twelve years earlier that proudly stated: PUSSY FOR SALE—INQUIRE WITHIN.

Sugar, her neck bandaged from the near-lethal cut she received in Detroit, sat down heavily on the steps that led up to the red door. Her sable-colored skin was ashen and chafed. Her once full figure was diminished by a good forty pounds, causing her clothing to hang and sag on her frame.

Never considered a beauty by anyone, she was now pitiful.

A round-faced little girl with large almond eyes, a small mouth wet and sticky with red Italian ice, stopped to stare intently at Sugar. Sugar hardly noticed the child, but when she did she asked her, "Mary Bedford still live here?"

The little girl was dressed in a red and white sun-flower dress, her thick hair piled up on top of her head; the ends curled under. She gave Sugar a small queer sort of smile and slightly tilted her head to the right, exam-ining the soiled rag that was wrapped around Sugar's neck. Satisfied, she plopped down on the stair step next to Sugar and began using her Popsicle stick as a shovel, digging out the dirt that lay between the cracks in the sidewalk.

Sugar looked at her, immediately reminded of the little girl from long ago who'd first asked her about her mother. The thought stirred deep emotions within her. Sugar looked around quickly and nervously, half expecting the little girl's mother to appear, snatch her up from the stair step and drag her away by the collar: We don't deal with the likes of them!

The little girl stopped her digging and looked up at Sugar. She shielded her eyes from the high noon sun and said in a distinctive Southern drawl, "Yeah, she live here. She be back soon, went down the road to the store." She considered Sugar a bit longer and then returned to her digging.

A heaviness consumed Sugar and she leaned into the hard stone stairs, allowing the heat to soothe her aching back. Her body, soul and mind were tired. She let out a loud sigh. Not one of relief but temporary contentment.

"You hurt?" the little girl's voice trailed up to her. She was pointing a tiny finger at the bloody rag that was tied around Sugar's neck. Her face was scrunched up like she was smelling something rotten.

"Yeah," was all Sugar managed to say and then sighed once again, looking off into the distance.

"Grandma, grandma!" The little girl shouted and bolted up and past Sugar. She ran into the waiting arms of a short, fat woman who looked like she'd seen better days. Sugar looked at them then turned away. Expressions of affection always made her feel uncomfortable.

The woman held the little girl tightly as she looked over at the bundled heap of a woman who sat on her stoop. She patted the girl's head and moved her behind her wide mass as she cautiously approached the woman. Mean was sparkling like diamonds in her eyes as she edged closer. Recognition quickly replaced the cold icy stare, and then pity.

"Sure nuff, if it ain't Sugar Lacey!" The short stout woman came toward her, the little girl behind her grinning and clinging to her skirts.

"She been waiting for you for a long time, Grandma," the little girl said and winked at Sugar.

It was Sugar's turn to shade her eyes with her hand. Was she seeing right? Was this Mary Bedford standing before her?

Grandma?

She looked up and into the aged face of Mary Lucille Bedford. It sure was Mary. Sugar had expected her to look older, but not as old as this. She certainly didn't expect to see her without one of her extravagant, flowing wigs. But there she stood, her thin silver strands pulled back into a tight bun. She wore a demure pink color on her lips and just a hint of blush on her cheeks. Gone was the heavy foundation, false eyelashes and light blue eye makeup that once graced her face.

Sugar thought Mary looked like life had slapped her around and then dumped her on the curbside to die. She looked horrible. The years of heavy smoking and drinking had taken their toll on Mary, but she was smiling.

"Mary Bedford, as the day I was born," Sugar finally managed to say. With difficulty she stood up, leaving her hands at her sides like limp weeds, staring at Mary and her grandchild. Mary's face gave away what she was thinking. It was a strange mixture of shock, pity and disappointment. "Come here, girl," she said, hugging Sugar. The faint smell of Evening in Paris filled Sugar's nostrils.

Three months came and went. August faded swiftly into the past and Thanksgiving was upon them. The three of them sat holding hands around a beautiful golden brown turkey. The lights were turned off and Sugar looked around at the faces illuminated by soft candlelight. Mercy was looking so much like her grandmother—pecan-colored skin and thick rosy cheeks. She smiled at Sugar, winked and bowed her head.

Mary began: "Thank you, Lord, for the food that we are about to receive and thank you for the life you allow me to have every single day. Thank you for my beautiful granddaughter Mercy and for my beautiful friend Sugar."

Sugar bowed her head lower. Even after three months of living with Mary and Mercy, she still couldn't get used to the kind words, the hugs and the kisses. She felt she did not deserve any of this.

"Please continue to rain your blessings down on us, amen." Mary ended and Mercy echoed her amen. Sugar mouthed the words, feeling the soundlessness of it quake her soul.

They ate until their fattened bellies stuck out comically in front of them. Afterward they sat in the small parlor that now held a brown, somewhat battered tweed sofa and two ivory-colored wing chairs.

Boarders came and went through the day, wishing them Happy Thanksgiving. Mary did not allow one of them to leave empty handed. She sent them off with slices of sweet potato pie, bowls of cole slaw, slices of ham and turkey. "Ya'll just better make sure you bring my plates back clean!" she'd yell as they went through the door and up to their separate rooms.

"You are too nice," Sugar said as she stroked Mercy's lolling head.

"Girl, they ain't got shit. Look at them, young and living on their own. They should be home at they mamma's house where they could save some money and get good cooking all the time. But these children nowadays in a rush to get out and be independent."

Mary shifted in her chair and wiped at her chin. "I try to help them any way I can. I got so much and they have so little, what's wrong with giving a little away? It's better than letting it go to waste, ain't it?"

Sugar nodded her head and looked down into the sleeping face of Mercy.

"She is out like a light. I'ma take her up to bed," Sugar said, and lifted the six-year-old up from the couch. She moved slowly to the back of the house where she and Mercy shared a bedroom. "We'll play cards when you get back," Mary whispered to Sugar's back.

When she returned, Mary was stretched out on the couch. "Oh, what happened to the card game?" she said with a laugh. "You got niggeritis now!" she teased further. As she came closer to Mary she realized that her position was a bit awkward. Coming still closer, she saw that her face was locked with pain.

"Mary!" she screamed, "what is it, what's wrong?"

Mary stared at the ceiling; white foam oozed slowly from her mouth. Her body shook violently as each bolt of pain ripped through her like lightning.

"Oh shit, Oh shit, Oh God, Oh shit, *Mary*!" Sugar was screaming and shaking the old woman. "Help!"

The waiting room of Cook County Hospital was dimly lit and filthy. Cigarette butts spilled from the standing ashtrays and littered the floor. The thick smell of smoke and sickness hung heavy in the air. Beige-and-green-tiled walls added to the misery of the people who had to be there.

People wandered in and out of the area, moving around restlessly as they awaited word of a loved one's condition.

Sugar sat stone still. She was tense and wary of everyone and everything around her. She'd never been in a hospital and after tonight, didn't want to have to return to one. Mercy was in a fitful sleep on her lap; a blanket encircled the two of them like black butterflies emerging from a cocoon.

The ambulance had come quickly. Sugar cursed herself for not having thought of calling for one. A boarder named Jonah heard the screaming coming from his landlady's apartment and rushed down to see what was happening. He was the one to call for an ambulance. It would be him that Mary would have to thank for saving her life … if she lived.

"Is there someone here with Mary Bedford?" a tall, white, wiry-looking man asked in a gentle voice. He had a white jacket on and a clipboard in his hands. He peered patiently over the glasses that sat at the very tip of his thin straight nose.

"Yes," Sugar said in a voice so low, even she hardly heard it.

"Are you family?" the doctor asked, looking at his chart.

Sugar froze. She wasn't family. Would they tell her anything if she wasn't family?

"I want Grandma, Mommy," Mercy said in a sleepy voice. Sugar's heart stopped beating. The child must be dreaming. Mommy?

"Oh, so you're Mizz Bedford's daughter?" the doctor said, now peering at her with tiny black eyes.

Sugar's head nodded yes, as if some unseen force was guiding it.

"Well … Mizz … uh … Mrs …" The doctor stumbled and looked to Sugar for assistance. Sugar, still in shock by the turn of events, could not read the doctor's face.

"Well, Mizz Bedford has suffered a stroke and—"

"She comin' home now?" Sugar heard someone say and turned her head to see who it was. All the eyes peered back at her. She had spoken those words. And then suddenly, they were coming again, like water flowing from a faucet. She wanted it to stop but it wouldn't. "Shecominhomenow shecominhomenowshecominhomenow."

Fear was thick in her throat like molasses, trapping the words.

The doctor was flustered. "Uh, no, she's suffered a stroke … not too severe, but she'll have to stay here for a few weeks until her condition improves," the doctor said carefully, aware that the woman he spoke to was on the verge of having a nervous breakdown.

"Can we see my grandma?" Mercy asked in a composed voice that stunned both Sugar and the doctor.

"Yes. Just for a minute, though," the doctor said and stepped back, pointing down a long corridor.

Mercy hopped off of Sugar's lap. She held her hand out to her. "C'mon Miss … uhm … Mamma. Let's go see Grandma," she said and winked.

How did this little girl get to be so strong? Sugar wondered.

Mary was in a ward with at least thirty other women. Some were moaning. Others were turned on their sides or stomachs, sleeping. Sugar was aware of the sound her shoes made as she walked down the long ward toward

Mary, sounding like a large clock inside her head. *Click-clickclick.* She wanted to run screaming from there, but she looked at Mercy and found the strength she needed.

Mary lay before them, her pecan complexion almost white. Her silver, silky hair dry and brittle. Her face twisted to one side.

Sugar was overwhelmed with sorrow. There were tubes running out of Mary's nose, mouth and arms; her eyes were closed and to Sugar, she looked dead.

It's funny, Sugar thought as she washed up the last of the supper dishes, *how life repeats itself.* Here she was once again, taking charge of the Bedford house. Collecting money and making sure the boarders conducted them-selves properly. No loud music after ten. No loitering on the stoop. She had handled it all quite well, just as she did twelve years ago.

Mercy was a tower of strength. She never complained, not even when Sugar overcooked the eggs or burned the bacon. Not even when her hair parts were crooked and her bangs drooped. She just smiled and went skipping off to school.

But Sugar knew the girl was torn up inside. She saw the tearstained pillow cases when she did the laundry.

People in the neighborhood, the former hustlers, pimps and prostitutes (some gone straight, others still living the life), came and did what they could when they could. They brought casseroles filled with baked macaroni and cheese, sweet potato pie, smothered pork chops and fried chicken. They took away loads of dirty clothes and returned them clean, folded and smelling of Borax. They did all of this for Mary, because over the years, Mary had done so much for them.

Sugar went to visit Mary every day while Mercy was in school. She fed her soup with a shaky, unsure hand, while she tried to keep a smile on her face.

She made light conversation about Mercy and what was going on in and around the house. But none of it came out sounding natural, it was always strained with the fear Sugar had lodged in her mind.

Suppose she never comes home?

Mary's speech was slurred and so she chose, most of the time, not to talk at all. She would just nod her head and offer a crooked smile.

One day, as Sugar was gathering herself to leave, Mary started to speak. It was difficult and clearly took a lot of effort to get out the one word she wanted so badly to say: Christmas.

It came out as "Kissmmmmas," but Sugar understood it. She had been worrying about that herself Usually it was just a day in a week for Sugar, but she knew that this was not just another week in her usual life. There was Mercy to think of now.

Sugar half hoped the holiday would come and go without the child noticing it, but the idea was shot down when Mercy came home from school with her scrawled pictures. Mercy had drawn a Christmas tree with tiny little gifts beneath it. She also had a wreath she'd drawn, colored brightly and cut out. Sugar saw the pride in her eyes as she presented her creation to her and asked her to take it to Mary. "This will make her happy and she'll get better soon. She won't want to miss Santa Claus," Mercy said, with a large smile and gleaming eyes.

The paper wreath now sat on Mary's nightstand propped up against the water container.

"Mary, won't you be home for Christmas?" Sugar asked, hoping her voice sounded cheerful. Mary shook her head slowly, painfully, from side to side.

Sugar was silent for some time, as she stared down at the large green and beige tile design on the floor. She eyed the Christmas wreath and could hear Mercy's excited babbling about the toys and dresses she hoped Santa would bring to her for Christmas. "Miss Shuga, I been a real good girl this year!"

Sugar squeezed her eyes shut and shook Mercy's voice from her mind. When she lifted her head to meet Mary's gaze, the eyes that looked back at her dropped responsibility heavy as stones on her shoulders.

"I'll try, Mary," she said solemnly, already convinced that her best effort wouldn't be good enough.

Sugar stood before the towering evergreen that practically swallowed the tiny parlor. There were ornaments of all colors, shapes and sizes hanging from its long, wide limbs. They gleamed and glimmered off the streetlamp light that filtered through the windows. The house was quiet except for the soft crooning of Nat King Cole's "White Christmas."

Sugar breathed in deeply, inhaling the sweet smell of the tree. It took her back to Arkansas, and she suddenly felt homesick, a feeling she'd never stumbled across before.

She turned to face Mary. "It's beautiful, ain't it," Mary said. It was still difficult for her to talk, but she was improving quickly. She'd come home by taxi just two days earlier, surprising both Mercy and Sugar.

"I just had to be here with my babies. I couldn't be in no damn hospital on Christmas, no siree!" she said as Sugar helped her up the front steps.

"I'm sure glad you're home. I didn't think I could have done it without you being here," Sugar said as she sat down in the wing chair across from Mary. She sipped her eggnog and allowed the whiskey it was spiked with to move through her, numbing the emotion she felt rising within her.

"Girl, what you talkin' about? Without me? You did it. *You* got the tree, the gifts. You did it all, girl, without my help," she said, and raised her own glass of eggnog in salute. "You didn't need me here, but I'm sure glad to be here. Thank the Lord," she added and bowed her head in a silent, quick prayer.

"I did use your money, though," Sugar said with a wry smile.

"My money is your money. You know that. 'Sides, it was all for my grandbaby."

Sugar looked back at the tree and for the first time noticed the ornament of the mother and child embracing. "Ahhh," Sugar uttered and moved closer to examine it. "I remember this," she said almost to herself as she touched it gently with the tip of her finger. "Do you remember this?" she asked, looking back at Mary, light dancing in her eyes, her finger still resting lightly on the gold and silver ornament.

Mary nodded slowly. She was the one who'd placed it there. It'd always been her favorite. It was special to her, given to her by her mother. She kept it wrapped in paper, in her hope chest at the foot of her bed.

"You tried to get me to hang it on that tree you had ..." She trailed off, recalling a long-ago Christmas. The thought of it brought a wisp of a smile to her face.

"Oh, look!" Mary shouted and sat straight up in her chair. Sugar jumped and nearly fell into the tree.

"What?" she yelped and ran toward Mary.

Mary was pointing a crooked finger toward her. "You having one. You having one I seen it don't try and deny it!" Mary was cackling and coughing like an old hen.

"I'm having what?" Sugar was confused, a puzzled look shadowed her eyes.

"You just looked up and smiled. You had one, thank the Lord, you done finally had yourself one!" Mary was laughing and slapping her thigh with glee.

Sugar smiled, finally understanding what Mary was excited about. It was true, the thought of that Christmas did make her smile. Yep, she'd had one. Christmas brings on all sorts of things. It was a magical season.

Sugar figured she'd be doing it quite often. She'd stored up plenty of good-time memories during the time she spent in the Bedford household.

"Sugar." The voice was hesitant. "Will you sing for me?" Mary's eyes were hopeful and pleading.

"Mary, I ... I told you, I don't sing no more ..." Sugar got up and walked back over to the tree. How could she deny this woman such a small request. She felt low down for doing it.

"Please, Sugar, it's Christmas. And as much as I need to hear it, I believe you need to do it," Mary said in a quiet voice.

They were silent. Sugar standing in front of the tree, Mary sitting staring at her back.

The song started small and muted with emotion, and then it rose like a wave coming out of the Atlantic. With every word, Sugar's voice stretched and grew until it was higher than the tree and overpowered the room. Mary had never heard "Silent Night" sung like that before. So much soul, so much sadness.

When she was done, both of their faces were wet with tears.

Spring came early that year. The streets came alive again with the sounds of squealing children and crying newborn babies. Sugar decided it was time. Mary was up and about. She moved a bit slower, but Sugar told herself it was age, not sickness, that slowed her movements.

By then, she was considering going west, where she heard the weather was always like a warm spring day.

"California? Who the hell you know out in California?" Mary asked, when Sugar announced her plans. "This time you won't just come back with your neck slashed, you'll come back in a damn box!"

Mary was yelling now, and Sugar tried to shut her mind to her words. She told herself—and for the most part it was true—that Mary just flat did not want her to go. Sugar didn't want to go either, but she needed to move on.

Mary ranted and raved for nearly two hours. Walking from room to room, slamming doors and cussing as she went.

"Them crackers out there don't like no kinda colored peoples. I hear they worse than the ones in the South. A soot-black girl like you don't stand a chance in hell in California!" she said before she slammed the bedroom door in Sugar's face.

That was bad, but the worst was yet to come. Sugar turned to see Mercy slipping silently into the kitchen, tears sparkling in her eyes. Up until then, Sugar had never mentioned to Mercy the fact that she would be leaving soon. The child had formed an impenetrable bond with Sugar. Sugar knew by the way she curled into her at night, matching her breath as they lay sleeping in the bed they shared.

Sugar felt like a low down snake.

Lower than she did when she lifted a can of beans from a store in Detroit owned by a gentle old man who had only the day before extended her credit.

Evening came in with a chill, and Sugar supposed this helped in cooling Mary down. She came into the parlor where Sugar was sitting and staring out of the window. Her eyes were heavy with apology.

She stood before her, leaning heavily on her cane, and reached into her bosom, pulling out a piece of paper that was aged yellow. "Here," she said and handed it to her with a shaking hand.

Sugar took it and her fingers began to tingle. "What's this?" she said as she rose from the chair.

Mary clucked her teeth and then began to ramble like a small child. "It came 'bout four years ago. I had all but forgotten it. Well, I ain't hear nothing from you in all them years. Didn't have a clue as to where you could be and I just now run across it again. Well, go on and read it."

Sugar tried to read Mary's eyes, but they held nothing but excitement. Sugar slowly unfolded the piece of paper that Mary must have folded and unfolded hundreds of times. Maybe hoping that the sheer ritual of it would someday draw Sugar back.

It was a telegram that read:

OCTOBER IST, 1951 *STOP* YOUR
MAMMA IS HERE *STOP* COME
HOME *STOP* LACEY *STOP*

Sugar read the words over and over again until they were no more than a black blur of nothing before her.

Mamma. Home.

Those two words seemed to burn into her mind.

Sugar looked from the telegram to Mary and then back again.

Mary stood in front of her, her breast heaving up and down with excitement. Sugar didn't speak. Couldn't speak.

"I almost forgot 'bout it, but like I said it's been quite a while." Mary stopped. She sat down because her legs were shaking. She breathlessly began again. "I sent word back sayin' you weren't here. I told them that you'd gone off to Detroit when you left here, but no telling where you could be by now."

Sugar blinked and reread the words again.

"Oh, Sugar, ain't it wonderful. Your mamma done come back for you. I know you grown and all, 'course it don't matter how old you are, you always need your mama. Lord knows I wish mine was still around. Lord have mercy, Sugar. It's like getting a second chance." Mary was grinning from ear to ear.

Second chance? I never had a first chance. I suppose this should be considered as my only chance, she thought to herself.

Sugar didn't know what she was feeling. Something was whirling inside of her, causing her to swoon. Was it happiness? Anger? Sadness? Did this woman who abandoned her, now after thirty years, deserve to have her?

She grabbed for the table to steady herself. Mary moved in close and took her face in her hands. "It's time," Mary said in a tender voice. Mary's face was so close to Sugar's that she could smell the Juicy Fruit gum Mary chewed by the pack. She could see the stained yellow teeth and the scar that was barely visible on the tip of her nose. But what she concentrated on were her eyes. Mary's eyes were calm and all knowing. "You got to go. Not to California, but Arkansas. Home," she said with such quiet strength it shook Sugar to the bone.

"Baby, everybody got their own reasons for doing things they do in life. It don't matter what her reason was at the time, what matters is she come back for you, and even though you might think it's too late, it ain't never too late where a mother and her child is concerned."

Chapter Ten

Weeks later, the banging was becoming irritating enough to drag Sugar kicking and screaming from the precious little sleep she could manage to steal. Sugar sat straight up and waited for the sound to come again, not sure if it was inside her head or outside her front door. It came again, a demanding knocking at her front door that caused her to jump, knocking over the nearby ashtray filled with butts and roaches.

Reefer was a new soothing friend in her life. A joint and a drink made everything okay. Veiled her vision and made the tricks she turned bearable. Yes, it was a magic plant and it was helping Sugar to play the greatest trick of them all on herself.

Lappy Clayton introduced it to her the first time they fucked. She liked the way it made her feel, how it lifted her out of herself while at the same time allowed her to go deeper into herself. It made her laugh uncontrollably until her sides ached and tears fell in floods down her cheeks.

He had taken to bringing her at least two joints every time he paid Sugar a visit, which was as much as twice a week now. "Consider it a tip," he said one early morning as he dressed, the morning sun rays dancing across his cream-colored back.

There was a part of Lappy that Sugar was comfortable with. The part that reminded her of herself, the part she wouldn't admit existed inside of her, the innocent side that at thirty years old still remained untouched by the type of life she lived. The side that came out and took in the sun and skipped rope on a St Louis sidewalk. She liked that side of herself and she saw it in Lappy Clayton too. Behind the slicked-back hair, fine suits, hip talk and gold tooth of the man Lappy, was the boy Lappy.

Sugar caught a glimpse of that boy, white on top, all black beneath. She saw it when he booked her for the whole night and showed up with fried chicken dinners and Coca Cola. The nights they laughed away. On those nights he didn't want to fuck, he just wanted to talk shit and laugh. He brought a record player over one night and a few seventy-eights. They kicked back and listened to T-Bone Walker and B.B. King. Lappy bragged that he had met both men. "They always be down at my man's place, the Memphis Roll. You can't come through Arkansas and not play the Roll."

Sugar found herself there too, among the hand clapping and loud laughter of sharecroppers, house mammies and uncles celebrating their blackness, full of their sires' spirits, getting down but not laying down for no one, not even the almighty whitey. Sugar was swept up in the raw, pulsating madness the people and the music produced. Liberated by drink and smoke, she found herself on stage next to a blind man that sang the blues so slow and sweet, people spoke on it for days afterward.

The blind man had other one-night gigs to do, the chitlin circuit was sixty-five nights of giving yourself over to segregated toilets and drinking fountains, and scared white people that suspected your lyrics carried something other than sadness or happiness. Suspected that maybe those words carried seeds of contention.

So they couldn't have him, but Sugar was just a forty-minute ride away, and her voice rocked the men like an over-heated lover and made the women fan beneath their dresses and decide against denial that night. The Memphis Roll claimed her for their own, and Sugar found extra income and a brief release for her troubled soul.

Then there were the other times, times when Lappy came in and said nothing, just walked past her and up to the bedroom. She could put it off on the tracks that ran up and down his arms—if it wasn't for his eyes, wild and raging with madness. During those times he did not seem to know her, and treated her like a whore, forgetting that they had broken wish bones together. During those times he rode her until she begged him to stop. When he could not find release and ordered her to take it into her mouth, he'd ram away, cussing her if her teeth got in the way. She'd have to swallow his seed; he would not allow her to waste it in the piss pan she kept beneath the bed, she had to digest it. He paid her to do it, he enjoyed watching her do it. And then he would leave, car screeching into the night, leaving Sugar shaking and bleeding.

Sugar swung the door open and was knocked back by the brilliant August sunlight.

"I been thinking that maybe we could try this here thing one more time," Pearl said, stepping in, sweet potato pie in hand, and closing the door behind her.

It'd been weeks since Pearl and Sugar spoke to each other. Each went about her life as if the other didn't exist, both miserable without the other. Pearl confided in Joe, leaving out the real reason she and Sugar had fought.

"You call her friend, Bit?" Joe asked when she mentioned that Sugar and her had had words.

Pearl nodded yes.

"Friends forgive," was all he said and the matter was solved as far as he was concerned.

Pearl made it clear to Sugar that coming to her home did not for one moment mean she approved of how Sugar made her money. She was there because she believed all of God's people could change their ways, save their souls.

Sugar stifled a laugh and lit a cigarette. *I ain't got no soul to save,* she thought to herself. "So I hear, Miss Pearl, so I hear," she said and exhaled enough smoke to cloak the doubt that she was sure was evident in her eyes.

"Miss Pearl, tell me about Jude," Sugar asked delicately, realizing that this was the cause of great pain for Pearl, and most recently Sugar. Sugar had felt uneasy after she and Pearl fought. Since Pearl had called her Jude, Sugar could not sleep without waking in a cold sweat and Jude's name on her lips.

"They never found the killer?" Sugar asked again, unable to believe that a person responsible for a crime so abominable would be allowed, by God himself, to walk this earth unpunished.

Pearl shook her head. Her hands were shaking and her voice was barely a whisper, but she assured Sugar she was fine. "It's still hard to talk about it even after all this time," Pearl said and wiped at the mist in her eyes. "Now you. Tell me about you. How you came to doing what you do."

Sugar's mouth opened and then closed. She got up to get her cigarettes. This wasn't going to be easy. She wouldn't start at the beginning but in the middle where the pain was numbing.

Sugar arrived back in Short Junction by bus. Fifteen years hadn't really changed Short Junction. It was still made up of clapboard houses and barnyard dogs, except now the dogs were older, their bark less threatening, and the houses slouched a little more.

People still moved like molasses and greeted each other with Mornin' or Evenin' whenever they passed you in town or along a quiet patch of dirt road. No, not much had changed.

Sugar paid a young, broad-necked boy to fetch her bags and to bring them on to the Lacey place. She wanted to walk. She needed to walk. Walk Chicago, Detroit and St Louis out of her soul.

She made her way down Route 4. The rain had come during the night and left the road muddy in some parts. Sugar's heels sank deep into the earth, holding her hostage for short periods of time. She removed them, allowing the cool earth to seep through her nylons and kiss the soles of her feet.

She stopped to admire a field of wildflowers, resting her head against the damp wooden post and plucking at the barbed wire that entwined it. She recalled her childhood and the easy joy she'd experienced among those brilliant flowers.

She stopped two or three times to ask for directions to the Lacey home. Not because she was lost, but because she wanted to exchange words with the people of Short Junction. She needed to re-connect with what she was before she'd become Sugar the whore.

They never answered immediately; they'd have to take her in first, allowing their eyes to travel down the blue silk dress with the Chinese collar. The one with the tiny red embroidery around the neck and hemline. The one that held Sugar like a calfskin glove, one size too small. They had to take in the six-foot woman with the jet black skin, heavily shadowed eyes and blood red lips. Only after they had traveled the world that was Sugar would they point or nod (in that way country people do) in the direction she needed to go. She'd thank them and begin walking again, leaving an overall-clad old man staring after her, watching her behind roll and wiggle beneath the dress.

As she traveled farther down Route 4, moving closer to the outskirts of Short Junction, Sugar noticed that where sprawling fields of cotton once grew, now stood large homes. Great white structures with windows that traveled from the floor to the ceiling.

Her mouth fell open with astonishment. "When the hell did this all happen?" she said aloud as she stopped to marvel.

A colored woman opened the front door and stepped out, waving at Sugar as she did. Two small dogs, barely taller than her ankle, rushed out behind her and started to jump and yelp happily about her legs. The woman waved at Sugar again, smiling broadly.

Sugar stood staring. The thought of a colored woman living in a house this fine in Short Junction, Arkansas, was overwhelming.

The woman was walking quickly down the long walkway that led up to the house, trying not to step on the small dogs that encircled her feet. As she came closer, Sugar could see that the baby blue dress the woman wore was not a dress at all, but a uniform. Sugar understood now.

"How you?" the woman said breathlessly, a genuine smile resting on her lips. The dogs stopped their yapping and sat obediently at her feet, watching Sugar with their small black eyes.

"Lord have mercy, it's gonna be a hot one today and only April," the woman in the blue uniform exclaimed and pulled a handkerchief from her bosom, dabbing quickly at the perspiration forming above her lip. She gave Sugar a sweet smile.

"You the new girl?" she asked and snatched a quick look at Sugar from the neck down. The smile remained, but not as sweet.

"New girl?" Sugar repeated stupidly.

"Yeah, new girl. This here is the Floyd house, we expecting a new gi—maid today. You her?" The woman's smile was visibly crumbling. "If you ain't the new girl then what you doing 'round here?" The smile was completely gone and the voice was turning rancid like week-old milk.

Sugar leaned back hard on her heels. "I ain't nobody's girl or maid. I was just admiring the house, is all," Sugar said, falling back into the Southern twang she'd so easily let slip away.

"Well, we don't need the likes of you sniffin' 'round here, so off with you," the woman said and waved her hand at Sugar as if she was a bothersome fly.

The likes of you.

There was that phrase again.

"You live too far South to be so damn uppity. You and me, we the same. The likes of me is the likes of you!" Sugar said, her voice gutted with anger. She threw her bare arm out before the woman's face so that she could see that their skin color was nearly identical.

The woman folded her arms across her bosom, rolled her eyes and clucked her tongue in disgust. Sugar's words had left her agitated and speechless. She swung around and started back up the long walkway to the house. The dogs, startled by her sudden retreat, began yelping and jumping about her feet again.

As the woman turned, Sugar was struck by her sharp features and small slanted eyes. Like a brick, it hit her. This was the same little girl who'd questioned her so many years earlier outside Short Junction's general store: *Ain't you got a mamma?*

The words stirred like a whirlwind in her head, preventing her from walking away. "Yeah I got's a mamma!" she yelled to the back of the woman and waved the aged telegram like a victorious flag.

The woman turned, giving Sugar a brief puzzled look.

Later, Sugar found herself standing on the porch of the Lacey home. The once-white paint was now graying with age and peeling in large thin slices. The porch, in desperate need of repair, slouched heavily to one side.

The yard was absent of the roaming, clucking chickens that once filled the front and back yards. Sugar bent her head slightly to the left and could see that the pen that once held Shelby the hog was now empty and overgrown with weeds.

The windows were open, allowing the light spring breeze to flutter the old lace curtains. Soft music sailed out and for a fleeting moment hung in the air over Sugar's head.

Pots and pans banged and clanged nosily inside as they were placed, moved and filled. This caused a slight smile to tickle at the ends of Sugar's mouth. It was a familiar and expected sound for a Friday—fish fry day.

Sugar rested her hand lightly on the door and then pulled quickly away when she realized, as if coming out of a trance, why she'd come in the first place.

She wanted to run. Run back to the bus and board it, begging the bus driver not to stop until they reached St Louis.

She wasn't ready. She wasn't ready to meet her mother. Coming had been a big mistake.

The broad-necked boy came up behind her, pulling a makeshift wagon filled with her belongings. He smiled, not at her, but at her legs and hips. He moved slowly and placed each case down carefully on the porch. All the while not raising his eyes past her neck.

"Ma'am," he said, his tone curious and strangely sexual at the same time.

Sugar nodded and dug into her pocketbook, pulled out a quarter and tossed it to him. The boy thanked her and took one last look at her long fish net-clad legs before he started down the stairs.

"Boy," Sugar said, not turning to face him.

"Ma'am?" The voice came from behind her.

"You got a mamma?" she said, her legs quivering now. There was a long pause.

"Yessum," the boy said.

"You live with your mamma?" Sugar asked.

"Yessum."

"She expecting you soon?" Sugar said, just wanting to keep him there with her, until strength came and moved her forward.

"Yessum, but if you needs me to … uh … do something else I'll be right able to do it," he said. His voice closer now. Hopeful.

Sugar said nothing.

"No. Don't keep your mamma waiting," she said more to herself than to the boy. He stood there for a while, bewildered by her strange questions. City women were funny that way, he thought to himself as he trudged away, his cart squeaking noisily behind him.

Sara Lacey, still small and fragile, but now wrinkled and gray, came to the door and swung it wide open. The sound of the retreating wagon had brought her to investigate who was on her property. Or perhaps it was the deafening sound of Sugar's heart beating hard inside her chest.

"Who you?" Sara asked, wincing her milky eyes.

Sugar just stood there, unable to utter a word.

"Who you, I said. Are ya deaf, dumb or both?" Sara demanded, taking a bold step forward.

Sugar parted her lips to speak and still nothing came.

"Gal, we don't like no strangers hangin' 'round this here house. Now, if you lost, say so. If you hungry, I'll be glad to feed ya and send ya on ya way." Sara paused, tilting her head slightly, trying to get her eyes to focus on the person in front of her. "If you selling somethin, I probably already got it, can't afford it or don't need it at all."

"Sara, it's me, Sugar," Sugar said in a small voice.

Sara winced again as if stung, and then took a few steps closer. At her tallest, Sara had only reached Sugar's chest; now, old and slumped, she stood up on her tiptoes until she was nearly face to face with her.

"Sugar? Well, lookee here … it sure nuff is you, ain't it! Good God almighty, come on in this here house." She snatched at Sugar's hand and led her into the large foyer.

The dilapidated exterior masked the beauty and order that remained within the Lacey home. It was just as Sugar had left it. High-polished dark wooden floors. Massive mahogany furniture. Nothing had changed, and Sugar felt like she'd stepped right back into 1940.

As they made their way past the dining area and on to the kitchen, Sugar saw that the large oak cabinet that sat in the wide hallway still held the stolen pieces of china.

The smell of frying catfish and simmering turnip greens accosted her senses and she was overcome with nostalgia.

When she was a child these food smells were always accompanied by hard-drinking, heavy-smoking men and women. Clinking glasses filled with white lightning, clay ashtrays overflowing with lipstick-stained cigarettes. The sound of a palm coming down hard on a thigh intertwined with glorious laughter.

The bedrooms may have made most of the money in the Lacey house, but the kitchen was its lifeline.

That was 1940, when Sugar walked away from Short Junction. That was 1940, when Joe Taylor had mistakenly placed his new shoes on the dining room table and sweet Jude lost her life. That was then and this was now.

Sugar did not find loud-laughing, good-time people in the kitchen. Instead what she found were two old women crouched over the large wooden table, peeling potatoes and fussing about something that only carried meaning to them.

When Sara and Sugar entered the kitchen, they stopped bickering and briefly observed the two women. After a short moment they went back to what they were doing, as if the two women were merely a passing wisp of air.

Sara left Sugar standing in the kitchen's entrance and joined her sisters in their potato peeling and bickering.

They don't even know who I am, Sugar thought to herself, as she watched them ignore her.

Sugar composed her thoughts and prepared to speak. But May, the eldest sister, beat her to it.

"Sugar, 'bout time your black ass got here," she said without looking up from her work. "I sent that telegram four whole years ago. Had I known that Western Union moved like a turtle I would have sent it regular mail," she said sarcastically, looking up to meet Sugar's gaze.

May spoke quick and emphasized each word by jabbing the air with the small pointed knife she held.

Like Sara, May's face was weathered and her hair gray. She now wore thick, black-framed glasses. From what Sugar could see, Ruby, who'd said nothing so far, was the only one who still had perfect use of her eyes.

"Go on and wash your hands and git with these here potatoes," May demanded, as she stared over the rims of her glasses. "It's Friday, gal, or have you forgotten what Friday is in this house?" she said and smirked.

Sugar hadn't forgotten. But she wasn't there to peel potatoes or fry fish. She was there to see her mother. There were no signs that another person was living there but she hadn't been upstairs yet. Her mother could be resting, Sugar told herself as she went to the sink to wash her hands clean of the road dust and perspiration.

She decided to humor the Lacey women and sat down to do what she had been told to do.

The Lacey women spoke amongst themselves, each sister picking up where the other left off. They were completely immersed in a world that Sugar had long ago lost her place in. She peeled potatoes and sat quietly, glancing up every once in a while to watch at their gray bobbing heads.

Sugar thought that the steady activity of potato peeling would keep her calm and focused until her mother came in, but it wasn't working. Distress clung to her like syrup, causing her, at times, to become short of breath.

Sugar stood up abruptly and the table rocked a bit as her knee hit into the side.

The other women gave her a quick look.

Sugar half walked and half ran into the parlor. The air seemed lighter there. She gulped it down like fresh well water and leaned, panting, against the wall.

There were beautiful crystal decanters, filled with rich dark brandies and whiskeys, set along the mantel above the fireplace. Sugar snatched one up, removed its bulb-shaped lid, held her head back and allowed the liquor to flow freely into her open mouth.

The liquid hit her stomach like acid and she staggered at the fire it lit there. Tears welled up in her eyes as she broke out in a sweat.

She sat down heavily on the velvet chaise, her legs wide open, decanter, half empty now, still in her grip. She leaned back and closed her eyes against the day.

May's calls from the kitchen for her to return pulled her back and she half walked, half stumbled out of the parlor, taking up a cheap tin ashtray from the table. At the center there were brightly colored letters written as palm trees screaming CALIFORNIA.

Sugar placed the decanter and the ashtray down on the table and moved to the cabinet to retrieve a glass. The women kept their heads bowed as they worked feverishly. Two large bowls were already filled with skinless potatoes.

She sat down and reached into her pocketbook that hung lazily on the back of her chair to pull out a wilted pack of Lucky Strikes. One stick remained and she breathed heavily at the thought of spending the coming hours without cigarettes.

She lit it and pulled deeply. Cigarette dangling from the side of her mouth, she tilted her head slightly as she poured a tall glass of whiskey. She was calming down now. The even flow of the brown liquid and the cigarette smoke that curled above and around her head helped her move into her old self. The Sugar that wasn't scared of much of anything or anyone. The Sugar who had worked the streets of Chicago and Detroit with just a switchblade and her own hard-hitting hands.

The women stopped to look at Sugar and then at one another. Disapproval coated their faces as they watched Sugar knock off three quarters of the whiskey she had just poured into her glass.

Sugar slowly licked her lips, savoring the warmth that spread over her entire body. She took a few more drags of the cigarette and then began peeling potatoes again.

The sound of the sharp blade removing the thick brown skins of the potatoes was the only sound to be heard for some time.

The day stretched into a smoky purple evening. The crickets started up a chorus that would last until dawn. The Lacey women had finally broken their wall of silence. A conversation erupted, filled with low tones and clucking tongues, as the Laceys spoke of Short Junction, past and present.

Sugar realized that their lives had settled into a grand-motherly pace. Friday and Saturday nights no longer found their home filled with loud music, men, women and sex.

They too, like Mary Bedford, had aged and changed. Their famous fried fish and potato salad was now served at church functions and sold at Friday night bingo games.

Sugar, who had finished the decanter of whiskey and who should have been stone drunk, experienced instead a type of relaxed hysteria. She said very little, attempting to keep her composure.

The back door swung open and an aged woman walked in shouting her "Good evening"s and "Howdy do"s.

Sugar stood bolt upright, toppling the decanter and sending the last drops of whiskey sailing the length of table. The woman gave her a quizzical smile and handed

May the town newspaper, exchanged a few pleasantries and left. They hadn't even bothered to introduce her.

Sugar felt like an idiot and told herself to stop watching the door. Stop waiting. You've been without her this long, a few more minutes won't kill you.

The Lacey women were nowhere near to giving an explanation about Sugar's mother. No, they wanted to know about Sugar's life away from Short Junction. They wanted to know why she never took the time to write. They wanted to know how she got a chipped front tooth and what about that split earlobe?

But they especially wanted an explanation for the long crooked scar that ran from beneath her chin and disappeared behind the small collar of her dress.

There was concern in their voices when they asked, but their eyes revealed other thoughts.

Sugar was ashamed to share her ordeal with them. Stories filled with abusive men, broken limbs and nights when her belly burned empty with hunger, her soul with loneliness.

She spoke quickly and briefly about her time in St Louis, Detroit and Chicago. She avoided the true stories that would explain her scars and made up tales that construed them as light mishaps instead.

The Lacey women eyeballed her and shook their heads as she spoke. They did not give birth to her, but she was their child just the same. They had raised her from a babe, and although she did not suckle at the breast of any of the three women, they knew her well and knew she was lying.

In the end, when Sugar was done talking, she looked up at them and tried to decipher what she saw in their eyes and what she saw frightened her.

Ruby was the first to speak. She started off slowly and softly.

"Sugar, I believes we've kept you waiting long enough. We know why you here and what you come for. But this was our way of letting you feel the way we done, when you ain't come four years ago. Now, we know that you weren't there in St Louis when the telegram come. But we raised you, and your whereabouts should have been known by us. You should have kept in touch.

"Now, before we go on and tell you 'bout your mamma, let me just say this: We did the best we knew how to raise you. We saw that you ain't go hungry, cold or unclothed. We treated you like you came out from inside of us."

She stopped for a minute. Looked Sugar from head to toe and shook her head, unable to continue. Sara placed a comforting hand on her shoulder and squeezed it tightly. Sara picked up where Ruby left off.

"Can't say we did everything perfect while you was here. We know that now. But we can't go back and change it now. The past is the past, and that's where it belongs— behind you."

Ruby leaped up from the table, suddenly remembering the fish, which was beginning to smoke. Her sudden movement startled Sara, and she lost her chain of thought.

"Uhm, oh yes. See, we feel we did our best where you were concerned. We gave you our name and our love."

Sugar's skin crawled at the word "love." What did the Laceys know of love? Whatever it was they gave her, it wasn't love. She'd seen what love was at Mary Bedford's house. She saw the hugs and kisses that were shared between Mercy and Mary. None of that went on at the Lacey house. Not without a price tag attached to it.

Sara looked down at her hands, away from the frigid expression that had settled on Sugar's face. May nudged her to continue.

"We know you been waiting to hear 'bout your mamma and we know that your feelings for her ain't what it should be. But we want you to understand that it ain't fair for you to judge her by what she done, 'cause she did what she had to do. She had her reasons for running off and leaving you with us like she did. But we glad she chose us, 'cause you brought a lot of joy to this here house."

Sara's voice thickened with emotion and she took the hem of her apron and dabbed at the corners of her eyes.

"When she showed up here four years ago, we was shocked to see her. We ain't heard nothing from her since the day she come and leave you with us. She look real bad. You see, she had the cancer, and that thing had ate her down to near nothing. She was no more than a bag of bones, and almost completely blind," Sara said, and her voice trailed off.

Sugar's heart felt like it had stopped beating a while ago. They were talking about her mother in the past tense. Like she wasn't around. Like she wasn't napping upstairs in one of the rooms or in town shopping for vegetables.

May was the first to see the turmoil in Sugar's face. The rage and despair was blending together and rising quickly to the surface.

"Baby, we are so sorry. So sor—" was all she was able to get out before Sugar exploded. Her fists were clenched so tight you could see the veins straining against the skin. She raised them and shook them in fury at the women.

"You're sorry? You're sorry! Sorry for what? Sorry that she ain't here? Sorry that you made me wait all day long before you told me she ain't here! Or are you sorry for the love you didn't give me the whole time I lived here? Exactly what in the hell are you sorry for? I'll tell you all something … you're a bunch of sorry asses, that's what you are!"

The women sat quiet while each word rocked them like a blow.

"Ya'll love me? Really? When I left here ya'll didn't even have the time to look over your shoulders to say good-bye. Ya'll just acted like I was heading down the road somewhere. Didn't even ask me to stay. Love would make you want me to stay." Sugar slumped back down into her chair. She picked up the empty cigarette pack and dug a shaking finger into it, hoping one would be there. There wasn't and she slammed it down hard on the table. "Just tell me where my mama is," she said in a voice that was low and tired.

May, who had been relatively quiet for the most part, stood up slowly. Anger was etched into her face. "Sugar, you don't forget whose house you in. We don't deserve that trash talk. Like we said, we done the best we knew how where you was concerned." She slammed both hands down hard on the table and sent potato peelings flying in all directions.

She walked around to Sugar's side of the table, and for the first time, Sugar realized the woman had acquired a limp. She walked past Sugar and retrieved her cane, which was set in the corner of the room next to the large black cast iron stove. She leaned heavily on the cane and walked out of the kitchen.

No one said a word. No one looked at the others.

When May returned, she carried an envelope, which she flung onto the table. It landed dead in front of Sugar.

"That there is what your mamma leave here for you. You know, the one you always thought ain't give a damn about you," May said sarcastically.

"What she do, write me a letter?" Sugar said in disgust. She would not look at the envelope. "What, she was too afraid to stay around and wait to tell me what she had to say?" Sugar didn't want to hear what she already knew to be true.

May sucked her teeth and said, "You telling me you expected your mamma to wait around for four years? Lord, child, she wasn't able to wait for four days! Weren't you even listening? Your mamma was sick. She was dying. Your mamma come here to try to set things right between the two of you. Your mamma came home to die!" May said and grabbed her hip in pain. She sat down next to Sugar. "She died right here. Right here in this house, waiting on you to come." The words dripped from May's mouth like poison.

There was a long quiet that was broken now and again by a passing car along the outer road. The guilt May's words inflicted welled up inside of Sugar and gushed forth in waves of sorrow. "Why ... why did she leave me?" Sugar asked between sobs and tears. Ruby shook her head in ignorance. The real story, the truth, would be too hard to repeat and just make it worse for Sugar. Ruby turned her eyes up to the ceiling and quietly asked the Lord for strength. Did she want to tell Sugar of the madness her mama, Bertie Mae, endured under the roof of Ciel Brown? The emotional and physical battering she lived with up until the day she left Short Junction with Ciel's man, Clemon Wilks?

No, she didn't want to tell it, but she did tell Sugar that the day she was born everyone in the Low came out to bear witness to her life. Sugar's wet eyes looked up at her. "True," Ruby said, and embraced her.

The truth be told, Bertie Mae ran scared. Scared that she would go mad and abuse her child like her mother abused her. She'd rather abandon her child than put her through that hell. But Ruby, May and Sara would keep that truth to themselves. Better that truth stay in the ground. Better for all of them.

That evening, when the house was quiet and the only sound to be heard was the muted sound of music traveling from the small radio in Sara's room, Sugar sat propped up on the bed in her childhood room staring at her mother's envelope.

The unmarked envelope stared back at her from its place on her lap. She traced its sharp borders with her fingers, and turned it over and over in her hands. Long after the music had stopped, she finally peeled it open and removed its contents.

There was a deed to a house and property in Bigelow. There was a will, that clearly stated Sugar as the owner of the house.

A small black and white photograph showed a woman leaning against a tree. Her hands were not visible, they were hidden behind her back, her long hair hung loose and wild about her face. The woman would have looked provocative, had it not been for the sad eyes. Sugar knew those eyes well. She had the same ones.

She flipped the picture over.

Bertie—Waco, Texas, 1928.

The scrawled writing told Sugar this was her mother.

She stood up and went to the large, square mirror that hung on the wall above the dresser. She held the picture up to her face and stared intensely at the vision before her. She wanted so desperately to see something of that woman inside her. Something other than the sad eyes.

Sugar lay back down in the bed, placing the picture gently down on her pillow. She looked down at her hands, and thought how much she wanted to see the hands of her mother. A tear escaped and slid quickly down her cheek.

The envelope also held a newspaper clipping from the Junction *Gazette.* It was an obituary:

Mrs Ciel Venita Brown

SHORT JUNCTION, ARKANSAS. (January 3rd, 1932) A colored woman was buried during the night in a casket furnished by the county. Wrapped in a shroud that had once been used as a tablecloth, the emaciated remains of Mrs Ciel Brown, who died Saturday morning, were taken to a private cemetery on the edge of town and buried Sunday night. No friends assisted in preparing the body for burial and no preacher spoke over the body or to the grief-stricken sons of the deceased, who stood by silently.

Mrs Brown died while in the confines of the Arkansas State Home for the Insane (Colored Section). She was taken ill while her son, Abel, visited with her. There she breathed her last breath.

She leaves to mourn three sons, Abel, Finis and Wylam. One daughter, Bertie Mae.

Sugar read the obituary twice. This was her grandmother. Sugar had uncles. Where would they be? The Lacey women didn't mention anything about family. Perhaps they didn't know anything about Bertie's family.

Sugar thought some things were better left as is.

She replaced everything except the picture in the envelope. She was disappointed that there was no letter. Some comforting words from her mother to her. She looked at the woman in the picture and the only word that came to her mind was: Why?

The following morning, as the jay birds perched themselves on the limbs of the great pine trees and oaks to sing the world awake, but not before slop jars were emptied or breakfast made and coffee brewed, the Lacey women pulled their robes tight against the early morning spring air and led Sugar across the dewy grass to the edge of the property where her mother was buried alongside the Lacey ancestors.

Fresh wildflowers, pink, yellow and vibrant purples, covered the grave like a colorful blanket. The Laceys stepped back a bit to give Sugar grieving space.

Didn't they know she'd been grieving her entire life?

She thought of the little picture of her mother with the sad eyes, now wrapped inside the Mary Bedford handkerchief and pinned safely inside her bra. She touched it gently as she stood over her grave.

A sudden breeze swept by and shook the weeping willow limbs that hung heavy above her mother's final resting place. Ruby looked up and pointed toward the branches that still quivered in the aftermath of the breeze.

"That's yo' mamma saying hello," she said, her eyes sparkling with wonder. Sugar smiled up at the sky and mouthed, "Hello mamma."

Knowing each other's past helped both Pearl and Sugar. Secret pains, now told, bonded the women together tighter than anything else in this world.

They held each other and assured each other that better days were coming. Sugar wanted to believe it, but life had taught her otherwise.

Chapter Eleven

"Bit, you sure you won't come with me?" Joe asked again as he and Pearl stood watching the train pull into the station. The rush of air it brought in teased at the hem of Pearl's dress, causing it to flutter about her ankles and threaten to rise to meet her knee.

"We done been through this already, honey ... we go through this every year."

Joe shrugged his massive shoulders in defeat. Pearl had not set foot out of Arkansas in fifteen years. The annual trip they took together each year to visit his family in Florida had come to an end when Jude died, but Pearl had insisted that he continue to go. "Joe, you acting like you gonna miss me or something," Pearl said and slapped playfully at the hand he rested lovingly on her shoulder.

The whistle sounded three times, signaling the departure of train #2438 to all points south. Young and old scrambled around them saying their good-byes. Redcaps moved swiftly through the crowd of people, expertly guiding dollies heavy with large black steamer trunks and beaten luggage to be loaded aboard the train. Children clung to the skirts of their mothers, crying to stay or begging to go along. Lovers pressed lips and bodies together as if it was the last time they would ever touch in that way again.

Joe and Pearl stood in the midst of tears, kisses and smiles and said their own good- byes. Joe kissed her gently on the cheek and Pearl squeezed his hand and smiled lovingly into his eyes. "I'll be back and blacker than ever before you know it." He tweaked her nose and winked and then he was gone on #2438 down the same tracks he helped lay so many years earlier.

Pearl found Sugar sitting on her porch and humming softly to herself. One leg folded beneath her, the other swinging back and forth like a long, brown pendulum trying to keep time with the rest of the world.

"Hey, Miss Pearl," Sugar called to her and waved her over. Pearl sighed heavily, not sure she was in a congenial mood. The heat had drained the little bit of energy it took her to see her husband off. She felt lonely and depressed. At the last minute she wanted to pull Joe back to her and beg him to stay, but she had fought that impulse and had waved instead, offering her biggest and brightest smile. Now she was hot and tired and wanting nothing more than to retire to her empty house.

"Miss Pearl!" Sugar called to her again. She was standing now, hands on her hips, annoyance in her voice. "C'mon!"

"Joe get off okay?" Sugar asked as she sipped slowly from a chilled glass.

"Uh–huh," Pearl answered in awe. "How you do that?" she asked, pointing at the frozen glass.

Sugar laughed. "Just put it in the freezer, Miss Pearl!" she said in lazy exasperation. She got up and walked into the house to retrieve another glass for Pearl. Moments later she returned. "Here you go, something to cool you off." She handed Pearl a frozen glass filled with yellowish liquid. Sugar sat down on the steps, giving her chair to Pearl.

They sat quietly for a while watching the day recede and the night stroll in on the back of the cool September evening. "What is this?" Pearl asked after draining the glass dry. The liquid, which went down cold, did not seem to cool her body; instead it ignited a small warm fire in her belly.

"Oh … Pike aid," Sugar answered. "You drank it too fast to really appreciate it, though," she said, laughing loosely.

"Pike aid?" Pearl said stupidly and pulled at her collar, allowing a space for the heat to ease out from beneath her dress.

"Uh–huh. Lemonade and corn liquor—"

"What!" Pearl shouted and jumped to her feet. "Corn liquor! Have you lost your mind, child? I don't drink!" She spat on the ground.

"Oh calm down, Miss Pearl, it's just a little dab of it in there, not enough to take any effect on you at all," Sugar said, trying hard to control her laughter. "It's just there to give the taste a little pick me up, is all."

Pearl calmed down a bit. "Well, even so, you should have told me." She looked at the glass. All of the frost had melted away, leaving behind the worn rose pattern that clung to its sides for dear life. "Want another?" Sugar asked innocently.

"I don't suppose I should," Pearl responded, but licked her lips in memory of the first glass.

Sugar smiled and disappeared back into the house to retrieve the pitcher of pike aid. Pearl leaned back in her chair, shaking her head at her own foolishness. "Here you go." Sugar was looming over her, refilling the glass Pearl still held in her hand. "Just a little bit, right?" Pearl's eyes questioned.

"Aw, go on, Miss Pearl, it ain't gonna kill you," Sugar said and stretched her body across the top step.

Pearl took her time with the second glass, enjoying the slight giddiness that was gradually taking over her mind. Her fingertips tingled and she felt a strange quivering in the lower regions of her body. She shot a glance at Sugar to make sure she wasn't watching her, then she squirmed in her chair, trying to quell the sensation between her legs. She patted the damp space between her chin and her chest and searched the sky for clouds.

"Ain't it beautiful, Miss Pearl," Sugar suddenly said in a breathless voice. "Just sky and land for miles, umph!"

Yes it certainly was beautiful. September days were unique in Arkansas. The sky was an enormous, pale blue pallet with white streaks and puffs. In September the horizon lowered itself and it seemed like you could reach up and touch it. The soil turned a deeper, richer brown and the trees, plants and flowers gave their all, knowing that in a matter of weeks fall would claim their brilliancy and tuck it safely away in winter's pocket, keeping it safe till spring.

"I didn't know you noticed those type of things," Pearl said.

Sugar didn't respond. She was beginning to notice quite a few things. Not only notice but appreciate them in a way she never dreamed possible. She smiled at the joy her small observation seemed to bring to Pearl's face.

Pearl sipped quietly and thought of the only other times she had ever digested alcohol. The first was as a servant in the McHenry home, during one of their infamous parties. It was the first party of the summer and rich white folks came from all over Arkansas and neighboring states to take part in the festivities.

Men in starched white and blue seersucker suits and women in long flowing silk dresses that captured every color of the season glided here and there hiding their smiles behind gloved hands or tilting their heads back in polite laughter. Clinking glasses resounded around the property and added to the comically composed festivities. Tennis, lawn bowling and croquet filled the daylight hours before dinner was served. At the drop of the sun, massive quantities of food were laid out beneath huge canopies. Whole pigs lay staring with dead eyes, their mouths stuffed with huge apples. Cornish hens, one for each of the two hundred or more guests, goose liver patés, English crackers, chilled cantaloupe soup, wild rice, pheasant and duck—Pearl saw that the white people certainly did have everything and so much of some things she never thought existed.

The mood would change after the meal. The band, brought in from Mississippi, would play ragtime and Dixieland music for the guests to kick their feet up to. Women would lift their legs to reveal seamed stockings. The liquor would flow like water, ice clinking against glasses; liquid falling out and over onto white patent leather shoes. Oh, a high time was being had.

Laughter became raucous, stories became full-fledged lies and Pearl watched as wives ran their long painted fingernails down the napes of other husbands' necks, while husbands whispered deep into the ears of their partners' wives—or their wives' best friends.

When it was all done, guests gone that could, others that couldn't retired to the many guest rooms, Pearl was left alone on the great lawn, gathering the delicate crystal that still held the liquids that made the guests talk louder and laugh longer. Cigar, cigarette and pipe smoke still clung to dew-wet eaves and the crying branches of the weeping willow trees. She didn't know why she suddenly tilted the glass up to her mouth. It was a quick and jerky motion, as if her hand was guided by something other than her mind. The drink traveled down her throat tickling as it went until it finally reached her stomach and settled there like glowing embers. Oh, the feeling was unique, and the only thing that came close to it was the feeling she got when she thought of her Joe and the way he kissed the under part of her arm.

She could think of the two at once and get a sharp pleasurable stabbing sensation in her womb, one that would keep her feeling silly for hours.

Even now as she sat and reminisced, her stomach contracted and she hid her smile behind a mock cough and her hand.

The second time had not been pleasurable at all. Her wedding night. She and Joe lay together in her own childhood bed, in her room that shared a wall with her parents' room. They spoke in whispers and giggled in the moonlit darkness of her room. She could tell the urgency he had for her. His sex organ pressed against her hip and throbbed there like a second heart. She would not, could not, remove her starched new cotton nightgown given to her by her mother as a wedding gift. She did allow his hands to travel beneath it and explore her virginal body. She was embarrassed by the moans that escaped her, heavier and even more sexual than the ones that emanated from Joe. When his mouth clasped hold of one of her erect nipples, she thought for one split second that her mind would snap.

He could not enter her, even though she was slick. The pain was too much to bear. He placed his hand between her legs and massaged her opening with his finger, he glided it effortlessly in and out until she thought her whole body would fall apart with pleasant convulsions. But when he mounted her again for the third time, she still squirmed against him, pushing him away instead of pulling him forward. He became desperate. "Take a little of this," he said. His voice was thick with want as he guided the small flask of whiskey to her lips. The smell alone intoxicated her, but to please her new husband she drank the whiskey. Moments later her head was spinning and her stomach turning. She spent an hour in the outhouse, puking up her wedding cake. Joe spent some time there afterward too, pleasing himself.

Pearl was consuming her third glass of pike aid, and wondering why the name began to sound familiar to her. She thought hard and long about it, but could not remember. She forced her attention on Sugar, who was smoking a cigarette. For the first time she realized that Sugar did not have on one of her many wigs. Her head was tied with a rag. Her face was absent of makeup, which was a rare occurrence. She looked normal for once, even fresh. Her scantily clad body seemed less threatening without all of the fixtures. In this chaste state, Sugar looked more like Jude than ever before. Pearl looked away and tried to consider something else, but again her vision was drawn back to Sugar. The cigarette smoke sailed over to her and invaded her nose. She coughed a little and fanned it away with her free hand.

"You need to stop that," she said, her voice lagging a bit.

"Stop what?" Sugar said.

"That smoking. You smoke too much and you don't wear enough clothes, either." Pearl was speaking matter of factly, her tone was less than accusing, just tottering on the verge of drunkenness.

Sugar, realizing this, just rolled her eyes and looked back toward the fields.

"Gimmesomemore to drink." Pearl's words spilled out like poor man's pearls, strung together and worthless.

Sugar looked over at her, and realized by the way Pearl was shoving the glass in her direction that she'd probably had too much already.

"I think that might be it for you, Miss Pearl. How about a Coke?" Sugar said, not moving.

Pearl set the glass down between her legs and leaned her head back against the house. "Sugar, don't it make you feel ashamed when you take off your clothes for everyone and anyone?" Pearl asked, curiosity lacing her voice.

"No," Sugar said quickly and shifted her body. She was uncomfortable, knowing what the questioning was leading up to.

"Umph," Pearl grunted and shook her head.

"It ain't no big deal. You take your clothes off in front of Joe all the time. That don't make you feel shame, do it?" Sugar said, a bit sarcastically.

Pearl had never disrobed in front of Joe, in fact when they made love, it was in the thick darkness of their bedroom and her gown was simply lifted above her waist. But that was so long ago; she had not been able to perform that wifely duty since Jude's death. It had been fifteen long years of nothing more than caresses and quick kisses, sleeping with even breath against a neck and a hand settled into the curve of a waist. Joe and Pearl simply shared a bed now and not each other.

Pearl did not respond.

"I feel free when I ain't got no clothes on," Sugar continued.

"How does being naked make you feel free?" Pearl sat up now, wanting to understand Sugar's words.

"I can't explain it, Miss Pearl, it just do."

"I think it's downright disgusting," Pearl said, frustrated because Sugar could offer no valid explanation.

"Well ... don't knock it until you've tried it."

Pearl huffed. "I don't know nothing about you, Sugar. You live next door and we spend time together, but you still a stranger to me."

Sugar laughed. "Miss Pearl, I see you one of those soupy drunks."

Pearl scratched at her nose. "I ain't drunk." Her words were slurred and she squirmed again against the warm feeling between her legs. "Tell me something, what you think your mamma woulda said 'bout what you do?"

Sugar stiffened at the words. They hit her like pellets. "Okay, Miss Pearl, I think it's time for you to go now." She stood and stretched her long brown frame. Any high she had was quickly seeping from her.

"Y-you think she woulda approved of you being a whore?" Pearl continued, oblivious to the anger that was building up in Sugar.

Sugar flinched at the questions and swallowed hard. She did not want to discuss a mother she never knew.

"She dead. How am I suppose to know what she think?" she said and bent down to snatch up Pearl's empty glass.

"I don't think she wouldalikeditverymuch." Pearl's bottom lip was stuck out and her head began to look too heavy for her neck.

Sugar just smirked.

"You think maybe she was a whore too?" The words fell effortlessly from Pearl's mouth and luckily Sugar had sense enough to realize that Pearl's words were only alcohol induced.

"Miss Pearl, if my mamma was a whore then she did what she felt she had to do. I ain't gonna judge her, cause I don't want to be judged. Anyway, we whores ain't all that different from the rest of you."

Pearl's eyebrows went up. "How you figure that?"

"Well we all got working pussies. We all whores in one way or another—"

"I ain't no whore. I know that for sure!" Pearl exclaimed.

"Yes, you is, Pearl, you and your mamma before you—"

"I ain't no whore!" Pearl was standing now.

"You lay down with your husband and in return he clothe and feed you—keep a roof up over your head. You stop laying with him, all those things disappear." Sugar snapped her fingers for emphasis.

That was not true. And Pearl shook her head insistently no, but she would not tell of what didn't go on in her bedroom. She would not.

"Look here, I do what I have to to put food on my table and clothes on my back and will keep on doing it same as you."

Pearl raised her hands in defeat. She did not want to argue again, but she had Sugar angry now. Sugar's tongue flicked words at Pearl like a whip.

"The only difference between you and me, Miss Pearl, is you began your whoring life in front of a congregation, dressed in white and with God's blessing!"

She slammed into the house, leaving Pearl sorry for speaking at all. Pearl heard the glasses crash into the sink. The refrigerator door opened and slammed closed three times and by the time Pearl's foot landed on the last step Sugar was back on the porch, huffing and puffing like a wild, angry boar.

"You right, Miss Pearl, you don't know me at all. I been on my own since I was fifteen fucking years old. Fifteen! And did you forget how I told you I survived? Have you forgotten!" Sugar's anger had the best of her now. Pearl turned to meet Sugar's enraged eyes but she did not utter a word.

"With my pussy, that's how! Men pay to fuck, eat or smell *my* pussy!"

Pearl blushed at Sugar's use of language; she wanted to throw her hands up to her ears.

Sugar was spent, the anger was mellowing down to simple annoyance now. Her breathing slowed and she sat down heavily on the steps.

"I ain't bad, Miss Pearl, I just ain't had no crossroads in my life is all."

Pearl traced Sugar's jawline with her hand. "Yes you have, child, you just wasn't able to recognize them when you came across them."

Chapter Twelve

Her headache was finally withdrawing. Just to be sure, she took another aspirin and kept the ice pack on her head. Her first hangover at sixty. She laughed out loud in the five o'clock darkness of her bedroom. She thought of Joe and her stomach trembled. She moved her hand across the empty space his absent body left in their bed. Not one full day had passed and she was already missing him as if he had been gone for twenty.

Her body was weak from the pike aid and lack of food. Cooking was something she did not want to consider after the heat and angry words from Sugar; the cans of tuna fish stacked in the cupboard would remain stacked until another day. Her mouth craved barbecue, but her feet would not carry her to town to get it. Perhaps buttered bread and a cup of tea, she thought.

Shortly before seven Pearl found herself eating exactly what she craved. Sugar appeared at her front door with two barbecue rib dinners, complete with corn bread and potato salad and Coca-Cola.

Sugar seldom visited Pearl's home, and when she did, she never left the confines of the kitchen; her visit was always short. Pearl felt they both preferred it that way. Pearl was uncomfortable having her around Joe; Sugar was uncomfortable with Pearl's apparent uneasiness having her there. But today they sat and listened to the radio.

Sugar bore another bag, a large heavy brown paper sack, its top rolled tightly closed. Pearl eyed it on and off, wanting to know exactly what it contained, but Sugar made no effort to disclose its contents to her.

"Miss Pearl, I got something I wanna do to you," Sugar said as they cleared the table of the dinner remnants.

"What?" Pearl was surprised at her statement. "What you want to do to me?" she said suspiciously.

"C'mon," Sugar said and grabbed the brown sack and headed up the stairs.

"W-wait a minute," Pearl said and rushed to follow her.

Sugar found herself standing in the upstairs hall of Pearl and Joe's house. The differences were few. Pearl's floors were bare, the unfinished floors dull against the old beige wallpaper with the tiny light blue flowers. Sugar turned into the bathroom. Unlike her own bathroom, Pearl's walls were painted white, and butterscotch towels, washcloths and hand towels added brightness to the room, even though it was dead darkness outside the window. "Sit down," Sugar said as she dropped the toilet seat down.

"What are you up to?" Pearl asked and sat down after a slight moment of hesitation.

"You need a new look, Miss Pearl. Not that there is anything wrong with the look you have now, it's just that it's too Bigelow," Sugar said, her hands fiddling with Pearl's tight bun trying to find the pins and release it from its present confined state.

"Stop it," Pearl said and tried to slap Sugar's hands away. "Ain't nothing wrong with my look." And then curious now, "What you plan on doing?"

Sugar stood back and placed her hands on her perfectly curved hips. She still wore the denim shorts and bright orange tank top she'd lounged in on the porch earlier that day.

"I plans on making you look forty instead of … fifty?" Sugar questioned and leaned forward, hoping Pearl would reveal her age.

Pearl blushed, joyful that Sugar had missed her true age by ten years. "I believe I look just fine," Pearl said and turned her bashful smile away from Sugar.

"I ain't say you don't, all I'm saying is that you could look better, better than fine."

They laughed together, and Pearl did not resist when Sugar went at the bun again. "Lord, Miss Pearl, you've got a whole head full of hair, pretty too," Sugar said as her fingers played in Pearl's long, thick mane. "Why you always wear it up? You hiding it from someone?" Pearl shook her head no and placed her hands over her mouth, hiding the smile that was plastered to her lips.

"First off, the gray has got to go." Sugar reached into the bag and pulled out a dark bottle of liquid.

"What's that?" Pearl said, looking around Sugar to eye the bottle.

"Dye. Dye for your hair."

"Oh no!" Pearl said, trying to stand. Sugar pushed her back down on the toilet.

"Just be still, Miss Pearl. Trust me, I know what I'm doing."

Pearl sat shaking as Sugar parted her hair into sections and squeezed the dark liquid onto it. She listened to Sugar talk about her time in St Louis, the time when Sullivan Place was hot and Mary Bedford's house was the place to be. She did not explain in full exactly why it was so, but Pearl got the gist that it was a whorehouse, and she held her tongue still from speaking against it. "I usta dye a lot of heads then. No one ever wanted to have their own hair color. Always red or blond. Ha, me, I never went in for all that, I was happy with my wigs."

Pearl listened and prayed that her hair would not simply slip off her head and drop to her tiled floor. The only person she had allowed on her head for years was Fayline. Every other Thursday at two, a wash and press and then back into the bun. She herself barely dislodged her bun, except to take it down to give her head a good scratching and greasing.

By nine o'clock Pearl came face to face with a woman that she'd known so many years earlier. She stood and stared open-mouthed at herself in the mirror, unable to believe that the woman who grinned back at her was indeed her.

"Oh my Lord," were the only words she could repeat over and over again.

Her hair hung limp and wet, shining blacker than night around her face. She stood that way for a while, running her fingers through her hair, and pulling at the curls that had begun to take hold of it as it dried in the humid house air.

"You look beautiful, Miss Pearl," Sugar said. She, too, was amazed. A bottle of dye had weeded out the age that had grown there.

"You miss her, she sure look like she been missing you, Miss Pearl," Sugar said as she coiled Pearl's hair into a French roll, leaving ringlets of curls to hang loose around her face.

"I ain't never seen her before," Pearl said in profound awe. She touched her face lightly, afraid that any contact with her fingers would cause the vision before her to waver and then distort, like a disturbed reflection in a pool of water.

"Joe is gonna love you, Miss Pearl!" Sugar yelled in delight and clapped her hands together like a gleeful child.

Joe's name brought Pearl back to reality. "Oh no," she whispered. Her face took on a fretful look. She turned to Sugar, wringing her hands, tears formed in her eyes. "Oh Lord … Joe?" How could she have forgotten that she had a husband? She'd made a decision, a drastic decision without consulting her husband. Suppose he hated it? Suppose he hated her for having done it?

"Oh Sugar, what have you done?" Pearl shrieked and dragged her hands down the length of her face, as if the very action would somehow change her black hair back to the ravaged gray it'd been just minutes ago.

Sugar looked on, bewildered at Pearl's sudden reaction. She was hurt.

"Miss Pearl," she started slowly, "what do you mean, what have I done? What I've done was make you look younger, beautiful. What's wrong with that?"

Pearl did not respond, she just stood staring at herself and shaking her head in dismay.

"What you want me to do, turn you back? Make you look old again?"

"I am old!" Pearl screamed and pushed past Sugar.

Sugar followed her into the bedroom. "You're older, not old, Miss Pearl," Sugar said. Pearl sat down on the bed and placed her head in her hands. Sugar leaned against the wall and examined the tight neatness of the room. The room lacked life. By instinct, Sugar knew nothing close to sexual passion had occurred there in a long time.

"You know what you need? You need to go out. Get away from this house, this town," Sugar said. She walked over to Pearl and knelt down beside her. "Miss Pearl, why you acting like your life is over? It's just a dye job. In time the gray will come back."

"Before Joe gets back?" Pearl asked hopefully.

"No, not by then," Sugar said with a wisp of a smile. "C'mon, we going out and show you off."

Pearl looked at Sugar as if she'd gone mad. "Out? Out where?" Pearl's eyes sparkled in spite of herself.

Sugar just smiled. "Just get dressed," she said. "I'll be back." And then she was gone. Pearl heard the front door close and quick footsteps move the few feet down the pavement to #10 Grove Street.

Pearl sat on her bed staring at the floor. Periodically she would look over at the worn Bible that sat conspicuously on the nightstand beside the bed. Its black cracked cover seemed to fill the whole room and dwarf her. There was nothing in the Bible that said you shouldn't dye your hair. There were no words that said, Thou shalt not befriend a whore. No, Pearl knew the Bible from cover to cover, and those shalt not's did not exist.

Pearl got up and went to the full-length mirror that stood in the corner of her room. She stood before it and looked at herself, the new her. She fingered her hair, soft, silky and black. She touched her face, ran her fingers over the face that was absent of wrinkles. Her eyes held her age, not the skin on her face. Slowly, methodically, without being totally conscious of her movements, she began to disrobe. She slipped her dress over her head. The slip followed, as did the brassiere and stockings and panties. She stood before herself, her naked self, and began to re-familiarize herself with her body.

The once flat stomach was rounded and protruded forward; it was scarred with motherhood marks three times over. If she could, she would not even sell those long, black marks that crisscrossed her abdomen, no, they made up who she was—a mother.

The breasts that once sat high and curved now sloped, but did not sag. Her hips were thicker, rounder, and so were her legs. She turned to examine her behind. It was large, expanded by time and good eating. All in all, Pearl did not have a body unworthy of wanting. She released the French roll and let her hair cascade down onto her shoulders. Wild, black waves of hair. She giggled to herself and hurriedly covered her mouth with her hands.

The night was dawning dark blue as the full moon took its place high above Bigelow, giving light to dark back roads and lost souls. A breeze kicked up, late-night September air that prepared you for October and beyond moved through the open window, provoking the curtains into shrill and frenzied movements. Without thinking, Pearl moved to close the window, and in doing so, exposed herself to the night. She stopped, but did not draw back. The night air moved seductively across her naked body. It was tantalizing and invigorating. Slowly, the night caressed her, transforming her nipples into resistant pebbles and teasing the small, pointed, pink flesh between her legs. Pearl parted the curtains and leaned the top part of her body out of the window, allowing her breasts to sway slowly in the night air. The night welcomed her nakedness. It felt so good, so right, so free. Suddenly, she understood.

This sudden empathy she felt for Sugar sent her reeling back from the open window. She snatched her clothes up from the floor and wrapped them, best she could, around her nakedness. What was she if she was able to take part in, understand and even enjoy an act that was clearly amoral? Had her acceptance of Sugar made her susceptible to her low-down traits? Was being a whore like having a flu—could you catch it like the diseases that hid and floated invisible in the air?

A shaken, unsure laugh bounced off the walls. "I'm being so stupid," Pearl said aloud and dropped her clothes back down to the floor. She started toward the closet door to retrieve her gown from the hook it hung on during the day. As she went, she caught, once again, the naked sight of herself in the mirror and something in her smiled.

"What you gone and done?" Sugar stood before Pearl, dressed in a dress so tight, it was as if her body was smeared with red paint and dusted with white gardenias. The tops of her breasts sat recklessly at the edge of the low curved neckline and jiggled like currant jelly with each draw of breath she took. "Why ain't you dressed, and why is your hair all undone?"

" 'Cause it's bedtime, that's why," Pearl said solemnly and looked back at the open Bible in her lap. Sugar shifted her feet and swung her tiny red handbag onto the bed.

"It ain't, either, Miss Pearl. You ain't gonna sleep on my hard work and time. We going out to show you off. I don't give a shit what you say!" She grabbed Pearl by the shoulders and pulled her into a standing position.

Pearl raised tired eyes to Sugar's face. A glint of new-found knowledge lingered in her dark eyes. Sugar recognized it, she'd seen it in her own eyes some time ago. She walked over to Pearl's closet and began rummaging through the frugal, dreary-colored dresses that hung there. Dress after dress she pulled from the closet, examined and then tossed to the bed. "Ain't you got nothing a little spicy?" Sugar asked in frustration.

Pearl was sitting again, flipping through her Bible. Every once in a while she would throw a look over her shoulder to see Sugar's progress. Her mouth was tired of saying no, she could not remember having to use the word so often in her whole life, except of course when she was raising her children.

"I guess this will have to do." Sugar held out a long pale pink dress. It was sleeveless, and had a large white collared neckline that came together as a huge bow in the front. The bottom was a million tiny pleats. Pearl turned to see what Sugar had found mildly approving. It was a dress her son Seth had given her for her birthday. It was a beautiful dress, but Pearl never wore it. She always imagined a younger woman wrapped in its silky cloth, but she could not bring herself to part with it, and so it hung at the back of the closet waiting for Pearl to remove it, admire its print and the sweeping sound of its material, only to place it back in the closet until she was moved to do it again.

"I ain't wearing that," Pearl said. She saw Sugar smile a little. "And I ain't going," she quickly injected and shook her finger at Sugar.

"I said you are."

"Ain't."

"Are too!"

"Ain't." Pearl was unmovable.

"Okay, Miss Pearl, what can I say or do that will convince you to go?"

"Nothing."

Sugar looked down at the old woman. Pearl's lips moved silently as she read her Bible. Sugar sighed and began surveying the room again. A small cross sat on the wall over the bed, and another, fashioned out of palm leaves, rested atop a jar of Vaseline on the dresser. Sugar suddenly realized how she could persuade her.

"If you go ... I'll come to church with you."

Pearl's lips stopped moving and she raised her eyes to meet Sugar's.

"You can have me for a month of Sundays," Sugar continued. She was grieving inside. Church wasn't the place she wanted to spend her free time, but she knew that was probably the only way Pearl would agree to go.

What she didn't know, was why it was so important to her that Pearl actually went.

Pearl closed her Bible and considered Sugar's offer. Sugar craved a cigarette, but instead bit her thumbnail in anticipation.

"Two months of Sundays," Pearl said, holding up a pair of fingers.

Sugar bit her lip, and then in surrender she said, "Okay, two months."

The dress hugged Pearl's hips a little too snugly, and embraced her bosom like an old familiar friend. She kept tugging at the material, hoping that she could stretch it loose.

"Stop it," Sugar said and slapped Pearl's hands away from the material. "You look just fine." She was applying a light dusting of baby powder to Pearl's face.

"That lipstick is too bright," Pearl said and shrunk back as Sugar tried to apply the flaming red lipstick to Pearl's lips.

"It ain't. That stuff you got there is too boring and too damn old," Sugar said, referring to the fifty-cent, doughy pink lipstick Pearl had tried to give to her. It *was* old, and was already in the beginning stages of decay.

"I ain't putting that loud color on my lips." Pearl turned her lips inside her mouth and folded her arms across her chest like a stubborn child.

"Okay, okay. Have it your way, then," Sugar said and threw the lipstick back in her bag.

Pearl looked like a doll. Her hair was back in the French roll, her eyelids lightly dusted with blue shadow. The color wasn't completely flattering to Pearl's skin color, or Sugar's for that fact, it was just a wild ocean that raged on your face and called attention to your eyes. Pearl put on her Sunday fake pearls, but Sugar made her take them off.

"You ain't going to church, Miss Pearl."

Pearl kept examining herself in the mirror, still unsure that it was her that looked back at her.

"So where are we going and how are we getting there?" Pearl asked. She was beginning to sweat and would need to move out to the front porch soon to try and catch a breeze.

"I gotta friend coming by to get us," Sugar said as they walked down the stairs.

"What kinda friend?" Pearl asked suspiciously.

"The kind that drives a brand new car and pays for everything," Sugar said, finally giving in to her craving and pulling her pack of cigarettes from her bag. They were on the front porch now, Sugar leaning over the railing and peering down the dark road. Pearl went into her own pocketbook, a hard black leather bag that she'd had for years, and pulled out a stick of Doublemint. "Umph," she said to Sugar's back as she popped the stick of gum in her mouth. She pulled at her dress again, and wiped at the blush on her cheeks.

"Will you stop that," Sugar screeched.

"Maybe this ain't a good idea." Pearl was having second thoughts. The night air had cleared her mind. She finally realized the extent of her commitment and the approaching headlights made her mindful of the possible consequences involved.

"Oh, Miss Pearl, you only gotta worry about one thing."

"What's that?" Pearl said, concern in her voice.

"You just gotta remember you is a married woman and tell all them men that's gonna be sniffin' around you that you already got a man!" Sugar laughed out loud, her laughter competing with the approaching car's motor. "Here he is."

Sugar walked slowly down the stairs, her body swaying in time with Pearl's quickening heartbeat. Pearl could see that with every step, Sugar was transforming into the Sugar that worked the night, the Sugar that appeared in the dreams of men and whose name, usually during heightened passion, suddenly rested on the tips of their tongues.

"C'mon, Miss Pearl." After a brief exchange with the man behind the wheel, Sugar called to her. Pearl looked up and down the dark street and half walked, half-ran to the car, hoping to get safely inside before she was spotted.

The driver's door opened and out stepped a white man. Well, what Pearl thought was a white man. The same white man she saw passing between their houses that early morning not so long ago. She took in too much air and began coughing.

"You okay, Miss Pearl?" Sugar was next to her now, patting hard on her back.

Pearl blinked the tears away and looked again at the man before her.

"This here is Lappy. Lappy Clayton. Lappy, this here is Miss Pearl Taylor."

Lappy smiled and his gold tooth sparkled under the moonlight. He took Pearl's hand, bent his head and tried to kiss it, but before his lips could brush against her hand, she snatched it away. Terror, then confusion, glistened in her eyes.

"Nice to meet you," he said, mildly annoyed at her reaction.

"Same here," Pearl muttered and looked down at the ground. What she'd seen in his face, or thought she'd seen, would not allow her to look directly at him.

"Well, ya'll ready to have a good time?" he said as he opened the driver's side door, pushed his seat forward and stood back so Pearl could climb in. She hesitated, but Sugar was already in, beckoning her to hurry.

Pearl sat quietly in the backseat trying to avoid looking at the sneaky eyes that watched her in the rearview mirror. She shifted her body, said the Lord's Prayer and looked out into the darkness.

Forty minutes later they came to a stop. Pearl was shaking; she looked out the window and saw a large wooden shack that was supported on slate-colored mason stones. Christmas lights—red and green—were hung around the doorway and carelessly from the sloping roof. It stood in the center of a wide open field. Large trees bordered the land and Pearl could hear the sound of water moving restlessly behind it.

The shack vibrated and shook under the weight of five dozen stamping feet, as the people kept time with the soprano and the piano that wailed away inside.

"It's okay, Miss Pearl," Sugar assured her for the hundredth time that night as they stepped over the threshold and into the smoky abyss called the Memphis Roll.

They sat down at a tiny round table that was covered with a purple-and-black-checked tablecloth. One lone candle sat in its center, the flame threatening to give in to the night wind that slipped in through the aging rafters.

Pearl kept her head bowed. She felt nothing but pure shame for being there; it pulsed through her body, contaminating her arteries, threatening to extinguish the remnants of her moral character.

"Drink?" Lappy was leaning over her, the candlelight illuminating his gold tooth. Pearl could smell his cologne and the stink of his breath. "Uh, no—no thank you." She responded without raising her eyes to meet his.

"Bring her a beer, and you know what I like," Sugar said as she lit a cigarette.

Pearl looked at her over the dancing flame. Sugar avoided her and turned her attention to the large mass of people swirling around them. Too much skin and loud let-go laughter clothed in hot tangerines, blood reds and hot pinks made up the women. Quiet, slanted-eyed Negroes that moved like serpents through the crowd and sported slick suits made up the men.

Lappy, dressed in a saffron-colored suit, pushed through the crowd, making his way toward the bar, stopping every few feet to shake an outstretched hand, slap a back or pinch a curved tight ass. Pearl watched him disappear into the crowd and wished that it would swallow and digest him, finally discharging him as the shit she knew he was. She tried to convince herself that Joe's leaving and the heat of the day were to blame for the departure she'd obviously taken from her senses. But now, she felt something else had a hand in things. It would have to be the case—either there was a greater force at work, or she was going mad, because what she saw, or what she thought she saw when Lappy took her hand in front of her house, was unsteadying enough to make her want to have the drink that Sugar had requested he bring back for her.

Men circled the table like vultures; their eyes caressed Sugar's body, their hands took brief liberties on her knee. They knelt down beside her and spoke into her bosom, or had a conversation with her leg. Her face and who she was were of no concern to them, and they made no attempt to pretend that it was.

Upon Lappy's return, the men scattered. He set a bottle of beer in front of Pearl and a glass of whiskey before Sugar and took his seat.

"This your first time, Miss Pearl?" Lappy asked. He spoke to her in a loud, slack voice usually reserved for friends.

"Yes," Pearl said. She did not want to talk to this man and absolutely did not want to look at him again, especially his hands—those pale long things, adorned with gold and glass. No, to look at his hands again would send her screaming from the Memphis Roll and down the dark road that brought them there. Because when she looked at his hands, she saw fresh, dripping blood.

"Thank you all for being here at the Memphis Roll. For all of you who ain't never been here before, welcome. And for the rest of you—ain't you got noplace else to be?"

The short, dark, round-faced man had a booming voice; it rolled like thunder over the lofty levels of laughter and conversation. People waved their hands at him in amusement and begged him to bring on the band. He told a few more jokes, none that even brought a wisp of a smile to Pearl's face.

A group of men entered through a side door and took their place on the small makeshift stage that was directly in front of Sugar and Pearl's table. A piano, guitar and drum set awaited them. The shack was quiet, except for the sound of people ordering drinks and chicken frying in a room behind the bar area. The band struck up and played tune after tune that ignited the shack, causing men and women to grab at each other and then send each other in wide, wild circles. They separated and came together again in a slow steady grind.

The temperature rose as the music became more feverish. The band members were soaked with sweat, but did not seem to tire beneath the music they put forth. The floor was alive beneath Pearl's feet and more than once she caught herself bopping her head or tapping her feet to the music, before she quickly composed herself.

Sugar yelled obscene praises to the band while slapping her thighs and keeping time with their frantic harmony. "Ya'll is too damn hot tonight!"

The music had hold of the people, compelling them to dig deeper into the rent, bill or mortgage money they foolishly carried with them. "Shiiiit! Pour me another!" reverberated throughout the shack as people slammed dollar after hard-labored dollar on the bar, pushing further and further back the consequences of their pleasure. Eviction, screaming wives, hostile husbands and hungry babies. They would deal with that when the sun fulfilled the promise of another day. For now there were good times to be had, and good times cost.

The band took a break, and people retired breathlessly to their tables, dark corners and the comfort and support of a wall.

"Ain't they hot, Miss Pearl?" Sugar's voice was filled with excitement and she continued to snap her fingers to the memory of the music that lingered in her mind. Pearl nodded in agreement. During the chaos, Lappy had disappeared. Pearl searched the crowd and spotted him pushed up against another woman. Pearl looked quickly away. Her watch told her it was almost three a.m.

"You think we could get going?" she said above the noise.

Sugar couldn't answer, the round-faced man was back.

"Right about now we gonna have our girl belt out a couple of tunes for you." His eyes fell on Sugar. Pearl blinked, and was sure she misunderstood his meaning.

"C'mon people, and give the lovely Miss Sugar Lacey a nice Memphis Roll welcome!"

Hands came together at a quick and deafening rate. Sugar turned, faced the crowd and did a little curtsey. Pearl's mouth dropped wide open.

Three songs later the crowd begged for more. The fifth and final song brought down the house and Sugar had to fight her way off the stage. "Let's go," she said and grabbed at the hand of a dumbfounded Pearl. "Miss Pearl, you better close your mouth, you likely to catch something other than flies in here."

They fought their way out of the Memphis Roll, the exit continually interrupted by someone who wanted to commend Sugar on her performance. Once outside, beneath the flushed dawn, Pearl finally found her voice.

"Why ain't you never said you can sing?" she asked in awe. Sugar shrugged her shoulders.

"You got a voice worthy of angels and you choose to do ... what you do?"

"Let's not start." Sugar's voice was stern.

Pearl shook her head in utter bewilderment. They walked across the field that was wet with morning dew. The car was gone, and Pearl found solace in that. She'd rather walk back to Bigelow than get back in that car with Lappy Clayton.

"Shit," Sugar said under her breath. They turned and started back toward the shack. People were spilling out now. Some stumbled and fell flat to the ground, while others linked arms with friends, shoes in hand, and started down the road home.

Isaac, the round-faced emcee who was also the owner of the Memphis Roll, took them home in his beat-up pickup. The ride was bumpy and the truck slow. Discarded soda bottles and candy wrappers littered the floor and the seats.

"I been trying to get Sugar to let me manage her. She could make a lotta money with her voice," Isaac confided in Pearl. "I got's a lot of connections in the music business and everyone that work the chitlin circuit gotta play at the Memphis Roll!"

The truck groaned as Isaac shifted into third gear.

Sugar sat sleeping between them, her head resting on Pearl's shoulder. In her sleep she was the image of innocence—not a whore or flashy juke joint singer—just Sugar.

"I dunno, I'm all talked out ... maybe you can talk some sense into her hard head," Isaac said in exasperation.

"I'm gonna try," Pearl said as the sun followed them into Bigelow.

Chapter Thirteen

The shop was filled with searing sounds as hot combs killed kinks in the Bigelow women's hair. The radio brought sounds from the world that mixed in among the Saturday conversation. Women complained about the dryers being too hot, flinched at the sting of the relaxer placed on an over-scratched head, but most of all, they talked about the happenings in and around Bigelow, especially Grove Street.

"Fayline, you say that woman been in here?"

"Naw, ain't come in, just walked by. Sometimes stopping to look, but ain't never step in."

"You wouldn't let her in, would you?"

"Hell no!"

"Good thing."

"Sure 'nuff."

"She been spending a lot of time with Pearl."

"Pearl Lawrence?"

"No, girl, Pearl Taylor!"

"Is that right?"

"Right as rain."

"Hmmm, ain't Pearl heard 'bout that woman?"

"Ain't you heard? Of course she has ... probably just don't believe it though."

"What's there not to believe?"

"You know how Pearl is. Naive 'bout lots of things. Life things. Anyways, she got Pearl doing all sorts of strange things."

"Really, like what?"

"Well you should know ..."

"Me? Know what?"

"Well didn't you dye her hair? Fayline? Fayline, honey, I think that curl is done now, you can take the curling iron out. Fayline!"

"Oh, s-sorry."

"Jeez ... damn Fayline."

"Don't mess with it, just let it cool off. It'll be okay. So you say she dyed her hair?"

"Black as night."

"Well, shit on me."

"Shit on that woman."

Ring—Ring—Ring

"Hey girl."

"Anna Lee."

"Josephine. Fayline."

"You got a wait ahead of you."

"I ain't here to get my hair done. I'm here to tell you something about someone."

"Oh, who?"

The women looked cautiously at Josephine. "Aw, you don't have to worry about Josephine."

"Yeah, well, when the shit hits the fan, and it will, I don't want nobody bringing it back to me."

"Talk, girl."

"I seen Pearl and that woman last night."

"We was just talkin' 'bout them. Audrey! Go get Miss Mable from under that dryer, she about done. Go on girl, tell it."

"I seen them at the Memphis Roll last night."

"Pearl?"

"Uh-huh, her and that whore."

"Pearl at a juke joint? You sure your eyes seeing right?"

"I ain't blind, Fayline, I know what I saw. She was dressed all loose and drinking up a storm."

"See?"

"See what, Josephine?"

"I was just telling Fayline about Pearl's strange behavior since that woman moved here. Her hair was dyed, wasn't it?"

"Now that you mention it, there was something different about her hair. She had a lot of makeup on too."

"Get out of here, Anna Lee! Pearl Taylor?"

"She was dancing around and hiking up her dress. It was a shame."

"What were you doing there?"

"W-what … We ain't talking 'bout *me*, are we?"

"Where Joe at?"

"He outta town, Red told me he went down to Florida to visit with his people."

"And he ain't take Pearl?"

"You know she don't go nowhere since Jude."

Silence.

"Well, he better hurry on back here and set his wife straight."

"Well, shoot, he ain't gotta if 'n he don't wanna. Plenty of women be ready to take her place."

"Like you, Anna Lee?"

"Humph."

"I hear you wouldn't mind being Mrs Taylor, Fayline."

"Go on with that bullshit!"

"What ya'll talking 'bout over there?"

"Shoot."

"Ain't nothing, Shirley."

"It's something all right, ya'll been huddled whispering and cackling like a bunch of hens over something, not nothing, and I wanna know what it is, so tell me."

"She ought to know, she know Pearl better than the rest of us."

"That's true."

"What you say about Pearl?"

"She was at a juke joint last night."

Shirley stumbled forward as if the words themselves shoved her. "Shirley, you all right? Sit down, sit down and breathe. You need some water, Miss Shirley?"

"What you say?"

"She said Pearl was at a juke joint. Her and her *new friend*!"

"Anna Lee, please."

"Well she ain't heard you the first time."

"The devil is at work."

"Sure is."

"Shirley, she done dyed her hair, too!"

"Stop it, Anna Lee."

"She should know."

"Lord have mercy. Lemme use your phone, Fayline, I gotta call my sister. We gotta go on over there and reintroduce the Lord back into Pearl's life."

"Sure, Shirley, you know where it is."

"She was wearing makeup and drinking too."

"Enough already, Anna Lee!"

"Uh, Shirley, you want me to doll up your wig a little before you go?"

Pearl's character was stretched, tugged and pulled until her name only left grainy particles of soil on the tongue of anyone who spoke it. She had become, in the eyes of the most influential women of Bigelow, nothing more than dirt.

"You sick? You look terrible." Shirley was peering through the screen door at Pearl, patiently waiting for her to open it. "I came right over when—" She stopped herself, she really had no good reason for being there except to pry. "You sick?" she said again.

"No, just a little tired." Pearl's voice floated through the gray that surrounded and concealed her from Shirley's bulging eyes. It was nearly two in the afternoon and she had not parted the curtains or opened the windows to let in the sunshine and warm fall air. Sleep had not taken her until late in the morning, when her body and mind were finally able to put aside the events of the evening.

She reluctantly opened the door; her better sense told her to send Shirley away.

"Jesus, Mary and Joseph, what have you done to yourself!" Shirley shrieked as she stepped through the doorway,

Minnie following close behind. Pearl sighed; she had not noticed Minnie. Now she would have to contend with the two of them.

Shirley and Minnie scrutinized the woman that stood before them, her eyes red and swollen from lack of sleep and from watching wide-eyed at a world she'd never known. Pearl's hair was wild about her head and its newfound blackness almost sparkled against the rays of the sun. They followed her to the kitchen, looking over their shoulders to see the dress thrown over the banister and amber brown stockings lying like driftwood on the staircase. The women exchanged glances and wondered what awaited Pearl at the top of the stairs, in the bed. Thoughts of infidelity ran wild through their minds and their mouths watered at the illicit image.

"Why your clothes thrown all over the stairs, Pearl?" Shirley was the first to ask. She questioned her in a wary voice.

Pearl breathed in again, and turned the flame on under the teapot.

"Is Joe back yet?" Minnie had not ventured completely into the kitchen, she stood in the doorway staring up the stairway, trying to hear the heartbeat of the man she knew for sure lay in waiting.

"He ain't due back till next week sometime." Pearl's response was sober. She didn't want to play the game with them. She was all too familiar with how they handled things, asked questions, heard the answers they wanted to hear and then went out into the small world of Bigelow and told the story they wanted to tell.

"I—I called you last night and you wasn't here. Where were you?" Shirley adjusted her glasses and folded her arms across her breasts, waiting for Pearl to lie.

" 'Round what time?"

"What?" Shirley hadn't expected a question to her question. She was thrown off. "I believe it was about eight or eight-thirty." Her voice was unsure and she looked back at Minnie, who'd taken a step closer to the stairway.

"Oh, I was here." Pearl began clearing the table.

"Maybe it was later then." Shirley pulled out a chair and sat down.

"Hmmm, how late?"

Another question. Shirley scratched at her wig.

"Listen, Pearl, I heard you was in some juke joint. Is that true?" Shirley's voice came out as a controlled scream. Veins stood out on her chicken-thin neck in frustration.

"Do you think it is?" Pearl looked directly at her. The look alone was persuasion enough to get Shirley moving. She stood quickly, upsetting the chair and sending it toppling to the floor. "That girl done put some roots on you! You ain't use to be like this. You done changed, Pearl, and it ain't for the better either! I can't believe Joe would approve of what been going on here in his absence—"

"What you know about what *my* husband approves of?"

Pearl's words were hot. Shirley backed away from her. She would not turn her back on Pearl and so she walked backward to the front door. Minnie, who'd made it to the third step, quickly moved in behind her sister.

"So nice of ya'll to come by. See you in church tomorrow," Pearl said smiling and softly closed the door.

Before visiting Pearl the women had made a decision. Shirley, Minnie, Clair Bell and a few others, each for their own reasons, decided to confront the evil spirit that had entered their town. They discussed their plan of action amidst the shampoo, hair grease and plastic curlers of Fayline's Beauty Shop. Words of discord, unlike any that had been spoken in Bigelow since slavery times, flew between them like cat-o'-nine-tails.

Anna Lee had only seen Sugar in town, buying vegetables or picking up packages. She'd thought nothing more of her than as a brightly clad woman, cursed black. To Anna Lee's dismay Sugar did not seem to mind this at all. Anna Lee's suitors, men that once lined up at her door just because she was half of something they could never own outright, now ignored her, choosing instead to pay Sugar for whatever it was they needed, rather than come to Anna Lee.

She had not had a long-stemmed rose left on her porch since Sugar's arrival. No small wrapped surprises left between the letters in her mailbox, or midnight telephone calls from men who professed their love in hushed tones, while their wives slept beside them. Sugar had taken all of that away from her. Anna Lee felt it was her birthright to have all of the attention of the Bigelow men. She was the half-breed of the town, the illegitimate child of Abraham the white storekeeper, the silky-haired girl with the dove gray eyes, tight high ass and abundant bosom.

She should be the pinnacle of Bigelow's black male desires, so she felt, not Sugar. Anna Lee wanted her gone.

Fayline wanted Sugar gone. At least six of her customers had started wearing wigs they'd ordered from the back of a movie star magazine. Sugar was taking food out of her mouth. Those women no longer needed to come in every other week for a wash and press.

To make it worse, Sugar had also taken a man out of her bed. Or she assumed as much. Cyrus Green wasn't a man of substance or good looks, but he had shared her bed twice a week for the past ten years. She was barren and would not bear him children, which meant he could do anything he wanted to Fayline and the only thing she would produce for him would be groans of pleasure and squeals of delight. Groans and squeals did not require feeding or clothing.

Over the years, Fayline had grown used to seeing his overalls hanging on her bedpost, his large straw hat resting on her bureau. She was accustomed to kissing his fingers, the nails dense with dirt, and the way his tongue tickled her thick belly. She boiled over at the thought of Cyrus smiling down on the ass of Sugar Lacey.

Yes, Fayline wanted her gone.

Shirley, Minnie and Clair Bell wanted her gone because Sugar represented all that was wrong with Bigelow, and nothing had seemed wrong with Bigelow until right before Sugar Lacey had waltzed into town. They still consoled the women who'd lost their children during the spring. The Bigelow five. And now those same women and quite a few more confided to them amidst tears and wringing hands the fact that their men were often absent from their beds, paid little attention to their living children and always seemed too tired to slop the hogs or clean the barn.

Shirley, Minnie, Clair Bell and the rest of the Bigelow women all wanted Sugar gone.

Things had not gone well at Pearl's house. Shirley and Minnie returned to Fayline's and it was decided. The four of them: Fayline, Clair Bell, Minnie and Shirley, climbed into Fayline's old Ford and were off to Grove Street. Faces set in hot contempt, adrenaline pumping, they did sixty from one side of town to the other and arrived on Sugar's front step just minutes later.

Sugar opened her door and came face to face with Shirley. She had her arms folded across her sagging bosom and her foot thumped impatiently on the wooden porch. Sugar was surprised, and her face gave it away, but then she saw the rest of the women milling around the porch, looking at her, through her and behind her into the house.

"Yeah?" Sugar said. Her voice was pure St Louis street. "What ya'll want?"

"We wanna talk to you," Shirley said and pushed her head forward until her forehead was near to touching Sugar's.

" 'Bout what?" Sugar said and stood back on one leg.

"About Pearl. You and Pearl and where you all was last night," Minnie chimed in from behind Shirley. The women moved in closer.

"Pearl know ya'll here?" Sugar asked and nodded her head toward Pearl's house.

"No, it ain't for her to know," Fayline said and flicked grit from under her nails in Sugar's direction.

"Can we come in?" Shirley asked and took a step forward.

Sugar put her hand up. "No. Anything you gotta say can be said right here on this porch."

"This here is private talk, not for anybody and everybody who pass up and down Grove Street. Just you and us." Shirley looked over her shoulder at the women for support. They all nodded their heads in agreement.

"Don't nobody hardly come down Grove Street, ain't but seven houses between the corner and the field, so I don't think we have to worry about people passing by and hearing what you got to say. But if it's so important for you all to be on the inside, why don't I come over to one of ya'll houses, we can talk and you can serve me lemonade and sweet cookies. How's about we do that?" Sugar's eyes challenged them.

If the look of horror that swept across the women's faces also made a sound, then all of Bigelow would have been on Grove Street.

"I wouldn't 'low nothing like you on my porch no less in my house!" Minnie yelled out. Shirley turned around and threw Minnie a warning look. "Hush up, Minnie," she whispered to her and then turned her attention back to Sugar.

"We all Christian women here—"

"Not all," Sugar corrected her. Shirley cleared her throat, nodded her head in agreement and continued.

"We don't want no trouble, we just concerned about what you done gone and done to Pearl, is all. She ain't use to nobody of your sort. You know what I mean, don't you? She a Christian woman like us and ain't never been exposed to your kind of people—"

"My kind of people? What kind is that, black people? Nah, can't be black people, 'cause all that live around here is black people, so what kinda people you talkin' about?" Sugar stepped out onto the porch, forcing Shirley to take a step backward.

"Girl please, you know what kinda people we talkin' about." Fayline stepped up, moving Shirley to one side. "You a whore and worse of all you a whore with bad luck as your pimp. Now we come over here to ask you to leave Bigelow, just pack your shit and be on the next train outta here."

"A whore? How you know I'm a whore, somebody done told you so or you been with me to know so?"

Again the sweeping silent look of horror.

"Uh-huh, thought so." She stared at them, those faces that could no longer look directly at her. "Ya'll need to go on back home now. Go on." She waved them away.

"You're influencing Pearl to be with other mens, just like you do. It ain't right."

Sugar was puzzled. "What you talkin' about, what other mens you talking about?"

"Don't act like you don't know, you She-Devil, you! I seen it with my own eyes. Clothes all over the floor, a shadow at the top of the stairs, hiding. I seen it! And she done gone and colored her hair too!" Shirley was yelling and spewing saliva as she spoke. Her wig vibrated on her head as she shook uncontrollably.

"You old and crazy, ain't no man over there." Sugar waved her hand at them again.

"Who told her she should go and dye her hair?" Fayline asked. She had a sly look on her face.

"I did, but that don't mean she's fucking for money now too!" Sugar's patience was running out.

"You a devil!" Shirley said and shook her two balled fists at Sugar.

"Yeah, well, so are you," Sugar replied, her voice rising.

"God's gonna damn you to hell!" Shirley was screaming now. Minnie was tugging at her, trying to get her to follow her back to the car where Clair Bell was already waiting.

"Shirley, I been in hell all my life."

"C'mon, Shirley, let's go." Fayline turned and descended the stairs. The fight was over. It didn't go at all the way they'd envisioned it. For some reason they thought the sheer number of them against Sugar would be enough to send her packing. They were wrong. Shirley gave Sugar one last long look and then she turned her back on her. Before she could get her foot firmly rooted on the last step, Sugar called to her.

"Shirley, are you jealous of me? Hmmm, jealous that ain't nobody been sniffin' around your skirts for a while? Even that man you got don't come sniffin' anymore. Well, I guess maybe you ain't pay no mind to it. Maybe you thought you and him was past that stage in your lives. You and, oh, what is his name again?" Sugar raised her head and scratched her chin. "What is his name?" She searched her mind or pretended to. Shirley turned around, his name escaped her mouth as soon as she thought it.

"Herbert."

"Oh yes, ole Herbert! He okay? I ain't seen him for a while." Sugar smiled smugly and was more than satisfied with the look of despair and hurt on Shirley's face.

"Tell 'em I miss him," Sugar added gleefully.

"Y-you ain't never had my man. You ain't never had my man," Shirley chanted. She was moving back up the stairs toward Sugar.

"Sure I have, he a nice old man. And you know what, I don't even mind that his dick don't stand up no more. Shoot, there are a hundred other things I can do to get his juices flowing." Sugar's head tilted back with laughter.

"You lying. You lying," Shirley whispered as she edged dangerously closer to Sugar.

"Am I now? You sure about that? Think now. Think about them nights when he claimed he was hangin' out down at the Rib Shack with the rest of them old men, think now. Could he have been with me? Could he have?"

"He wouldn't," Shirley said. Even as the words left her mouth she was unsure about them.

"How would you know? You too busy minding everyone else's business except your own. Counseling people on how to take care of their men and here you ain't even taking care of your own man."

"Shut up, you whore!"

"Oh yes, you fucking in everyone's life except your own!"

It was sudden and quick. Shirley's handprint seared scarlet on Sugar's jet black cheek. The echo of the slap reverberated through the fields that surrounded them.

Sugar wasn't sure what had happened. She saw Shirley's hand rise and then hang suspended before her, she heard the sound and saw Shirley's mouth form a large circle and then she felt the sting and knew she'd been assaulted. She stumbled backward, tears clouding her eyes, her anger increased.

"Did you smell me on him, Shirley? Did you smell my pussy all over Herbert? Think! Think hard now!" Sugar's voice was loud and hysterical. "Ya'll better think about it!" She pointed at each woman and shook her head knowingly at them.

"Fuck you," Shirley said as she turned to walk away. She had never used that word aloud. Did not even find it suitable to use on the worst of God's two-legged creatures. Never thought she would be saying it to another woman. Would never know she had said it to her own great grandchild. Nevertheless, those words felt comfortable and familiar as they flowed from her mouth. "Fuck you," she said again.

Chapter Fourteen

Pearl squeezed Sugar's hand as they ascended the three steps that would lead them into Bigelow's First Baptist Church. They were late, and the place where she and Joe usually sat was already taken. The minute Pearl and Sugar walked in heads turned and stayed turned. The men slid down low into their pews and the women followed Sugar's hips with hot contempt. Sugar had dressed in the most demure dress she owned, a midnight blue sleeveless sheath that clung to her body, the neckline a flurry of sheer silk that cascaded like a waterfall down the front. The dress was supposed to sit open revealing the side curves of her breast, but Pearl had taken the time to pin it closed.

Pearl and Sugar had an argument about the wig earlier. "Why can't you wear your own hair sometimes? You got a good head of hair. Healthy and shiny," Pearl asked as Sugar donned her short red wig. "You don't need so much of that paint on your face, either. Why can't you just be yourself, Sugar?"

"I guess I don't know who that is, Miss Pearl."

Eyes, both male and female, burned into them. Pearl avoided the stares and opened her Bible instead. Sugar leaned back, crossing her legs, allowing one arm to rest on the back of the pew while she fanned herself lazily with her handkerchief.

Even the Reverend stumbled through his sermon. Reverend Foster, whose words always flowed smooth as buttermilk, was having a noticeably hard time; it was clear his attention was somewhere else. Sugar smiled and shook her head. What would his dedicated flock think if she stood up and told them that their beloved Reverend Foster liked to rub his nose in between the soft mounds of her breasts and paid weekly visits to her house, without his Bible, hours before he stood in front of the good people of Bigelow?

The idea tickled her to death and she laughed again. Pearl nudged her in the ribs and gave her a quizzical look.

Sugar amused herself by counting the men who'd visited her. Almost all of them had been in her house at one time or another; socks on, boxers curled around their knees, drooling and wanting Sugar so badly they said it hurt. And now they didn't even look at her. They kept their heads forward or lowered in shame.

Sugar saw Shirley. She sat almost directly across from her, and had not moved her eyes from Sugar's form in the hour they'd been there. Sugar smiled at her, winked and blew her a kiss and even then, Shirley's death stare did not waver. She saw that Clair Bell, who sat two rows ahead of them, and Minnie, who sat beside her, were doing the same. The heat and their perpetual staring eyes were taking their toll on Sugar, making her uncomfortable and causing her to shift restlessly in her seat.

"When's the choir going to sing?" Sugar whispered to Pearl. Her behind was going numb against the hard wood.

"Soon," Pearl whispered back, and dropped her eyes back down to her Bible.

The choir was made up of six women, three men and ten young girls and boys. And when they sang their voices climbed up into the rafters and spread out like blue flames. Sugar perked up and the heat that pulled at her skin was gone. She felt an autumn breeze sneak in through the windows and embrace her.

It started with one tapping foot and built up to the hand clapping, foot-stomping, screaming frenzy that could only be found in small-town Baptist churches. Sugar was swept up in the music, and had forgotten about the staring, hateful eyes of the Bigelow women. And they had momentarily forgotten about her. People jumped up and danced down the aisles, calling out to the Lord. Some fainted while others bent over and wept.

When service was over, the congregation, emotionally drained and spiritually fulfilled, walked out into the September sunshine, still humming. Smiles stretched wide across a rainbow of black faces, and hands that shook in greeting, gripped longer, harder. It was Sunday and it was a feel-good day.

"Now that wasn't so bad, was it, Sugar?" Pearl said as she adjusted her hat and stepped back to let a running child pass.

"Not at all, Miss Pearl," Sugar responded.

People dressed in their Sunday best positioned themselves in front of the church, exchanging small talk, waiting for the Reverend to appear so they could compliment him on his strong sermon. Children ran around adult legs, laughing and forgetting that a torn stocking or soiled pants leg could mean the switch.

"Oh, hello, Fayline," Pearl said when she saw Fayline pushing through the crowd of people toward her. Guilty, her hand went directly to her hair and then dropped back down again.

"Pearl," Fayline said coldly as her eyes expertly traveled around her head like it was a familiar road. "So I see you've dyed it black." Her words were clipped and she threw Sugar a dirty look. Sugar just crossed her arms and smiled.

"Oh, um, yes. Do you like it?" Pearl asked hopefully.

"Not really, Pearl. A woman your age don't need to have no jet black hair. A rinse would have done you just fine. But then it ain't my hair, so to each her own." Fayline turned, exchanged one last nasty look with Sugar and walked away.

"Well," Pearl huffed. "That's Fayline, you know. She owns the beauty shop in town. Have you met her?" Pearl spoke to Sugar but her attention focused on the crowd and the three women who stood huddled just beyond its border.

Sugar had chosen not to tell Pearl about the words that were exchanged with her friends earlier. Some things were better left unsaid, and that was one of those things. "I—I've seen her in town, but we have not been formally introduced," Sugar responded, following Pearl's eyes to the huddled mass of women just a glance away. Shirley, Clair Bell and Minnie stood, shoulders touching, mouths moving, looking directly at them. It was obvious that Pearl and Sugar were the topic of their conversation. Pearl shaded her eyes with one hand. "Good Lord, what are they up to now?"

"Morning, Sister Pearl." Reverend Foster's voice was moving past them, but Pearl caught him by the arm and gently pulled him back. Her smile said, "See, Reverend, I did what you asked me to." She nodded in Sugar's direction.

"Reverend, I'd like to introduce you to Miss Sugar Lacey. Sugar, this here is Reverend Foster."

Sugar stepped in and extended her hand. All eyes were on them. The Reverend took her hand in his cold, shaking palm. He did not look her full in the face.

"So nice to meet you, Su—Miss Lacey." His voice was uneven, swiftly changing from adult to adolescent in pitch.

"So nice to meet you, Reverend. What a beautiful service, just wonderful. You certainly are a *powerful* man."

Reverend Foster pulled at his collar and cleared his throat. "Thank you, Sister." He wanted his hand back, but Sugar wasn't letting go. She wanted everyone to see, see their beloved Reverend holding the hand of Sugar Lacey.

"Will you be attending next Sunday?" he said in mock optimism. He did not want to ever see Sugar sitting in his church again, and he would be sure to make that clear to her during his next visit.

"I sure will, Reverend. Miss Pearl got me for two months of Sundays, but I'm sure I'll extend it beyond that." She released his hand, and he fought the urge to wipe it against his robe. One final nervous smile, a nod of his head and then he was gone.

Sugar's smile was mischievous as she turned to face all of those who'd been watching her. She looped her arm through Pearl's and they began the walk home. Women turned their noses up at them, grabbed at their children and moved back, giving them plenty of space to pass. Men watched sideways, risking a slap on the back of their heads from the heavy hand of a watchful wife.

The air was dancing by the time they pulled up to the house. A storm was coming for sure. Black clouds fragmented the beauty of the pink slashes that could usually be seen right before pale yellow painted the sky.

They laughed together in Pearl's kitchen and put an extra cup of sugar in the last batch of lemon pound cake. "This gonna ruin that figure you got, girl!" Pearl said and snapped the dish towel off of Sugar's behind. "Sure will," Sugar responded and then laughed, not caring if she spread twenty sizes bigger. Life suddenly meant more to her than a small waist and perfectly shaped hips.

The two women had spent every waking moment together. Talking, cooking or just sitting quiet together and marveling at the world that lay out before them. Sugar had never in her life taken the time to adore a tree or dote on a splendid blade of grass, but her growing friendship with Pearl was changing that.

Mornings found a trick from the previous night dressing in the background of her room and Sugar eager to get him gone so she could watch the dawn break alone.

"Joe coming back today or tomorrow." Pearl smiled it more than she said it.

"You miss him, huh?" Sugar questioned, looking up from the chicken she was cleaning.

"Sure do," Pearl said, looking into the bright light the sun lent to the kitchen.

Sugar was happy that Joe was coming home. Happy for Pearl. She tried to push her selfish feelings aside, knowing that what they had now would change or maybe disappear altogether once he was home.

That afternoon Sugar continued to bare her soul to Pearl in painful slivers. From her time growing up in Short Junction, to her migration to St Louis, Detroit, Chicago and then back to St Louis. She spent a long time speaking about Mary and Mercy. The scare that almost took Mary from her, the comforting feeling she got from Mercy's tiny arms encircling her neck at night and the pain that plagued her still for leaving them. Once or twice Sugar turned away while she spoke and Pearl was sure she saw tears in her eyes.

Over the past week Pearl had taught Sugar how to bake, and Sugar showed Pearl, with the help of a large ripe cucumber, the technique of giving hand and giving head. Pearl wriggled her nose in disgust and shook her finger at her in reproach, but her eyes never left the cucumber. Sugar saw that Pearl had finally allowed curiosity and possibility to couple.

Pearl told Sugar about her happy childhood, meeting and falling in love with Joe. The birth of her three children and the hideous, aching loss of one.

"Jude," Pearl said and her voice quivered. To Sugar, that name and the way Pearl breathed it out sounded like a great work of fiction. Pearl straightened her back, pulled back the years and finally began to tell Sugar about Jude.

"You know, you remind me so much of her." Pearl's eyes were gleaming and they seemed to smile and cry all at once. "You got her color, you know. Like Joe, strong, black skin. The old ones call it pure African skin. They say when you the color of darkness, your lineage is pure, never been touched by a white man." She laughed and waved her hand. "That's what they say anyway."

"You always calling me by her name," Sugar said, wanting to keep Pearl talking about her daughter. She still woke from wild dreams with Jude's name pressed to her lips like a lover's kiss.

"Do I." Pearl's reply carried no surprise. "I suppose that happens when someone is always on your mind."

"Tell me more about her." Sugar wanted to hear about the daughter that took so much of Pearl with her when she died.

"I done told you about her already," Pearl snapped. She did not want to dwell on it now, not when her life was beginning to take on some joy again.

"You told me about what happened to her, not about her." Sugar touched Pearl's face with a gentleness she did not know she possessed. "Please." She turned soft, soothing brown eyes on Pearl's own.

"She—Jude was my only girl, my last child. I didn't mean for her to be the last, God made that decision for me." Pearl wrung her hands and spoke in quick bursts. "We all doted on her. Me, her daddy, Joe Jr and Seth. She was a sweet dark thing. Joe usta call her his sweet licorice stick. Hmmm, she was sweet, but don't be fooled, she was a tough thing. Jude ran before she walked, you know? Humph, always trying to keep up with her older brothers. I tried to keep her feminine, but Jude was a hard one. Always tearing her dress, losing her ribbons, ripping and running like a new colt all over the place.

"But we loved her anyway. Can't help but love a child that lived inside of you for nine months. She was smart as a whip, could out-spell both of her brothers and add up big ole numbers without using paper or pencil. Joe and I told her she was gonna make a fine teacher or doctor. We were saving to send her to college after she finished her schooling here. One of them fine Negro colleges. I was gonna go back to work to bring in a little extra." Pearl sighed and looked at her hands.

"The boys ain't have no interest in schooling," she continued, "Joe Jr was talking about going in the army; and Seth, well he had big dreams, was going to start his own business. He said 'Mamma, I ain't going in no white man's army to get killed for a country that don't want me to piss in the same toilet they do. Me, I'm gonna start me my own business, one that the white man gonna find a need for and when they come into my place of business they gonna have to call me Sir!'

"That Seth was always talking big. Still talking big. Always got ideas that go beyond normal colored people's dreams."

Pearl showed Sugar a picture of Joe Jr and Seth. Handsome men. Joe Jr in his service uniform and Seth, all teeth, handpainted sign in hand that said SETH'S FIX IT SHOP.

"Another dream that never made it." Pearl traced a finger over the letters and grimaced.

"Where's Jude's picture, Miss Pearl?" Sugar flipped through countless photo album pages that held black and white pictures of picnics and birthday parties, hoping to find Jude.

"I—I took them out. I couldn't bear to look at them, at her. It was just too painful, so I took them out and put them in here." Pearl went to the closet and retrieved a large white jewelry box from the top shelf. The age-old paint was yellowed and chipped at the corners, revealing the pale pine wood. A smiling ballerina stood gracefully on its top, her painted lips pursed in perfection. "This use to be mine when I was a little girl and I gave it to Jude on her eighth birthday. She loved it so, would lift the top and let the music play for hours. It don't play music no more, it stopped the day ..." Pearl trailed off.

"It's okay, Miss Pearl." Sugar gently took the box from Pearl and went back over to the bed.

"I only look at them when I feel I need to have her near me. When I miss her the most."

Sugar lifted the lid and saw herself staring back at her. She jerked as if struck. Her hands were shaking as she lifted the first of many pictures from the box. Jude rolling in the grass, Jude swimming in the lake, Jude sleeping, Jude laughing. Sugar's head was swimming. If someone had brought these pictures to her and said, "Here you are in the life you can't recall," she would have believed every word of it and ignored the slight differences that remained between Jude and herself. Jude's smaller nose and thinner lips, her rounder eyes and fuller brow. But the smile was the same; sure and solid. Sugar knew that smile, it was her own.

"You see," Pearl said, standing over her. Sugar shook her head yes. She did see and it scared her to death. "They say everyone got a twin, you hers, I guess," Pearl said and sat down beside her. "God done sent you here to soothe my hurting heart. I see that now. He could have sent you anyplace else, but he chose Bigelow. He sent you here to put a smile back on my face and laughter back in my mouth. He knew I had turned my back on him after Jude, I told him I would continue to serve him, but I couldn't trust him no more. That was, until you showed up." Pearl placed her hand over Sugar's. "I love you for helping me trust again."

Pearl's words melted over Sugar, coating her in warmth and sweet affection, but simple acceptance was hard for Sugar after so many years of rough callused hands handling her body.

"You think you love me because I remind you of Jude," Sugar said quietly.

"That may have been so in the beginning, but now I love you for you, not who you remind me of."

Chapter Fifteen

Joe stepped into his home just as the long hand on his watch skipped past the two, dawdled a while and then landed squarely on the short hand, which comfortably kissed the three. Welcomed by an empty home, Joe was immediately aware of the untidiness of his house. Thick dust covered the coffee table and the plastic lampshades. There were dishes in the sink, an unwashed bowl, batter still clinging to its inside walls. Clothes were strewn across the unmade bed and globs of blue Pepsodent littered the bathroom basin.

He unpacked, and carefully placed his clothes in the closet. All the while he wondered where his wife could be.

He moved to the lower parts of the house, discovering the warm smell of lemon pound cake. Joe scratched at his chin and walked to the living room. He thought about calling Shirley to see if Pearl was there, but as his hand made contact with the phone, large yellow headlights traveled quickly across the room, blinding him for a moment and then disappearing. An engine hummed contentedly outside his door and he heard loud, loose laughter that for some reason reminded him of the French brothels he visited during the war.

He opened the door slowly, not realizing he had moved to do so, and what he saw made him catch his breath. A woman he thought to be his wife, but was quite sure she wasn't, was ascending the porch stairs; her smile, painted burgundy, was fading quickly until it was just a line. "Joe?" She must know me, he thought, she's called me by name. The first drops of rain began to fall, within moments it was driving, drenching the stranger before him. Pearl was thankful for the rain, for it hid the tears of sudden shame that sprung as if on cue when Joe opened the door.

Blue and black ran down her face and washed over the painted burgundy lips. "Joe?" Why wasn't he saying anything? He was tormenting her with silence. She was misreading his eyes, and for the first time Pearl felt fearful of her husband.

Sugar was standing in the background, her off-white dress soaked through revealing her naked breasts and bright red French cut underwear. Darkness had swallowed up Bigelow, thunder clapped loudly behind its curtain, but Sugar remained. Isaac was gone before the first drop fell, barreling his beat-up pickup down the road, one hand hanging out the window waving good-bye. Sugar looked around to see if there was something she could use to protect Pearl, should Joe strike her. Nothing. She clenched her fists and summoned up every bit of strength she had. She would take him with her bare hands if she had to. She waited.

"Joe, I got's a lot to tell you. Uhm, something's done happened since you been gone." Pearl was yelling over the driving rain and booming thunder. Bolts of lightning sliced through the damp darkness, lighting up her frightened face, reflecting the terror that was eating its way out.

"Bit?" Joe leaned forward and Pearl flinched. "Jesus Christ, that you, Bit?" His voice was pure amazement. "Bit, w-what, where you been? Come inside before you catch cold, woman!" Joe stepped forward and grabbed Pearl's hand, pulling her to him in a quick, wet embrace.

Sugar's racing heart began to slow. Her fists relaxed and then laughter, nervous at first, bubbled out until it poured like the rain that soaked her.

Pearl sat in the warmth of the kitchen, her grandmother's quilt wrapped around her damp body, her feet soaking in a warm tub of water. Blue and yellow flames danced below the kettle encouraging the long, high scream that pierced the quiet calm of the house.

Joe was moving about; mixing eggs for scrambling, bending over and looking in the refrigerator to check for slab bacon; shaking his head in dismay when he found none. Searching cupboards and finding a half-empty box of grits and flour for biscuits. "We got buttermilk?" he questioned and looked over his shoulder.

"Some left," Pearl responded. She had insisted that he sit while she made breakfast, but Joe would not have it. He'd pause every once in a while and fold his arms, shaking his head, marveling at the beauty that reclaimed Pearl's face. "You sure do look different, Bit."

Slowly, as the grits cooked and her tea cooled, she unfolded for him the two weeks spent with Sugar. The helpless connection she felt toward her, the affection that grew beneath it. Her face moved in angry waves as she told of her so-called friends' disdain for Sugar and their relationship; the threats and warnings that would certainly befall her should she continue on the path she'd chosen to take.

Joe listened intently as he scooped the grits onto two plates and stirred the eggs. She used her words carefully, side-stepping exactly what Sugar was and always had been. But Joe knew, he'd heard talk from the men in town. She described in detail Sugar's time in Short Junction, growing up at the Lacey home. Joe's mind cringed at her words and he stood quickly, attempting to avoid the question he knew would come.

"You know about that place, the Lacey place over in Short Junction?"

"Yep, heard about it when I was there." Joe knew he'd answered too quickly. They both heard the false composure in his tone and fell silent. Over the years he'd tried to expel the memory of the beautiful brown woman with hair that touched her shoulders and a smile that seemed to warm the air. Her name had passed his lips once since he married. And that was while he slept beside Pearl and dreamed of the time he spent with the woman beneath the sycamore trees.

Bertie Mae.

Even now as he sat remembering what he'd tried so hard to forget, he could taste the sweet dew that was her lips.

He'd met her while laying railroad tracks just on the outskirts of Short Junction only days after he'd decided to marry Pearl. His days in Short Junction were long hard ones. Lifting steel and laying steel was not an easy task for any man, but the black man seemed to complain less and accomplish more. Those long hard days laboring beneath a relentless sun were made bearable knowing that the sun would set, the heat recede and evening would find him at the Lacey home.

His path crossed daily with the beautiful Bertie Mae, since she'd taken to sitting up on a grassy incline beneath a sycamore tree. She said that was her place of solitude. Later it would become their place of passion.

Joe was not a man who took advantage of women. It wasn't in his character to do so, but Bertie Mae did something to him that tested his morals and caused his stomach to quiver. When she touched his cheek, her hand hot with desire, he knew that he would not, could not deny her.

Evening fell and she slowly undid her blouse. He had all intentions of saying no. He saw the first button slip and disappear from its opening and then the second. He'd found his voice by the third. "No, Bertie, please don't." He reached his hand up quickly to still her movements and found his palm pressed against the swell of her breast. She shuddered and covered his hand with her own, pushing it down hard.

Joe was still. He felt her nipples harden and strain against the thin worn fabric of her dress. He reached up and undid the remaining two buttons of the blouse. The material fell away to reveal two full, round, brown breasts. Bertie's breathing quickened and her chest seemed to beckon him.

He leaned forward and kissed each jutting nipple gently. Flicking them with his tongue, causing Bertie to moan aloud, grabbing his head, anchoring his mouth on her hot breasts. Joe sucked like a hungry newborn, and pushed Bertie down to the ground.

He ran his tongue lightly up and down her neck. He came to her chin and nibbled at it. He moved to one ear and then the other, exploring it with his tongue and teeth. He kissed each eyelid and her nose. Joe paused when he came to her mouth. It was open, wet and ready. "You are so beautiful," he said as his mouth came down on her own burning lips. Their tongues danced together for what seemed like forever.

Quickly and awkwardly, Joe removed his boots, overalls and thin white T-shirt. He stood before her, nude, his body as strong and dark as the trunks of the century-old trees that surrounded them. Bertie ogled at his penis. It stood long and erect, throbbing before her like his second heart. He removed her skirt and slip. She wore no panties, as she had only two pair and both were drying on the line in her yard.

Her stomach was flat, smooth and as unblemished as a river stone. He bent and kissed her navel, inhaling the sweet musky scent of her. Bertie gasped.

His tongue made circles on her thigh and then found itself between her legs, relentlessly toying with her womanhood. Bertie moaned and called his name over and over again. The grass beneath her was slick with her liquid. He pulled himself up and straddled her, placing her legs over his shoulders. As he entered her he kissed her, softly at first, and then with more urgency. Bertie winced in pain, pulled him closer, deeper until the pain was replaced with pleasure.

He slid in and out of her and breathed her name heavily in her ear and neck until they both cried out to the heavens.

They lay there beneath the sycamore tree, its branches whispering above them in the receding twilight.

They parted, no promises between them, not knowing their union had spawned a new life.

Pearl watched her husband remember some long ago indiscretion and as she was about to question him about the look in his eyes she heard her mother's voice in the back of her mind: "What you don't know won't hurt you." Pearl obeyed those words and went on with her story.

"... and Joe, she sing like you wouldn't believe! Her voice just lifts you up and takes you where it wants to. It's powerful, you know?" Pearl's eyes danced when she spoke of Sugar's singing. Joe smiled and touched a small damp curl that clung to the side of Pearl's cheek.

"That's how she make you feel?" he asked, realizing now how much Sugar had played in his wife's transformation.

"Me and a whole lot of other people. Joe, I been to a juke joint. Twice." Pearl's eyes were lowered, avoiding the disapproving look she was sure Joe was casting on her.

"Is that right," he said between bites of food. Pearl heard the surprise in his voice and replayed his words in her mind to locate the anger that she expected to be there.

"You heard me?" she said and raised her eyes.

"You been to a juke joint. Yes, Bit, I heard you," Joe replied, stuffing another biscuit in his mouth.

"Well, ain't you got nothing to say about that?" She was looking full in his face now.

"Uhm, no I don't. You went 'cause that's what you wanted to do, right?"

"You think it's all right for a Christian woman to be keeping time in a juke joint?"

"Well, I never thought about it before, but I do know there are worse places than a juke joint a Christian woman could be spending her time at."

"Like where?"

"Like Shirley Brown's!"

They laughed together over Joe's little joke and finished the remainder of their meal by discussing his trip to Florida. In between Joe's words and her questions, Pearl thanked God that she had picked correctly, and had been picked correctly. There weren't many men who could come home to an unkept house to find his woman, mother of his children, climbing out of another man's car (morning or night) and not knock her clear out of her skin first and ask questions later. Not many men would cook breakfast for that same woman and listen with interest about the time she spent with a whore.

The rain fell all day long that day. The sky was a gray ceiling. Bigelow children moved restlessly about the rooms of their homes, stared despondently through rain-streaked windows or bounced a ball impatiently against a wall.

Young lovers pulled each other closer, delighting in the patter of the raindrops and the colorless day that looked in at them. Old lovers would once again feel the fires of passion and desire take root and remain tangled in each other's arms until night fell.

The rain had that effect on people. And so did Sugar's presence.

They were both tired. Joe had hardly slept during the long train ride home. Pearl had been up since six that morning. They walked upstairs, arms linked, whispering instead of talking in normal tones. They each took turns washing up over the basin. Pearl washed her face and brushed her teeth twice. The Memphis Roll's homemade beer and the early morning breakfast had left a steely taste on her tongue.

Looking up from the basin, Pearl caught sight of herself in the mirror and laughed aloud, a light silly chuckle reserved for soft young mouths of school girls just discovering the magic and mystery of a boy's touch. She cast a guileful smile at the cotton gown that hung expectantly on the back of the bathroom door and her eyes moved back to the woman smiling in the mirror.

After a moment, she flicked the light switch off and walked stark naked from the bathroom to her bedroom.

In the gloomy gray morning light of the bedroom, Joe lay on his side. His mind was slowly being pulled into the darkness of slumber and he barely heard Pearl enter the room. He would marvel later at the absence of the swishing sound that usually accompanied Pearl's entrance and the giggle that replaced it. He would enjoy recalling how Pearl climbed in beside him and pressed herself hard against his back, her legs thrown across his own, her breath, heavy with lust, against his neck. He would lick his lips in retrospect on the exact moment her lips brushed against the nape of his shoulder while her hand found the slant opening in his boxer shorts. He would not know that at the exact moment he realized his wife was naked against him and demanding in hushed, heavy tones that he fuck her (those were her exact words) while she expertly guided his organ up and down between the soft palm and fingers of her hand, the memory of that moment would, for the rest of his life, dance across his mind causing a small smile to cross his face.

Chapter Sixteen

The first November morning was a warm sheath of fog that wrapped itself comfortably around Bigelow. People moved about cautiously, barely able to see their hands in front of their faces, much less an approaching car or person. The willow branches hung eerily over the main roads and brushed invisible against brown cheeks, causing women and some men to shriek at its touch. The sun was a dim lightbulb in the sky and the soil a deep wet brown that oozed beneath feet.

Summer had battled autumn and won and now it threatened to drag into war the approaching winter. Only the calendars that hung on kitchen walls and the daily newspaper confirmed that winter was quickly approaching. Thanksgiving would soon be upon them and frost had not yet replaced the morning dew that settled on the thin blade grass.

Talk about Sugar had not completely ceased, but had melted into a low hum. People had less of a reason to stop and point at Sugar. In fact, she had blended into the woven cloth that was Bigelow, like a small imperfection or crooked stitch. Brightly colored dresses, pedal pushers and cropped tops were slowly replaced with cool calm blues, whites and greens that hugged Sugar's figure more like an old friend than a lustful one-night stand.

She replaced the blonde and red wigs with subtle auburns and ravens that complimented her face and brought attention to her eyes.

Joe and Pearl accompanied Sugar to the Memphis Roll practically every Saturday night now. The bartender, waitresses and quite a few of the customers called Joe and Pearl by name, and they even had their own table, center front. The more time Sugar spent with the Taylors, the less time she spent with Lappy Clayton. He'd cornered Sugar on one occasion, grabbing her roughly by the arm as she stepped down off the stage. "Where you been?" His breath was sour and his eyes bloodshot. Sugar snatched her arm away from him. "I been around," she said in disgust and started to walk away from him again. He stepped in front of her. "Yeah, you been around, but you ain't been with me." Sugar threw a quick look over his shoulder and saw Pearl's worried eyes looking back at her. Pearl's hand was resting on Joe's shoulder, pushing him gently back down into his seat.

"Look Lappy," Sugar said between clenched teeth, "this ain't the place or the time—"

"Yeah, it is the place and the right goddamn time!" Lappy was yelling, spit flew from his mouth and his eyes rolled in his head. "You ain't never home and when you here you with them." He turned and glowered at Joe and Pearl. His words were slurring and he stumbled back a step. "Who they to you now, huh? They your pimps now? Ma and Pa pimp!" He let out a reel of crazed laughter.

"You have had too much to drink, Lappy," Sugar said in a low voice. People were starting to look at them. "You need to go on home and sleep it off." She stepped around him and he turned and grabbed her again. This time Pearl could not keep Joe in his seat. He was up and on Lappy before Pearl could say a word.

"Problem?" Joe asked. He stood a full foot taller than Lappy and outweighed him by at least one hundred pounds. Lappy stepped backward and looked up into Joe's angry face. "I said, is there a problem?" Joe repeated himself and took a step toward Lappy. Lappy's hand fell from Sugar's arm.

"Naw, man. Ain't no problem here," Lappy responded in a small voice that made Sugar turn her eyes away. Even though he didn't deserve her pity, Sugar still felt ashamed for him.

"You gonna pay," Lappy hissed at Sugar. Sugar rolled her eyes and dismissed his threat as drunken rhetoric.

Joe stood his ground until Sugar moved past him to the table and Lappy sulked his way out the front door, swearing vengeance.

Sugar sat beside them every Sunday in church. She understood the words Reverend Foster read from the large worn Bible that sat on his podium and little by little she began to apply them to her life. But her greatest joy, the thing that made her sit straight up in the pew, was the some-times gentle and more often turbulent voices of the choir. They left her shaken, wet-eyed and weak with happiness. "You should join the choir," Pearl suggested this each and every Sunday. Sugar smiled and shook her head no, each and every time. Bigelow definitely was not ready to see her stand before them singing the Lord's praises.

Shirley, Minnie and Clair Bell offered Pearl short acknowledgments whenever they had the unfortunate pleasure to stumble across her path. Pearl told Sugar that they would eventually come around. Sugar knew they wouldn't, but agreed when she saw the slight sadness that misted Pearl's eyes as she stared at their swiftly retreating backs.

"Something's going to happen," Pearl said, mostly to herself. Her hands moved quickly, snapping the long firm green beans in half. She was halfway through the bowl and her eyes moved from her work to the window and back. She shook her head and mumbled to herself.

"What you say?" Sugar asked, lowering Sam Cook's crooning voice on the transistor radio.

"Nothing," Pearl said, and looked nervously back at the window. The fog was becoming denser, the humidity increased and the temperature rose by at least ten degrees. "Lord, Lord," Pearl uttered and quickly wiped her hands across her apron. She walked to the window and peered out into the solid gray. Unsatisfied, she moved to the front door and swung it open. Hesitatingly she stepped onto the porch and was swallowed by the smoky heather. She stepped back quickly and promptly shut the door.

"What in the world is wrong with you, Miss Pearl?" Sugar was less than concerned. By now she was used to Pearl's minor panic attacks, the way she got herself all worked up over the smallest things.

"It just ain't right," Pearl whispered as she walked back into the kitchen, throwing a worried look over her shoulder as she did. "I ain't never seen no fog like this in my whole life."

"It's just fog, Miss Pearl." Sugar's hand moved to turn the volume on the radio back up, but Pearl shook her head. Disgruntled, Sugar returned to cleaning the bucketful of chitlins that rested in the sink.

"Humph! Things just *ain't,* you hear me? Everything got a meaning and purpose. Ain't you learn that yet?" Pearl's eyes shone. Her words were felt like daggers in Sugar's heart. She rolled her eyes at the pig intestines, knowing full well that she could run from her past, but never hide.

Joe Jr had called early in the week to advise his parents that once again, he would not be joining them for Thanksgiving. Maybe Christmas, he said, before hanging up. Pearl swallowed hard after she replaced the receiver. Joe said nothing, just cleared his throat and left the room, leaving Sugar and Pearl alone.

"Joe Jr been gone near thirteen years now. Been home maybe three times. Jude's death shook him up a whole lot. He said the South ain't noplace for colored people. I told him colored people *are* the South. I know he's just scared, thinking the same thing might happen to him that happened to Jude. Can't blame him, really, but I sure do miss him." Her voice dripped with grief. "It's like I done lost two children instead of one."

"Well, why don't you and Joe go on up North and visit him, then?" Sugar voiced, her tone light and carefree. She wanted to try to avoid the melancholy she saw quickly enclosing Pearl.

"He ain't never invited us," Pearl said.

"Well, what about Seth?" Sugar smiled brightly. She sang her words instead of speaking them.

"Ain't heard from Seth for about four months. Who knows where that boy might be now. He always chasing his dreams and they never lead him home." She walked upstairs, her last word bouncing off the loneliness she felt, leaving Sugar alone.

The kitchen oozed cinnamon and nutmeg aromas; with each whip of the large wooden spoon through the sweet potato mixture, the smell became stronger. In between football quarters, Joe visited the women, looking over their shoulders and examining their progress. Pearl shooed him away like a bothersome child, but not before allowing him a taste of dressing or a fresh baked biscuit drenched with sweet butter. For the moment Pearl's attention was taken up by her work, the heavy fog outside her window forgotten.

The knock came late in the evening, just as Sugar was grabbing her sweater to go home. The day was done and the fog remained stubbornly in place like a cell block wall. Joe offered to walk Sugar to her door, but Sugar declined. "It's just across the way, Joe," she said in a bashful voice. She had only recently started calling him Joe, at his and Pearl's own urging.

"I'll get it," Sugar yelled out as her hand reached for the doorknob.

"No you won't, either!" Pearl was beside her before Sugar finished her sentence. She looked cautiously out the slim windows that framed the doorway. "You don't know who or what is out there in that fog," Pearl whispered. The knock came again, urgent now. Both women jumped. "Miss Pearl, you got me all spooked now," Sugar said in mild annoyance. She sucked her teeth and once again attempted to open the door. Pearl slapped her hand away. "Leave it alone. Joe." Pearl turned and called to Joe who was dozing in the living room. "Yeah, baby," he called back through a sleepy voice.

All three now stood at the door, Sugar and Pearl behind Joe as he swung the door open. The fog moved in first, long tentacles of mist that wrapped around their ankles. Pearl looked down and kicked at it, then she grabbed Joe's arm and began to shake. "Someone there?" Joe said and took a step forward. "No, Joe!" Pearl screamed and pulled him backward almost toppling him to the floor. "Pe—" Someone or something jumped out of the fog. Sugar, in the middle of trying to steady Joe, caught sight of the form and fled. She was up the stairs before she was sure she'd seen anything at all. It seemed her legs were reacting on their own, without the help of her mind. Pearl had not released Joe, but dug her fingers in, locking her hold on his arm and squeezing her eyes shut against the horror that was sure to be standing before her. Joe reacted by bringing his free arm up and out, his fist making quick impact with the face of whatever it was that then lay groaning at his feet.

"Seth! Oh, my God, Seth!" Sugar heard Pearl's squeals of surprise and concern. Her trembling legs brought her slowly back down the stairs. "Oh Joe, look what you done!" Pearl and Joe stood huddled over the heap on the porch. Sugar saw Joe shake his head and then reach out to help the man up and then she heard a deep laugh. Pearl turned and Sugar saw that there were tears rolling down her face, but she was smiling. Closer still, she saw Seth's strong jawline, a nose that at the moment was bleeding, long thick eyelashes and wide-set eyes that were so dark and deep, she was sure that women had lost themselves in them forever.

She was staring at him, his long fingers and the strong large hands that she wanted to lay on top of her own. She shook her head against her thoughts.

"Sugar, this here is Seth." Pearl plucked him on the back of the head and went to retrieve the ice trays from the freezer. "Seth is my son and a fool!" she said with a laugh. "Seth, this here is my friend, our friend, Sugar Lacey."

His head was tilted back in order to thwart the flow of blood. He held a handkerchief to his nose that obstructed his view of her. "Hey," he said and raised his hand in a hello gesture.

"Hi," Sugar said and dropped her eyes.

"He is the biggest fool! Now what kinda person gonna jump outta nowhere like that? When you gonna grow up, Seth? I done told you over and over again that everything can't be a game. Now suppose your daddy would have had the shotgun? You woulda been dead already!" She plucked him again on his head.

"Ow, Mamma! Daddy, tell her to quit!" Seth yelled in mock pain. Joe just chuckled and stood with his arms folded across his chest in fatherly admiration.

"Why didn't you call and tell us you were coming, Seth? We could've met you at the station.' Pearl wrapped four blocks of ice in a new dishtowel with a red and yellow turkey on it and placed it on Seth's nose.

"I wanted to surprise ya'll and—"

"But how did you get here from the station? You get a lift? Oh, Seth, don't tell me you walked here, in this fog?"

"Mamma, no, I—"

"Well how did you get here then—"

"Pearl, would you let the boy talk," Joe firmly intervened. Pearl threw an exasperated look at him, but said nothing else.

"Thank you, Daddy. I drove here, Mamma."

Pearl did not seem to understand what Seth was saying.

"In a car," he added and shot Sugar a look of mild interest.

"A car? Whose car?" Pearl asked.

"My own. I done bought me a car, Mamma!" Seth was excited and looked at his beaming father for approval. Joe patted him firmly on the back.

"You did what!" Pearl screamed with glee, finally understanding what Seth was saying. "Oh, that's wonderful!" she said and kissed him on the cheek.

"It's right outside. I cut the engine when I was halfway up the street and coasted it the rest of the way, that's why you ain't hear me pull up."

"Sure 'nuff. My baby done bought himself a car. You doing okay then, huh? What else been going on with you, baby?" Pearl asked excitedly and pulled up a chair to sit next to her son.

Sugar listened for a while as Seth talked about New York and Harlem. He told them about the trains that moved hundreds of people all over the city and into Brooklyn, Queens and the Bronx. "Underneath the water?" Pearl said, her eyes wide with amazement.

Sugar was uncomfortable. She felt forgotten by the people who had, over the past few months, become more than friends, but family. "I gotta be going now," she whispered beneath the laughing and talking sounds that emanated from Seth and his parents, and moved quickly on tiptoe to the door. Once again, just as her hand was about to grasp the doorknob, Pearl's voice blocked her escape. "Sugar!"

She stopped cold. "Yes," she said, but did not make any attempt to turn around.

"Where do you think you're going?" Sugar knew the tone. She knew that Pearl was standing behind her, her hands placed firmly on her hips, her lips a straight line.

Sugar spoke to the door. "I got to go, Miss Pearl. Uhm. Things to do, you know?" Sugar felt the air move and then Pearl was beside her, speaking into her neck. "You said you wasn't gonna be doing *that* for a couple of days."

Sugar had agreed that she would not take in any work for the next week. She had enough money to live on, and anything she needed but couldn't afford, Pearl would supply. "I want you to stop this foolishness. You got other talents that don't require you to lay down and spread your legs." Sugar listened to Pearl and half heard her. She'd been told this before but all it got her was a small, big-teethed Jewish man chasing her around his desk, trying to take advantage of her.

Sugar knew it was useless to argue with Pearl. The energy involved was more than enough motivation for Sugar to just nod her head in agreement.

Pearl had asked Joe to ask around about other places in the county that offered what the Memphis Roll offered.

To Pearl's surprise there were quite a few. But the places there were, were only willing to let Sugar sing for tips or were too high up on the chitlin circuit to consider an unknown.

"Don't worry, baby, you keep doing what you do at the Memphis Roll. Word gets around and those people who said no will be banging on your door begging you to come sing at their place." Sugar had wondered when Pearl moved from Bible carrying Baptist to music industry mogul.

"I ain't doing *that*," Sugar hissed back now. "Ya'll don't need me around. I know you all want to catch up with one another."

"You stay right here. You are family now so you and Seth need to get acquainted." She grabbed Sugar firmly by the elbow, ignoring her rejections, and led her back to the kitchen where Seth and Joe were in deep conversation.

"Oh," Seth uttered. The smile that held his lips wavered, faded and then reluctantly reappeared. Sugar knew that look. It was the same look the good Bigelow women threw at her. A look that made it quite clear that she was not wanted or needed. A look that said: Clutch your children, watch your men and don't let your pocketbook hang too loose from your shoulder when she's around.

Those looks, the ones from the women, did not bother Sugar. She'd worn blinders against that sort of intimidation for far too long.

But from a man, from Seth Taylor, the look was wounding. Sugar staggered and almost doubled under the intensity of it. "Just wanted to say good-night," she said quickly and turned to rush out of the house.

"So mamma, what you got to eat?" Seth said, rubbing his palms together.

The gray wall began to recede against the stubborn rays of the high morning sun. Slowly, slowly the thick rays of light sliced through it until it was nothing more than fine, thin strips of mist and then nothing at all.

Thanksgiving morning had ushered in a winter chill that took all by surprise and sent people scurrying to chop firewood for heat, squirrels scampering to gather food for the winter and Sugar wondering about her life in Bigelow.

Seth's reaction to her had haunted her for most of the night, causing her to twist and turn through small intervals of sleep, until finally her unrest sent her from the bed to the top drawer of her dresser and the joint that awaited her there. The marijuana muffled the noise in her head, fragmented the looming face of Seth Taylor and allowed her to sleep. But her sleep was filled with Jude. The haunting pictures of a child that looked so much like her. And Jude, as always, spoke to her from those black and white still lifes, pleaded with her to go away from Bigelow before a tear would fall from one almond-shaped eye and roll down the glossy photo finish, leaving blue and pink scars in its wake, finally falling off the rippled white border and into the vast darkness of Sugar's dream.

She woke with that very same tear in her own eye and wiped it quickly away. Why was Jude coming to her, asking her to leave? Was it jealousy? Sugar balled her hands into fists and beat at her head and yelled at the walls of her room, "What! What! What!"

It could be jealousy. A jealous spirit looking in from the great beyond. Pulling back the layers of time and space and seeing that her mother's pain had finally lifted. Sugar supposed that Jude's spirit felt threatened. If the pain had lessened and become a distant memory that brushed against your thoughts every blue moon, then a memory of a child taken could walk in pain's retreating footsteps.

Sugar was a fighter, had been all of her life, but how do you fight the soul of a dead child and her brother?

If eating was a sin, then all that sat around the Taylor table would surely have been sentenced to hell. The table creaked beneath the weight of heavy ceramic bowls filled with sweet sausage dressing, collard greens, potato salad, macaroni salad, chitlins, candied yams and roasted potatoes. A turkey, baked to golden perfection, sat beside a glazed ham adorned with bright red cherries. Biscuits, so light and flaky they threatened to rise to the ceiling if not for the melting sweet butter that dripped and ran across their swollen bellies, restraining their flight. Music filled the background and the temporary voids that opened up when talk and laughter were put aside for a forkful of macaroni and cheese or a sip of plum wine.

Sugar smiled on top of the festivities, never quite feeling a part of them. No matter if she was quite often the subject of conversation. Seth and Joe retired full-bellied to the living room to watch the football game. Sugar and Pearl sat quietly at the table, picking at bits of sweet potato pie, their ears tuned in to the heavy male laughter a room away.

"Mamma, seeing that you cooked all this here food, I figure the least I can do is wash the dishes." Seth stood at the doorway, his arms expanded as wide as an eagle's wings. He yawned loudly. "If I don't do something, I'm gonna fall asleep." He smiled and walked toward the sink piled high with dishes. His eyes never touched Sugar.

"Joe asleep?" Pearl asked as she removed her apron. She didn't seem to notice Seth's apparent aversion to Sugar.

"You know he is." Seth laughed and twisted his hand up to his mouth in a drinking motion. "I think he had too much plum wine."

Pearl tied the apron around Seth's waist and kissed him lovingly on the cheek. "Well, then I will certainly take you up on the offer." She swatted him smartly on the behind and went to clear the remaining dishes and casseroles from the table.

"Miss Pearl, I'll take care of that," Sugar said and grabbed the plate from Pearl's hand. She didn't want to help. Would have been perfectly happy going home, running a bath and smoking a joint or having a tall glass of pike aid. But she wanted to show Seth that she was useful and not just a piece of garbage his mother had dragged in off the street.

"Well, okay," Pearl said with a wink. "I'm going to sit down and watch myself a little television."

At first the silence that surrounded the flowing water and clinking silverware was uncomfortable. Seth washed and Sugar dried. No talk. No eye contact. No brief smiles. Sugar reached to grab a plate from Seth and their fingers brushed, finally their eyes met and held. There was nothing for a long moment. Just a soundless circle around them.

They could only hear the beating of their hearts. Not the rushing water or the static sounds of the television. Seth's lips moved and the sound came rushing back in. But it was warped and confusing and Sugar found herself leaning closer to Seth, desperately wanting to know what those lips were trying to communicate.

Seth's eyes widened and he pulled his head back. He too had been hurled into a zone of soundlessness. "What?" they both said in eager unison.

"You look a lot like Jude," Seth said. His eyes walked carefully across Sugar's face, pausing to examine her nose or to rest in the dip of her lip. Sugar returned to the table, answering him over her shoulder. "Yes. I know. I saw pictures."

"I guess that's why she likes you so much." Seth cut the water off and turned, leaning his back against the sink, crossing his arms over his chest. He watched her walk away, sway away. Her movements brought a slight smile to his face. "She talks about you all the time."

She smiled in spite of herself and was glad to hear the softness in his voice, the calm that for some unknown reason stirred and heated her insides. She did not respond; if she had her voice would have been light, her words a swirl of pink and white cotton candy on a May day. She couldn't risk the silly in her, answering for her.

"Daddy seems to like you too," Seth added and she heard his approaching footsteps. "Got my mamma to dye her hair and paint her fingernails," he noted in mild amusement. He was beside her now, looking down on her, through her. His eyes voicing so much more than his mouth was prepared to say.

Sugar nodded her response but kept her eyes lowered, staring hard at the table, as her hand continued wiping at the invisible crumbs.

"I like it." He leaned in and spoke close to her neck. She could feel his hot breath heavy with the scent of sweet potato pie. "I like it a lot. She looks twenty years younger. I think Daddy likes it too, although he probably ain't never said nothing to you about it. Just ain't his way." And then his breath was gone. Sugar closed her eyes and longed for its return.

"Mamma says you from Short Junction, but spent most of your time in St Louis." He was sitting down, his long legs stretched out before him, his hands crossed over his chest. He was looking at Sugar, wanting her to look back. "She says you a singer. Is that so?"

"Why would your mamma tell you a lie?" It was out before she could stop it. She almost slapped herself right there in that kitchen. Right in front of Seth Taylor. Why couldn't she just answer the question like a normal human being? She was being malicious for no reason. She raised her head to look at him, to apologize. But then she remembered his reaction toward her the night before and most of that afternoon, and decided he deserved it.

His eyebrows were hitched so high up on his forehead that they were touching his hairline. Her lashing words had caught him off guard. "W-well no, to the best of my knowledge, my mamma ain't never told me a lie." His words were surrounded by light laughter. He sparkled when he laughed. Sugar smiled.

"Oh, you something, ain't you?" He paused to consider his next set of words. "So you sing. That's nice. Maybe you'll sing for me before I go?" He winked at her and laughed again.

Sugar was still standing, but had dragged her hand from the table, stopping the mechanical wiping movement her hand had found comfort in. She stood there like a plank, her eyes darting from Seth to the table and then back to Seth. She felt like an idiot. She couldn't remember a time she was so uncomfortable in front of a man. Too much of who she was was exposed to him. She didn't have on a lot of makeup; just a little powder for the shine and a bit of lipstick. The thought brought her hand up to her face and she ran her fingers quickly across her cheek. Perhaps it was the bulky sweater and faded ankle-cuffed denims. She felt more naked in that than any of her skin-tight, low-cut dresses. Maybe it was because she hadn't had a cigarette since she walked in Pearl's house. She'd purposely left them at home and now she questioned her decision.

"Ain't you tired? You and mamma done cooked up a storm and ate up a bigger one. C'mon now, sit down." Seth moved the chair out from beneath the table with his foot. "C'mon," he coaxed and then flashed a smile.

"No, I gotta go," she said quickly. Her behind just brushed the plastic covering of the seat before she straightened up again. Too many weird thoughts and feelings were swirling around inside of her. She couldn't trust herself to be herself around Seth Taylor. Because at the very moment she wasn't sure who *herself* was. It was best she leave.

"Where?" he asked innocently.

"Home."

"Home?" Pearl walked in the kitchen and Sugar jumped like a child caught doing something wrong. "You going home now? I just talked Joe into a game of cards." Sugar detected the disappointment in Pearl's voice.

"I—I think I ate too much," Sugar said and tapped at her swollen belly. "I'm not feeling too hot," she lied and dropped her eyes.

"Oh no." Pearl's face filled with concern. "I think I got some seltzer around—"

"No," Sugar raised her hand in protest, "don't trouble yourself, Miss Pearl. I just need to lay down."

"You sure?"

"Uh-huh. I'll be fine. I'll see you tomorrow."

Sugar said good-night to Seth and went to wish a half-asleep Joe the same. Pearl and Seth met her at the front door. "Seth going to make sure you get home all right," Pearl said and gave Seth a little nudge. Sugar eyed mother and son suspiciously. "I just live right next door," she said, wondering if Pearl was going senile. She turned to face Seth, trying to gain some support. "You could spit the difference between here and there."

"I know where you live." Pearl rolled her eyes at Sugar's ignorance to the obvious. She was well aware of the attraction between the two. The previous evening Seth had asked a thousand questions about Sugar. He slipped them in the conversation, hoping Pearl would not notice his obvious interest in her neighbor. But she had. "Seth gonna see you home anyway. It's late and a lady shouldn't be out and about alone after dark."

No one had ever referred to her as a lady. It was a role she never thought she would play. She liked it. "Okay," Sugar surrendered.

The evening sky looked far above them. It was cobalt blue with a heavy dusting of tiny twinkling stars. Seth's and Sugar's breaths preceded them in tiny puffs of white that appeared and disappeared quickly. The temperature had dropped with the setting of the sun, and all around Bigelow fireplaces burned, sending billows of smoke up into the dark. Surrounded by silence, they walked the short distance down the road and to #10 Grove Street.

Sugar's mouth moved to say good-night when they reached the porch, but before she could utter one word his feet were already walking up her stairs, his body was settling down into her porch chair and his eyes were turned on the large Arkansas night sky that surrounded them. She moved hesitantly up the stairs and silently took a seat beside him on a beach chair made up of green and white strips of material wrapped around the metal frame. A Sears catalogue special that she'd seen and taken a fancy to. She would sit there and pretend that she was by a pool or on a beach, her feet lazing in the surf. It was her dreaming chair.

They sat there for a while, just staring at the sky and breathing in the new winter air. His voice startled her, although she had been waiting for it to come. "Short Junction is so close. You know, I ain't never been there? Been to most of these towns around here 'cept that one. I hear Short Junction smaller than Bigelow. Shoot, Bigelow ain't the size of nothing so Short Junction gotta be less than nothing." He laughed at his little joke. Sugar laughed too, and covered her mouth when she did.

"Daddy said you done woke something up in Mamma." The words came suddenly, his tone turned serious. Like his father, he spoke to his hands. "You know, after Jude died, she just went inside of herself, you know what I mean? It was like she was my mamma, but she wasn't. She was doing the same things she always done, after a while anyway. She took care of us and all, but her eyes were empty and she just stopped smiling altogether." A long time filled with quiet passed before he spoke again. "And then Joe Jr went into the army. He wasn't doing nothing but running away. Still running I suppose. Me, I hung around for as long as I could, but couldn't stay here forever, not in Bigelow." He looked around him as if he'd forgotten where he was. "Daddy say she smile all the time now and laughing too. Singing to herself in the kitchen and all! He say, he done got the woman he married back again."

Sugar was listening, enjoying the sound of his voice washing over her like a velvet wave. She didn't care what he said as long as he kept talking.

"Sugar." He was calling her name. Slow and then again, "Sugar?"

"Yes," she answered and turned to look into those deep brown eyes.

"I wanna thank you." Once again, his eyes finished his thoughts and Sugar found herself, as she knew she would, lost inside of them.

The winter air left as quickly as it had arrived. The next morning's air and every morning after that was warm and brilliant. Children skipped happily to school and streaked home to finish homework and enjoy the remaining dwindling daylight. People smiled broadly and spoke loudly, needing to be heard over the tumultuous joy that entered Bigelow.

Sugar was caught up in that joy. She had become a living, breathing part of it. Seth had become another limb she never knew she needed. The hours she spent away from him were crippling and made it, if not impossible, extraordinarily difficult to hold a teacup or flick a light switch. He was a third lung. Her breathing was labored without him. He made it possible for Sugar to see the beauty she possessed inside and out.

She was Sugar Lacey, born in Short Junction, Arkansas, thirty years ago. Abandoned by her mother, father unknown, raised by three women who took pity on her and took her in, giving her their name and calling her their own. She was Sugar Lacey, St Louis night club singer, come home.

That is what he had been told and that is what she was to him. No more. That's what his mamma told him, and that's what Sugar had attested to. His mamma didn't lie, to the best of his knowledge. Life went on.

Pearl sat back in her rocking chair and watched Joe climb into his truck, back it out and head down the road. She waved goodbye and turned her attention to the November sky and silently thanked God for her life and the lives of her family and friends. Her lips moved soundlessly as she spoke to her Jude, as she often did now. Running down for her the events of the past five days.

"Jude, I know you know all about Sugar, what I done told you, and what you've seen for yourself. I believe you had a hand in guiding her here to me, and I thanks you. I guess you know that Seth is sweet on her, and she sweet on him too. He don't know what type of life she done led, the things she allowed men to do to her body, and I ain't gonna tell him. We all got our scars to bear, every single one of us. Sugar ain't spoiled, she just a little bruised, is all. Bruises can heal and fade away to nothing. He don't have to know.

"What good would it do? He's human like the rest of us, he's gonna automatically judge and that ain't for him to do. You know that, Jude, that's gotta be left to the Almighty.

"Seth likes Sugar for who she is now, and as far as he is concerned, she always been that person, no one else. Maybe when you sent her you ain't expect her to touch no one else but me. Maybe you ain't all for Seth and Sugar getting together, probably wasn't in your plan. But you gotta know that she done changed for the better, she halfway out of what she used to be. I think Seth can pull her out the rest of the way.

"I know he's your brother, but he's my son and a mother knows best. Seth done had his own hard times. A wife that ain't care about him. That Viola treated him like a dog. She wasn't no kinda wife for my Seth. I ain't never like that child, but I let Seth make his own decision and learn the hard way. And what happened? She crushed his little heart into dust and let it go on the first strong wind that passed by. Hurt him so bad, that he ain't never talked about another woman since then. Well, up until now. You see how his eyes light up when Sugar come around? You see how he just can't stop grinning at her? She make him happy and he make her happy. He make her want to be respectable.

"A man should have a wife, and a woman should have a husband. It ain't natural any other way. He need someone to love and she need to be loved. I wants this to work! Lord knows I wants this to work!"

Her face was wet with tears when she was done.

Seth's time there was coming to an end. A few days more and Sugar knew she would be standing alongside Pearl and Joe waving good-bye to Seth as his car cut through the road dust and headed toward home. The thought disrupted the comfortable happiness he'd brought to her. When things were bad, time had a habit of taking its time to pass, making sure you experienced every painful moment. When things were good and contentment abundant, time moved like the wind, hurrying precious moments along and forcing things that normally require nurturing to grow and forge quickly.

Seth and Sugar's talk was light, supported by laughter and hand holding. Seth told Sugar about his dreams and asked her about her own. His hopes and dreams rolled effortlessly off his tongue, like the dew off a leaf under the yellow heat of the sun. She had very few dreams, and the few she had had only just blossomed within her, and they all included him. She shrugged her shoulders. "I don't know, tell me more about yours."

"This old man I know, he's got a small diner up in Harlem. Does all right business, I know I could make it do better. Anyway, his wife died some years ago, children all grown and gone. He wants to come back South, live out the rest of his years in the house he grew up in, says he'd sell me the diner..." He trailed off then, bending to pick a wildflower.

"You gonna buy it, right?" Sugar asked, her eyes wide.

"Want to." He placed the flower in Sugar's hair above her left ear. Taking a moment to make sure it sat just right. His actions always surprised her. They seemed so out of the ordinary to Sugar. But Seth treated it like it was a part of everyday life. And maybe it was—Sugar never really had a normal everyday life against which to measure his actions.

"Well, it ain't that easy, takes money. I got some, but not enough."

"How much more you need?" she asked innocently. Not realizing that a man's business was his pride.

Seth raised his eyebrows. "Not too much, about five hundred, but more than I'll be able to get my hands on in the next month or so."

"Will he take less?" Sugar's mind was working. She had a little money left, not near five hundred, but almost two hundred. She would give it to him in a second. It was the least she could do for all he'd given to her during the past few days. Knowing Seth, though, he wouldn't take it.

Again his eyebrows rose and then he smiled. "Sure, probably."

Hodges Lake was a huge fluid mirror that the trees peered down into, witnessing their lush summer greens turn into deep reds and fiery oranges, until finally, unable to hang on any longer, they'd crumple. Dry and brittle, they'd float weightlessly down, littering the liquid spectrum.

Sugar thought, if not for Seth, she would have definitely felt uneasy. The tall looming trees, and weeds thick as branches, clasped tight around anything that stood still long enough. Birds moved suddenly and quickly from the treetops, their feathered bodies temporarily blocking out the small patches of blue that fought through the wooded canopy.

It was cold there. No one had informed the backwater woods that summer had decided to hang around a little bit longer. Sugar pulled her sweater closer to her body. An icy chill sliced through the thin blanket she and Seth shared, causing her to shake and her teeth to chatter. He wrapped his arm around her shoulder and pulled her close. "You cold?" he asked, the warmth in his eyes caressing her face.

"A little bit," she said and gave him a brief smile. They were alone for the first time since Thanksgiving night. No one in the next room or backseat. Just them. She was glad and nervous all at once.

"Me and Joe Jr use to come here all the time and play when we was kids or fish alongside Daddy. Farther down," he pointed south, "the lake gets shallow. Daddy would let us swim there. We'd stay in the water so long that we'd look like raisins by the time we got home." He laughed at the memory. "Mamma would be mad. Fussing with Daddy about letting us stay in the water for so long."

"Was Jude with you?" Sugar asked. She was staring at the spot Seth pointed to and she could envision the three children, two boys, one girl, splashing happily around in the water.

"Sometimes," Seth said quietly. His mood was serious now. Sugar had felt it when she opened the door to his solemn face this morning. A massive change from the wonderful time they'd spent together the night before. They took in the new James Dean movie, *East of Eden*. Broward County held the only colored movie house in the state of Arkansas. It was a place where people could lose themselves to the imagination of the silver screen without having to be subjected to the confines of an overcrowded colored section of a white movie house balcony.

Sugar sat through the movie, barely conscious of what was going on in front of her. Seth's arm was wrapped around her, his hand softly, rhythmically stroking her shoulder. He gently guided her head to rest in the curve of his neck. Her heartbeat eventually slowed and her breathing evened, as she allowed her mind and body to become comfortable with his affection and tenderness. Seth's actions felt as foreign to her as another country. Afterward, when the movie was over and they filed out, blending amidst other black couples, he found her hand and held it tightly in his own. She could think of nothing else as they sped along the dark country roads, the moon lighting their way, Nat King Cole serenading them from the car radio. She wanted nothing more than to have him near her again, she wanted to return to the safe darkness of the movie theater, the drifting scents of buttered popcorn and the soft space between Seth's jawline and shoulder. And as if reading her thoughts, he pulled her to him once again.

Neither of them wanted the evening to end so they found themselves in the sultry, sexy darkness of the Memphis Roll, hungry for passion but settling for two fried chicken plates and Cokes. She introduced him to some people, glad that he'd been absent from Arkansas and Bigelow long enough not to be familiar with more than two faces. Thankfully, two faces that she'd never known in the darkness of her bedroom. She took the stage to sing and although the Roll was filled to capacity, her songs were for Seth alone.

When the sun rose up to kiss the sky, Seth Taylor's own lips were brushing gently against Sugar's forehead. They said goodnight, even though morning was in full bloom, and went reluctantly smiling to their separate beds, holding themselves tightly until sleep slipped in and took them to the land of dreams.

Now they were seated close to the lake's edge, wanting so much to look directly at each other, to touch, but satisfied for now with the reflections that bounced off the deep blue belly of the lake.

"This lake mean a lot to me." Seth was speaking again. His tone was muddled, and made it more difficult for Sugar to decipher what he was feeling. She listened intently. "As a child I came here to play and then to mourn my sister's death. As a man, I loved here, asked Viola to be my wife and when it was over, I came here and tossed my wedding band into the water. I've come here to think things out, to be alone and to pray."

Sugar knew he was talking around what he really wanted to say. She knew that he was searching for the right words to express his real thoughts. If only she could look into his eyes, then she would know the truth. "What I'm saying is, this been the place where I make all my life's decisions, right here in this spot." He jabbed the ground with the piece of wood he'd been fiddling with.

"Sugar, I ain't felt this way about a woman for a long time. I—I mean, you make me feel special and warm all over, you know?"

She did know, she was experiencing the same feelings. "I can't explain it. I feel like somebody done cast a spell on me or something." He laughed nervously. "What I means to say is, I'm heading back North the day after tomorrow and for the first time I don't wanna go, but I knows I gotta go, and what I wanna know is, well, will you come with me?" He said the last few words fast. His voice cracked like a pubescent boy, his hands shook.

Sugar's face was hurting. It was as if something was pulling the skin around her mouth in two different directions. It took a moment before she realized the wincing pain was from the wide smile that stretched across her face. Her heart exploded with joy and her soul sang hallelujah, but her mind dwelled on the truth of her life and she questioned her emotions.

His question shocked her mute, and she could not find her voice to answer, and if she could, she would have asked: *Why me?* Because happiness like this was not usually reserved for people like her and she knew it.

He read her face wrong, and assumed her smile meant yes. He embraced her and held her in his arms until she herself felt that yes could be the only right answer. She was going to take Pearl's advice, and stop looking behind her and set her eyesight straight ahead.

He kissed her, gently, timidly, on the lips. Unsure if he should, but unable to stop himself from doing so. His fingers found her scar and moved lovingly over it. She waited for him to ask about its origin, but he didn't. His hands slid down her back and branched off and up her sides, brushing innocently against the curve of her breasts, and then he pulled away suddenly, clearing his throat and averting his eyes. She felt it too, the fire and desire. For the first time in her life she *wanted* to give herself over to a man, and not because the rent had to be paid, or her stomach was touching her back, but because she loved him.

They walked, hand in hand, out of the woods and into the full bright light. The world looked so beautiful that she felt her life ahead couldn't be anything less than wonderful.

Chapter Seventeen

Sugar's mind was whirling as she moved quickly through the house, gathering what few things she owned and shoving them into her worn suitcase. They'd decided that they would tell Joe and Pearl tomorrow, the day before he was leaving—they were leaving.

Lunch was tough. Seth and Sugar were bursting with their secret and they couldn't help but grin stupidly every time their eyes met across the table. "What in the world is wrong with you two?" Pearl had inquired more than once. Joe just looked up from his cold chicken sandwich and shrugged.

"Ain't nothing wrong, Mamma, everything is all right," Seth answered, his mouth half full of food.

Pearl turned her eyes on Sugar. "Ya'll acting silly. Like a bunch of schoolchildren!"

"Leave it be, Bit," Joe said and winked at her. Pearl shrugged her shoulders in defeat. She changed the subject. "Ya'll going out tonight?"

"Yes ma'am, gonna go down to the Rib Shack and hang out down there for a while with them boys. Say my good-byes and all," Seth said and reached for the pitcher of lemonade.

A ghost of sadness crossed over Pearl's face. She didn't want her boy to go.

"Can't you stay a day longer?" she pleaded. "One more day, Seth."

"Mamma, I done stayed too long already. You want me to lose my job? I got's things to do, Mamma." Seth was smiling, trying to keep the mood jovial. "'Sides, I'll be back before you know it!"

"Ask him not to go, Sugar," Pearl was demanding her. "Go'on, maybe he'll listen to you." She folded her arms stubbornly across her bosom.

Sugar shot Seth a look—she wanted to tell Pearl and Joe about their plans. It wasn't fair keeping their decision a secret; Pearl was gonna suffer all the more when she found out Sugar was going to be leaving with Seth. He shook his head no and looked at his father for help.

"Bit, c'mon now. The boy said he got's to get back to work. Do you want him to lose his job?" Joe intervened.

"He could always come back home to Bigelow, plenty of jobs 'round here."

"Like what? Working canning fish or cutting the white folks' lawns? He don't want that. He want better than that," Joe said and returned to his food.

His words made Sugar uneasy. "He want better than that." Was she part of the *better* he wanted? She quickly pushed the thought from her mind. Of course she was.

She helped Pearl wash and dry the dishes. Her mind was wrapped around so many things that she was getting a headache. She didn't have much to say and Pearl, overwhelmed with her own concerns about Seth's imminent departure, didn't notice.

"I'll be by to get you about nine." He was standing close, his hands enclosing hers, both of their hearts beating wildly. They wanted each other, but resisted. Sugar supposed that's what was called keeping it pure. He kissed her eyelids and the lobe of her ear then walked slowly home, looking back twice to make sure she was real and his.

The clothes she would take were packed. The others, the reminders of who she used to be, would be burned. She opened the small drawer to the nightstand by her bed, she didn't know why, and found herself looking at the small Bible Pearl had given her, a rosary and a wilted pack of Luckys. She stared at these things for a long moment until she finally picked up the Bible and opened it to the place that held her mother's picture. It had been a while since she looked at it and now she sat down and stared at the woman who'd given her life, as if it was the first time she was seeing her.

"I gotta man, Mamma. He say I make him feel happy. I'm gonna keep making him happy, Mamma. And maybe we'll get married and have us some babies."

The thought of having babies tickled her. She'd never imagined herself as a mother. But then she'd never imagined herself more than a whore.

"I ain't never gonna leave my babies, Mamma," she added and placed the picture safely back between the Bible pages.

She placed the Bible and the rosary on top of her clothes and closed the suitcase.

She slipped twice running for the phone. Dripping wet, she left soggy footprints across the floor. "Hello?" she answered breathlessly, hoping it was Seth.

"Hey, baby!" The voice was low, haunting.

"Seth?" she said and pulled the towel around her.

"Naw, girl … it's your tootsie roll, your nigga … Lappy!"

Sugar stood stark still. She hadn't heard from him since he cornered her at the Memphis Roll more than a month ago.

"Yeah?" Her voice was granite.

"Baby, where you been? I been calling you but you ain't never home. I even drove by there the other night, knocked on your door, nothing. Started to go over to that old woman and ask her if you were still living, but it was late. You know I respect the elderly." He laughed a twisted laugh that caused the hair to stand up on Sugar's neck. "I got to bust a nut, girl. I been saving it just for you. Got a little weed, a little whiskey. What you say to that!"

The shaking started in her knees and rose quickly, until it was in her stomach churning like sour milk. She sat down and covered her mouth, trying to resist the urge to puke.

"Sugar?" His voice was like poison.

"No," she managed to say.

"No? C'mon, girl. You know uh, me and this cat named Lou figure maybe you can take us both. You know what I mean?"

"No!" She was screaming. "No! No! No!"

There was silence. Sugar thought the line was dead and then his voice came again like a coiled cobra poising to strike.

"You listen here, bitch, I'm the one who got you most of your customers. If it wasn't for me you would be blowing farm boys for fifty cents a pop. I'm the one that got you hooked up at the Roll! So don't you go telling me no. Because I don't much like that word. And people that done used it on me, ain't walking around to tell about it and neither are their old lady friends. You get what I'm saying?

"Now we both businesspeople, I ain't trying to come and get my goodies off for free. Naw, I'm willing to pay, just like always. Things been good for me and I'd like to share the wealth. Now we willing to pay you one hundred dollars for your time, now you know that's more than you make in a month. We'll be over there about ten, so if you ain't wash your ass, I suggest you do so."

Click.

The dial tone buzzed in her ear. She opened the nightstand drawer and pulled out the pack of Luckys.

Pearl jumped as the front door slammed shut. "Oh, Lord! Seth is back!" Pearl squealed and scrambled from the bed.

"Bit, Seth is a grown man. He done been married his ownself, he know what married peoples do." Joe was laughing as he watched his wife run around the bedroom, her hefty behind jiggling madly as she rushed around picking up her bra and panties and trying anxiously to shove herself into them before her son made it to the top landing of the staircase.

"Yeah, but it's the middle of the day!" Pearl giggled in spite of herself and tossed the bra aside, opting to throw her house dress on over her bare breasts. Sex had become a daily routine with them. They found themselves breathlessly wrapped in each other's arms at least once a day. They had probably had more sex in the past two months then they did in the entire thirty or more years they'd been married. With each union, Pearl became less inhibited with her body and her actions toward Joe. It was wildly passionate, sometimes lasting for what seemed like hours, other times it was short, sweet and terribly satisfying, but right now it was interrupted.

Pearl rushed from the room and met Seth at the bottom of the stairs, practically slamming into him. "Oh, hello, baby," she said, her voice too high and sing-songy.

"Hey, Mamma," he responded. He noticed that her house dress was buttoned wrong, her hair tussled and her cheeks inflamed. "Where's Daddy?"

Pearl's hands came up to her face, brushing away the wild strands of hair from her eyes. Joe's scent lingered on her fingertips and caught her off guard. She quickly shoved her hands into the pockets of the dress.

"Uh, we was taking a ... well, a nap."

"Uh-huh," Seth said and decided to return to the kitchen. It was obvious what was going on. He hadn't decided how to feel about his parents taking care of business as much as they did. Since he'd been home he'd heard the late-night groaning. The light tap, tap, tap of their headboard as it made insistent contact with his bedroom wall.

"You hungry. Want me to make you a sandwich?" Pearl spoke quickly, her movements swift and fluttery like a small bird.

"Okay, Mamma." Seth knew she needed to occupy herself.

They sat across from each other, enjoying the quiet mother and son moment. Pearl reached out and brushed her hand across his face, picking a piece of lint from his thick mass of hair or just rubbing the back of his resting hand. Seth talked a mile a minute; every other word was "Sugar." Pearl smiled. She knew by the way Sugar's name always seemed to find a place in his conversation, and how it rolled off his tongue like honey, that the two were smitten.

"You like her something awful, huh, Seth?"

"I likes her well enough," Seth said, still wanting to keep their announcement a secret until tomorrow.

"You likes her more than well enough," Pearl said as she removed his plate from the table.

"Well, to tell the truth, I thinks a man could do real well with a woman like that." Seth leaned back and rubbed his stomach heartily.

"Sure could," Pearl said, watching him sideways. Her heart was hopeful.

At nine, Sugar heard Seth come up the porch steps and knock softly on the screen door. Everything he did was soft. Like how you'd expect a woman to be. Gentle. She heard him calling her name from beneath her bedroom window, over and over again. But she wouldn't answer. Couldn't answer. She just lay there enjoying the sound of her name in his mouth.

The shame of what she was about to do had taken her voice away, left her mute with remorse. She didn't know that at the time. Sugar thought she was doing it for Seth. Told herself the money would come in handy, help him to buy that business up in New York, help fulfill his dreams and make a better life for the both of them.

Then Sugar convinced herself that she was doing it for Pearl. Lappy wasn't a man to play with and he had told her that if Sugar didn't oblige him Pearl could be the one to suffer. She didn't want that.

But looking back, being open and real with herself, Sugar realized that she did it because of who she was and you can't change a person overnight or during a week home on holiday. What she was had been hammered into her.

The woman who Seth fell for, well, that wasn't Sugar. Not the real Sugar. The one he loved was a lie someone conjured up on the front porch of #10 Grove Street.

He would have found out sooner or later. Life is just that way, there's only so much you can do in the dark before it comes to light. If nothing else, Sugar learned that much. Who's to say his best friend in New York wasn't a customer of hers in St Louis?

But that realization hadn't come yet. Even as she lay there and listened to Seth calling her name she still knew that she would let Lappy and his friend use her body one last time, and then she could just disappear. Their money in her pockets, Seth on her arm, the two of them burning up the road to New York, to a new life.

She heard Seth half walk, half run back to his house and she knew he was going to try and phone her. That phone rang a million times and then stopped and rang a million more times before he ran back and started banging on the door, Pearl and Joe with him this time. Six hands banging on her door. She thought she would go mad. But she lay there, sane as could be, still as the night.

Lappy Clayton's car pulled up and Pearl, Joe and Seth stopped calling her name.

She heard the car door slam, his footsteps as he left the car and approached the house and the breeze as it wrapped around the dogwoods.

"She ain't there," Seth said. He was mad that she ain't answer him. Mad that he didn't know if she was dead or alive. Mad that some high faluting, half breed nigger was walking up her front porch.

"C'mon, Seth. C'mon, now." Pearl's voice was scared. Sugar couldn't see what was happening, but she knew Pearl was pulling at him, coaxing him back over to the house. Last thing she wanted was her baby tussling with the likes of Lappy Clayton.

"Go on, son," Joe commanded him.

"Daddy, I'm trying to tell the man she ain't there! So he might as well head back to where he come from!"

Sugar whispered in the darkness: "Please, Seth."

Maybe she was talking to God. She didn't know. All she knew was didn't nobody step to Lappy Clayton and expect to walk away unmarked.

Lappy ain't said a thing. He didn't even take a moment to snuff at 'em. Didn't even look Seth over more than once. He just called Sugar's name out one time, loud and sharp, and there she was opening the door.

Seth's face changed instantly and his lips moved to form the question, why? Sugar didn't respond. How could she? She knew he was thinking all the wrong things, and whatever his thoughts were, were far better than the actual truth.

She wanted him to say her name one more time, not that it would have made a difference in the life she'd chosen to keep when she swung that door open for Lappy, but so she could feel something, for the last time.

Seth stood in the yard and watched as Lappy Clayton stepped into Sugar's home and closed the door behind him. Seth couldn't stop shaking his head. He couldn't stop clenching and unclenching his fists.

What had just happened?

"Lying bitch! If she had a man, why didn't she come out and say so?! Why!"

His parents stood behind him, saying nothing, not even breathing. Pearl's mouth hung open, and disbelief spread quickly across her face as she watched the scenario unfold before her. What the hell was Sugar doing?

Seth stormed past them and slammed into the house. By the time Pearl and Joe got up to the door of his room, half his clothes were already in his suitcase. His face was filled with anger.

"Seth." Pearl wouldn't cross the threshold. She felt that Seth's anger would surely blind him and possibly cause him to mistake her for someone else. "Seth?" she called again, above the slamming dresser drawers.

"Mamma." He answered between clenched teeth, then held up one hand and looked at her like she was the enemy.

Joe placed his hands firmly on her shoulders and backed her away from the room. She turned questioning, concerned eyes on her husband. "He a man, let him deal with this as a man," Joe said. His words usually made sense to Pearl, but now they were meaningless bunches of letters.

"Seth, baby, please. What you doing? You ain't planning on leaving right now, tonight?"

Seth moved past them like the wind. Joe and Pearl followed. He was halfway out the door before his father's voice stopped him. *"Boy!"*

Seth's face was wet with angry hot tears. What he wanted was to just keep moving, let the cool air dry his face and maybe settle his soul. He wanted out of that house, away from Sugar, Bigelow, and all of the bad things that always seemed to happen there.

"You ain't gonna disrespect me and your mamma by just slamming out of this house and not saying good-bye, I don't care what's paining you." Joe knew his son was hurting, he felt the pain his son was experiencing. It spilled from Seth, infecting both of them.

He wiped at his tears, and turned to face his parents. His face was a pot of emotion, swirling and bubbling, threatening to boil over. He brushed his trembling lips against his mother's cheek, moving quickly away from her so as not to get caught in her embrace. He shook his father's hand. Pearl wept as Seth sat in his car, engine running, staring at the shadows that moved behind the thin curtains of Sugar's bedroom. He heard Lappy's laughter and then the lights went out. Seth's tires screamed against the black tarmac, and then he was gone.

Chapter Eighteen

Pain was an unwanted friend of Sugar's. She couldn't seem to get away from it, no matter where she went. Sugar looked behind her and pain was there. Looked beside her and pain was there, looked ahead and pain was beckoning her to hurry and catch up.

From the moment Lappy entered her house, she knew he had been drinking and drugging for most of the day. His face was haggard and his eyes bloodshot. He smelled of booze and reefer. When Lappy lay down on top of Sugar, pain came and lay down on top of him, making Sugar's burden and misery greater. Sugar just pulled in as much air as her lungs would hold and let them both get on with what they had been destined to do.

She didn't ask where his friend was, or if she was gonna get the same amount of money for just doing him. She didn't want to speak because she was still hearing Seth's voice calling to her in the corner of her mind. It was a light echo that was quickly fading into the darkness that surrounded her and she strained to hear it over the creaking of the bedsprings and the howl of wind outside her window.

She looked up and over the shoulder of Lappy and caught sight of the dry leaves flying by like wingless birds. The cold that followed the morning gale was seeping in fast and all she could think of was, she should have lit the fireplace. But then she remembered she didn't have any firewood. And then she remembered she didn't have no Seth either.

"Who you think you are, huh? Who you!" He yelled and raised his hand as if to strike her. Sugar cringed and waited for the impact. "You bitch. I set you up at the Memphis Roll, I get you your customers and you treat me like some junkyard dog! Nah, baby, it don't work that way. You hear me, Sugar? I'm the man and you the bitch!" His words were hot and angry.

Lappy lowered his hand and turned Sugar roughly over, taking her from behind. She didn't even stop him when he began to get rough and scream obscenities at her. "You gonna learn your place. You hear me, you whoring bitch!"

She felt his hands on the back of her thighs and the only thing Sugar could think of were clusters of black-berries. She felt his tongue on her back and she saw the smooth stones that sat in the shallow part of Hodges Lake. With each of Lappy's thrusts Sugar could hear Seth calling her a lying bitch.

"Look up at me, gal," he says. "You embarrassed me. Made me look like a piece of shit. Everybody saw it. You and your *friends.*" "Friends" came out wet and obscene. "Sitting up in the Roll like they own it. Like they had something to do with you being there." Lappy was breathing heavy like he needed air, sweating like the temperature just rose forty degrees instead of dropping twenty. He clutched his stomach as if in pain, but the smile that spread across his face said something different.

Sugar looked up past that mouth and into his eyes and there she saw what Jude saw fifteen years earlier, and she wasn't even scared.

Poor Sugar lay beneath Lappy waiting for the end, but realizing, after he began to speak, that she was just at the beginning. His words would have left her emotionally handicapped had it not been for the faith she did not know she possessed.

Lappy laughed with glee and began his tale where he should have climaxed. His voice was thick and he dribbled hot spit into the folds of Sugar's ear. His breath was like fire on her cheek and she could feel his heart beating so hard against her chest that she thought he would drop dead on top of her. But the more he spoke, the faster he slammed into her. It was as if the words alone motivated him, but Sugar was no more than a hole in the mattress by then. Her body had gone numb a lifetime ago.

He spoke of a car trip. A ride through the Arkansas countryside. Drunk and speeding down a lonely country road in an almost new 1936 Ford. He remembered the heat of the day and the sound of the car's engine as it suddenly shut down. Not knowing much about cars except how to drive them, he cussed most of the two miles he walked up the road in the hot sun toward Bigelow. He was just rounding a bend in the dirt road when he saw the ribbons, yellow and light, appearing for brief instances above the tall colorful wildflowers. Had the girl stopped jumping, the flowers would have hidden her completely from sight, but he saw the ribbons and evil propelled him toward her.

The girl smiled when she saw him coming, pushing the flowers aside and down, crushing them beneath his fine leather shoes. She wouldn't have been there, but she was supposed to meet a friend. A boy from Sunday school who'd passed her a note that said she was pretty and that he liked her. Liked her very much. She liked him too and had liked him for a good many years of her youth. She thought it was funny how they'd been in the same Sunday school class for years, and only this year had he finally noticed her.

Can't tell Mamma and Daddy, she'd thought as she stuffed the note into her brand-new white laced brassiere. She liked the way the paper felt against her budding breasts. "Knobs" her mother called them.

No, they would forbid it. "You don't meet no boy no wherever. A well-raised young man would come to your house, sit down with your family." She'd heard it a million times from her mamma's mouth and had never defied her, but today, today was different.

The girl wouldn't have been jumping up and down either, but she couldn't see the road over the flowers, couldn't see if he was coming along. She was too scared to stand too close to the road, too far out in the open, someone would see and tell her parents. So she stayed hidden in the thick field of flowers and jumped up every once in a while, snatching peeks at the road.

She smiled at Lappy because she was young and innocent. Nevertheless, her heart had jumped a bit at Lappy's approach and the smell of liquor that preceded him. The path through the flowers was a popular shortcut among the locals, but the girl did not find his face familiar. And if he was not familiar to her, then she was not familiar to him and he couldn't tell on her. And if he could, who would he tell? He didn't know whose child she was.

The thought of running like the wind did not even cross her mind until Lappy's heavy hand was crushing her windpipe.

Lappy's hands were closing hard around Sugar's own wind pipe as he told her how Jude's scared eyes pleaded, how her knees buckled under his strength.

"She didn't die quick, you know," he said quietly, his eyes turned up, remembering his deed. His hand went slack around Sugar's throat; just enough to let a piece of air through. She gagged and felt her stomach turn over.

It was true, the girl's life stubbornly left her body in spastic jerks and twitches that rustled the long fragile stems of the flowers and drove her body deeper into the soft earth, soiling her white and yellow dress.

Lappy watched until death had replaced life and then he raised the child's dress above her waist and stared down at the clean white cotton panties that seemed to glow against her smooth brown skin. He reached into his pants pocket and pulled from it the switchblade he carried for protection and slowly cut the material away from her body. She was still a child and only barely a woman. Hair as light and sparse as the coat of a newborn cat covered the flesh that sheltered her womanhood.

Lappy lowered his face and inhaled her scent. He hurriedly unzipped his pants and removed his penis. He tried to enter her, but her flesh was young and did not give enough to allow him inside. He cussed in frustration and spat in her face. His hand was up now, up over the girl, the blade glimmering in the high afternoon sun and then it was down, slicing through her skin, splintering her pelvis bone. Over and over again, until he'd separated her life-producing organs from her body.

Then he looked at her, lying there, her dress rolled up to her neck, a pool of blood covering her lower section, and he saw the eyes, wide open and staring. He saw himself in those eyes. He looked down at his life-taking hands and tried to shake away the murderous qualities they now possessed.

Lappy threw the young girl's vagina beside her, and walked away, looking back once only to see if anyone was witness to his crime before continuing down the road toward Bigelow.

He'd found out the girl's name a day later when the news of the murder spread like wildfire through ten towns.

Jude.

His hand tightened around Sugar's throat again and then loosened. He did not want to choke the life from her, he wanted to beat it out of her.

"I'ma do you just like I did her. This time though, it's gonna be sweeter 'cause you done gone and given me a reason to kill your ass!" He slapped her hard across her face and laughed.

It seemed as though the laughter went on for days. Sugar's ears were filled with it and then suddenly he stopped. His face changed and he leaned in close to her until their noses touched. "You know," he said with a slight look of wonder in his face, "you kinda look like her." They remained like that for some time. Noses touching. And then he laughed again and yelled, "Jude's waiting for you!"

Heavy-fisted blows rained down on Sugar's face until her nose spouted blood and her eyes swelled shut. His hands wrapped around her throat for the third time, stopping the passage of air, causing her chest to swell hot and the darkness behind her eyes to come forward and pull her in.

The howl of a wild animal is what yanked her back from death's grip and into the swirling gray room. Sugar could not open her mouth and she believed it must have been cut away from her face, because she felt nothingness there. The howling increased and held on until the pitch became unbearable and then it faded, only to gain momentum seconds later. She realized, after some time, that the howling was not that of a wild animal, but the combination of wind and wild man.

Fire gauged itself through her navel, long flaming fingers reached out and ignited her womb so that no life would ever live there. The pain was a hurricane raging through her body seeking release in a scream that would never come.

She saw Jude's eyes. Those young wet eyes. Like buckets of water, looking down on her. Looking sad for her. She wanted death and asked for it out loud, "God please let me die!"

Pearl saw Lappy leave beneath a black and mournful sky. The moon was hidden and not a star lent light. He left from the front door, same door he came through, except this time he didn't close it. He left it open, swinging hopelessly in the wind.

Pearl huffed and shook her head in disgust. She'd not slept. Not even one wink. First sadness kept her awake, then anger, then concern and finally dread. Joe would not leave her, and so he settled himself in the living room on the couch.

Pearl looked out the window again. Lappy's skin was glowing dim in the vast dark purple of the departing night. Red splattered his back, neck and hands, giving the illusion that *he* was wounded. Pearl watched, wondering if the lack of sleep was playing tricks on her eyes.

Lappy was whistling, his shirt thrown over one bare shoulder as he walked slowly toward his car. He stopped short of the driver's side door and bent over and puked. Pearl's hands came quickly to her mouth and her eyes widened. He turned around, feeling her presence, her watching eyes, and stared directly at the curtain that hid her. Puke dripped from the sides of his mouth and clung to his lower lip. His eyes seemed to glow, and the sight of them sent icy shivers up and down her spine. He smiled and then waved gaily at her.

Pearl's heart was beating so loud and fast, she thought she would faint right then and there. He looked up toward the silent second floor of Sugar's house and then climbed into his car and drove off.

Fear should have kept her welded to the spot behind the curtain. Fear should have sent her running to Joe's sleeping side, but instead fear sent her running from the safety of her home and straight through that open front door up to Sugar's room.

Pearl stood at the threshold of Sugar's bedroom as the predawn light melted away the gray of the room. There was a smell like wet steel lingering in the air. Her heart began to sink, sink deep into her chest, trying to hide from the sight it was sure awaited. She stepped in, and a feeling so familiar and horrible took her by the hand and led her to a place she had been fifteen years earlier.

Among the crumpled, blood-soaked sheets lay Sugar. Pearl reached down to touch the purple, swollen face of her friend and it was 1940 all over again.

This time, however, Pearl's sanity was saved, by the grace of God, her sanity was saved. Sugar's eyes fluttered and then opened.

Her voice found her, after fifteen years her voice came and Pearl screamed until her throat closed up and Joe stood beside her, shotgun in hand.

Hours later, Sugar heard voices around her. "She needs to be in a hospital."

The voice came from above her. It was a stern disinfected voice. The sharp snap of rubber gloves followed the stringent words and then she heard Joe. "Well this here is the way we want it. No hospital, just home."

"She could set up an infection in any number of places on her body. Was the police notified?"

"Dr Williams, maybe you've forgotten where you are. This here is Bigelow. The law don't care none about us and what we do to one another. It just don't make no sense getting them involved in something they could only make worse, now do it?" Joe's voice was calm, but his annoyance at the doctor's ignorance was evident.

Sugar could hear footsteps and the voices of Joe and Dr Williams fading as they traveled down the stairs and out the front door. She felt a cool wet cloth move slowly across her forehead, a hand constantly brushing against her own and the sound of rapid prayers.

She was alive. For some reason God had spared her. But Sugar would never look at it that way. She had asked God for only one thing in her entire life, and he had not granted it.

God had sent Sugar to the brink of death, dangled it before her and then snatched it away, hurling her back to Joe and Pearl Taylor. Three weeks and four days passed before Sugar was able to stand. Lappy had done a job on her. Cutting deep into her stomach, but somehow missing her vital organs. Bruised purple fingerprints remained wrapped around Sugar's throat, broken skin around her cheekbones and the soft underside of her eyes would heal and scar blacker than her midnight skin.

She dropped down in weight, unwilling or unable to eat. She did not speak or let her eyes wander across the soft faces of her saviors. Joe's strong arms lifted her from her bed and carried her gently from the room and into the bathroom. He sat her on the toilet, holding her body erect as Pearl undressed her, before he placed her into the warm soapy water of the bathtub. They washed her together. Husband and wife. Father and mother. They washed her as if she belonged to them.

They took turns feeding her or speaking small words of hope, faith and encouragement. The hugs came often accompanied by quiet easy kisses on the slope of her cheek and the brim of her head lulling her to sleep or waking her to the breaking day.

Time's seamlessness enwrapped her and when the blue haze of hopelessness finally faded away into the morning mist of the twentieth day, Sugar decided that her time in Bigelow had come to an end.

"Miss Pearl." Sugar's words were not spoken, but seemed to be a part of a weary breath taken years earlier. Pearl turned slowly toward the dark living room and her heart stopped and started again with the first step she managed into the room.

"S–Sugar?" she said warily. "What you doing out of bed child." She tried to make her tone light and rushed as if she had better things to do, but would take the time anyway. "C'mon, back to bed, you ain't near well enough to be—"

"Pearl, please." Sugar's words came stronger now. "You look worse than me." Pearl half-laughed, and moved into the small light that spilled in from the hallway. The swelling had gone down in Sugar's face but it was easy to see it had been used as a punching bag. Her brown eyes were nothing more than brown pools of water. Her lips were puffed and black.

"You, well, you and Joe have done all you can for me. Look at you, here all day every day. All night every night. You got your own to worry about." She coughed and Pearl took a step toward her. Sugar raised her hand to keep her away. "Stop, Pearl. You been doing for me for a long time. I don't even know how long, but I knows it been a while. I want to thank you." Her voice cracked. "Ain't many people would have taken the time to care for the likes of me, and at first I gotta say that I was mad at ya'll for doing it. Dead was the only place I wanted to be, but in time I realized that no matter how much I wanted it, I wasn't getting it. Life's funny like that sometime. I also wanna thank you for keeping the law outta this. It would have made no sense, really. Lappy like to be the devil himself, reporting what he done to me could only bring more harm than good. Thank you."

She moved slowly to the couch and sat down, leaning forward briefly to put out her cigarette. Pearl was shaking. She had wanted with all her heart to call the police. She wanted Lappy Clayton to be hung from the nearest tree and his body left to whatever would have him. But Sugar had whispered no in her ear so many times after Pearl found her that she'd dreamed the word dancing around her for two nights straight. And so she did nothing, but hoped that Sugar, after she healed, would think differently and want justice to be done.

"I'm better now, not good as new, but I ain't never been new, just borrowed, lent and given like secondhand things usually are. I am who I am, Miss Pearl, can't no amount of soap and water change that."

"Sugar." Pearl felt despair clogging her throat, forcing tears from her eyes.

"I ain't deserve a lot of what I got here in Bigelow," Sugar continued. "I mean the good things, the things that made me smile, laugh and sing. I ain't do much good for people in my life and so I really don't know why so much good has come to me." She shook her head in disbelief. "But I suppose that will all end now, seeing what I went and done to Seth." Sugar found it hard to say his name now. Saying it was like a blade being dragged across her heart. "I ain't get a chance to say sorry." Her voice choked with emotion.

"You planning on leaving. To go where?" Pearl asked, trying to sound casual, to masquerade the panic that was growing inside of her. She wiped at her tears and forced a smile.

"Don't know yet."

"When you thinking about going?"

"Soon."

Pearl looked around her. She tried to imagine herself without Sugar. She didn't know who that might be, the person that existed before Sugar's arrival was buried deep into the hard, dry memory of Bigelow next to the rotting bones of her baby girl. How could she be anything more with the loss of two in her life now?

It would do no good to beg against Sugar's decision. Just as it had done no good to force Sugar into a role that she was unprepared for. Look at the damage that had been done already. Pearl could have kept Sugar close and not changed a thing about her, she was really fine as she was. Dark, loud and full of energy and song. Who said she had to be demure, low-key, with an unpainted face and a Christian clean soul? Does that make a good human being, a good and decent friend?

They would all have to learn to live with the misjudgment they'd made.

Sugar had another burden to bear, another secret to hide. Every time she looked at Joe or Pearl she heard Lappy's words echoing in the forefront of her mind. Her decision had been made as soon as the words rolled out of Lappy's mouth. If she lived she would never tell. Telling would only open old wounds that were still healing. Pearl and Joe didn't deserve that kind of pain.

Jude was there all the time now, popping up beside her, hiding behind her eyelids and inviting herself into her dreams. The mirror reflecting her face, sometimes with those sad eyes, sometimes just her sweet face with deep black holes where her eyes should have been.

She was always there. A piece of lint on the blanket, a moon ray on the wall. Just there, floating and waiting. Taunting Sugar with her presence.

Sugar didn't know whether she was trying to get her to stay or push her away.

"What!" she would yell. "What do you want from me!"

Those sad, wet eyes just stared back at her.

Sugar sat slumped on the bed. Staring at nothing in particular. Her sight was turned inward. Every once in a while her body would quiver and tremble, but just for a moment. And then her head would lift and she'd survey the room with quick darting eyes. She was afraid to take too much of it in at one time. The room where she carried out the business of pleasure, the room where Lappy Clayton had tried to carry out the business of killing. She blinked back the memory and shuddered.

It was during one of those episodes that she spotted the box. Small, wrapped in brown paper, resting on the dresser. Probably brought in by Pearl or Joe during one of their vigils. She walked over and examined it. It was a package, delivered through the mail. Her name and address was scrawled on top:

Sugar Lacey
#10 Grove Street
Bigelow, Arkansas

In the far corner, the return address was written:

Mae Lacey
Duncan Road
Short Junction, Arkansas

Sugar stood there for a moment, not sure if she should open it or not. She cocked her head sideways, trying to help her mind tell her what to do next.

She felt the room cool. The wind suddenly died outside her window, but she felt a breeze pick up around her ankles. It swirled slowly, almost lovingly around her calves, edging its way up her thighs, hips and waist, until finally she was enwrapped.

"Mama?" Sugar muttered and then jumped at her own voice. Her hands went up to her mouth and her fingers touched her lips in awe.

With trembling hands she tore at the brown paper that secured the box. Tore through its many layers—layers that at times seemed like skin—until she reached the lid. She removed the top and her nose was accosted with the scent of lavender. Dozens of aged yellow envelopes that carried her name in delicate, fading black ink lay before her.

She removed the envelopes, one by one, first bringing them close to her nose and smelling the lavender, then moving them across her cheek and down her neck. She could feel her mother. For the first time she could really feel her mother. She laughed, a tearful sorrowful laugh as she opened the letters.

Each envelope held thin sheets of paper that carried words so unbelievable, yet so believable that there would be no decision for her to make. It had been made while she lingered in her mother's womb, a wisp of balled flesh, a secret not yet known.

They all began the same: "My dear sweet child."

And closed simply: "Mother."

The letters revealed a life filled with suffering. They told of a sliver of time when Bertie took love for herself beneath the watchful eye of the moon and her glowing children. It explained her choice to abandon a perfect ebony child because of her fear of inherited madness and the cancerous guilt that manifested itself into the tumor that consumed her body and finally extinguished her life.

"... He knows nothing about you and I hope he never will."

Sugar's hands trembled violently as she held each letter and read aloud the life of a woman she never knew. She hoped her father's name would be revealed to her among the words that spilled out in jagged black ink. But it never was and then she came upon the picture.

There was her mother, young and beautiful, her hair pulled back, her skin glowing, a shy smile across her face, nothing like the sadness that blanketed her in the first picture Sugar had. A young man stood bashfully beside her, tall, dark and incredibly handsome. Their bodies didn't touch as they posed awkwardly for the camera. Sugar pulled the picture closer to her face, even though it was quite evident who the man was. She saw her own features sketched in his face. She saw Seth's features in his face. She turned the picture around and her mother's handwriting confirmed what she already knew to be true: *Me and Joe 1924.*

Days later, Sugar set her bags just inside the entrance of the church doors. Visible for all to see. She wanted them to know that they'd won. Their God had heard their prayers. She was leaving.

"On the eve of our Lord's birth." That's what the Reverend called it, and that's the way Sugar would always remember it.

Pearl looked up in surprise when Sugar appeared beside her. She nudged Joe to scoot down some so as to make room for Sugar in the pew. Even when the space was made Sugar stood staring at them for a good long while. Her focus moved slowly from Pearl to Joe, resting on him for some time before it moved back to Pearl.

She looked as she did when she waltzed into Bigelow behind the crazed winter of '54—'55, except her skin was the color of what flames leave behind after they danced across the walls of a poor man's house. Her eyes, never much to sparkle, were now black holes.

Pearl's hands went up and across her mouth. Sugar looked so vulnerable and at that moment she looked more like Jude than ever before.

Whispers filled the spaces between the Reverend's words as the people of Bigelow muttered under their breath. Word had gotten out about the attack, and no one was up in arms about it. Who was Sugar? Certainly not a Jude. She belonged to no one and nowhere. A whore.

At the height of the Reverend's sermon, Sugar stood up. Tiny waterfalls of sweat spilled down his face and his voice rose to a holler while his hands gripped the sides of the podium, steadying his Jesus jumping. He caught sight of her and stopped dead. The congregation was thrown and turned to see what he was looking at. Sugar was walking now. Straight toward him. Her feet hit the floorboards hard and with great intent. The Reverend had taken more than a few steps backward. His heart raced. His thoughts filled with the memories of the wicked, stolen pleasures he'd shared with the woman that was now in his face. He held his breath and felt the blood drain from his head down to his feet.

Sugar was looking at the Reverend, but not seeing him. She turned on the congregation. A combined breath was taken and for a moment, there was no sound at all. Sugar looked down on the people of Bigelow and they looked back at her. Waiting.

Then suddenly, like a fledgling breeze before an approaching storm, whispers rose up from the pews, filling the emptiness until the church walls groaned and the whispers became a raging gale of shouts and screams.

"Sit down, girl!"

"You done lost your mind? The Reverend is preachin'!"

"Lord, she ain't got the good sense God gave her."

Sugar stood before the congregation, her head hanging heavy on the stick that was her neck. And then she spoke with a voice that betrayed her grief and disguised the hopelessness that was eating away at her senses.

"Ain't but two of ya'll in this church ever made me feel welcomed here," Sugar began. She raised her hand and pointed a shaking finger toward Joe and Pearl.

Clair Bell, Minnie and Shirley twisted uncomfortably in their seats, and pulled at the collars of their dresses. "I'm leavin' here tonight," she continued, "but not without sayin' some things that need to be said."

The men who'd laid down with her squeezed their legs shut and scratched at the spaces behind their ears and beneath their chins, bracing themselves against the truths they thought she would tell.

"I wanna say to Joe"—she raised her head high and looked directly at him—"and Miss Pearl, that ya'll been like family to me. I appreciate you looking on me with warm eyes, talkin' to me like I was somebody, treatin' me like I was your own." She choked on "your own," giving it all the meaning it deserved. The sound of those two words placed together caught some people's attention as they slipped from her mouth.

Sugar's eyes did not welcome those faces into view. Her eyes rested solely on her Joe and Pearl. Her words were meant for those two only. "I wanna say sorry for the things I did and the things I didn't do and I wanna thank you, for everything."

Anna Lee smiled and turned her head to exchange a triumphant glance with Fayline.

Sugar walked slowly down the aisle, away from the pulpit and toward the door.

A quiet peace had settled over Sugar. A peace she had never known in all her years. Even as she walked past the sad staring eyes of Joe and Pearl, the good-riddance looks from the Bigelow women and the forlorn glances of the Bigelow men, she was not fazed. Her hurt had been replaced with tranquility. The anger that had laid heavy in her heart for so many years was no longer present in her mind and soul. It had dissolved with each step she took toward the pulpit and each word she spoke to those who cared for her.

Pearl willed herself to stay seated. She kept telling herself, "She ain't yours. Let her go." She repeated these words over and over in her mind until they escaped from her mouth in a moan. She dug her fingers deep into the soft underside of Joe's arm and rocked herself back and forth.

Joe's eyes teared for the third time in his adult life. The first time was when he promised himself to his wife. The second time, when he lifted the cold, dead body of his baby girl, and now. He could not give reason as to why he felt so impassioned. It would be one year later before he would understand why his heart had opened and allowed his emotions to slip down his face.

Pearl was losing another one. Only this time, she would not have to bend over a pine box to say a final good-bye.

No, this was worse.

This time the sound would come like a flood. It started deep in Pearl's belly and rose in her throat like lava; hot and steaming. Fifteen years of loss. Fifteen years of grief. Fifteen years of anguish finally spewed forth and shook the church's insides and everyone who had the misfortune of being there.

Black John braced himself. He did not have the comfort of his straw hat. His hands moved around his lap, searching for consolation, until finally clasping on to those of his neighbor.

Sugar, already out the door, never heard the great wail of emotion released at her back. If she had, the depth alone of Pearl's sorrow would have spun her around.

Sugar barely noticed the biting cold and brutal wind that had its way with her as she walked down the path that led from the church to the street that would place her firmly back onto the familiar road of her life.

One step forward, two steps backward. Two steps backward. One step forward.

AFTER

Fall 1956

"I got some people from over in Carnery wanna come on over here and check out the house." A white man with a beet-red face and a tan plaid jacket looked in at Pearl through the screen door. It was barely ten o'clock and the temperature had already soared to eighty degrees. "They told me that you all got the keys to the place," he continued.

Pearl couldn't tell if the heat was making him uncomfortable or the fact that he was talking to a black woman with a blank face. She looked him over and without a word, turned and walked away.

"Ma'am?" The white man was confused. He took out his paper and looked down at the name and address again. He was at the right place. He cussed under his breath and was about to turn to go back to his car when Joe came to the screen door. The white man was short, so he had to tilt his head way back to meet Joe's eyes.

"You need the keys to number ten?" Joe pushed the door open a crack.

"Uh, yes," the man said, scratching his head.

"Just a minute." Joe let the screen door close again. When he came back he had one lone silver key in hand. "Lemme come on over there with you, the lock is a little funny, you gotta jiggle it just right."

The white man nodded and pulled his handkerchief out of his back pocket to wipe at his forehead and the back of his neck. He had to half run and half walk to keep up with Joe's long strides. He finally caught up and stuck out his hand. "Tommy Cathers," he said. Joe considered his sweaty palm and then took it into his own. "Joe Taylor."

"Uh, this house been up for near a year now. We just got this listing two weeks ago. You had a lotta people out here looking at it?"

"A few." Joe hesitated before he took the steps up to #10.

"Really. You know the people that usta live here?"

Joe didn't answer; he was jiggling the lock. He hadn't been in the house for almost as long as Sugar had been gone. A month after she left someone came and placed a FOR SALE sign in the front yard.

The door was open and Joe stepped back to let the man in.

"Thanks ... Joe," the man said and hesitantly stepped into the house.

Joe stood, peering into the dusty emptiness. He half expected Sugar to come swaggering around a corner or down the stairs. He closed his eyes and wished it hard, because Sugar had taken part of his wife with her. But when he opened them all he saw was the white man's red face staring back at him. "You okay?" the man asked, genuine concern in his voice. That's all he needed was this colored man to pass out or drop dead with no witnesses. Not with all of the civil rights stuff going on down there; he didn't want to be blamed for anything.

"Yeah," Joe said and turned to leave.

He was halfway back to his house when the white man came out to the porch, calling to him. Joe looked down and realized that he still had the key clutched tightly in his hand. "Probably want to keep it," he thought to himself and turned back toward #10.

The white man was grinning and holding something in his hand.

"It was laying on the floor near the fireplace. Burnt a little 'round the edges, but still clear." The white man's voice was excited. "I almost threw it in the trash, but I looked at it and realized it was you."

Joe sighed. The heat and this man's babbling were toying with his patience. He took the picture from the man and stared at it. His heart skipped a beat. His breath shortened and then he turned and sat heavily down on the stairs.

It was him. Him and Bertie Mae.

"That's you, ain't it?" the man bellowed and slapped his knee in triumph.

Joe stared long and hard at the picture. Stared into the truth he'd tried to avoid the whole time Sugar was there. He didn't need a picture of him and Bertie Mae to see that she was a clear product of the two of them—he'd thought it the first time he saw her, but had convinced himself otherwise. Now he stood, his stature a bit stooped, and placed the picture safely in the breast pocket of his shirt.

He took the first step toward home, where he would speak the first word of an age-old story and ask, for the first time in his life, for forgiveness from his wife.

CONTENTS

AUGUST

SEPTEMBER

OCTOBER

NOVEMBER

DECEMBER

ACKNOWLEDGEMENTS

This book would not have happened without the support and encouragement of Paul Field, editor in chief of the *Irish Daily Mail* for most of the period covered in these pages. I would like to thank him for his enthusiasm for the project from day one, for his help when I felt swamped on occasion during the selection process and for his professional guidance and advice throughout. I would also like to thank Ted Verity, Paul's predecessor, who first entrusted me, when I joined the newspaper back in January 2007, with the commissioning of The Saturday Essay.

Many other colleagues in the *Mail* have contributed in some way – either to the success of the Essay slot on an ongoing basis or to the taking of this specific publishing venture from an idea to a reality. So, in no particular order, I would like to acknowledge the input of Paul Henderson, Regina Lavelle, Sebastian Hamilton, Paul Drury, Eric Bailey, John Cooper, Conor O'Donnell, Leslie Ann Horgan, Michael Kealey, Michal Hefer, Garrett Brennan, Claire Hyland and Ross Bowden. Thanks also, on a professional and personal level, to news editor Ronan O'Reilly for his unfailing humour and no-waffle perspective.

I am grateful to Edwin Higel of New Island whom I have known for more than a decade, a valued and trusted friend in the world of Dublin publishing. Thanks also to New Island editor Deirdre O'Neill for her patience, professionalism and genuine interest in this book.

Then there are the writers, without whom there would be no book. Thanks to all for their wonderful writing, their co-operation and their can-do attitude.

Acknowledgement and thanks are also due to Christy Moore for permission to use lyrics from 'Lisdoonvarna' in an essay by Shay Healy.

And finally, a big thank you to my husband, Gerry Sandford, who sowed the first seed when he said to me one day last year, 'You know, all those ideas and all those great writers would make a terrific book.'

He was right. I hope that you agree.

Roslyn Dee
September 2010

INTRODUCTION

By Roslyn Dee

It usually starts on a Sunday. The tiniest flicker of an idea. Something that just starts to float around in my head. Maybe I'm standing on the side of a hockey pitch watching my adult son perform his magic, maybe I'm sitting around the dining table at home with my husband, in the genial company of good friends, dissecting home and world events, shooting the breeze, talking about new books or films, the latest shenanigans in the Dáil, how Vincent Browne had made mincemeat of some poor eejit on his television programme a few days before. Maybe I'm listening to the radio, or eavesdropping on the Dart, gleaning from whatever source I can the things that, in any given week, are becoming talking points, with the potential to make us happy or hopeful, sad or downright angry. To engage us in some way.

Whatever way the seed is sown, it's usually around Sunday that the process begins. It ends on The Saturday Essay page, six days later.

When I joined the *Irish Daily Mail* – where I am Associate Editor – in early 2007, the commissioning of The Saturday Essay became part of my brief. At first I found it rather daunting. The Saturday Essay. What did that mean exactly? I wasn't entirely sure. Oh, I knew what an 'essay' was, all right – I'd written enough of them in my time, albeit usually about two hours from an already extended deadline and following an exasperated conversation with an out-of-patience university tutor.

But a newspaper essay is different. This, by its nature, is a great piece of writing that is of the moment; that captures that which is engaging us, as a nation, on any given week of the year. It is a snapshot in time. Yes, it can, and – as you will see when reading the essays in this book – it does often speak of the personal. But look closer and you will see that that 'personal' story is often your story too. In the context of the individual lies the universal. Like an inkblot on a page, that which starts small spreads far. From the personal portrait springs forth the bigger picture.

Two elements are crucial to the success of The Saturday Essay. First, there's the idea. Then, there's the writer. But it is the marrying of the two that is the secret to ultimate success on the page, to making it a compelling read, week in, week out, for our readers.

I have been privileged to work over the years with many of this country's finest writers. Some – like Joseph O'Connor, Nell McCafferty, Peter Cunningham and Fiona Looney – I have known for many, many years, while others I have developed a relationship with more recently during my time as an editor at the *Mail*. And so I have grown to understand – albeit in a steep learning curve kind of way! – which themes will bring out the best in which writers. It's about knowledge and passion for a subject, and in the end it's that connection that is the vital element – that fusion between writer and idea.

In this book you will find writers who are master wordsmiths, philosophers and commentators. Some of those represented here are celebrated novelists, playwrights or poets. Others are journalists or academics. But the human factor is vital too. Most are mothers or fathers, brothers or sisters, husbands or wives. All are sons, or daughters. And it's that humanity, that sense of kinship, that informs many of the pieces here, with each writer conveying their particular understanding of despair, or anger, or joy, or hope, having experienced all or some of these themselves. As we all have.

Reading through the list of essays in this book is like holding up a mirror to Irish society over the last few turbulent years. The good, the bad and the ugly are all represented. The people and events that inspired us, and those that let us down.

The Church looms large – in both a positive and a negative way. There's Mark Dooley's marvellous piece about Pius XII, the Pope who took on Hitler, while Tom Inglis casts a somewhat colder eye and gives us his take on why he feels the Church is finished. There's politics, of course – be it Eamon Delaney on Bloody Sunday or Richard Waghorne on the architects of our current malaise – and there's the enduring importance, and poignancy, of family, captured beautifully by the likes of Dermot Bolger and Joseph O'Connor. There's the power of sport in this country, and there's our ongoing love of the land. Destruction and desolation is balanced by redemption and renewal. Obama is there, on the cusp of hope, in the spellbinding words of Colum McCann, and, a year later, there he is again, the election euphoria over, in an eloquent and measured assessment by Marion McKeone.

There's a pervading 'we can fix this' attitude, a sense that all is never completely lost, that even within the negative there's a positive waiting to happen – or a positive that must be *made* to happen.

Perfection is not essential – sometimes it is only when the flawed is acknowledged that you can see the way forward. It's that old Leonard Cohen thing: there may well be a crack in things but isn't that, after all, how the light gets in?

It was the sixteenth-century French writer Michel de Montaigne who first used the term 'essay' when making an 'attempt' ('*essai*') to put his thoughts about given topics into written form. His first collection – *Essais* – was published in two volumes back in 1580. The English writer Francis Bacon followed the form, as did Ben Johnson in the early seventeenth century.

More recently Aldous Huxley, a noted essayist, described the writing genre fairly succinctly when he said that 'the essay is a literary device for saying almost everything about almost anything, usually on a certain topic. A collection of essays,' he went on, 'can cover almost as much ground, and cover it almost as thoroughly, as can a long novel.'

It's a definition, from someone who was himself, of course, a novelist, that manages to truly convey the potential, in depth and scope, of the essay format.

Not every Saturday Essay idea is mine. Sometimes the Sunday and Monday I spend mulling over ideas draws a blank – or throws up an idea that, when properly discussed and dissected with colleagues, just runs out of steam or takes off in another direction. It is therefore, in the main, a collaborative process. And in that collaboration with fellow editors on the paper – and with writers – is sparked great debate. In the editor-in-chief's office every week sit five or six senior editors, all of us with one objective in mind – to come up with the very best possible Saturday Essay that we can. We discuss, we argue, we tease out the ideas. Once the theme and the thesis is agreed upon, then we discuss and argue all over again until we have the correct writer. There's nothing 'woolly' about The Saturday Essay. What exactly is this piece saying? is the question.

Sometimes an essay comes about on the back of a book that a particular writer is already working on or sometimes there is an anniversary that begs to be marked in some way – like Susan O'Keeffe's beautifully crafted but hard-hitting essay, written twenty-five years after the death of Ann Lovett, or Dave Hannigan's about how the death of so many Manchester United players on an icy Munich airfield exactly fifty years previously forged a bond between Old Trafford and Ireland that remains unbroken. I am a sucker for anniversaries – on the basis, largely, that if I am amazed and interested that it's been twenty or thirty years since such-and-such a memorable event, then readers will be equally amazed and engaged with the subject. It has that compelling 'remember that?' factor. Like the old people in poet John Montague's 'Dolmens Round my Childhood', they stand, these never-to-be-forgotten moments, like dolmens along the road of a nation's shared history.

Certain months bring particular allegiances – and so in the landscape of March, for instance, with its Mother's Day and St Patrick's Day landmarks, you'll find essays exploring both motherhood and our national psyche – but not in a Hallmark-card type of way. There's nothing sentimental, after all, about our relationship with alcohol in this country – just read Peter Cunningham's essay on the subject if you are in any doubt about that one.

This book is exactly as it is described – it is a 'selection' of the Saturday Essays that have appeared in the *Irish Daily Mail* from 2007 until the summer of 2010. It was the selecting bit that I found so difficult. From more than one hundred and sixty essays, we have here, in this volume, the chosen sixty-one. (I hate round numbers.) It was an extraordinarily hard task and I should point out that two of my own essays are included here only at the insistence of Paul Field, the newspaper's editor-in-chief. You don't argue with the boss!

Many, many fine essays that appeared in the newspaper over the past three years have not made it into the book. I had to make decisions for all kinds of reasons – balance of topics and the numerical balance within any given month of the year being just two practical examples. Then there were some essays that worked wonderfully well on the given Saturday on which they were published, but which simply did not travel in terms of ongoing reader appeal.

Some writers are represented here with a number of essays. Inevitably I have built up a 'bank' of writers over the past few years, those whose writing style suits our essay page, wonderful writers who can turn their minds and their hands to myriad topics. To them I say a special thanks for their superb pieces, for their patience at the editing stage, and for, on occasion, their speed – necessitated when my mulling-over process has extended itself way beyond Sunday and Monday, and Saturday's deadline is approaching fast.

It has been a tremendous privilege for me to be so involved with The Saturday Essay for the past few years. I have learned a great deal – about writing, about editing and about this country of ours in all its grief and its glory. The essays in this collection give us, by way of fine writing and argument, an opportunity to look at ourselves in the mirror.

Like it or loathe it, they offer us a snapshot of Irish society, a potent image of ourselves. They show us, in effect, who we are.

Roslyn Dee
September 2010

JANUARY

DEATH OF THE POST OFFICE

Peter Cunningham

My old friend is on the phone to England. He's in the horse business and for the last forty-five minutes he's been negotiating the sale of a racehorse to a trainer in Yorkshire. Several hundred pounds still separate the parties.

The English trainer insists he will pay not a penny more. My friend has reached a crucial pass in the deal. He appears to hesitate. Suddenly, out of the ether, a third voice enters the fray. A female voice. 'Hold firm!' she hisses to my friend. 'Hold firm!' It is 1960 and the local postmistress through whom all calls must flow has not been able to resist entering the negotiations on whose every moment she has eavesdropped. (My friend held firm and sold his horse for the price he wanted.) Despite the advent of modern telephony which has made such stories quaint anecdotes, the rural post office has until recently held firm against the ravages of the open market and the global pressure to justify the existence of any organisation only by reference to its annual profit. Not anymore. As well as having eighty-four full post offices, Ireland has 1,300 sub-post offices, the highest number in the EU measured by head of population.

Over the past four years more than 400 post offices have closed in rural Ireland, a trend which is likely to continue as EU full liberalisation of postal services looms in 2009. The closure of rural post offices mirrors the decline of rural Ireland.

The termination of vital local services on grounds of efficiency and economics dismays local communities whose ability to stand their own ground has become increasingly tenuous.

In Lombardstown, County Cork, a small community beside the River Blackwater, the local post office is on death row. Catherine Healy-Byrne, the postmistress, works five and a half days a week for less than €11,000 a year from An Post.

Her post office also doubles as the local shop, the normal arrangement found in rural Ireland. The closure of Lombardstown post office, Catherine says, 'would be a terrible loss. [Lombardstown] would be like a ghost town.' But in Dublin, Richard Ryan, a spokesman for An Post, argues that his company must prepare for the liberalisation in 2009 and has to think commercially rather than socially.

'An Post cannot be seen as a company that simply provides a service, primarily because of the social function. We have to look at the business side of it,' he says.

Rural Ireland is under siege. The barrage comes from all sides and without respite. Countrymen who have always driven for a quiet pint now either stay at home or chance the trip but do so in dread of being put off the road. (More likely, their local pub, like their post office, has closed down. A thousand pubs in Ireland have closed over the last three years, mainly in rural areas, a trend that looks set to continue.) The sons and daughters of farmers who have traditionally built a house on the family land now find their efforts blocked by unyielding planning authorities.

Broadband access for many parts of rural Ireland is merely an aspiration – the same as mains water or a public sewerage scheme. Medical services are hit and miss, with long-term treatment for such illnesses as cancer only available in Dublin. Public transport is a bad joke.

Even traditional country pursuits, such as hunting and shooting, many a rural dweller's only means to alleviate the grey infinity of the Irish winter, are under threat from government ministers obsessed with politically correct views of the environment.

'Post offices occupy [a vital place] in the social infrastructure of the local community,' says St Vincent de Paul national president, Mairéad Bushnell, commenting on the recent closures of rural post offices.

Pointing to Bus Éireann's transport system to areas of low population and to the ESB's provision of electricity to offshore islands as examples of State-owned companies providing important social but commercially unprofitable services, she says, 'There is no reason why An Post's mandate cannot be amended to support the post office network in areas where it is under threat.' The increased use of electronic funds transfer systems means that fewer people need to use their local post offices. Under an EU court ruling, the social welfare contract, worth in excess of €50 million annually to An Post, must be sent out to tender next year. The loss of this contract to An Post would be catastrophic for rural Ireland.

Inevitably, if the closure of post offices continues, deliveries to remote areas will also come under threat. The postman (and postwoman) in rural Ireland regularly circulates throughout the community. He is often the only one who meets the lonely and the ill in isolated locations and reports their wellbeing or otherwise to those who can take action.

The postman comes across burglars, and the dead, and sometimes helps deliver babies, as well as the post. The postman delivers the post in the country – he drives it up the lane, carries it in through the back door and puts it on the kitchen table. He then, as often as not, sits down and has a cup of tea – behaviour which must seem like a nightmare to suits with slide rules whose only goal is to cut the fat from time.

What are being witnessed in the closure of sub-post offices are the accelerated stages of the transformation of Ireland from a mainly rural to a mainly urban society. Power has shifted from the country to the town.

Rural communities, always viewed with suspicion by the urban, have become an inconvenience. People who choose to live at the end of a two-mile boreen have to live with their choice, the argument goes, and cannot expect to be carried as a burden by society. The provision of goods and services is shifting away from the country.

It is difficult to see how this seismic shift in Irish society can be halted. Ireland's history has meant that this decisive change only began a century or more after that of mainland Europe.

France, Germany and England were by the late nineteenth century well on the way to being transformed into societies of chiefly urban dwellers, drawn to centres of population by the work in new industries, by better housing, by the superior availability of goods and services and by the protection from outside dangers traditionally enjoyed by people who live together in large numbers.

The closure of Ireland's rural post offices, and pubs, is symptomatic of the pain arising from Ireland's delayed demographic transformation. The Department of Community, Rural and Gaeltacht Affairs attempts the Sisyphean task of supporting 'the sustainable and inclusive development of communities, both urban and rural'.

It does not enjoy good press, being associated mainly in the public mind with attempts to force towns to change their names into Irish – Dingle into An Daingean being one example. The department's mission statement, part of which is quoted above, is suspiciously unfocused, as the 'both urban and rural' phrase suggests.

The Community, Rural and Gaeltacht Affairs Minister, Éamon Ó Cuív, is reported as saying that he 'is concerned with any withdrawal of services in rural Ireland and believes the way to address these issues is by a comprehensive policy of rural development'. Lofty words, but short on specifics. If Ó Cuív's department was really concerned about such matters as the slow death of rural communities, then what better place to address this decline than in rural post offices?

Ireland has benefited more than any other country from the EU, which may explain our slavish obedience to its diktats. Anyone with the slightest experience of Europe will know the way in which the French or Italians choose to interpret European law on such matters as toilet facilities in bars and restaurants, food preparation, safety standards, the production and sale of farm produce – the list is long. Rural Ireland should take a lead from our European neighbours and insist that the liberalisation of the European postal service in 2009 is a pathetic reason to allow Irish villages to die.

Ó Cuív's department could use the local post office as the growth nucleus for the village, channelling its energies and resources through a physical entity that up to recently was on call twenty-four hours a day. It could do so in partnership with An Post whose mandate can be amended to allow it to continue in the social role it has played for so long and with such success. The ultimate financial cost of such a strategy is unlikely to be greater than having to set up a new rural network in place of the sub-post offices.

There is another cost. If we allow rural Ireland to die before our eyes, then romantic Ireland, too, will truly be dead and gone, and in the grave.

26 January 2008

THE BETRAYAL OF ANN LOVETT

Susan O'Keeffe

Ann Lovett was a teenage mum. That's what we would call her now. Back then, in the mid-1980s, we can only imagine what people called her for 'getting pregnant'.

In holy Catholic Ireland she was fair game for name-calling, fair game for gossip and she was on her own the minute her secret swelled out from her clothes. At 15, Ann had her life before her and she was just getting to the good part; old enough to enjoy it and young enough to enjoy it.

Was she pretty? Was she tall? Was she good at history? Did her school socks swivel round her ankles? Was she a Queen fan or did she prefer Michael Jackson's 'Billie Jean'? We don't know.

But nine months pregnant in January 1984, Ann herself would have been in no doubt of what she was. She was 'a disgrace'.

There would have been no cooing over pretty vests and cuddly toys, no friendly neighbours knitting booties, no proud family anticipating the great excitement of a new life. Ann was in an impossible position; old enough to be pregnant, too young to know how to cope in a community whose knee-jerk response was to alienate her.

There were no gaps in the fence of Irish Catholic sexual

repression for her or anyone round her to escape. Nobody could come forward to help her because nobody ever had. God's message from the altars, in the country's hundreds of Catholic churches, was not about building a loving, caring community which valued everyone as equals.

Instead, the priests rammed home a constant sermon of a God who would spurn those who broke his laws. And getting pregnant aged 15 was definitely a law-breaker.

And so, when the great mystery of birth occurred, she was on her own in the freezing cold of a January afternoon. Lost like an animal on the hillside with the town of Granard's great grey church looming over her. Except Ann was no animal and she was not lost. She knew exactly where she was. Abandoned.

And in her pain and fear, she chose a place of death to have her baby boy – right next to the graveyard in her home town. And so it was that, right under a statue of the Blessed Virgin, young Ann Lovett chose to lie down in the graveyard on that freezing cold afternoon on the last day of January, give birth and die. She chose to be at the very heart of the establishment which had so cruelly disowned her and her child.

And when she and the tiny boy were buried in that graveyard, the town folded them away, just as towns and villages around Ireland had been doing for years with their 'disgraces'. The gossip, the rumours and the slurs would fade eventually and the headstone would cover over in that grey-green lichen that obliterates all detail, all shame.

Granard's name would continue instead to be immortalised only with the hero, Michael Collins, who had met and fallen for Kitty Kiernan in the Greville Arms Hotel on Main Street.

Except that someone in the town understood the enormity of the events in the Granard grotto and saw fit to tell the media. Five days after the funeral, the nation learned of Ann's cold and lonely death; her school bag and her dead son found lying next to her as her life faded away. The rawness of the story hit straight between the eyes. We could feel the icy cold. We could hear the crows wheeling in the winter sky. We could hear the graveyard trees creak in the wind.

And of course, we could hear the dying cry of an abandoned baby, the stifled moans of a dying girl. There was no 24/7 news to dissect each morsel of the story. There was no need. Its barbarism was plain. Modern Ireland was medieval and our shame was palpable. This teenage girl should have been part of some antiquated past and here she was, at the tail end of the twentieth century, right before our eyes.

Of course, there is no public face to remember Ann Lovett by. Instead it's her name that haunts a generation of Irish men and women who remember that moment when Ireland's hypocrisy was laid bare, and who understood right then that the nation had failed thousands more secret Ann Lovetts down the years. We understood that because there could be no other explanation for a town to turn its back on a child in need.

This was our norm. This was our Ireland, a country which constructed a parallel universe of lesser beings: 'fallen' women and 'nuisance' children.

Defining moments in a nation's history are rarely carved with such immediate clarity. As the outrage of Ann Lovett's death gained momentum, the others stepped from the shadows. We didn't need to hear them on the radio to know that they were there but nothing – rightly – could have stopped them telling their stories – their own and others'.

They wanted us to know that women like Ann who had killed themselves or their babies or run away or given their babies away were friends, neighbours, sisters, daughters and mothers. They wanted to tell us of their pain and fear. They needed us to accept a new norm; that they would no longer stay where Church and society had pushed them. They were returning to our universe.

The open secret had spilled out and could never be pushed back to the dark corners again.

Twenty-five years on, Ann Lovett would recognise much in her native town. The stern grey church still commands a view of Granard but she might pause to check the modern building across from it offering childcare and crèche facilities. The Greville Arms has survived, but the town itself has few outward signs of the tide of prosperity that has rushed through the land since 1984.

She would find it more surprising to visit her old school, Cnoc Mhuire, where the 15-year-olds will be wearing make-up, their hair straightened, their skirts hitched up, chatting on their mobiles, arranging parties and sleepovers. Those young women are not likely to die in shame in Granard churchyard or any other Irish churchyard in 2009. They are more able to step out into the world and they have a better understanding of their own value and their self-worth. Their society no longer sees sex as a great secret; single mothers keep their babies and the smothering grip of the Catholic Church has eased.

Such progress is welcome in a modern democracy. That it is belated and won at high cost should not reduce its value. Nor should it blind us to how far behind we really are in valuing our citizens, especially our women and children.

We need look no further than the horror story in Roscommon that unfolded in the past few days. We still have not legislated for women's right to choose abortion and if there was a referendum in the morning, there is no certainty that it would be passed. Some remnant of us, the one that allowed a schoolgirl to die with her baby, still struggles with sex, women and the Catholic Church; is still fettered somehow to its traditional authority and values. No matter that we have seen again how the Church continues to fail children, very recently in Cloyne, recently in Ferns and with further revelations to come for Dublin.

Which part of us is able to accept this behaviour, these lies, these cover-ups, these denials, the secrecy, the obstruction? These are men of God, for God's sake.

But their actions, the actions of men like Archbishop John Magee in Cloyne, tell us clearly that Ann Lovett's ghost is alive and well and living in a parish near you. The hypocrisy that was laid bare on that cold afternoon in the waning light remains at our core, despite the twenty-five years that have elapsed since.

This is the hypocrisy which continues to ignore the voices of victims, the hypocrisy that prevents us screaming from the rooftops to rid ourselves of this ghastly Church with its ghastly ways that long ago lost its right to be enshrined in our constitution, influence our politics and run our schools.

Yes, Ann Lovett's death forced this nation around a very difficult corner and forced us to face horrific home truths about ourselves and our morals. But we cannot stand here now in a new century in a new Ireland and say her death was not in vain. It was. Her agony, her pain and her loneliness can be found in homes across Ireland today; in the memories of those who have suffered and in the minds of those who are still suffering.

The Catholic Church has still not owned up to its extraordinary catalogue of physical abuse and abuse of power and we as a society have failed to demand that it does both. And until we demand it and until it is given, the stain of Ann Lovett's blood and that of her son is on all our hands. We allowed her to die and that was shameful. We have continued to allow others to be abandoned as she was and that too is unforgivable, because we knew. Because she told us. And she chose to give birth at the church, in the shadow of Our Lady, so that we might listen.

24 January 2009

OBAMA:
ONE YEAR AFTER THE EUPHORIA

Marion McKeone

'Call no man happy till he is dead,' the Greek sage Solon counselled Croesus. Were he alive today, he might counsel the punditocracy to call no president competent until he is done.

It seems long ago now since Obama dazzled us with his oratory, his verve, his brilliance. And yet the memories of that freezing cold morning in Washington one year ago, when a throng of more than two million Americans braved the icy January dawn to witness history being made, are still crystal clear.

No one there could ever forget the spine-tingling wave of euphoria that engulfed the crowd when Barack Obama was sworn in as the forty-fourth president of the United States.

But we live in an era of instant gratification that has little time for incremental success. Global crises, recessions, even wars, are expected to be resolved within a 24-hour news cycle. Success or failure is judged according to daily sound bites and photo opportunities by experts that focus on tactics over strategy, style over substance.

It has been said loud and often that running a campaign is not the same as running a country, especially a country as diverse and ideologically disparate as the United States. A candidate plays poker. A president plays chess.

Imagine a presidency like a pixilated portrait. If a president is lucky and serves two terms, the portrait will be made up of thousands of pixels. In 365 days, however, that portrait is far from complete but, ready or not, the reviews are in.

And a slew of opinion polls suggest that Americans are split down the middle about whether or not Obama's first year has been a success.

By these standards, then, Barack Obama's first year in office has been something of a damp squib. It transpired over the past twelve months that the Icarus candidate wasn't after all a mythical figure on an ever-upward trajectory. Rather he was a mere mortal who walked into the propellers of government and one year later has managed to emerge relatively unscathed.

After Barack Obama's historic victory and the giant surge forward that it represented for a country that had been awash on a sea of anomie and self-loathing, it was inevitable that the subsequent progress, the laying down of the bricks and mortar of achieving his promises, would seem unremarkable, even regressive.

Obama, like his predecessors, has been forced to dance to Washington's legislative tune – a clumsy waltz with two steps forward, one step back. But Americans should not lose sight, amid the daily grind of compromise and capitulation that characterises government, of how far things have come – and how fast.

During the ten years I spent in America, which spanned the end of the Clinton era to the Obama presidency, the country was plunged into an era of hitherto unimaginable political and economic turbulence and disarray.

Ten years ago, the world's media filed reports on the farce that was the Florida recount from a variety of locations, ranging from car parks to 24-hour strip clubs that obligingly provided CNN with a backdrop of pole dancers. When a giant Disney character sidled up to one of the hapless judges, dropped the bottom half of his costume and mooned at the assembled throng of lawyers and political operatives, it was clear that pretty much anything could happen in America.

Pretty much anything – except the election as president of the United States of a black Chicago community organiser who was still repaying student loans. Eight years ago, that was still unthinkable. But in August 2004 it was apparent, even before he was elected junior senator for Illinois, that Barack Obama was going places. Fast.

After his electrifying address to the 2004 Democratic convention that all but buried the political cadaver that was John Kerry, I predicted in a political column that it would be Barack Obama who would be the next Democratic leader. Less than six months later, witnessing the display of petty triumphalism and score-settling that was George W. Bush's inauguration for his second term as president, that prediction seemed laughable.

It seemed improbable that America could recover from its lurch into paranoia and isolationism. There was no vision, only ratcheted-up fear, and no idealism, only self-interest.

Yet four years later, the country regenerated itself and ushered in a new era of unprecedented optimism. On the November night when Obama swept to victory, the shabby vestiges of the past two decades were swept away. Obama was the candidate onto whom they could project their hopes for a new era.

If George W. Bush's gut dictated his decisions to the detriment of the US, Bill Clinton's groin dictated his. Now with Obama in the White House it seemed as though once more the brain would be the organ of central command.

America was caught up in a Mexican wave of exuberance. Harlem threw a party and twelve million people came. For me, the image that has been distilled from a kaleidoscope of stoop parties, honking horns and millions of joyous Americans dancing until dawn in the streets, is one of cheering black sanitation workers waving American flags from the backs of rubbish trucks as they cleaned up the detritus of this unprecedented celebration.

Many of those who danced in Harlem and cheered on Washington's National Mall were old enough to remember a time when making eye contact with a white woman could trigger a violent death at the hands of a lynch mob. But amid the jubilation, there was trepidation too.

Obama may have been prodded forward by the finger of fate but, ironically, it was the chaos and incompetence of the Bush years that provided the necessary catalyst. The combination of raw political talent, verve and formidable organisational skills that tapped into the yearning for change propelled him to victory.

Appealing to a shared sense of idealism rather than exploiting cultural and ideological chasms excited a jaded America, but his election did not eliminate the ideological extremism that was turbocharged by the terrorist attacks of 9/11. Nor did it undo the economic meltdown, heal the havoc wreaked by Hurricane Katrina, or erase the consequences of a belligerent and isolationist foreign policy.

Nor would it change the political DNA of a country where 40 per cent of its inhabitants regard themselves as conservative and just 20 per cent would describe themselves as liberal.

The same conditions that allowed Obama the candidate to soar would quickly drag Obama the president back down to earth. Somewhere on the campaign trail in the frenzied months of 2008, Chris Lehane, a veteran Democratic strategist, cheerfully suggested to me that, given the public mood, the Democrats could nominate a refrigerator and win the White House. Many would argue that's more or less what they did. Obama's cool has become frosty for some. His equanimity is criticised as aloofness, his detachment as diffidence.

One year on, in its love affair with Obama, America has proven a demanding mistress. This is, after all, a country that craves Hollywood endings. And the daily grappling with recession, wars, political division and a resurgent Republican party, is certainly not the stuff of fairytales.

People feel let down. Those who believed most have lost most faith. The dream may be over but it was just that – a dream – and real substantive change will take longer than one term, much less one year, to achieve.

Whether America has the patience or the stomach for the self-sacrifice that will be necessary won't be apparent until after Obama has departed the White House. It will be some time before we know whether Obama has the courage and vision to deliver the sort of lasting change that America needs, where unity of purpose transcends cultural and ideological divisions, allowing America to transform its healthcare service, lead the battle against climate change, end the wars in Iraq and Afghanistan and restore America's standing as an economic superpower. He has shown himself to be a pragmatist, a conciliator, and a compromiser in the Clinton tradition.

Already, in my view, he has brought America to the brink of affordable healthcare, ended an era when America sanctioned torture, stabilised the economy to some degree and restored America's standing on the global arena.

But the changes he has so far brought about have been imperfect and incomplete. And with much of his capital spent, the year he now faces into will be even more difficult – his looming battle on climate change will be an exhausting one and his decision to ratchet up the war in Afghanistan has already disquieted a majority of Americans.

Congressional Democrats dread that, in the 2010 mid-term elections, they will pay the price for Obama's gamble with what they believe will turn into a no-win Vietnam-style quagmire that will destroy him.

How do you define success in Afghanistan? The obliteration of the Taliban? The capture of Bin Laden? The soldiers coming home?

One year on from that cold January morning in Washington, Obama is no longer divine. The mere mortal, however, has made a start. Call no president competent – or incompetent – until he is done.

16 January 2010

THE IRISH ANSWER TO EVERYTHING

Shay Healy

Some have lost millions in bank shares. Others have seen their pensions completely wiped out. Many have had their houses repossessed. Even more have had to finally pony up for the egregious loans they so casually invited on to themselves. But you won't find them sitting whey-faced in the Berkeley Court, drinking a brandy and Gaviscon, because, unlike others, when faced with disaster, the Irishman leans into the wind and tries to hold his pint steady.

In the face of disaster, why some kind of extraordinary self-hypnosis takes over is a mystery, but despite the horrors that surround him, he convinces himself that in the end, everything will be 'grand'.

Wouldn't you think that, given the financial apocalypse, the plummeting property prices, the floods in Cork and Galway and the recent disaster of the countrywide big freeze, with roads impassable, public transport at a halt and schools closed, that what we need is a snap of the fingers to bring us out of our hypnotic stupor.

Alas, we are still in denial. Even when people across the country this weekend are without a drop of water to call their own. Imagine, no water coming out of the taps. In 2010!

And yet, as each disaster unfolds, there we are, shrugging our shoulders to the same old chorus – 'sure it'll be grand'.

The story goes that Noah (for whom lack of water was not a problem) was sailing The Ark past Carrantuohill, Ireland's highest mountain, when he spied a Kerry farmer, sitting on the remaining three feet of dry pinnacle, defying The Deluge.

'Can I give you a lift?' asked Noah.

'I'm grand,' answered the Kerryman, 'sure 'tis only a shower.'

The joke is in the 'shower' of course, but in terms of study, the key word here is 'grand', which has five definitions in the English dictionary: outstanding or impressive in appearance, extent or style; ambitious and far-reaching; worthy of great respect by virtue of exceptional ability or high rank; wonderful, enjoyable or memorable; main or principal.

These definitions are adequate in their own terms, but none of them comes close to construing or interpreting what 'grand' might mean to the Kerryman in the joke, or for that matter to Noah, who surely had an awkward time trying to explain it to his fellow creatures on The Ark.

'Grand' sounds like a flabby word left over from the famous Oirish musical *Finian's Rainbow*. 'How Are Things In Glocca Morra?' goes the song from that musical. Sure, aren't they grand?

It's probably futile to tell them that things have never been worse here in our little twenty-first-century Irish Glocca Morra and no amount of saying it is 'grand' will make it any better. Yet we persist. There is no doubt that we Irish can proudly claim to have put the phlegm into phlegmatic and because 'grand' is such an all-purpose part of our national vocabulary, we tend not to hear ourselves doing it.

But it is a powerful word that can confirm the truth, or varnish a lie, in a way that keeps the social wheels permanently oiled.

It's great fun and very beguiling for a foreigner to hear the word a couple of times during their holidays in Ireland, but, in truth, our whole 'sure it'll be grand' attitude is a millstone around the neck of a meek populace, who hide behind it rather than speak their minds in their everyday lives.

English etymologists have rightly decided not to acknowledge the sixth possible definition of the word, because they recognise it for the bogus word it is.

Despite its suspect nature, some outsiders continue to be intrigued by the capacity of 'grand' to be so cunningly ambiguous. Depending on the inflection it is given, it can capture a variety of moods, all the way from total contentment to that dread moment when you hear the approaching swish of the scythe of the Grim Reaper.

The only place where 'grand' has any real currency is when it comes to matters of health. Queries about general health can be answered with a reassuring 'grand'.

Used in this effective manner, the word terminates the conversation on the subject. That doesn't mean there aren't still hardy stoics who will muster a 'grand' from the pit of their pain, even though they have just lost a leg to a hay-baling machine.

While the Irish rock legend Phil Lynott was lying on his death bed, the nurse leaned over and asked him, 'How are you, Philip?' Philo replied, 'I'm grand.' He wasn't grand at all. Ten days later he died, but in saying he was 'grand', he had deliberately diluted the anxiety of his loved ones.

I once met a real cowboy. His name was Jack Glover and he hailed from Sunset Ridge, Texas. Jack drove cattle all his life along the Chisholm Trail from San Antonio to Abilene. And now that he was too old for droving, he had opened a ramshackle cowboy museum in San Antonio.

Jack was full of fascinating stories of the cattle drives and a big smile lit up his grizzled features, especially when he talked about Irish cowboys on the drives.

'There were lots of Irish cowboys – everything was always

grand with them – and the funniest thing about them was that when they hadn't seen each other for a long time, instead of shakin' hands, they would punch each other out.'

Meanwhile, back in Ireland, two latter-day Irish cowboys who haven't seen each other for a while meet in secret, because they are lying low from their building suppliers.

There will be no punching. The greeting will be expressed as either a couple of air-kisses, a hug, or a desperate wail of 'why did I give those bastards a personal guarantee?'

The macho credentials of the Irish male have taken quite a battering since those crazy days of the boom time, when becoming a millionaire was a formality rather than a challenge.

A new breed of jackal politicians, bankers, developers and builders led a rampage through the fertile pickings of the property business, carving out new boundaries, erecting houses on flood plains and settling into a delusion that every spin of the roulette wheel would be a winner and things would be permanently 'grand'.

A bit further down the ladder of greed, the hoi polloi turned 'grand' into 400 grand, borrowing huge amounts of money to buy fancy houses and SUVs. The self-confidence of those who were allowed into the game became almost objectionably overbearing, so when the crash did come, it was an extreme corrective for the honchos and the worker bees.

Our leader of the time, a man who said he was an accountant, never saw it coming. When people questioned him about the headlong dash to a new, improved poverty, he advised the whingers to commit suicide because they were wrong. As far as he was concerned, everything was 'grand'.

'Grand' is also such a deceptively warm word. It wraps itself round you like a comfort blanket. When people say things are 'grand', it can mean that everything is okay, or that they are at peace with the world, or that they are satisfied with their lot – or that they are lying through their teeth.

As a term of evasion, adopting the attitude that 'everything will be grand' is also unsurpassed. It is the straight answer that is never straight. It is a barrier to inquisition. It is an ameliorated complaint.

As a nation, we are slow to speak up and even though the steak we are wrestling with could be used to mend a hole in your shoe, when the maître d' queries how the steak is, invariably we pronounce it to be 'grand'.

Yet it could never be said of us that we're a timid people by nature. Socially, we are good-humoured, noisy and garrulous, but somehow in the wake of the biggest financial con job of all time, our anger has been diffused and our young men have been emasculated by business failure and unemployment.

Where is our Michael Davitt, our Parnell, our James Connolly, our Big Jim Larkin, our Michael Collins? There is so much grief in this recession and so many lives have been wrecked, isn't it time to call a halt to saying everything is 'grand'?

The health service isn't grand. Our education system isn't grand. The way the floods wreaked havoc on people's homes and lives isn't grand. The government fiddling while Ireland was freezing wasn't grand. Families and businesses left without water isn't grand either. Yet the government manifesto might as well be exactly that – 'sure, everything will be "grand".'

The fat-cat bankers getting off scot-free isn't grand. Why we still subscribe to this philosophy is due to a malignant apathy in the body politic. The voters continue to surrender to the dismally trite write-off that 'those hoors up in the Dáil are all the same'.

And yes, they will continue to be, if we continue to let them.

I suppose I shouldn't allow myself to get too het up. As long as Bertie isn't elected Lord Mayor or President, I should be grand.

23 January 2010

MURDER ON THE HILL

Roslyn Dee

Some day we'll build a home on a hilltop high, just you and I
Shiny and new (that two can fill)
And we'll be pleased to be called
'The folks who live on the hill'
Peggy Lee song by Oscar Hammerstein, 1957

In a hushed courtroom, the defendant leaves his seat and walks slowly across the floor to take the stand. In his early fifties, he is well groomed, in good shape and smartly dressed; an attractive man with an air of privilege about him.

The courtroom is packed, has been every day throughout the trial. This, after all, is box-office viewing; this is someone from the right side of town, someone who had it all – the model wife, the wealth, the adored child, the fabulous house on the hill of Howth and the lifestyle to match. This is not a man struggling through the world on a daily basis, with a dysfunctional family background, no money and a drug problem. This is not a man with a messy past and no future to speak of, a man for whom jail would be an upgrade.

No, this is Mr Perfect, with the kind of life that many people watching this drama aspire to themselves. This is respectable, middle-class homicide. This life could be yours – this death could be yours. Unfolding here, playing at a courtroom near you, is the story of the unravelling of a seemingly perfect existence. Unfolding here is the story of Celine Cawley and Eamonn Lillis, the folks who lived on the hill.

My grandfather, who died a very old man more than thirty years ago, was obsessed with Perry Mason, the American defence attorney who sprang to life on television, from the pages of the novels of Erle Stanley Gardner, in the shape of the actor Raymond Burr. I remember, as a young child in the early 1960s, watching the black-and-white courtroom drama with him, week in, week out. The crime was always, absolutely always, one of murder and although the master defender invariably proved his client not guilty, he always succeeded, in the course of the trial, to deliver the real killer.

Back then I couldn't really understand my grandfather's fascination with the series. Years later, I understood. There was glamour, there was passion, there was greed, there was love and hate, there was jealousy and despair. This Californian drama might have been playing out on small black-and-white TV screen in my grandfather's small, terraced house in County Derry, but the emotions, the instincts and the inner lives were universal. This was human drama, this was people's lives. With a Californian suntan, a neat little suit and a 1960s hairdo, this could be you.

Disintegrating marriages are nothing new. We all know people for whom it is a sad reality. For some of us, it has been our own reality. Some falling-aparts are less dramatic than others, but it is, nonetheless, the proximity to our own circumstances that makes a trial like that of Eamonn Lillis such compelling viewing. Remember that time you lost your temper with your wife? Remember how you shouted, threw that plate? Or how about you? Do you not remember how you had been thinking for months that there must be more to life than this? More to love than this? Of course you'd never hurt her, never raise a hand to her. In all the years of your marriage you've had arguments – loads of arguments – but you'd never lose control, never, ever strike out. Would you? You sure?

Crimes of passion, as the French call them, don't exist as a 'category' under our law. But they do exist, however difficult it might be at times to define them as such. When does love become hate? Is it just a moment, just a flash when control and all human empathy vanish? But if you pull back from that precipice, can you repair and build again? Can hate ever turn back into love? One thing is certain, where there is passion there are rarely any rules. When spur-of-the-moment passion is absent and violence is planned, however, it is, as William Shakespeare put it, 'murder most foul'.

According to one eminent FBI profiler, retired officer Candice DeLong, a great many premeditated murders, where the husband kills his wife, occur because the men are narcissists. 'Life is all about them,' she says, citing one wife-killer she had come across as showing more joy over his great haircut than over the impending birth of his child. When that self-obsession takes over completely, the narcissist's mind doesn't turn to divorce – it turns to murder. Divorce, after all, is messier for them than a body on the bedroom floor.

That's certainly what Joe O'Reilly thought when he savagely killed his young wife, Rachel, in the bedroom of their bungalow in north County Dublin just over five years ago. O'Reilly, now serving life for murder, was the classic narcissistic killer.

I remember hearing him on the radio, talking to Pat Kenny, just a couple of days after Rachel's death. I was in the car at the time and my husband was driving. We were actually lost in the back roads of Wicklow, somewhere between Enniskerry and Roundwood. I remember that detail so specifically because when something strikes you or affects you very forcibly, you can always recall the specifics of time and place.

I was rooted to the car seat that day, stunned by Joe O'Reilly's composure and by the fact that, at the end of the interview, I had more of a sense of him than I had about his poor, dead wife.

Her death was somehow secondary, it seemed. He had the floor, the lights were on him and he was in his element. It was, classically, all about him. From that day on, through the infamous *Late Late Show* appearance, during the long, tortured months before he was finally charged, and then during the show-stopping trial itself, we were all reeled in, fascinated by the lives of Rachel and Joe O'Reilly.

Why? Because they were Mr and Mrs Average. Young, with a few bob, with two young kids, with their own comfortable home. A young married couple doing well for themselves with a seemingly enviable life. They could be your daughter and son-in-law, for goodness sake. Rachel could be your sister, Joe the guy you worked with, knocked a soccer ball around with once a week.

There was the affair, of course. Joe O'Reilly's affair with Nikki Pelley. Then these last few weeks we discovered that Eamonn Lillis too had had an affair – albeit short-lived – with Jean Treacy. That also drew us in, adding another layer to the plot. But isn't that what happens? Don't people have affairs all the time? It doesn't make you a killer.

Brian Kearney wasn't having an affair. Nor was his wife Siobhán. Now there was a couple who really seemed to have it all. Siobhán, whom I knew, was stunningly beautiful. She and her husband had material wealth – an up-market home in south Dublin and a small, boutique-style hotel in Mallorca. They had a gorgeous little boy. Siobhán's own family – her parents and siblings – adored her. But beneath the veneer she was unhappy in her marriage and was planning to leave her husband.

For controlling men like Brian Kearney, for whom material assets are the Holy Grail, this was unacceptable. Divorce, let's not forget, can be messier than a body in the bedroom. And so Brian Kearney killed Siobhán, in her bedroom, on the last day of February 2006. And then began the soap opera of Siobhán's life and death, the final scenes holding us all in thrall for weeks as we witnessed grief, despair and lives laid bare in a Dublin courtroom. Middle-class lives, a drama with a beautiful, doomed young woman as its central character; a cold, controlling husband who snapped; a grieving family; a little tousled-haired boy, motherless. How appalling, how truly sad, how utterly compelling.

We seem to have had more than our fair share of wife-killers in this country. That's the perception at any rate. But have we? I don't think so – you only have to take a trawl through other jurisdictions to see that it is, sadly, a relatively common occurrence. In America over one-third of all murdered women in the country are killed by an intimate partner. So no, it's not about numbers, it's about the profile, the lifestyle – it's about middle-class homicide and that's what makes it box-office, that's what fascinates us, whether we like it or not.

Celine Cawley's death, or Rachel O'Reilly's or Siobhán Kearney's are no more tragic than that of Baiba Saulite, shot dead in Dublin in a 'hit-style' killing in 2006, or that of any poor young prostitute murdered by pimp or client. Death is death, after all. People are left bereft. But most of us can't relate to the murder of a prostitute, or to someone killed in a 'hit'.

But when we sit in the Lillis or the Kearney courtroom, and we read the newspapers day after day, we are looking in the mirror. Not in every detail, of course, but in the killing of the Rachel O'Reillys, the Celine Cawleys and the Siobhán Kearneys we see fragments of our own lives. And we are drawn to the detail because there is a morbid – and somewhat smug – fascination in having a ringside seat to a drama that shows us that sometimes perfect lives aren't so perfect after all.

And there is relief – boy, is there relief – that, although similar to us, this is not us. This is not my life – or yours. We would have taken our daughter to school, walked the dogs, and yes, maybe we too would have had a row, but we would never, ever, have gone that far. We wouldn't be capable of that. Would we?

30 January 2010

FEBRUARY

THE CHURCH OF MAN UNITED

Dave Hannigan

As the British European Airways twin-engine Elizabethan RMA readied itself for a third attempt to take off from Munich Airport, it was Johnny Berry who articulated the fears that up until then had remained largely unspoken among the Manchester United players.

A fearless winger by reputation, Berry offered the opinion that the way things were looking they might all die here on this German airstrip. Liam Whelan, such a religious man it was once rumoured he might leave football for the priesthood, remained stoic at the suggestion.

'If that's going to happen,' said the Dubliner, 'I'm ready for it, I hope we all are.'

That February night in 1958, three of the first-team squad were Irish. Harry Gregg proved the hero of that darkest hour, dragging some of his friends from the burning wreckage, Jackie Blanchflower suffered injuries that prematurely ended a promising career, and Whelan, well, he was one of the eight players who in death turned a mere football club into something much more important than that.

As the fiftieth anniversary of the tragedy looms this Wednesday, the date also marks the point in history when the relationship between United and Ireland was changed forever.

Irish supporters of a certain age have always invested the demise of the Busby Babes with the same significance others accord the assassination five years later of President John F. Kennedy.

That the mercurial midfielder Whelan, cut down in his prime at 23, was among the dead, only added to the poignancy in Ireland. The outpouring of grief during his funeral on the northside of Dublin was the defining moment for a prepubescent Bertie Ahern.

The future Taoiseach was brought along to watch the cortège make its way towards Glasnevin Cemetery. After that, there could be no other club for him, nor for so many thousands more of a similar age.

'My affection for United dates back to my earliest days, when as a young lad kicking a ball around on the streets of Drumcondra, I used to pretend to be Liam Whelan,' Ahern wrote some years ago.

'There always seemed to be an Irish connection at United. I was always impressed by Matt Busby. He was a charismatic and dignified figure, a devout Catholic, and United were considered to be a Catholic club, which is another reason Irish people identified with them.'

Other English clubs have had fond and lengthy associations with Ireland, but none has endured and grown quite like this one.

The first Irishman to play professional soccer anywhere was a Belfast-born left-winger by the name of Jack Peden. A petulant type, he plied his trade in Manchester in the 1890s, when the team that would be called United was still known as plain old Newton Heath. Seventy years later, an even more gifted left-winger from the same town as Peden, a kid by the name of George Best, would encounter success and excess in almost equal measure.

Between those two eras came Munich, and after that everything was different. The powerful symbolism of the catastrophe and its impossibly tragic storyline, stretching all the way to Whelan's native

Cabra, meant Irish people were inexorably and romantically drawn to United.

Decades before Ryanair made cheap day-trips such an intrinsic part of the modern supporters' culture, the Friday-night boat trip to Old Trafford was already a type of hard-core pilgrimage for fans from all over the island.

Protestants and Catholics. From the North and South. Even in the worst of times, United provided a church where every Irish denomination found common ground and, to its credit, the club has always acknowledged this rabid constituency far across the sea.

It is difficult to think of any other English outfit asking a Dubliner to parade his freshly won World Snooker Championship trophy at half-time on the pitch as United did with Ken Doherty (a devout red) back in 1997.

Of a different timbre, the monetary value of the link can be gauged by the match programme in recent seasons containing a Mastercard advertisement urging Irish fans to get a credit card with the slogan '*Ar aghaidh libh*, lads'. Way before the intrusion of slick marketing, however, this bond went deep.

'Matt Busby loved Ireland and I think he felt that Manchester United should go over there at least once a year,' said Paddy Crerand, a Scot of Irish descent. 'Our first game after winning the European Cup was a friendly in Dublin, a testimonial for Liam Whelan's brother. You have to remember that one in three people in Manchester claim some sort of Irishness. Matt was honorary president of the Irish club in Chorlton, and he didn't hold the position just for the sake of it.'

That the city had long-standing historical ties with Ireland no doubt helped in the strengthening of the union. Even before the Great Famine struck, one in ten Manchester residents were Irish-born, and today the city hosts Britain's largest annual Irish festival.

That a preponderance of Irish men has worn red at crucial

junctures through the decades also explains the intensity of the rapport. While every United fan has his or her own personal epiphany, there are games that remain landmarks for all, and nearly every one of those came with Dubliners, Corkonians or Belfast boys operating in key roles.

Ten years after Munich, more than a quarter of the first XI that defeated Benfica in the European Cup Final were Irish, and one of them, the peerless Best, was the hero of the hour.

Thirty-one years later, Roy Keane sat out the Champions League triumph over Bayern Munich through suspension, but his outsized heroics and Denis Irwin's quiet brand of excellence made such a contribution to the treble season that somewhere along the way Sir Alex Ferguson picked up an impressive knowledge of Cork geography.

'Denis says Roy is from the rough part of Cork, and Roy says Denis is from the rough part of Cork,' said Ferguson. 'I don't exactly know who to believe here, but there is obviously a little bit of competition in the parts of Cork they come from.'

Funny as it may seem to hear him discussing the merits of Keane's Mayfield and Irwin's Togher, there was a time Irish fans worried about Ferguson. In the years after the departures in quick succession of Frank Stapleton, Kevin Moran, Paul McGrath and Norman Whiteside, before the arrival of the Cork duo, a bizarre legend grew up that Ferguson had something against the Irish.

Ignoring the obvious fact that Whiteside was a Protestant from east Belfast, the ludicrous notion was predicated on Ferguson's perceived anti-Catholicism. In its way, this was as misguided and wrong-headed as the belief in a different time that Busby's faith caused him to discriminate in favour of the Catholics in his charge.

Busby's staunch personal Catholicism, and his closeness during his formative years to his maternal grandfather, an Irish immigrant by the name of Jimmy Greer, formed the unwieldy premise for that fallacy. In practice, Busby, like Ferguson, picked the best players, regardless of affiliation.

As with any longstanding affair, there have been some rocky spells. When J. P. McManus and John Magnier began buying up shares in United through their company Cubic Expression, it looked for a time as if the Irish were finally, officially, going to take over Old Trafford.

Unfortunately, that whole episode degenerated instead into an unseemly and drawn-out soap opera involving Ferguson, the fertility rights to a horse, myriad protests, and the eventual selling-on of the stake to American Malcolm Glazer, a final act that didn't exactly endear the Irish investors to the United faithful.

If having so many Irish stars has always provided a lineage to which supporters could lovingly adhere, there is also a sense of genuine comradeship between the players themselves too.

Despite coming from very different backgrounds, Whiteside and McGrath became fast friends once they met at Old Trafford and Eamon Dunphy tells a wonderful story about himself as a young apprentice being taken into the confidence of the veteran Cork centre-half Noel Cantwell for no other reason than that they shared a nationality.

The different eras tend to interact. Thirty years or so after making his United debut in a friendly against Bolton Wanderers in Cork in 1963, Crerand was introduced to a man who claimed to have lost his job because he took a half-day from work to go to that game at Flower Lodge. The man's name was Mossie Keane. His son Roy ended up with his face plastered on to the white part of the Irish tricolours that vendors sold outside the ground on match days.

From Peden to Best, from Cantwell to Keane, the line is drawn and somewhere in the middle stands Liam Whelan. Back when he first arrived at the club, the 18-year-old neophyte met Johnny

Carey, another Home Farm alumnus, and the then club captain asked the kid his name.

'Liam, is it?' enquired Carey. 'Well, hold on to it for as long as you can. They're sure to take it away from you here.' The boy who had been christened William but was known as Liam became Billy Whelan by the time he died.

And that's the name they etched on the memorial plaque at Old Trafford, the one that remembers the tragic day when United and Ireland were changed forever.

2 February 2008

THE NATIONAL MUSEUM OF COUNTRY LIFE

Áine Ryan

Rural Ireland is dying. It is terminally ill and in chronic decline. Forget the government spin, the corporate codswallop. Within another two decades all traces of traditional Ireland will be the preserve of the National Museum of Country Life. Like in the past, vast tracts of lands will be the playground of the rich and the national parks of designer-heeled hillwalkers.

It is immaterial that in a recent Western Development Commission survey, more than half of respondents stated they would have a better quality of life in the west than they have in Dublin. It is nothing more than fanciful that 41 per cent of the same group, who were aged under 35, claimed they would like to move from the city to the west. Dream on. What do they expect to live on? Fresh air, idyllic land and seascapes, leprechauns with crocks of gold?

Tellingly, 43 per cent of this group also believes they could work remotely if they moved across the Shannon. That's not what the Irish Farmers' Association claims this weekend. Findings from a survey across the association's 945 branches show that more than 75 per cent of Irish rural homes cannot get access to an affordable broadband service and still await the roll-out of the government's National Broadband Scheme.

Naturally, from the vantage of the grey urban jungle, the notion of life amid wild Atlantic storms, bracing rustic walks, friendly farmers trundling by in rickety tractors, pungent turf-smoke wafting from modest cottages, has an allure. It provides an escape from the shackles of gridlock, cluttered car parks, long supermarket queues, crime, crowds, commuting, car cramp, road rage, the M50, the Red Cow roundabout.

It is almost 65 years since our former longtime Uachtarán and founding father Éamon de Valera made that iconic St Patrick's Day 'dream speech'. You know the one – it has been popularised by the notion of comely maidens dancing at the crossroads. In his stilted and starched voice, Dev boomed out over Radio Éireann on 17 March 1943: 'The Ireland which we dreamed of would be the home of a people who valued material wealth only as a basis of right living, of a people who were satisfied with frugal comfort and devoted their lives to things of the spirit; a land whose countryside would be bright with cosy homesteads, whose fields and villages would be joyous with the sounds of industry, with the romping of sturdy children, the contests of athletic youths and the laughter of comely maidens, whose firesides would be forums for the wisdom of serene old age.' With the benefit of hindsight, the political naivety and innocent idealism of Dev's myopic vision for dear old Cathleen Ní Houlihan is patently clear and utterly hilarious.

No place for David McWilliams' Deckland – the suburban mindset – in this panacea. Nor is there a sign of Breakfast Roll Man or Low GI Jane in this rustic reverie. Rather, the comely maidens have transformed into Bebo clones and the athletic youth are now boy-racers whose favourite pastimes are deadly 'chicken' and 'doughnut' manoeuvres.

Notwithstanding the seismic changes that have occurred over the last half-century, contemporary Ireland still retains a significant cultural romanticism about the appeal and mystique of the rural and pastoral way of life. Of course, reality was always and still is much starker.

All that a series of ivory-tower decisions – made by faceless EU bureaucrats in Brussels and Strasbourg in the 1970s and 1980s – managed to achieve was fatally to wound the integral sustainability of a traditional, peasant and partly self-sufficient way of life.

These bungling pinstriped Merlins changed the face of farming and, behind the wand of brown-enveloped subsidy cheques, anaesthetised an historic way of life. They introduced the Common Agricultural Policy, sheep subsidies, headage schemes, tax incentives. Their planning and policy excesses subsequently led to overgrazing, beef mountains, milk lakes, pollution and landslides.

Ironically, thirty years later it is the once-lampooned, muesli-eating Green Party politicians who have become the evangelical messiahs heralding the inevitability of a return to such a simple lifestyle. After all, carbon footprints tread lightly on the small holding, with its organically grown vegetables, milking cows or goats, squealing pigs, clucking hens and bank of nearby peat.

Of course, for thousands of years this island's most peripheral outposts challenged and tested its human populations. Such rich archaeological remains as Inis Mór's Dun Aengus and Clare Island's Cistercian Abbey are stone testaments to clusters of ancient habitation forged out of a raw and unwelcoming environment.

Nevertheless, mass frontier stretching didn't occur until after Sir Walter Raleigh's introduction of the potato in 1565. By 1800 more than three million people in Ireland depended on the tuber. Its ability to proliferate in boggy, poor soil had allowed the many landless poor to move west and colonise every rood and perch of ground in Connacht.

By 1841, this meant that County Mayo, for example, had a population of 388,887– three times more than it has at present. Large families lived in primitive hovels and eked out subsistence liveli-hoods. They subscribed to a higgledy-piggledy farming method known as the rundale, or clachan, system. It was primarily depend-ent on the lazy bed, the loy and the Connacht Lumper potato.

The horrific legacy of the Great Famine of the mid-1840s has been well documented. The cruel exigencies brought about by the potato blight were often matched by the intransigence of medieval landlords, who casually used the battering ram and eviction as their preferred husbandry tools. Often death on the side of the road or the dreaded emigrant coffin ships were the only alternatives.

However, as the west of Ireland slowly escaped from the grey cloud of famine and centuries of oppression, it became intoxi-cated by the charisma of Michael Davitt and the political potential of the Land League. By the 1880s, the so-called Celtic Dawn was firmly on the horizon; the establishment of the GAA, the Gaelic League, co-operative societies, literary soirées and folklore groups ensured a frenzied wave of cultural revivalism.

Ironically, those at the helm of many of these initiatives were members of the Anglo-Irish ascendancy class. It was poet William Butler Yeats, for example, who suggested to John Millington Synge to go to the Aran Islands. His iconic peasant character, Christy Mahon – *The Playboy of the Western World* – was based on a notori-ous Achill man, James Lynchehaun, who went on the run after as-saulting a local landlady. The anointing of such characters as heroes still pervades in our contemporary romanticism of rural Ireland.

From about the 1850s the splendid and scenic isolation of Con-nemara and the west had become a regular refuge for an illustrious caravan of artists, writers, politicians, actors and even philosophers. By 1917 the famous Dublin surgeon, writer and wit Oliver St John Gogarty had bought a mansion near the pretty village of Leenane, situated on the edge of Ireland's only fjord, Killary Harbour. Gogarty described Renvyle House as being in 'the fairyland of

Connemara, at the extreme end of Europe, where the incongruous flowed together at last.'

One of Gogarty's many visitors, the artist Augustus John, said the house was located in 'the most beautiful landscape in the world'. Yeats, Lady Lavery, Churchill and Lord Beaverbrook were among his colourful list of guests.

Seventy years later, the late Richard Harris stayed in Renvyle House, by then a hotel, during the filming of *The Field*. Reportedly Harris's adherence to method acting meant that he only ate traditional fare – porridge, bacon and cabbage and Irish stews – during filming. Many of the scenes from *The Field* were shot in Gaynor's bar in Leenane, using local people as extras. John B. Keane's simple and raw story of the Bull McCabe's clashes with a rich yank who returns to a small village, throws his money around and gets the clergy onside, still resonates deeply in rural Ireland.

Nowadays, in another cruel twist, elderly, lonely bachelor farmers crouch over dying embers in isolated holdings, far up remote boreens, off the main tourist trails and away from the urban havens of Westport and Clifden. Stringent drink-driving laws now preclude them from the comfort and company of the pub. The local sub-post office has recently been closed. Masses have been cut back to a minimum due to the collapse of vocations and shortage of priests.

An incongruous satellite dish rattles in the gales that batter the side of the house. In recent years, it has become the elderly farmer's main companion.

Undoubtedly, the Western Development Commission's 'Look West' campaign has real merit. Around 1,000 people check out the website each week. But without sincere, significant and radical backing from across the Cabinet table, it too will be consigned to the shelf where Charlie McCreevy's decentralisation plans and the National Spatial Strategy gather dust.

Meanwhile, young Dev – Minister for Community, Rural and

Gaeltacht Affairs, Éamon Ó Cuív – cannot reverse decades of neglect and short-sighted policies alone.

In September 2001, his cousin, former Minister Síle de Valera, officially opened the National Museum of Country Life in Castlebar. She observed that the many artefacts and items housed in the museum told the rich story of an Ireland that had existed until fifty years ago. Síle de Valera was wrong. Rural Ireland still whistled a lively tune, albeit in the remotest places, a decade ago. Today, the banshee hovers as its death rattle echoes over windswept glens and mountains.

23 February 2008

ALL HUMAN LIFE IS PRECIOUS

Mark Dooley

It is a night I shall never forget. Half asleep, I heard commotion, and then those terrible words: 'Dad has had a stroke.' They were uttered by my tearful grandmother in reference to her dear husband. Both my grandparents had been watching television in February 1982, when my grandfather suddenly slumped in the chair beside her. She fetched my mother, who found herself powerless in the face of tragedy.

The ambulance soon arrived, and my dear old granddad was carried from his chair for the last time. Hours later, we knew things were very bad. Death, which had so nearly claimed him that night, took leave of my grandfather at the threshold. In so doing, it left him in that twilight zone between life and extinction – a person dwelling in a corpse.

Gone was all power from one side of his body. Gone was his voice. Gone was his capacity to think, feel and eat. Yes, death could have seized him, but for its own reasons it did not. And so we were left with the awful consequences of that cold February night.

Now, the petty problems of yesterday had suddenly been eclipsed by this, and it would be another four years before the gentle rhythms of 'normality' would once again resume.

As the months slowly passed, my grandfather gradually recovered consciousness. But he was never to walk or talk again. He was fed and washed like a child, the monotony of his condition being eased only by our regular visits to his nursing home, and, of course, by his cigarettes.

Financially, the burden of nursing care took its toll. But that did not stop my mother from doing what she could to keep the funds flowing, or from caring for my grandmother. Throughout those years, she proved that the greatest of saints often go unnoticed and unrewarded.

Yes, for four long years he lingered in that place. He could not read, watch television, play a game or chat. But he was alive and, in his eyes, you could see that he was grateful for it.

By the time a second stroke finally delivered him to his grave in 1986, we were not relieved. During those years of his captivity, we loved my grandfather and did our best to answer his every need. We were blessed that he was still with us, which is why, when it came, his death was still a shock.

Still, the whole experience was challenging on many levels.

But not once did we ever think that it would be better, either for him or us, to end my grandfather's life. Even though we knew he would never get better, and that whatever life he had would be severely limited, it was still for us a human life worth preserving to the end.

I say this in light of the recent clamour for change in the law regarding assisted suicide for the terminally ill. Leave aside the fact that doctors have just discovered that those in a so-called 'vegetative' state have the capacity to communicate through brain activity. Vitally significant though that breakthrough is, there are deeper reasons for retaining our legal and moral prohibitions against euthanasia.

First, we are not animals. When I looked into my grandfather's eyes, I did not see only flesh and blood. I saw a person who, despite all his infirmities, was still a source of love and meaning. He could not be 'put down' in the way of all other creatures.

It is easy to sneer at such a view in this age of scientific reductionism. We are told that the only thing that separates us from the beasts is more sophisticated adaptation skills. We are told that moral and religious values are not things which mark us off from the rest of creation, but can be reduced to pre-cognitive neural activity. We are told that the only moral consideration which should guide us regarding the 'end of life' debate is that which seeks to diminish pain and suffering.

For most of us, however, human life cannot be reduced to its organic essentials. Yes, we can agree that we are creatures who have evolved from what one philosopher calls the 'simple chemistry of the oceans'. But that is only a single dimension of a very complex story. Let me try to explain it like this: science will tell you how things were caused – how, in other words, they came to be and how they physically function.

That is why, for its most ardent exponents, death has no real meaning. For them, it is simply the end of the anatomical process, which is why the merciful response to prolonged suffering must be termination.

You do not have to be religious to be repelled by such a view of the human condition. It is easy for anyone to observe that there is much more to life than is accounted for in scientific explanation. For one thing, human life transcends its biological conditioning to create a world of meaning, where things are endowed with sacred and moral significance.

In so doing, we do not deny science, but testify to the fact that there is more to life than is dreamed of in Darwin's theory. Or, as my intellectual hero Roger Scruton puts it: 'When we see another's smile we see flesh moving in obedience to impulses in the nerves. No law of nature is suspended in this process; we smile not in spite of, but because of, nature. Nevertheless, we understand a smile in quite another way: not as flesh, but as spirit, freely revealed. A smile is always more than flesh for us, even if it is only flesh.'

No animal can smile, but we can. And it is his beaming smile which, until the very end, characterised my grandfather's final years. I remember visiting him during that time, and his reaction was always the same: his face would light up with a smile which cast aside all facial distortion, and then he would serenely sob for sheer joy.

Here was a man whose life ostensibly seemed without purpose. And yet, it was a life full of meaning. In spite of everything, he had meaning for me and I for him. Here before me sat someone who was an essential part of my story, an individual who loved me like only a free being can. In those moments, what I experienced was not an ailing organism that would be better off dead, but a being entitled to his place in what Kant once called 'the Kingdom of Ends'.

When it comes to creatures like us, creatures with moral significance, there are, in other words, limits to what we can do. As a centre of moral judgement, a person cannot be treated as a means to someone else's ends. Rather he is, even when rendered physically or mentally incapable, an end in himself.

That is why, when his death came, it was not for us a mere physical event. It was one replete with meaning, in as much as it testified to a life less ordinary. To have cut that beautiful life short, on the basis of costs and calculations, would have been a crime against the moral law.

Now I am not saying that mercy has no role to play in considerations of assisted suicide. Mercy is, of course, central to the moral life, and it should drop, as Shakespeare teaches, like 'the gentle rain from heaven'. But there already exists a culture of mercy in the Irish medical system which, it seems to me, obviates the need for any move towards euthanasia.

Five years after the demise of my grandfather, I noticed my

grandmother trying to spread milk on a slice of bread. A few days later she was diagnosed with inoperable brain cancer, and would be dead within weeks. Her short illness was borne with dignity, and when she arrived at the hospice there was no attempt to unnecessarily prolong her life. Such is the merciful nature of palliative care, and it is something which is widely availed of by the terminally ill.

Why change this noble regime, except to introduce a culture of rights into a sphere where duty should prevail? Strange as it may sound to modern ears, this is one area of human existence that should never be reduced to a lifestyle choice.

For even when dying, we still have duties to those who love us, and for whom our lives have essential meaning.

My dear old grandfather taught me many lessons in life. But the greatest message was one he imparted long after he had lost the power to speak. He showed me, in language more profound than any I have heard, that we undermine the Kingdom of Ends at our peril.

And now, as we face this brave new world in which we clamour for death on demand, I think of that little old man in his wheelchair. I think of his tears and his smile as they triumphantly announced the person trapped inside his physical prison. And then, with tears in my own eyes, I give thanks that he lived in a very different age – one in which he was loved and valued even when he had nothing to give in return.

6 February 2010

PARENTS:
THE LOVING TIES THAT BIND

Dermot Bolger

Forty-one years ago, in the summer of 1969, our family physician, the late Doctor Fagan, took the unusual step of summoning my mother to see him at his practice in Finglas village. A truly decent, and also frank, man, he was characteristically blunt.

As a mother of four she should know that her husband, who worked as a cook at sea, had such chronically high blood pressure that in all probability he would drop dead soon. My mother should prepare herself for the fact that she would, in all likelihood, become a widow. At 10 years of age, I was her youngest child. I do not know what future she expected on that day when she walked home, but the future rarely unfolds in expected patterns.

This coming May my father will hopefully celebrate his ninety-second birthday in the excellent care of Beneavin Lodge nursing home in Finglas. He led an independent life in his own home – albeit with a huge input from his children and carers – until just three months ago. In contrast, within a few months of her conversation with that doctor, my mother would die just days before Christmas in 1969, following complications that arose from an operation on a brain tumour.

One parent has been an ever-present in my life, the other has been an enduring absence. No relationship is more complicated and multifaceted than the relationship between parent and child. You glimpse aspects of your parents as a child; on one level you get to know them in intimate detail. But you need to become an adult too before you know them fully, when the seemingly huge gap between you in terms of age and experience shrinks. But the age gap never totally closes, because for as long as your parents are alive you are never allowed to fully grow up; in that one relationship you remain defined by being someone's child.

Indeed, you may even have become a grandparent yourself but remain part of a generation that is young in relation to someone close to you: the person you once depended upon but who now – as the pendulum swings – depends more and more upon you.

With longer life expectancy now you can find four generations simultaneously existing within many families, each generation making different demands on your time and bringing different responsibilities and rewards. It is important to us what our children think of us and what our grandchildren think, but – even though we think that we have moved on – we remain trapped by the fact that it is still so important to us what our parents think.

Because while we are magnified in our children's eyes by the fact that their first impressions of us are shaped when small, we are invariably reduced in our parents' eyes, back into the role of children again. Our parents hold the key to our most vulnerable memories: they (along with our older siblings) are the only people who can truly see the entire graph of our lives.

My childhood was in no way literary, although my eldest sister would also become a novelist. But my fellow author Carlo Gébler was born to the sound of a typewriter as his mother Edna O'Brien wrote novels by day while his father Ernest Gébler wrote novels by night. Carlo and I often talk together about the business of parents and I find his take on what it means to be a son fascinating because our early experiences were so unalike.

Carlo's parents had a fractious, short-lived marriage and, aged 10, Carlo was sat down by his father – an idiosyncratic, dogmatic man who could have given master classes in how not to be a parent – and forced to write a letter that declared which parent he wanted to live with. He chose his mother, but his troubled relationship with his father still defines him.

'At 21 I felt I was forging my own destiny,' Carlo confesses. 'But at 55 I know this is absolutely toss and nonsense; it was all predetermined from before I was born. Mum and Dad were the primary predeterminants. They made me what I am. So it is more than just being shaped – you are invaded, contaminated by your parents and you can't escape them. We are definitely driven psychologically to win our parents' affection. Everything we do is directed at our parents.'

Gébler is absolutely right, but, hand-in-hand with our early desire to win approval, every child also starts the process of breaking free, of finding a way to make their own declaration of independence. Some do it by moving to the far side of the globe, some by immersing themselves in political or artistic or religious movements that directly contradict what their parents believe in, others by emotional stealth, a slow process of withdrawal.

But at some stage every child needs to stand apart, no longer defined by what their parents stood for.

I am fortunate in having always enjoyed a close relationship with my father, though we often have healthy divergences of view about politics or history. But I am aware that there are other people utterly estranged from their parents, who bear too many wounds from being casualties of awkward childhoods, who have ceased to have contact but are still defined by their experiences in the cockpit of family life, often the location for the most uncivil of civil wars. People for whom the gradual realignments within the relationship between parent and child can never occur because one party will never be able to meet the other party halfway.

Yet even such estrangements can be a defining, unbreakable bond because none of us ever truly breaks free of family life. We think we can control our destinies but we cannot control our memories or dreams.

Noël Coward noted that living your life was like being forced to give a violin recital in public while only learning to play the violin. By the time you have mastered the art, the recital is already over. Perhaps it is the same as being a parent or being a child.

I never knew my mother properly because the cycle of your relationship with your parents is only complete when you have undergone some similar type of life journey. In that way you begin to understand them and they see you in a new light.

I know my mother was born on a Monaghan farm and came to Dublin with her sisters to find work during the war. She met my father when he was sailing on those tiny Irish ships that made incredibly dangerous voyages to Lisbon to bring vital supplies back to Ireland, despite frequent attacks by German planes. In 1949 they moved to what was then the countryside of Finglas where the first houses were built.

It was undoubtedly hard for any woman to raise a family with her husband at sea, but my memories are warm and loving. My last memory is of her smiling and waving from her hospital bed on the night before her operation, when she must have known there was a strong possibility she would not see me again. My memories of her are relatively few but they stay with me and they still burn bright.

Your relationship with an absent parent is always fixed, to some degree, but my relationship with my father is richer and deeper because for the past forty years it has constantly changed as we have changed, as our views diverged on some issues and merged on others, as he has kept his children in touch with the past and we try to keep him abreast of the present.

Three times a week I bring my sons to Ben Dunne's gym in

Ballymun and we bench-press together. Until recently we played on the same football team. I nudge them towards the books of Paul Auster and Cormac McCarthy and they introduce me to the music of Jape and Architecture from Helsinki and Thomas Truax. We don't share identical tastes, but we can find room for common ground as we discuss music and books and sport and politics.

I feel that my father's generation rarely got this chance to find common ground, they were often bounced into absolutist positions by de Valera's closed society that felt so threatened by change. Scandals in the Church and political establishments have now allowed such blinkers to fall away.

But my father's generation is still shaped by a world where a boy was a boy until he donned his first pair of long trousers to earn his first wage and then suddenly became a man.

Having an elderly parent brings difficulties and responsibilities, as their independence is gradually eroded, as confusions set in about time, the distant past becoming clearer than yesterday's events.

Yet because I never got to know one parent, I recognise these years as precious, as a chance for the shifting dynamic of the relationship between parent and child to deepen again. Not everyone gets to say what they want to say to their parent or child. For some people wounds are still too raw and the only way to be free of the past is to remain separated from it.

But life works in unexpected patterns and, during the years when the person you once depended on comes to depend on you, things left unsaid can then be said. Because, when the day comes and both our parents are gone, it is then that we will have to confront the reality that, at last, we ourselves are no longer young and that we need to redefine ourselves again.

20 February 2010

MARRIED TO BEING IRISH

Fiona Looney

So the sky didn't fall down. Some thirteen years, to the day, after divorce was introduced – that's almost two full seven-year itches – we can finally say, with statistics at our backs, that those ubiquitous 'Hello Divorce, Goodbye Daddy' billboards were totally, irresponsibly wrong.

According to the ESRI report on family trends, released last week, the rate of marital breakdown in this country actually slowed after 1997.

Some thirteen years, and what was predicted to be a slew of disappeared daddies later, just 3.3 per cent of Irish marriages fail – a rate that places us squarely at the bottom of a 31-state European league, alongside Italy.

So why didn't the floodgates open, the skies darken, and plagues of frogs descend from the heavens? During the first – failed – divorce campaign, I interviewed a briefly famous young American woman who warned that if the referendum was carried, women here would break fingernails and demand a divorce over it. Well, there have been a hell of a lot of broken fingernails since then, and none, as far as we know, have made it all the way to the High Court.

But even those of us who agitated in favour of divorce would have to admit to being taken aback by the ESRI's findings.

We might have bullishly rejected the flood warnings, but even the most optimistic of us expected a steady stream into the courts. Instead, we have barely a trickle. Rather than bask at the bottom with an I-Told-You-So expression, perhaps we should ask why.

That we join the Italians at the foot of the table of marital breakdown is surely more than mere coincidence. The last couple of decades might have seen us become a largely secular society, but in common with Italy, we retain a firm grip on Catholic tradition – or perhaps, it retains a hold on us.

Most Irish couples still marry in a Catholic church, even if few are what the Church would consider 'practising'. For all that these couples might not darken the church door again until it's time to have their children christened, the permanence of marriage, as enshrined in the Catholic rite, perhaps lends a solemnity to the whole business that couples marrying outside the Church don't experience to the same degree.

That's not to suggest that couples who opt for civil weddings don't take their vows as seriously as those who marry in church; rather, there's a sense of generational tradition about a church wedding that perhaps bonds couples to its promises where otherwise they might part. In other words, if Mammy booked the church and bought the hat, then it might be rude not to stay the distance.

Of course, this is not necessarily a good or healthy phenomenon: but in considering the ESRI statistics, it might account in part for our surprisingly low divorce rate.

But to my mind, there is a more persuasive, if more elusive, explanation for those numbers. And it's an argument that, had we thought of it back in 1986, might have brought divorce to our shores a decade earlier. Back then, and again in the 1997 re-match, the anti-divorce lobby screamed that if we allowed divorce into Irish law, we would end up 'like America or like Britain'.

Those of us on the other side of the debate tried to muster

scant statistics and hollow reassurances that we wouldn't, but we failed to land on the most obvious counter-argument of all. We would not end up like America or Britain simply because we are not American or British. We are Irish. We are unique. Or, to look at it another way, we are peculiar.

Even back then, the land loomed large. Property rights represented a powerful weapon in the arsenal of the No lobby, and arguably won them the day, first time out.

What neither side grasped, in retrospect, was that property is so disproportionately important to Irish people that *it* – rather than the law – was and would remain the single biggest barrier preventing couples from splitting. Even after boom and bust, we still buy ahead of renting; we still bring up our families in two-storey houses with gardens rather than in apartments.

When I lived in London, in common with the vast majority of home-buyers there, we were leasehold tenants. Here, when we bought our family home my parents strongly advised that we buy out the 1,000-year lease, just as they had done a generation before.

Social historians will no doubt point to colonialism and throw in some penal laws. But whatever the reason, the result is that we are inordinately consumed with owning property in this country. Splitting it, selling it, leaving it – they all go against the Irish psyche and since at least one of them is inevitably involved in divorce, it was always going to be a final, drastic resort. Those who threatened us with floodgates forgot that, for an island nation, we are unusually land-locked.

What also marks us apart from our near and Atlantic neighbours is our puzzling tendency to settle for half measures. Until Noel Dempsey put his foot down, we had nearly a million L drivers breaking the law daily.

A similar attitude prevails where marital breakdown is concerned. Just as our parents' generation included many, many couples who maintained cosmetic marriages for parish and priest and never spoke to each other behind closed doors, so our generation is notable for the number of separated people without any intention of divorcing.

For my part, the only Irish people I know who are divorced have all re-married – it is, in effect, the only reason they concluded their first marriage at all. Everyone else I know whose marriage has ended, from former taoisigh downwards, is simply separated.

Some judiciously – some, we might argue, less than judiciously – but it seems that we retain a suspicion of divorce, even when the chances of marital reconciliation are absolutely non-existent.

Separated-but-not-divorced is not a uniquely Irish condition, but the ESRI figures suggest that our rates of divorce are disproportionate to our rates of separation. Both are extremely low, but the phenomenon is worth noting nonetheless – if only to tax the social historians with a harder question. Is it a financial issue? Hardly – most of the undeniably expensive business of marital breakdown is taken care of in judicial separation. Is it about the priest, or even the Mammy?

Perhaps, but again, the trickier business surely arises from acknowledging that the marriage has failed in the first place, something that the separated have surely already conceded. Perhaps it is a poignant effort to hold on to a failed marriage, even if it is only by a tenuous thread.

Many separated people still refer to their estranged spouses as their husbands and wives – I can recall being taken to task on *Liveline* by Marguerite McDaid, many years after she and Jim separated, because I referred to the Donegal TD as her 'ex-husband' – a term she clearly found unpalatable.

The divorced, of course, have no real or legal claim on the title. Maybe, for many, divorce is simply still a step too far.

And perhaps it is worth reminding ourselves that it was ever thus. The referendum was, after all, passed by the narrowest margin in the history of Irish referenda – less than 1 per cent. So although the law makes divorce available to everyone, it is arguable that in these, its early years on the statute books, half the population will never go near the courts, no matter what state their marriage is in. Maybe it is only the Yes voters, memorably dismissed on the day of the referendum by Úna Bean Mhic Mhathúna of the No Divorce Campaign as 'wife-swapping sodomites', who have known the courage and the despair of their convictions.

So where does that leave us, thirteen years after us wife-swapping sodomites popped champagne corks and toasted the unhappily married? The American woman who warned us about broken fingernails is divorced (though not, I gather, because of anything to do with her nails). We elected a taoiseach who was separated and even if he never left that halfway house, it wasn't his marital status that brought him down. Jim McDaid is divorced and remarried. The hysterical anti-divorce lobby has been proved emphatically wrong in its dire predictions.

So why does this ESRI report feel like a hollow victory? Perhaps it is because none of us, however emotional we became at the time, expected a seismic shift in the human condition that would suddenly give rise to a marked increase in happy marriages.

The fact that thirteen years after legislation we have such a low divorce rate might feel like another champagne-popping event, but the fact is that the statistics must also suggest that there are still many, many unhappy marriages out there.

In a naive way, many of us who voted for divorce did so simply so that people could be happy – the realisation that many are still smothering in bad situations is a disheartening one.

The divorce lobby was never an anti-marriage movement. On the contrary: in carefully crafting legislation to allow couples who had exhausted every other avenue in trying to keep their marriage viable to separate legally and as painlessly as possible, we underlined the value we placed on marriage and striving to make it work.

Some thirteen years on, some of us still believe in marriage and we still believe it is worth preserving. But we are glad that when it is irretrievably broken, the law now allows for shattered lives to be fixed.

And for the many whose lives, hearts and minds have been healed by this most hard-fought-for legislation, this, and every, weekend is worth celebrating.

27 February 2010

MARCH

THE RISE OF THE IRISH EMPIRE

Mark Little

There has always been something vaguely imperial about the Taoiseach's annual St Patrick's pilgrimage to the White House. Our humble leader rendering onto Caesar that which is Caesar's: a cut-crystal bowl of shamrock.

For all the lofty talk of mutual friendship down the years, there has never been any doubt that the US president always played the Emperor in that set piece. But this year, when you look at those pictures of Bertie Ahern and George Bush, reverse the roles. Just for a moment, think about that piece of diplomatic theatre as a high watermark for the Irish empire, a point somewhere between rise and fall. You don't have to imagine Bertie Ahern as Caesar, just the figurehead for a global Irish identity travelling at full throttle.

As the Kennedys, Clintons and McCains play the green card in Washington this week, think of them as competitors for that Irish imperial endorsement. You may ask how much that endorsement means in modern American politics. The answer is enough that they would seek it so diligently.

In his latest book *The Audacity of Hope*, Barack Obama recalls how his first major outing as a candidate for the US Senate was at the tail end of Chicago's St Patrick's Day Parade: 'I found myself marching just a few paces ahead of the city's sanitation trucks, waving to the few stragglers – while workers swept up garbage and peeled green shamrock stickers off the lamp posts.' It is a sign of how far we have come, that we don't let ourselves get carried away with such desperate attempts to impress the broader Irish family.

Not too long ago, our entire economic future depended on money and jobs from America. Today, we live with a changed equation. US companies still employ 90,000 people in Ireland, but the number of American workers employed by Irish companies is now 70,000 and rising fast. Indeed the boundaries of the Irish empire extend all the way to Fifth Avenue. A chunk of the €9 billion extra that Irish consumers will spend in 2007 will fund this year's Christmas shopping campaign in New York. (Personally, I had not understood the march of the Irish empire until I had witnessed the arrival of a bus load of Irish shoppers at the Timberland factory outlet in Manchester, Vermont.) At the heart of the imperial advance is the conquest of those who used to shape our destiny. In Britain – the largest traded property market in Europe – one in five investors is Irish. Perhaps that is part of the reason we were so magnanimous towards the English in Croke Park just recently: they may have a claim on our past, but we own the long-term lease.

Any Irish person who spends time travelling will return with tales of the Irish property buyer, internet pioneer, boutique hotelier, new-age guru or surf-champion. The sheer penetration of the empire occasionally defies belief.

I have spent some time in Iran over the last few years. In hotel lobbies, I've bumped into Irish businessmen specialising in investment opportunities in pariah nations. I have listened to talk of Sam Beckett in the Godot cafe near Tehran University. Beside state-sponsored slogans denouncing the 'Great Satan', I have read graffiti extolling Boyzone. I have heard repeated testimonials to the greatness of Roy Keane. And, in recognition of a dark history, I have seen a burger shop named after Bobby Sands.

Forgive the imperial hubris, but this must be our fifteen minutes of global fame and fortune. In fact, I wonder if I am part of the last generation who will know what it is to be an Irish loser. Twenty years ago I part-funded my education by delivering newspapers, flipping burgers and cleaning toilets in various European cities. While working in the car park at Heathrow's Terminal 4, I was called 'white wog' by a customer with a cheap car and a red face.

When *The Commitments* was published, my contemporaries had a bleak laugh at Jimmy Rabbitte when he said: 'the Irish are the blacks of Europe.' Not because it was charming, but because it felt true.

No one who came of age in the 1980s will ever mourn the passing of Ireland's old global identity. You will hear few people of my generation seriously complain about what we left behind as we rapidly ascended to the status of imperial power. That said, there is also confusion about where we are going; we, the citizens of the fourth most globalised nation in the world, proud owners of holiday apartments in Cape Verde and patrons of the Irish bars of Phnom Penh.

But enough about our perspective. What does the rest of the world make of our new Irish imperial identity? Once again, if you travel to any degree, you will hear a sea-change in international attitudes towards Ireland.

When I was 18, I asked an Israeli girl I met in a Copenhagen youth hostel what Ireland meant to her. 'U2 and the IRA,' was the answer. Today Bono may still come up, but only as part of a much broader conversation. The secret of the Irish empire is that it trades a cultural brand that offends nobody and can be safely adapted anywhere in the world.

An empire spread by consent rather than conquest. In truth, you would be surprised just how persistent the old clichés can be. In the United States around this time of year, you will not hear ordinary people extolling Ireland's innovative corporate tax regime.

It's still all Paddy McLeprechaun and his endless appetite for green beer and violence.

Even where the new Irish brand is well rooted it is often Irish in name only. I recently came across an American music critic who blasted America's manic demand for 'pop Celtic lite' music in the wake of *Riverdance*. He quoted a music promoter in North Carolina: 'The more it doesn't sound like authentic Celtic or Irish music, the faster the tickets are snatched up. I'm thinking of forming my own band called the McPhakes and playing nothing but *faux* Irish music.' In fairness, we shouldn't expect an accurate appraisal of Irishness from those who haven't lived here. That is why we need to pay close attention to the views of those who have settled among us in the last two decades.

What strikes me when I talk to my 'New Irish' friends is the prevailing weariness I hear. Many of them were drawn in by the promise of *craic* and good humour but discovered it is often a façade. Friendships they thought they had formed over a pint seem to dissolve once they leave the pub. Most of the people I know are happy they came, but many feel Ireland promised a familiarity it didn't deliver. In the words of an English friend of mine, 'the longer I spend here the more foreign things become to me.'

In so many ways, the duelling emotions you hear from the 'New Irish' reflect genuine insecurities in the new Irish psyche. On the face of it, the developing Irish identity is based on self-confidence and self-declared happiness. In an EU survey published late last year, 56 per cent of Irish people said they believed things were going in the right direction – exactly twice the European average. Yet this is the same nation where 300,000 people at any one time are being treated for depression. This is the same happy-clappy bastion that this week emerged at the top of Europe's binge-drinking league table.

You get the feeling that the dizzying rise of the Irish empire has left many of us trailing in its wake, not quite sure of how we relate to all of the change, all of the time.

Such statistics do prompt plenty of angst-ridden bouts of self-analysis, but they tend to focus almost exclusively on money. The national conversation quickly gets sidelined into ideological debates about the distribution of wealth or the materialism of Irish society. Even well-meaning debates about the 'quality of life' come back to the same old question: 'We're rich, but are we happy?' Just maybe, it is not the economy, stupid. Perhaps the greatest source of confusion is the sheer speed of our transition from provincial zeroes to global heroes. In a matter of years, we lived through a transformation our Western peers took generations to achieve. The only constant left at the end of that transformation is change itself.

Our collective orgy of creative destruction has removed any benchmark by which to judge progress. Very soon, the dominance of the Catholic Church, sexual repression, emigration, sectarian chaos in Northern Ireland, will be lessons in our children's history books. And so too will the homogenous Ireland of the past. The single ethnic, racial and religious standard that once defined us is dead. We are a nation in flux, dragged in a different direction by the forces that continue to drive our global advance.

At its most basic level, it has given us a cosmopolitan edge, delivering fresh ideas, new blood and – yes – decent food. It has an irritating side as well. Just as we drift away from the United States in a political sense, our default pop culture is ever more blingtastic, our accents ever more Californian and our lifestyle ever more 24/7.

In the new, splintered reality of Irish life you only seem visible if you are setting trends or willing to buy into them. If you are not one of the key demographics to be leveraged, you no longer have a part in the great big makeover of Irish life.

Last week, I spent a few days in a Dublin hospital recovering from a bad skiing accident. I shared a ward with five men who came of age a long time before skiing holidays were all the rage. It was fascinating to hear them share stories of a past Ireland, to hear tales of the Emergency when air-raid shelters were built and tea was rationed.

One morning, we were shifted to the day room and left in front of a flickering television. For ninety minutes the six of us watched a morning show full of items about the latest bikini designs in Gran Canaria and the facial treatments available in Brown Thomas.

The version of Irish identity unfolding in front of our eyes could have been produced on an alien planet for all the relevance it had to the lives around me. A few days inside the public health service give you an alternative vision of life inside the Irish empire, shining a light on the daily battles of elderly men and women to retain their dignity and relevance, the constant struggle of doctors and nurses – the 'New Irish' among them – to preserve some humanity at the heart of a dysfunctional world.

All of this has to be constantly set against the genuine scale and depth of Irish progress. But it does point us toward the essential irony of our situation. At the very moment Ireland conquers the world, we have lost our shared identity.

Different groups now have very different experiences of this moment in Irish history. All of us have benefited from transformation, but some have more control than others. Some of us are driving the march of an empire while others sit in the back seat wondering why on earth we are driving so fast.

During the rise of an empire, the destruction of shared certainties is a creative act. It will not feel that way if, God forbid, we ever live through its fall.

17 March 2007

I AM A PADDY; ERGO I DRINK

Peter Cunningham

It was the expression 'drunken mob' used in media reports earlier this week to describe what occurred in Finglas that was surprisingly shocking. Last Monday, St Patrick's Day, the Garda riot squad moved into an area of south Finglas that had been taken over by young thugs running amok. Cars were hijacked and torched, their occupants beaten up. Children as young as 10 years old were reported to have been intoxicated.

Loutish behaviour on St Patrick's Day, particularly in Dublin, has become pretty much standard in recent years and therefore to hear about it again shouldn't come as much of a surprise. Yet, nowadays in the wider world you don't hear much about 'drunken mobs'. Riots and political demonstrations that get out of control, yes. Crowds of rampaging dissenters where the abuse of power has provoked despair and violence, certainly. But drunken mobs? Crowds whose behaviour is fuelled by drinking so much alcohol that the riot police have to be called in? It's a modern rarity – except in Ireland.

When it comes to doing drunk, we still do it better and more consistently than anyone. Alcohol abuse is an Irish epidemic. We binge drink on an epic scale and we pay the consequences: at least half of all fatal and serious road accidents are linked to drink-driving. Drunken brawls are commonplace. Recently, two Polish men were murdered in Drimnagh when they refused to buy drinks for local youths. Drunkenness in Ireland is not new, but the link between drink and violence is a worrying modern phenomenon.

It wasn't always like this. Drink has truly become the demon in our midst. Alcohol abuse has devastating consequences: depression, anxiety, suicide, marriage breakdown, criminal behaviour, unemployment and poverty all come after the hangover. The community too pays a high price. Alcohol misuse is estimated to cost the economy more than €2.7 billion a year in health costs and lost productivity. Irish men cannot moralise about excess drinking, and I am no exception. We have all grown up in what is known as the drink culture, in reality a dingy subculture where alcohol is the major form of recreation; where the system of measuring alcohol in units is seen as a scorecard rather than a medical imperative.

Alcohol is Ireland's biggest public conspiracy. We are all in it and we all sustain it. We laugh knowingly at the booze-soaked fossil that is Father Jack, but the truth is, we all know a Father Jack, and many of us either are or have been in the same place as Frank Kelly's deadly accurate depiction. Drink is everywhere in Ireland and in the battle to try and weave a path through it and not be swallowed up, we have eulogised and celebrated 'the jar' for generations. We have presented ourselves to the world as the only people who truly know how to have fun and are mystified when we encounter cultures who seem to have fun without getting legless. We feel sorry for such people. They haven't discovered the magic potion, as we have. They don't understand that being pissed is the supreme definition of happiness.

Yet, the fact that a drunken mob can take over a residential area of Dublin in 2008 should ring alarm bells in the heads of anyone who cares about Irish society. This image, like a throwback to that of a medieval mob, should at the very least cause us to have a long hard look at ourselves. Isn't it high time that we admitted that our freewheeling alcohol consumption is both personally ruinous and a devastating example to the younger generations? We are the inheritors of centuries of alcohol abuse, but we are not alone. In Georgian London it was estimated that a quarter of all households were used for the production or sale of gin. 'Drunk for a penny, dead drunk for twopence', was the catchy advertising slogan of the day.

By 1838, the caricature of the drunken Irishman was well established when Father Theobald Mathew went on a nationwide crusade to exhort people to take a pledge not to drink. At its height, just before the Famine, Father Mathew's temperance drive had enrolled nearly three million people. The abuse of alcohol was so widespread and destructive in the United States in the early twentieth century that a national prohibition on the manufacture and sale of alcohol was imposed from 1920 to 1933.

Today the sale of alcohol is still outlawed in many towns and communities across the United States. In Norway, Sweden, Finland and Iceland, the sale of liquor to consumers takes place only through government monopolies. Many countries of the Middle East, North Africa and Central Asia either partially or totally ban the sale and consumption of alcohol. Similar restrictions exist in South Asia and South-east Asia. And even parts of Australia have a tradition of alcohol prohibition. What all this is saying is that alcohol is a dangerous drug that most societies feel it necessary to legislate for. Not here. In Ireland today, where taking the pledge and Father Mathew sound like embarrassing sound bites from an era of ignorance and poverty best forgotten, alcohol roars in the ears of the nation. We all enjoy it, we are all complicit. If a home team wins a coveted trophy, or a horse trained in the home village wins a big race, the media interview with the locals usually ends with the line: 'And I've no doubt that there'll be plenty of sore heads here tomorrow!' We take it for granted that celebration and drunkenness are natural companions. The *craic*, that term that seems to encompass all any of us could ever wish for, means only one thing.

The myth of drink is rooted in us as fiery, goblet-swilling Celts. Drink was long celebrated too as being synonymous with genius: Brendan Behan and Flann O'Brien, both of whom I remember as sad and paralytic, were writers whose genius was overtaken by their tragic alcohol-led destiny. This Irish-drink myth gets carried forward by the likes of Shane McGowan, whose self-destruction from alcohol is worn as a badge of distinction. It is carried forward too by the 'hell-raising' antics of Colin Farrell. I am a Paddy; ergo I drink. And I am a Paddy and I drink, but when I hear about drunken mobs on the rampage, attacking innocent bystanders and 10-year-old kids throwing up because they're drunk, I have to wonder where we all went wrong.

It's as if Ireland is still in the era of Gin Lane or Oliver Twist. There's no point in complaining that we're victims of our genes or of our tragic past. There's little pride in blaming the Irish weather, or the lack of alternative activities to being in a pub in Ireland, or the wisdom found at the end of a row of pints. We need to try and think our way soberly out of this mess, which is no longer just a drunken mess but has become a murderous one as well.

Adjusting the attitudes of the nation is not easy when it is estimated that over one-third of Fianna Fáil TDs have connections to the pub trade and are therefore dependent on us all continuing to suck our pints from their high stools. Look at what happened to former justice minister Michael McDowell when he tried to introduce café-bar type legislation, which might have provided a European-style solution to an Irish problem. McDowell's proposals were savaged by Fianna Fáil TDs with vested drink interests and went down in flames.

'People are no closer to the acceptance of alcoholism as a disease than they were when this centre opened in 1978,' says John Donohoe, senior counsellor at the Hanly Centre in Dún Laoghaire. 'The focus now is all on drugs. It goes without saying that drink is the biggest drug of all but, of course, the government gets a lot of money from alcohol sales.' More than €2 billion every year, to be exact.

What the government should do, but won't, is ban all advertising and sports sponsorship of alcohol. What else can kids think of but a future on the booze when whatever sport they have chosen to play or watch is intrinsically interwoven with intoxicating liquor? It comes at them from every quarter. The television commercials equate camaraderie, sex, strength and the good life with watching the head form on a pint. Sport has largely become a euphemism for the jar.

We have made things this bad. I wish we hadn't. But there comes a time when we should stand up as a nation and assert ourselves as more than just part of a drunken mob.

22 March 2008

MAMMY *NUA*

Joseph O'Connor

The great Irish playwright, John Synge, died 100 years ago this week. He was a man who knew a thing or two about how we think.

'There is nothing in the world better than a single-hearted mother,' he once wrote to his fiancée, adding in a remark that must have caused raised eyebrows: 'I hope you'll be as good to me as she was.' In a context where the nation itself was usually embodied as a mother whose brave, strong sons would fight for her liberation, the statement may not seem all that surprising. America had Uncle Sam, the French had Lady Liberty, but here we had the National Mammy.

From Joyce to Sean O'Casey, from Frank O'Connor to Liam O'Flaherty, the image of the Irish mother didn't change. She was kindly, reliable, capable, stoic, the wise and resourceful martyr in the kitchens of Irish fiction and on the stages of our motherland's theatres.

In jokes, she had a special relationship with her sons but not her daughters. ('How do we know Jesus was really an Irishman? Because he loved being with the lads, he thought he was God, and he lived with his mother until he was 30.') And there was another species of Irish Mammy joke in which the mothers of the country were remembered for their long-suffering sense of victimhood.

('How many Irish Mammies does it take to change a lightbulb? Ah sure, don't mind me, son, I'll sit by myself in the dark.') The Irish Mammy of these incarnations was a descendant of Patrick Pearse's mother as embodied in that strange genius's last short poem, penned on the night before his execution.

He wrote that she had contentedly sent her two sons out to be shot by the British, secure in the happy knowledge that it had to be thus. One wonders if Mrs Pearse herself felt the same way.

A while ago I was looking at an old copy of the Irish Constitution as part of research for a novel I was writing. If you looked up the word 'mother' in the remarkably thorough index, the entry read 'see family and sex'. It must have been nice for Irish women to know just what they were for.

No confusion of gender roles there.

But as a kid and as a young man, it always struck me as strange: Ireland's so-called love for its mothers. Like most famous love stories, the truth was more complicated.

Irish mothers, in reality, often seemed the prisoners of an ideology that imprisoned them by constant flattery. We sang songs about them, wrote poems about them – exalted them to the heavens. The heavens, indeed, were particularly interesting in this regard.

Not for nothing was the mother of Jesus deeply revered in Ireland, held up as an example to all Irish women. The fact that she had given birth without sexuality or even biology being involved made her a difficult role model, to say the least. But the Virgin was the go-between who brought our desires to God. It was as though the function of a mother was to be maker of intercessions to a dictatorial father whose punishments we feared.

All Irish mothers were to aspire to be like her. But when you looked at our culture, for example our legislation, you wondered what kind of double-think was going on. Small things and large ones. Little exclusions and great. No woman, therefore no mother, could serve on a jury, which meant that the definition of crime was exclusively male. Women were forbidden from serving on the censorship board, the body that banned literature about birth control.

Divorce was outlawed by an almost all-male Dáil in 1925. All contraception was made illegal in 1935, thereby ensuring the Irish Mammy remained a mammy. In 1937, the number of women TDs was three. When they dared speak up for women's rights they were excoriated.

One editorial of the era is typical of the general view: 'Many men (including, it is whispered, the President) think that a woman cuts a more fitting and useful figure when darning the rents in her husband's socks than she could hope to cut in a parliamentary assembly.' Married women in the civil service had to surrender their jobs.

The Criminal Conversation Act meant that a man who lived with another man's wife following marital breakdown could be prosecuted.

Until 1965 a wife could be disinherited by her husband (a theme explored often in the fiction of John McGahern). An Irish mother had no right to unemployment benefit for most of the twentieth century; indeed her only legal status was as a dependant of her husband's. Even children's allowance payments, when first introduced, were paid to fathers not mothers. It's a far cry from the warbling of ballads about the grey-haired, gentle mammy.

Patrick Kavanagh's bitter epic, *The Great Hunger*, may have been nearer the mark of what was felt by some Irish men about their mothers. Maguire's mother is a vicious crone whose refusal to die conveniently and bequeath him the farm is advanced as the reason for the protagonist's misery. Remarkable that it never occurs to him to get off his arse and find a job.

How useful to have Mammy to blame. It's one thing fighting for the motherland and roaming the hills with the guerrillas, but you sometimes sense that if the generation of Michael Collins had stayed home and changed the odd nappy, we might have been better off.

As recently as my own childhood in the 1970s, the notion that fathers might do childcare tasks traditionally performed by mothers was ridiculed.

I remember being on a school trip in about 1975, and seeing a young man pushing a pram down Henry Street. The resulting explosion of laughter was led by the nice priest accompanying us. He often wore what he himself called a '*gúna*' while saying Mass, and he would pirouette before the altar boys, enjoying every moment of the twirl.

But such ironies were not to be discussed. In the subsequent three decades, our notions of motherhood (and fatherhood) expanded. While some of the 1960s feminists had seen motherhood as an oppression, women of my own age tended to regard it as an aspiration, but desirable on fairer terms.

The recession of the 1980s and the period of recovery saw many mothers returning to part-time work. The election of two mothers as successive Irish presidents marked a sort of coming of age. Motherhood became funny, a subject we could laugh at. Mrs Doyle in *Father Ted* was an explosion of the Irish Mammy figure, which is why we found her so hilarious when our grandparents would have found her depiction so shockingly disrespectful as to provoke a Sean O'Casey-style riot. And motherhood became trendy, somehow sexier than before.

Internationally, icons of popular culture from Princess Diana to Victoria Beckham spoke about their varying understandings of motherhood. In Ireland, birth rates rose as the Celtic Tiger arrived. Indeed, during the late, lamented boom, you sometimes even heard it said that couples with larger families were indulging in a kind of economic boasting, since having more than one or two children proved you could afford it. The Yummy Mummy appeared in Irish suburbia, piloting an SUV intended for military or agricultural purposes.

She fulfilled the part in popular iconography that Old Mother Ireland once had. These days, an Irish mother needs to be qualified in many fields, including accountancy, taxi-driving and psychotherapy.

The new Irish Mammy also has to endure being partnered by a man who has realised he is supposed to talk about his emotions. He talks about them with the extensiveness and passion his own father reserved for Shamrock Rovers. Indeed, so open are Irish men about their feelings these days that you sometimes sense they are about to form a support group called Men Are Misunderstood in Ireland ('MAMI' for short).

If I were an Irish mother myself, I'd be pining for a bit of reserve, of the kind our granddads used to have. I remember my beloved paternal grandmother telling me that while she and her husband had cherished their children, you didn't talk about love too often in those days.

With the huge families Irish mothers tended to have, simply feeding them was the main aim of the day. She told me her greatest ambition had been to raise her eleven children without any of them ending up in prison. That she managed to succeed in this gave her enormous satisfaction.

She felt she had done her job.

Irish mothers still do their job, but it's more complicated. In the car park of my kids' school, I see the mothers every morning, more admirably capable than I will ever be: freighted with hockey sticks and football gear and guitars and schoolbags, dancing-shoes, basketballs, communion dresses.

To realise most of these women are about to go from the school to an office or other workplace, following which they will drive home and do most of the housework, is to realise that while feminism had eked advances for Irish mothers, there is still a shamefully long road to travel. There is the gloss of equality but it is still just a gloss.

Pay is not equal, discrimination continues, and out of the 166 TDs returned in the most recent election, only twenty-two are women. In that sense, the Dáil is about as representative of the nation as is a Village People video. Ireland's relationship with its mothers continues to be ambiguous and multitracked.

While the traditional platitudes and pieties are still uttered about motherhood, mothers like Kathy Sinnott found that the State raged against them when they fought for their children's education.

We're tongue-in-cheek about the Irish Mammy. She's a part of our past, like showbands, scapulars and *The Riordans*. Being a mother in Ireland today gets you nothing you didn't earn. Sometimes it doesn't even get you that.

When Mother's Day was first invented, in about 1908, it was a day for one's own mother, not mothers in general. (That's why it was spelled 'Mother's Day' with the singular apostrophe.) But somehow, along the line, it became the deeply plural Mothers' Day, a celebration not of your own mother but of motherhood itself.

That's what we've tended to be good at in Ireland: honouring the very general while ignoring the specific.

But if the motherland is ever to become a place where motherhood is authentically respected, rather than sentimentalised in a way that actually demeans it, we'd want to start growing up.

21 March 2009

A MORE UNITED IRELAND

Susan McKay

It took a moment to identify it, that waking feeling, but only a moment. After all, it was something we'd lived with for decades. It was dread, familiar and sickening. All the days this week, all over this country, but particularly in the North, people were turning on the morning news and bracing themselves, once again, for horror.

It had pounced on us unannounced last weekend, when we heard that self-styled dissident republicans had murdered two soldiers in Antrim. It had laid its slimy hands on us again on Tuesday with the news that another faction had murdered a policeman the night before in Craigavon. It is still there, lingering and unsettling.

But there is something new in the air as well after a week that plunged us back into the kind of feelings we wish we could forget.

There is hope.

Last week the people of the North became a community. Not the two communities, but one, and one that saw the people of Britain and of the Republic as our neighbours.

We became truly united in grief and rage, and together we told the murderers that we are not going to let them take away our peace.

On Tuesday, I listened to Peter Robinson's address to the assembly at Stormont with growing astonishment. I have listened to speeches from our now First Minister for many years, and on just about all previous occasions, I have disagreed with just about every single word he uttered. Last week, he spoke for me. 'Today a dark shadow hangs over our province,' he began.

He spoke of the callousness of the murders, and offered our collective condolences to the bereaved families of the soldiers, Mark Quinsey and Patrick Azimkar.

'It was an act intended to divide us. It was calculated as a means to raise fear and hatred and planned to cause us to stumble,' he said. It was the next line that was most impressive. 'This is not a time to raise the flag of narrow interests,' he said. Instead, it was a time to unite: 'We must never return to such terrible days.' The future depended on our struggle for a shared society. It was a 'moment of truth', and the answer to the challenge posed by the killers had to be: 'We are not turning back.'

Within hours of this powerful call for unity, gunmen ambushed and killed Stephen Carroll. His wife's anguished statement will be remembered. 'A good husband has been taken away from me and my life has been destroyed,' she said. 'And what for? A piece of land that my husband is only going to get six feet of.'

All over the country, people were talking to friends and to strangers about how awful it all was, and ending up in tears. We had heard so many of those eloquent, grief-stricken statements of the harsh truth about the Troubles.

It was simply unbearable that another woman was having to wrench such words from her broken heart.

But other memorable words were spoken that day too, and there were images to amaze: the chief constable, Hugh Orde, flanked on one side by Peter Robinson and on the other by Martin McGuinness. While Robinson spoke again of the power of unity, McGuinness listened.

Then it was his turn.

'We are going to remain united in our approach and ultimately we will prevail,' he said. 'These people are traitors to the island of

Ireland. They have betrayed the political desires, hopes and aspirations of all of the people who live on this island. They don't deserve to be supported by anyone.'

The murders brought something home to me. How traumatised we still are by what we lived through, and how close to the surface that trauma is. Back when political murders were an everyday occurrence, we had to steel ourselves to be able to go through the motions of normal life.

Since the ceasefires of 1994, the Good Friday Agreement of 1998 and, finally, what looks like a settled regime at Stormont, we've relaxed, we have let down our guard. And yet, this week, we cried like frightened children.

I recently became friendly with a woman whose son is a British soldier based in Antrim but who was about to go to Afghanistan. When I heard about the murders at Massereene barracks, I sent her an email. She wrote back to say that her boy had already left, and was fine, but devastated.

He'd told her it was a sort of rite of passage the night before you went to Afghanistan or Iraq, to get takeaway pizzas, since you wouldn't be getting them out there. It was seen, he'd told his mother, as a kind of lighthearted last supper.

Those who feel most keenly the pain of the families bereaved last week are the people who themselves lost loved ones to the violence during the years of conflict. I spoke with Kathleen Gillespie, whose husband, Patsy, was murdered by the IRA in Derry in 1990, when he was used as a 'human bomb' in an incident which left five soldiers dead as well.

Patsy worked in the kitchens at a British army base in Derry, and had refused to be intimidated out of his job after IRA warnings that such workers would be seen as collaborators and 'legitimate targets'. The atrocity was seen as a turning point in the Troubles.

Many in Derry had joined the IRA or at least saw the choice of joining it as understandable after the slaughter of ordinary Catholic civilians by the British army on Bloody Sunday 1972.

But for the IRA to use an ordinary working man as a bomb shocked and revolted the entire population. We couldn't see it at the time, but the early 1990s were the darkness before the dawn.

In the years since her husband's death, Kathleen has supported many others through bereavement, and has spoken at conferences around the world, sometimes sharing platforms with ex-combatants, about the difficult reality that lies behind words like truth and reconciliation.

She's talked about what it is like to have to rebuild your life from such ruins. She's a strong, vibrant woman, and highly respected. 'Everybody's distraught,' she told me this week. 'I was in tears watching the TV the other night and I just thought to myself, "Holy God, here we go again".' She'd been out with friends one evening during the week and a rumour had swept through the pub that someone had been shot in Derry.

'The place was in uproar,' she said. 'But it was only a rumour. I don't relish the thought of seeing more families going through the same pain as my family went through. I don't think I could stay here. It is just a nightmare to think that a few people who want to start the whole thing up again can do this.' Like many of us this past week though, she was impressed by the politicians. At last, she feels, it looks as if they really mean it.

That is the essence of the hope. That they mean it. That when they come back from their investment trip to the US, the First and Deputy First Ministers will start to work together in a real sense, and that they will instruct the more recalcitrant among their colleagues to do likewise. Because while it is true that a majority of the people voted for the set-up at Stormont, what we have seen so far has not given power-sharing a good name. Too much point-scoring, too many stand-offs, too much obstruction.

Precious little rebuilding of a society ravaged by conflict, the sectarian undertow left well alone. Fine minds have applied themselves all week in this paper and elsewhere to explaining the ideology which supposedly motivates the dissident republicans who carried out the murders.

By contrast, Hugh Orde described them as 'criminal psychopaths'. As a reporter during the Troubles, I met a good number of combatants from both the IRA and the loyalist paramilitary armies. Some spoke at length about Ireland and its liberation, or about Ulster and its defence. Some were ignorant of the most basic facts of our history.

Some were clearly motivated by pure hatred dressed up as politics. What they did have was the support of significant elements of their communities. That is certainly not true of those now swilling the bitter dregs within the Real and Continuity IRAs, with their silly videos and their grandiose fanatical claims.

I interviewed one of these a few years back, when they were attacking Catholics who were on policing partnerships. He stank of urine, talked aggressive rubbish and was full of grievance.

I've met similar loyalists.

One of those arrested after the murder in Craigavon last week is a young Catholic who is only 17. A few weeks ago, an 18-year-old Protestant was jailed for a brutal sectarian attack which left a young Derry man in a coma from which he will never recover.

Bitter people full of atavistic hatreds are still poisoning the minds of some among the post-Troubles generation.

This week we have seen unspeakable sadness. But we also saw real leadership, from the politicians and from the trade unionists who gave the people room to grieve publicly and in silent solidarity. What we need now – and urgently – is for the young to be inspired by a sense that the community that McGuinness and Robinson spoke about, and which most of us, in those remarkable moments, felt part of, can be a good place, a place where they want to live. In peace.

14 March 2009

THE WEZZ GENERATION

Fiona Looney

The night-time temperature is barely bothering single digits, but the girls gathered in groups around the street corner seem impervious to the cold. Passing car headlights illuminate their bare legs, rooted in towering high heels and eventually disappearing under tiny skirts not much longer than elasticated belts. Others are wearing shorts, paired with bra tops just visible beneath their flimsy leather jackets.

On another street corner, in another part of the city, these girls might easily be mistaken for prostitutes. But this is a smart part of Dublin and the girls are lining up for a disco that caters specifically for 13- to 15-year-olds.

There are many of these discos around the country; all, it seems, come with their share of deeply disturbing stories that filter out into the consciousness of worried parents. One, the Wesley disco, known by the middle-class youngsters from private schools who frequent it as the Wezz, is particularly notorious. Here, breathless parents report, 'new' girls are approached by boys, and asked if they 'do' oral sex. If they consent, they are guaranteed instant popularity; if they decline, they're banished to the sides of the hall with the other wallflowers.

Men who have worked as bouncers at these discos tell of

finding discarded underwear in the toilets and under benches, and teenagers giggling about complicated codes involving jewellery and lipstick that give out signals of a girl's sexual availability. One, called 'rainbow kisses', involves a group of friends all wearing different shades of pink and red lipstick, liberally applied, which telegraphs to a boy that the whole group is willing to fellate him, administering a rainbow effect on his genitalia.

Many of the stories are, no doubt, apocryphal – designed purely to give parents sleepless nights – but there are enough of them to suggest that within these teenage discos, there is indeed some very grown-up behaviour going on.

Last week's Pfizer report on adolescents and sexual attitudes found that while the majority of Irish teenagers now lose their virginity between the ages of 16 and 17, a common theme to emerge across all groups surveyed, irrespective of social class or geographic region, was the perception that a higher percentage of people aged 14 to 15 years are now sexually active than was the case five years ago.

It concluded that 'although we must be careful not to attach too much significance to what are in effect second-hand accounts of sexual activity of younger teenagers (12 to 14 years), the fact that this view emerged across all of the groups means that we must be careful not to dismiss such information as merely "hearsay".'

It's not just in Ireland that young girls are becoming sexualised way before the legal age of consent. The phenomenon spreads right through Western society and begins long before puberty. Little girls these days are as likely to attend 'makeover'-themed birthday parties as they are to see clowns and magicians, and dolls like Bratz, all short skirts, pneumatic breasts and attitude, are beating Barbie (one boyfriend, a zillion careers) hands down in the toy shops.

When my older daughter was a toddler, I found it impossible

to buy a pair of black tights for underneath her Christmas dress –
now, little girls' Christmas clothes are miniature versions of adult
women's party wardrobes, all single-shouldered shimmer and slit-
skirt smoulder.

Since most five-year-olds have not yet formed pressure groups,
the only conclusion to be drawn from these gauche marketing
trends is the sexualisation of children begins with adults – or at the
very least, our collusion at the onset of the phenomenon cannot
exonerate us from responsibility for what happens in teenage discos a few short years later.

In the meantime, our daughters are bombarded with pencil
cases sporting the Playboy bunny logo, teenage sensation Miley
Cyrus – adored by the 7 to 10 year olds – posing in her underwear
and Britney Spears running a chaotic personal life while barely
dressed as a raunchy schoolgirl. By the time they make it to the social networking sites, spawning grounds for overt sexual behaviour,
little wonder that so many young girls have already concluded that
they exist purely to be sexually available and to pleasure boys.

It is no coincidence that over 25,000 Bebo users have deployed
the term 'slut' as part of their user name. Psychologists labelled
this hyper-sexualisation of adolescents as 'raunch culture', fuelled
in a large part by an image-driven media but also, significantly,
hugely influenced by young boys' access to online pornography.
Teenage boys' ability to circumvent the ever-improving filters on
home computers means that many have effectively free rein over
increasingly graphic pornographic content – with a recent British
Home Office report finding 54 per cent of boys concluding that
pornography was 'really inspiring'.

'The access to pornography by young boys is proving harmful
to them,' says UCD-based psychologist Marie Murray. 'It's distort-
ing their understanding of sexuality, and it's entirely without the
context of relationship or love, that then objectifies women and

themselves. It is a huge issue as pornographic addiction replaces relationships or it becomes an expectation within a relationship.'

Another psychologist, Linda Papadopoulos, who authored the Home Office report, elaborates: 'This isn't the type of pornography that was around when we were teenagers. What kids are seeing today is often violent and it has no intimacy, no respect, no context of sex within a loving relationship.' It is this sort of soulless, graphic experience of sex that would seem to drive the raunch culture. The trend towards waxing away pubic hair comes entirely from pornography; so too, does the popularity of breast enhancement. Teenage boys now expect teenage girls to look and behave like porn stars and many teenage girls, it seems, are only too happy to comply.

Others simply feel pressurised to follow suit. A popular practice now among girls is to photograph themselves topless on their phones and send the pictures to boys they like, who then share the images among themselves. This is not parental paranoia in the car park of the teenage discos – this is actually happening, all over the country.

And, worryingly, it seems to be happening here in an environment peculiarly devoid of any real regulation or parental influence. Speaking at the 'Self, Selves and Sexualities' conference in Dublin last weekend, history professor Diarmaid Ferriter suggested that we as Irish people have effectively replaced our fear of being too sexual with a fear of not being sexual enough.

Contrasting the sexual repression of the past century with the current premature sexualisation of girls, he conceded that 'there is huge pressure on people to be sexually knowledgeable in so many ways'. This is hardly the fault of its young poster girls, who, realistically, are more au fait with Lady Gaga's hair removal techniques than with the history of sexual repression in Ireland. Again, we must look to ourselves. Addressing the same conference, Sara

Stokes of NUI Galway suggested that 'raunch culture and the attitudes it perpetuates have not been widely challenged in Ireland and very little discussion exists regarding alternative models of sexuality, aside from those informed by traditional Catholic values and moral panic.'

She said: 'Acceptance of this hyper-sexualisation can be read as a backlash to the culture of fear and silence that has plagued Irish sexuality traditionally – as a result, in the interim between a dominant anti-sexual regime and one which is overtly sexualised, there was no forum in which to openly discuss sex and sexuality and no room for the formation of an autonomous sexuality in Ireland.'

Mr Ferriter suggested that perhaps we Irish are simply 'not very good at moderation'. But while the quantity of sexual behaviour is of concern where our children are concerned, it is the quality that is truly disturbing. For women, the genuinely depressing reality is that having spent two generations agitating for women to be sexually liberated, we now find our daughters trapped into patterns of sexual behaviour that are demeaning and infinitely more exploitative than anything our repressed grandmothers might have experienced. So however much we might choose to despair of 'them' and 'their behaviour', when it comes to the corrupting sexualisation of our children, the buck stops squarely with us. Our children are the first generation of Irish people to grow up without being taught that sex before marriage is a sin.

For us, their parents, that is a formidable precedent. The trouble is that in our eggshell-walking efforts to avoid burdening our children with the same sexual guilt that repressed our generation and previous ones, we have failed to offer any example at all.

We rightly rejected one sense of repressive values, but we have neglected to replace them with an alternative set of guidelines. A key finding of the Pfizer report is that there is a lack of dialogue between parents and children where sex is concerned, with a majority of parents arguing that either their children were reluctant to engage or they were satisfied that it was being dealt with in school.

Neither excuse exonerates us. We need to find what Miss Stokes called 'an autonomous sexuality' – and if we can't do it as a nation, then we need to do it as individual families – through dialogue and through example. We also need to concede that much of what we find challenging about our children's behaviour is a direct result of our own efforts to escape our repressive, sin-obsessed past.

We, after all, are the generation who fought hard so that women could dress however they wanted without the law or anyone else deeming that 'they were asking for it' – now, we see our daughters coming down the stairs and we struggle to think anything else.

But again, that is our problem, not theirs. It is neither realistic nor fair to expect a whole generation of young girls to change their style of dress just because their parents are uncomfortable with it (though I would suggest that hiring a clown instead of a make-up artist for a 5-year-old's birthday party won't break any hearts).

It is not too late to sit down with these barely dressed children and set down parameters of acceptable sexual behaviour with them. As Miss Murray says: 'Those who are more protected by parents can get through the phase with the counterbalance of parental sense and boundaries around it.'

We need to engage with our children – however uncomfortable that might make them and us – and offer them a positive version of sexual behaviour to which to aspire. We need to tell them that in spite of our own obvious lack of porn-star bodies and attitudes, our experience of sex has been loving and fulfilling for both partners.

It might make them so embarrassed that they won't even be able to face the disco. But we owe them nothing less.

27 March 2010

AMERICA, OUR NEXT PARISH

Joseph O'Connor

When I was a child in the suburban Dublin of the early 1970s, my father used to take us on holiday to Connemara. We loved it. Summer would arrive and the talk would turn quickly to the matter of when we would make for the West. The preparations, the small ceremonies of the annual pilgrimage, simply became part of our lives.

The Atlantic was the essence of Connemara's allure. At home in Dún Laoghaire, we lived near the coast but our local version, for all its charms, seemed tame. We had chippers, a public baths, American-style ice-cream parlours, with Gene Vincent on the jukebox, faded posters of Elvis on the wall and a statue of the Child of Prague on the counter. Old ladies shuffled down the pier, arm in arm, tutting at the cornerboys and their bell-bottomed motts.

But it wasn't the real thing. It was Brighton with nuns. You could walk from Glasthule all the way to Booterstown and not see a grain of sand. You didn't see the breakers roar in from the horizon, those thunderous whitecaps born in Boston Sound, or feel the shocking tang of spray in your mouth. In Dublin we had the sea. In Connemara they had the ocean. The people spoke of America as 'the next parish'.

If Connemara's history is a ghost story, its phantoms are sea-ghosts, poignantly in love with the promised land of freedom:

the emigrants who went to Illinois; the political refugees forced to flee to Boston; the Princess of Connemara, Mary Martin, who voyaged to New York only to die in a cheap hotel.

This coastline seemed to me then, as it seems to me still, a storybook of spectres that is waiting to be opened, a place that says more about the unique relationship between Ireland and America than any history textbook ever will.

Yet for all that it was an annual part of our lives, Connemara felt exotic too. I remember sitting in the back of my father's Hillman Hunter on those wearisome, annual westward drives, reading the place-names of coastal Connemara from his crumpled AA roadmap. Bunnahown, Rosroe, Kilkerrin, Tawnaghbaun, Aillenacally, Aillebrack, Curhownagh, Ardnagreevagh.

If you said them aloud the result was poetry. And as an adult, I would often experience precisely the same feeling in America, the beauty of American place names. Montana, Baton Rouge, Mississippi, El Dorado, Lake Pontchartrain and Dublin, Ohio.

How ethereal that vowelly geography sounded, how thrilling its music on an Irish tongue.

It often seems to me our greatest gift to America: that sense that the poetry of the everyday, the music of the common man, is capable of touching the deepest places of the heart. You know it listening to Springsteen, to Dylan or Johnny Cash, on each of whom the influence of Irish music was astonishingly deep, and it shines from the pages of American literature, as from the country songs borrowed from Irish folk melody.

America in the nineteenth century was an idea more than a place. A laboratory where men and women would attempt to discover for themselves if this strange notion called 'democracy' was possible.

They would live without kings, without bishops participating in legislation, and the citizens would be assessed not on the basis of where they had come from but where they might want to go.

It had terrible imperfections, including the obscene fact of slavery, and it had xenophobia and a persecution of its native peoples. But if you were Irish and poor in the nineteenth century, America's possibilities and its sense of its own power must have made it seem a land of dreams.

It was the only country on earth where the language of simple human joy was included in its constitution. It was where 'life, liberty, and the pursuit of happiness' became a new sort of holy trinity.

Again and again in the traditional Irish songs of the era, we see the language of freedom applied to America: 'Come to the land where we will be happy / Don't be afraid of the storm or the sea / And it's when we get over, we'll surely discover / That place is the homeland of Sweet Liberty.'

When you see what was going on back in colonised, ruined Ireland, those images can be more clearly understood. You would not think today, as you amble the impossibly beautiful waterfront at Clifden, that you might be walking through a space that was once a disaster zone: the Ground Zero of Victorian Europe.

These beaches, those pebbled strands, saw astonishing suffering. This sea-land that would be hallowed by generations of Irish-American writers witnessed tragedy so immense that many of those who observed it would be traumatised for ever.

The narrative revealed by Connemara's coastline is not part of modern Ireland's love affair with itself. But it is still the essential chapter in the story of Ireland and America, the braiding together of two peoples. We thought it important not to go on about that horrendous decade in which millions of the Irish underclass died of famine or were driven from their country to America.

How old-fashioned, how uncosmopolitan to mention all that. Impolite to the neighbours across the water, perhaps; inconvenient in a new age of peace. If we didn't forget the victims, we stewed their bones into propaganda, the meat of the murderous ballad and the beer-fuelled come-all-ye.

But behind all the evasions were real men and women, children starved and dumped into pits. Their graves can still be dimly discerned around the shorelands of Connemara; unmarked mounds, like middens for rubbish. They were called scrounging layabouts by the commentariat of their day, a good number of whom regarded the landless Irish as literally subhuman.

Those who took them in, in their hundreds of thousands, and finally in their millions, for over a century, were the people of the United States of America, and that should never be forgotten by Ireland. Nor should we forget the stories of the hundreds of thousands of Irish Famine-era immigrants who took up arms in the American Civil War.

Often enough, they knew their deaths were absolutely certain, yet they continued to sign up and fight. And often they fought their own countrymen on America's battlefields, these desperately poor people who had crossed half the world in the hope of a new life and freedom. Was it hope for acceptance in the Land of the Brave that led so many to the killing grounds of Gettysburg and The Wilderness? As for the long time it took for the Irish to truly gain that full acceptance, a remark made by Joseph Kennedy to New York journalists in 1952 is revealing: 'I was born in America. My children were born in America. What the hell do I have to do to be called an American?' Perhaps the election of JFK, the direct descendant of Famine-era emigrants, was the high watermark of that process that had begun centuries earlier.

Certainly, in the 1980s, as perhaps in the years that face us now, the cities of the US were thronged with Irish-born migrants, still in search of a better life. The book that tells us everything about Ireland and America is no novel, no historical survey, no textbook. It is the telephone directory of any American city.

There, in lines, are the endless Irish names, the people who bear my own surname and probably yours.

On Cashel Hill, Connemara, there is a Famine-era cemetery that is still in use today. Ard Caiseal looks down on a rock-strewn inlet that opens, dramatically, into the Atlantic. It is one of those loftily lonesome places that the folk music shared by Ireland and Appalachia somehow translates into sound. Oceanic windstorms buffet Cashel Hill; the trek up is dizzying and arduous.

On the wintry afternoon I last made the climb, a small stars-and-stripes pennant had been placed on a tombstone. It marked the grave of a young local man whose family had Massachusetts connections, as have numberless Connemara people.

He was 21 when he lost his life, too far from home. He should be alive today, dandling grandchildren, but that was not to be his emigrant's fate. Locals recall that on the icy morning when the military came to bury him, the vehicle that bore his casket could not manage the steepness of Cashel Hill. So he was carried up the mountain to his final resting place, up the rocks to Ard Caiseal, as his ancestors had been.

He lies among those others whose names are long forgotten, who were abandoned in the latitudes of hunger.

His grave, and the desolate coastline that enspaces it, is a powerful reminder of many things: among them, the awful cost demanded by patriotism, the wrongs we have done to one another for love of country, the dreadful waste that is racism, all those unaccepted friendships, but the hope that the world can yet be a fairer place when those who have plenty, as they did in America, help the poor to have a measure of dignity.

If the text of Connemara's coastline includes any moral, it is a potent forewarning about hatred and bigotry. The sea divides. It also connects. All who have found peace on this silent shore have something to learn from the stony words that commemorate that young man. In some sense they remember not only his own short life, but all the nameless who lie around him, wherever in the coastland of Connemara they lie, and in other Connemaras, across other seas.

On St Patrick's Day, the date on which we commemorate the lonely slave who became the national icon of our country's possibilities, I will remember that young man of Connemara and Boston whose epitaph speaks volumes still.

L/CPL Peter Mary Nee
Galway/Connemara
United States Marine Corps
Born 15 August 1947
Died 31 March 1969, Vietnam.

13 March 2010

THE CHURCH AND ME

Kate Kerrigan

When I was a child, I prayed to God every night. I had a deep devotion to the Blessed Virgin, so I joined the Legion of Mary and used to make the tea after Mass, help with jumble sales, visit old people and try to persuade our Italian neighbours to go to church more regularly, and not just for the dress-up days of their First Holy Communion.

An aunt was a nun in a convent not far from where we lived and we used to visit her one Sunday in every month. I remember the smell of the dark, polished wood in the elegant, sparsely furnished room where we would sit and wait for her.

Then she would glide out to us, a stout, friendly woman, all smiles and hugs. The nuns gave us iced biscuits and made us feel so welcome and special, showering us with gifts of miraculous medals and Rosary beads that never lost their significance for me.

I went through a period in my pubescent years when I dallied with the idea of becoming a nun. I was taken into the canteen to meet some postulants, and while I loved the warm, jolly, boarding-school atmosphere, in truth the real world – of boys, eyeliner, leg-warmers and smoking cigarettes – already was calling me.

By the time it came to the bell, book and candle grandeur of our wedding, I was more or less lapsed. Shocked by the hypocrisy of the Church, I had decided I did not want our first child christened, but my husband persuaded me. We live in a Catholic country, he pointed out. Suppose he wants to get married in a church? We should give him the option.

I decided he was right but the event itself meant very little to me and I felt hypocritical. My integrity, if not compromised, had somehow shunted out of whack. So to school. With our inquisitive son nearing the age of reason, I made a decision, based on my own faith as a child, to bring him up as a Catholic. Not a sometimes, when it suits, à la carte Catholic, but a proper, churchgoing 'God is watching you; Jesus was a great man altogether' Christian. Minus the homophobia and the misogynist attitudes, of course, and with the addition of the theory of evolution, we are pretty much on the button.

The older I get, the more I enjoy all the pomp and ceremony. As a sceptic, I believe that most things that aren't fact are, by and large, superstitious nonsense. As somebody who has struggled with loss in the past year, and who had enjoyed the comfort of faith in the past, I know the value of believing in something.

And so I choose to believe in the superstitious nonsense I grew up with, rather than crystals and Buddhas. In any case, I appreciate the weekly routine of worship. I like my 8-year-old child sitting in enforced silence for forty minutes; kids never get the chance to be bored these days and Mass is the only excuse I can find to not have him constantly entertained. It's good for him, and me, to have some quiet time together.

At other, private times, for me it's yoga. I say decades of the Hail Mary to myself. It might as well be a Buddhist chant but when life is tough, it works for me. Plus, my local priest is too good an opportunity to pass up.

If God had a catalogue where you could order village priests, Father Paddy Hoban would be in the gold membership version.

He has curly, snow-white hair, and is a humble, mild-mannered, deeply holy man who also is fantastically clever, a brilliant liturgist and has something of a dry, measured wit. His sermons are always short, inspired, topical and on the button.

His brother, Brendan, the parish priest in our neighbouring town and a writer and historian, isn't far off him. Local atheists envy me. So I should be living in a kind of spiritual idyll, except for one thing. The religion I practice, the religion I am rearing my children in, has become so darkly associated with the very worst kind of sin imaginable.

The word 'Catholic' itself has become synonymous with the word 'abuse'. As an ordinary Catholic mother being outraged from within the cloistered conservatism of the Church itself, I feel completely powerless and used. If I didn't have such a great set-up, I'd certainly be joining the ranks of the outraged defectors, especially after the week that has been in it.

I'm afraid to ask my priests, 'what are we going to do?', in case they say, 'pray'. I don't want to pray. I want to march. I want to rebel and break away and start again. It is their misfortune to be trapped by and in an organisation that has revealed itself as rotten to the core, which has a homophobic fossil as CEO.

The website offering people the chance to formally defect from being counted among the Church's number worldwide (www.countmeout.ie) claims that 7,500 people have downloaded forms – I'm surprised it's not a lot more. One wonders why more clergy don't stand up and speak out, but then one only has to look at Father Brian D'Arcy, a natural leader who should be Cardinal D'Arcy by now, or Father Kevin Hegarty, banished to the westernmost point of Mayo after consistently speaking out about clerical abuse long before the press got hold of it.

Integrity is not a byword for career success in the Catholic Church. Some of the most vigilant defenders of clerical silence have been the laity, people alongside whom I sit in my Sunday pew.

Again, I am afraid to discuss the subject among the old faithful in my parish, in case they tell me something I cannot bear to hear. The ones prepared to make themselves heard plead for no change, but their arguments are underpinned with the desperate clang of denial.

Deep down, they too feel responsible. The Church's crimes are our crimes. We are guilty by association. The most resonant truths we heard this week were uttered by priests themselves, the courageous voices of Fathers D'Arcy and Hegarty when they told us, the astonished laity, 'the hierarchy just don't get it'.

No point in getting angry, ranting and asking questions and raving on. Their moral consciousness just won't compute. You only have to look at how watery and terrified Diarmuid Martin seemed when he came home from Rome.

The men at the top just don't get the whole human consequences thing. In their own minds, they have risen above us ordinary mortals in both their political and spiritual stature. The opinions and struggles of the ordinary clergy mean little to them; the needs of the laity, even less.

My loyalty towards my priests and my daily experience of the Church has been strengthened by three deaths this year. The local priests know where my biscuits are kept. I made friends with a priest and nun in London who had helped my brother before he died.

There is no doubt in my mind that the Catholic Church has attracted good men. The evil paedophiles were able to exist because of a rotten system. The majority of the priests and nuns doing God's good work on the ground have nothing to do with the Church hierarchy except as a kind of laundering service for ordinary parishioners' money.

If every priest in every church in Ireland stood up and told his parishioners he was giving this year's collection money to victims of clerical abuse and not sending one single penny of it over to the bosses in Rome, the Vatican would soon perk up and listen.

It makes me angry and sad that the oldest Christian Church can be accurately defined in such cynical, worldly terms. Shame and confusion that I should be thinking in these terms about my, and my family's, spiritual welfare. I feel so betrayed, returning to a Church I knew was outdated but was prepared to give the benefit of the doubt to, out of sentiment and loyalty.

I have pledged a new member to them through the education and spiritual care of my child, and as a thank-you, I now am faced with this moral quandary. At the end of Leo's First Confession, Paddy invited the children's parents onto the altar to take the places they had practised during a rehearsal earlier in the week.

The parents were then asked to stand with one hand on our child's shoulders. Paddy then led us in a prayer of love and appreciation, a public acknowledgment of how precious our children are, how we will always protect and cherish them. In the light of all that has happened, it would have been easy to be cynical, but this is my child and I have promised him God and a big day out in May.

I hope neither of them let him down.

20 March 2010

APRIL

THE HIGH COST OF CHEAP FOOD

Tom Doorley

Food takes on a different significance in a time of global economic gloom. Eating, after all, can be a great source of comfort when we are feeling down. And cheap, feel-good food is what many of us crave these days.

Domino's Pizza reported a staggering 15 per cent increase in their UK sales over the first six weeks of this year. And in January, a new record was achieved by a drive-through branch of KFC when it did £110,000 (€122,000) of business in just one week. No wonder then that this vast provider of deep-fried, battery chicken bits is planning another 300 outlets (with the creation of some 9,000 jobs) before the end of this year.

The fast-food business has never had it so good: consider how the Subway franchise in Ireland has worked. When it started in 1997, the plan was to open seventeen outlets. Now, there are 189, generating over €100 million in revenue every year and sustaining some 2,500 jobs.

Subway's latest move is to announce the opening of more than 100 new outlets in Ireland before the end of 2010. Having tasted their 'sweet onion chicken teriyaki' sandwich, I take my hat off to the people who run this business. I had no idea that something I find so unattractive could appeal to so many people. But I dare say I spend too much time in my ivory tower.

Not that I am immune to the charms of fast food. As I have said before in this newspaper (and it got me into trouble with the food fascists) I am quite fond of an occasional – a very occasional – Big Mac. And I also have a certain admiration for the way that McDonald's has reinvented itself and bolstered its share price having been almost written off as being in terminal decline less than a decade ago.

Now, McDonald's too has announced plans to open additional Irish premises outlets in the course of this year. Ennis, Wexford, Portlaoise and Maynooth will be the beneficiaries. Indeed, we learned this week that the Ennis outlet, which is being built at present, has attracted job applications from a number of out-of-work architects, doctors and bankers. It seems, however, that irrespective of who is actually serving up the burgers and fries, there are more and more people on the other side of the counter looking for more and more food that is bad for their health.

So why is this the case? Well, it's tasty, it's comforting, it offers instant gratification and, above all, we know that it's frowned upon, that it's the kind of thing the healthy finger-waggers and the food fascists despise. In a perverse way, it's the very badness of fast food that makes it such a pleasure – and such a guilty pleasure.

But it's a dangerous guilty pleasure. If fast food were a mere distraction from our usual – and hopefully reasonably balanced – diet, there would be no cause for concern. We could let the gastronomes get on with their tut-tutting.

After all, many of these people imbue food with a kind of moral marker: people who roast rare breed pork are obviously good; people who wolf down low-fibre, industrial rubbish are obviously bad and, what's even worse, poor. Food as a lifestyle accessory is alive and well, in a way that our European neighbours would completely fail to understand.

Fast food is cheap food. You can fill yourself up at McDonald's or at KFC for the kind of money that wouldn't even buy a cappuccino and a croissant in the kind of café where the chattering classes like to gather.

And while it is a very good thing that we can now buy porridge, fruit and freshly brewed coffee at McDonald's, we all know that nobody really goes there for that. The entire *raison d'etre* of McDonald's is hamburgers and fries, which is what they do best. And nobody goes to KFC for the coleslaw. No, the appeal is the intensively reared chicken, dipped in batter and crisped up in the deep-frier.

Fast food, by definition, is not whole food. And it's not just the fast food outlets that are to blame here. Take a look at the 'specials' on offer in your local supermarket this weekend. You won't find any wholesome organic chickens with their prices slashed. No, it's the highly processed foods that are going cheap in an attempt to attract buyers. Just as in the burger outlets, this too raises the issue of health.

It was an Irish doctor, Denis Burkitt, who produced the first really convincing hypothesis that linked sugar and refined carbohydrates with disease. After training at TCD and the old Adelaide Hospital in Dublin, he worked as a surgeon in Africa in the 1950s where he was struck by how rarely he encountered patients with conditions like diverticulitis and appendicitis; and he concluded that this must be due to the relative absence of refined foods. He became one of the most convincing proponents of the high-fibre diet.

Curiously enough, another Irishman, Dean Swift, had hinted, two centuries before, in the magnificently titled essay 'Of Human Ordure', that dietary fibre might be a good thing. Our attitudes to food and fatness have changed over the centuries. Early humans had it tough in the days before we started gorging ourselves on sugar and fat and white flour. The taste of wild honey was a very rare treat; meat did not come their way every day. Indeed, our ancestors probably realised that sugar and fat not only tasted good but also tended to extend the waistline.

Many aeons before WeightWatchers and its ilk, people believed that putting on a few pounds was a happy and a wholesome thing to do because they had noticed something in their battle for survival; when food supplies grew scarce, it was the skinny people who perished first.

Even into the last century, a certain plumpness was regarded as an attractive feature, perhaps even something of a status symbol. There was a real sense that famine and poverty were never very far away. Corpulence, especially in Ireland, given our history, went with affluence.

Plumpness, however, is now more or less the norm in Western society. Indeed, morbid obesity, or life-threatening fatness, is becoming common. Only this week we saw Dundalk woman Bernadette Treanor challenge her insurance company, Eagle Star, on discrimination grounds because they had doubled her critical illness cover. Why? Miss Treanor is 5ft 2in tall and weighs fifteen stone. As a result, she is, says Eagle Star, a higher health risk.

So why, as a nation, are we putting ourselves at risk by getting fatter? Undoubtedly our sedentary twenty-first-century lifestyles play a part. But diet is crucial, and our diet – along with our actual eating habits – has changed. Fast food is bad enough if it regularly substitutes for one of our standard three meals a day. But there is mounting evidence that a hamburger and fries, for example, is seen more as a snack, a kind of comfort-eating pick-me-up.

Snacking at home, usually on processed foods that are high in fat, sugar and salt, has skewed our instinct as to what we actually need to eat. Some 40 per cent of households no longer possess a table at which the whole family can eat together. Such a family occasion, therefore, where food is celebrated, no longer exists in almost half the homes in this country. Mealtime has given way to a form of grazing and a kind of dietary anarchy now reigns. When appetite is perverted into a kind of itch that needs constant scratching, it is obvious that such an overabundance of refined carbohydrates and saturated fats will lead to obesity.

Some years ago a man in the US sued McDonald's because he had become grossly overweight as a result of being one of their best customers. The court's sensible reaction was encapsulated in a newspaper headline which read: 'Too Many Burgers Make You Fat? No Kidding, Rules Judge'.

While its causes may be cheap food, obesity is an expensive business. It leads to type 2 diabetes and to cardiovascular disease, which in turn put enormous pressure on our shrinking health services.

So, fast food, cheap food, carries a significant hidden cost. And now Professor Michael Marmot of University College, London has identified obesity as a major cause of cancer, stating last month that there are clear links between certain common forms of the disease – such as that of the breast, bowel and oesophagus – and being overweight.

Low-fat diets and exercise appear to be linked to a decreased risk of developing cancers of the cervix, gall bladder and prostate, so it is reasonable to suggest that obesity is implicated in these too. Indeed, thanks to the obesity epidemic in our industrialised nations, the World Cancer Research Fund has predicted that deaths from cancer will double over the next forty years.

As we head further into this recession we must call a halt right now to our soaring level of fast-food comfort-eating. You don't have to go to McDonald's or fill your supermarket trolley with this week's 'specials' in order to eat cheaply. It is possible, after all, to grow a few potatoes in a bag or a dustbin, or indeed to use a small corner of your patch of garden to grow a selection of vegetables.

In the end it is about balance.

An occasional Big Mac won't do anyone any lasting harm, but if high fat and highly processed food becomes our comfort blanket, then the ultimate cost of what seemed like a cheap diet option will be far, far too high.

4 April 2009

OUR SHANGRI-LA

Helen Rock

There's nothing like a week away in the noise and chaos of downtown Manhattan to make you appreciate once again the joys of Éireann. Okay, New York was good in parts and except for a noticeable dearth of building cranes on the cardboard cut-out skyline, and a few lacklustre mid-season sales, there were few visible signs of recession.

And yes, the city did shine at times, with whole streets filled with beautiful white plum blossoms and shimmering displays of star magnolias set against dark red-stone Gothic churches.

But despite conservationists' best efforts, nature is still very much on the run on the island that the native Indians called Manahatta, meaning Land of Many Hills.

Even little bits of man-made garden that they have caged in here and there on the sidewalks, and which are signposted as 'wildlife conservation areas', are poorly planted and harbour aggressive grey squirrels, while a few brave little speckled birds peck nervously in the thin grey earth.

So it was sheer bliss to fly in a long direct line across the Atlantic Ocean to Dublin in the red and gold dawn of last Monday morning, with a strong tail wind at our back pushing us ever faster towards what began to look increasingly like Shangri-La, Nirvana, the Land of Plenty.

As the plane came off the sea and flew over Clare-Limerick and up across the midlands, the pink-lit clouds parted and there we were, looking down on a vast expanse of barely marked land of the sweetest, softest, brown-green colour. It was as though Ireland lay at the beginning of time.

All you could see was a rather mystical landscape punctuated with big gleaming silver lakes and coiling rivers. Not one building was as yet visible and that made it easy to believe that there were none, ever, except maybe those vernacular buildings made from indigenous materials taken from the quiet landscape around them – clay and slate, wood and stone, all well married in and leaving no scars.

And in a way we are almost at the beginning of a new time, now that the hysteria and bad manners and loss of reason associated with getting rich quick by fair means and foul are all fading, and the fool's gold has turned to dust.

Now spring has truly sprung and is dancing along in the sunlight and growth is all around us in this land of milk and honey. And yes, there's a lot to celebrate in the flourishing beauty of this country of ours.

A third of our public water may be contaminated, according to a shocking new EPA report, but we still have plenty of clean water and lots of unused land. Put the last two together, add seeds, plant billions of trees and rear poultry and livestock in humane, organic conditions, and we'd soon have not only the means to feed ourselves with the best of food, but a source of wood for building – for furniture, for hurleys and, if coppicing was practised properly, renewable wood for burning and keeping ourselves warm.

If the government really cared about the country and not just about themselves (and this includes the straw men and women of the Green Party) and if, for example, the mass planting of broadleaved trees that we desperately need in this still underwooded country was taken seriously, it would stop ongoing erosion and flooding, take carbon from the atmosphere and make oxygen.

If heavy-duty agricultural chemicals were banned completely and taken out of the food chain, if slurry was not allowed to run off land into the rivers and streams, if dumping of toxic industrial waste into the water sources was a complete no-no, if certain county councils were not so careless about sewage systems that you'd half-believe they're trying to kill us off, if all the hired hands of the State were answerable for their actions, then we could all sleep safely in our beds, secure in the knowledge that there will never be another famine on this island, that now we control the means of production we will not want again for the basics to sustain us in life.

Earlier this month, after many years of campaigning by An Taisce, the government – in the form of John Gormley, Minister for Environment, Heritage and Local Government – finally announced the formation of the Environmental Pillar of Social Partnership (it doesn't exactly trip off the tongue, but it's a start). It will be represented by a range of non-governmental groups, including An Taisce.

While the latter has come in for some bad maulings over the years by vested interests, it is an excellent body and should be supported. Set up in 1948 by the legendary Robert Lloyd Praeger, botanist and author of the best book ever written on the Irish landscape (*The Way That I Went*), An Taisce has been fighting the good fight from its inception, beginning with Praeger's inaugural address on Raidio Éireann in October of that year.

He spoke passionately back then about our over-reliance on monoculture in our plantations of exotic conifers, which make up a staggering 79 per cent of our forests, mostly managed as a purely commercial affair by Coillte.

The main environmental consequences of our forestry policy, said Lloyd Praeger back in 1948, are habitat loss, deterioration of water quality and aquatic biodiversity, landscape and amenity impacts and changes in archaeological setting of particular sites.

Well, things have deteriorated since then, despite the laudable aims of the Tree Council. Once upon a time, we had a tree culture unrivalled in Europe. Now, after ninety years of self-governance, we are still denuded. It's time we got back to the forest.

We are a good people. We take care, to a large extent, of our most vulnerable people. You would never see here, as I did in New York last week, a poor middle-aged man with full-blown cerebral palsy living alone on the streets, his bed and only means of transport a bockety old manual wheelchair, a chair that was so difficult to manoeuvre that his big hands were swollen and badly blistered from trying to turn the unguarded wheels.

We must teach our children well and show them the ways of unsentimental nature, and that includes human nature. We should introduce them, as a matter of policy, to the notion of helping those who need it, of growing fresh food and taking nothing, except our parental love, for granted. Happily, this veg-growing trend is now back again, with every old Green hack and media babe jumping on the bandwagon, claiming to be leading the revolution.

But don't let that put you off.

Look instead to the good things that are there – and much of it for free. Take the marvellous Botanic Gardens in Dublin's Glasnevin, and its offshoot at Kilmacurragh Arboretum in Wicklow which is in spectacular bloom right now.

Under the Botanic's dynamic director, Peter Wyse-Jackson, the gardeners there are leading the way with their magnificent new organic vegetable garden – opened by a rather red-faced, bumbling Bertie Ahern over an al fresco lunch one hot Sunday last year, just after his fall from grace but before the bubble had burst for the rest of us.

Both Glasnevin and Kilmacurragh also have great programmes of lectures, walks and workshops for children (including pond-dipping for creepy crawly things, which they love) as well as for adults, and most of them are free.

Then, of course, there's the Phoenix Park, and the lovely gardens of Farmleigh, and Airfield in Dundrum, and all the beautiful parks, museums, galleries and model farms that are open to the public free of charge around the whole country.

Indeed, despite the gloom merchants and naysayers who predicted its demise, a pared-down Bloom in the Park is scheduled to go ahead for its third annual outing over the June bank holiday weekend.

And guess what? The highlight being billed for that is a vegetable garden – in this case a reproduction of the White House kitchen garden that the cook Alice Waters, of Chez Panisse fame, has made for Michelle Obama.

It's time to get back to the earth. To take joy from all that's good about this country of ours. Maybe we did nearly destroy it all forever in our heedless and headfirst pursuit of wealth, and in cherishing that above the things that really matter. Things like compassion and truth and beauty.

So now, as the landscape bursts with life and we see before us what we have, we should learn to cherish it.

25 April 2009

HEANEY AT SEVENTY

Joseph O'Connor

I can remember the first time I read a Seamus Heaney poem. It was called 'Punishment' and it was part of a sequence he wrote out of the captivating experience of seeing photographs of ancient bodies that had been preserved in the boglands.

It was strange and unforgettable, incredibly daring in what it was doing. It implied a connection between the body of a girl who had clearly been the victim of some kind of human sacrifice and the bodies of women who had been attacked in Northern Ireland for befriending British soldiers. Wider comparisons seemed to suggest themselves also: to collaborators in France at the time of the Second World War, who were stripped or had their heads shaved or were tarred and feathered, scapegoats from the crimes of a whole society.

I was 18 at the time, a student in UCD. The year was 1981 and the poem, although written a good while previously, seemed to speak for the times I was living in. It was the era of Ann Lovett, of the nightmarish story of the Kerry Babies, of debates about abortion and contraception and divorce.

The poem's way of connecting an ancient ritual of degradation to the contemporary and rapidly changing country I knew seemed absolutely revolutionary, but it seemed so by accident. It is the genius of Seamus Heaney.

Then there were the beautifully crafted lyrics, the gorgeous evocations of countryside, the constant and delicate counterpointing of present and past. His first book was entitled *Death of a Naturalist* and he seemed uneasy about the idea of the old-fashioned poem in which everything in nature is good. He was no Ulster Wordsworth, warbling about daffodils. His work had a kind of impatience. But for all that, he had an accuracy of description no Irish poet of his generation has ever rivalled.

To read him is to stand in the Irish rain, to know what it feels like to go wintering out through the fields. He doesn't describe; he incarnates on the page. Yeats wrote that it is hard to know 'the dancer from the dance', perhaps echoing an old saying still current in Connemara, that a really great singer does not sing the song but allows himself to be sung by it, always. In the work of Seamus Heaney, the truth of that motto comes alive. You sometimes have the feeling he is simply revealing what is there, rather than conveying anything artificial through art.

His poems have the sense that they grew on the page, like wildflowers sprouting out of a limestone outcrop in the Burren or rushes on a windswept strand.

And for me, Seamus Heaney is the spiritual inheritor of Patrick Kavanagh, not Yeats. He has Kavanagh's innate sense of what is loved by the ordinary reader, the small, precious moments of everyday life that somehow clarify to us what we actually are. Not for nothing does every book of Heaney's regularly top the Irish bestsellers' list. He is that rarest of creatures: a poet whose work is widely beloved, garlanded with literary awards from critics and academics all over the world, but simultaneously read in every Irish home where poetry is even slightly valued.

His poems zero in on events other poets wouldn't notice: a boy watching his mother peeling potatoes by a sink, an old man meeting a friend with whom he once went to school, a son driving his father to confession, a bricklayer at work, the small rites and observances by which lives are lived in Ireland, the ways in which we speak to one another, or fail to. Like Austin Clarke and Thomas Kinsella, like Paul Durcan and Derek Mahon, and like the great Paul Muldoon, his fellow Ulsterman, he has taken the realities of this tiny island on the western outpost of Europe and found in them truths that have touched people everywhere.

In other ways, he reminds me of an ancient Irish bard, a druid who knows the secret rhythms and rhymes of his tribe, the underground water of his community.

His line 'Whatever you say, say nothing' is perhaps the most achingly sad and toughly accurate reflection of Northern Ireland's tragedies and evasions. And yet his observation that there are instances 'when hope and history rhyme' has been quoted from the halls of Stormont to the lawns of the White House, an intimation of what is truly best in us, a kind of acknowledgement of a people who have always deserved better than the hatreds in which they have struggled.

His work contains constant echoes of the earlier Irish poets and he stands in that great tradition that stretches back so far into the past that we know almost nothing of its anonymous geniuses.

We will never know who wrote something as staunch and powerful as 'The Rocks of Bawn' or 'I Wish I Was in Carrickfergus', but Heaney's scrupulous sense of place and getting the details right places him in the company of that extraordinary pantheon.

Yet he has been no narrow or purely local intelligence. While he has proved himself a magnificent, capable translator of ancient Irish texts, his work has been alive to American and European poetry, to the verse forms of Japan, the geography of the United States. 'District and Circle', the title poem of a recent collection, makes a journey on the London Tube an extraordinary adventure in meditation and recollecting the past.

He has reminded us that we are citizens of the world while reminding us too that we belong to a part of it that is unique. A remark he made during a 1996 interview puts it with the quiet power that is typical of him: 'If you have a strong first world and a strong set of relationships then in some part of you, you are always free; you can walk the world because you know where you belong, you have some place to come back to.'

Ireland, as we know, is undergoing a trauma. For many years and decades we thought we were failures, denizens of a place that had given little to the planet with the exception of its great writers and poets. Heaney is always aware of the special richness of this tradition. He has the scrupulousness of James Joyce, the wry humour of Beckett, and the Yeatsian sense that there are times when a poet can somehow touch the DNA of an entire society and turn it into something beautiful.

More even than that, there has been an integrity to the work that every reader recognises and responds to. With its values of love of language – of words and their musicality – and its insistence that the everyday is worthy of celebration, Heaney's work has somehow come to belong to us all in Ireland. If we have a national poet, in any meaningful sense of the term, he is the only contender for the mantle.

And in these times of challenge and austerity, of recent dreams being smashed as violently and as permanently as Éamon de Valera's once were, Heaney speaks of an older and deeper set of priorities as well as being urgently contemporary.

He has written often of the dignity of labour, of things of the land, of those who sow and reap and hammer and harvest, no matter the madness of the world around them. He has roved through the kitchens of all our Irish childhoods, noticing and immortalising the women who haunt them and who speak of weather and children and the preparation of food as a way of speaking about something else.

My late father-in-law, John Casey, a man who left Roscommon in the 1950s to work on the building sites of Coventry and

Manchester, loved only one poet, and it was Heaney. He saw him as a figure who had given a voice to a whole mass of Irish people often forgotten by literature.

And it never surprised me that John would be sometimes so touched by a Heaney lyric that tears would appear in his tough eyes; for Heaney's heroes, if he has them, have been the people whose principal inheritance has been their courage and precious little else. And he has written with a modesty and non-attention-seeking poise ordinary readers find exemplary and touching. We see in his work a kind of subtle transmission of many of the solidarities we used to think were important in Ireland.

He doesn't do chat shows or celebrity photo shoots. He sits at a desk and writes. A friend of mine who is an Irish novelist is fond of remarking that whenever he is invited to do something embarrassing to market one of his books, he asks himself, 'Would Seamus Heaney do it?' before responding. I think he's only half-joking.

Heaney has become a touchstone to a whole generation of younger Irish writers, and in some ways, I believe, to his readers.

In one of his earliest and most frequently quoted poems, a youthful Seamus Heaney sees his father digging in a field that may or may not yield too much. He resolves that the pen is also a kind of tool, a way of getting down deep. 'I'll dig with it,' he remarks. It was a noble manifesto.

This is what he has succeeded in doing throughout a life in poetry. He has excavated what we are, found remnants of what we were, and somehow suggested with immense skill and beauty a notion of what we could be, and still might be. He has written that poetry can be redemptive. His own certainly is. That he is still, at the age of seventy, making work of such extraordinary grace and relevance is a cause for celebration indeed.

11 April 2009

MAY

EUROVISION:
A REAL ROCK REVOLUTION

John Waters

Thursday night's semi-final outcome seems a little encouraging for those who would like to see the Eurovision remain a song contest, rather than become an exercise in silliness or spectacularity or gay subversion.

The bookies had been hedging in all three directions, placing Switzerland and its vampires near the top of the list of favourites, in accordance with one interpretation of Lordi's victory last year.

As of today, the analysis that Eurovision will in the future be all about vision seems once again unnecessarily pessimistic or premature, though, this being Eurovision, it remains to be, as it were, seen.

The general consensus about the semis was that the overall standard of song was lower than usual, with an excess of disco and flat-earth rock, and too many countries relying on flamboyance, costumes and dance routines. But there is a consensus, too, that the voting public weeded out the dross in a forensic and decisive manner.

Switzerland's vampires were buried at the crossroads with the stakes of good taste driven deep into their hearts. Israel's advice to the texting public to 'Push the Button', was, it seems, disregarded, as voters plumped for songwriting values rather than controversial opportunism.

Several striking songs emerged, including Serbia's haunting 'Prayer', Hungary's 'Unsubstantial Blues', Slovenia's 'Flower of the South' and Latvia's 'This Night'. Thursday night's outcomes seem also, incidentally, to bode well for Ireland. Our song is distinctive and, in several senses, traditional. Had we been in the semi-finals, we would almost certainly have made it through on the patterns of voting that emerged.

But the final may well be a different matter. For one thing, the (unclear) age profile of voters may shoot downwards on Saturday, since children and teenagers don't have to get up for school the next day. Such are the matters that otherwise intelligent adults found themselves speculating on in Helsinki in the early hours of Friday.

Of course, the semi-final results bring into play another old chestnut, the one about the 'Eastern-bloc' block vote. Nine of the ten qualifiers are from Eastern Europe, apparently giving succour to the conspiracy theorists who tell us that it is all nowadays about politics and tribal affinity.

They miss that Poland didn't make it, even with its babe-factor ten. I have from the outset sensed the voting patterns which have emerged since the arrival of the Eastern-bloc countries are less about politics than cultural recognition.

Eastern European countries vote for one another not because of tone-deaf neighbourly loyalty but because they share a culture which, though derivative of the culture of the West, is nowadays in-scrutable to most of us on the other side of the melted iron curtain.

It used to seem like Eurovision was a long way behind the pop mainstream; that, in seeking a common denominator, it plunged rather than soared. In part this was a consequence of the in-eluctable fragmentedness of Europe and its popular cultures, which tended to exist in separate compartments at varying levels of advancement.

The old voting system, based on panels of hand-picked specialists in the various entrant countries, tended to consolidate this tendency, creating and maintaining a particular Eurovision thing – in sound, look and attitude. But latterly, the breaking down of political barriers and unification by technology has drawn the strands of European pop culture more closely together, broadening the scope of what is possible and plausible.

Last year, the victory of Lordi with 'Hard Rock Hallelujah' offered a possibility of an opening up. For a metal band to win Eurovision had until then seemed implausible and unacceptable. Lordi changed that, in one sense breaking all the existing moulds, but in another creating a possibility, a danger, that visual spectacularity might become the norm, reducing Eurovision to a single lane.

Thursday night's results seem reassuring on this score. The sub-Lordi hard rock acts, like Iceland and the Czech Republic, were consigned to the flames, and Switzerland's early exit seems to demolish the condescending view of voters as ironic nihilists with eyes only for effects and raised eyebrows intent on ironic mischief.

Last year's contest was interesting for reasons that transcend the implications of either the Eurovision or pop music – one of those moments when pop culture tells you something that you hadn't previously taken on board. One of the byproducts that arises from the separation by snobbery of Eurovision from the pop mainstream is that there is little or no intelligent punditry to be found.

There are many Eurovision anoraks who can tell you the colour of Dana's frock or Sandie Shaw's toenail polish, but none, it seems, capable of translating the experience of Eurovision into a set of implications for pop music in the real world.

The cynics, of course, say that Eurovision has absolutely no implications for pop in the real world, but this is just another layer of the cynicism that locks us into the problem. Indeed, the absence of such analysis is handing this potentially amazing cultural event into the hands of those, like the gay lobby, who glory in its kitsch and its disconnectedness.

Some predict that, within a decade, the Eurovision could be an exclusively gay event. This would be a ludicrous waste.

There is an argument that, because Eurovision has seemed so predictable, so set in its ways, so self-regardingly shallow, that it is unproductive if not impossible to extrapolate from it any useful sense of direction. But is this true?

Last year, Lordi drove a coach-and-four through the pundits' predictions. The trouble is that nobody seemed to feel sure what Lordi's victory actually meant. Was it the triumph of grotesquerie or the emergence of a tactical understanding of where the centre of European pop gravity actually lies?

In Helsinki, the consensus during the week veered towards the former analysis, perhaps driven by the bookies' insistence in picking as favourite the appalling transvestite ditty from the Ukraine's Verka Serduchka. But what people tend to forget about Lordi is that they had much more going for them than masks.

They seemed to understand something about the taste of the voters, reprising a particular period in the rock pantheon – Purple, Led Zep. etc – that endures after more than three decades. They seemed to understand that, although this music continues to appeal to a certain substantial cohort of young people, it is not something that can readily be admitted to. But coated with a sugaring of irony, it became both palatable and admissible.

If this, rather than the spectacularity dimension, is what is significant in the Lordi phenomenon, the lesson to be learned relates somehow to new encountering of past pop values. It is, in the end, about the difference between east and west.

In the movie *Lost in Translation*, Bill Murray's character is a deadpan American actor who, regarding himself and his life with an irony so light he can barely move, is bemused to find himself adrift for a weekend in a city where lately-landed Western pop culture is celebrated with an enthusiasm born of recent discovery.

It is as though Tokyo caught a passing glimpse of Western pop culture since the 1950s and recreated it in its most intense and literal form. He feels like he's experiencing a genetically enhanced version of his own cultural past.

What we missed about 'our' opening up of 'our' borders to the east was that this would be a two-way process. We thought only of how we could exploit our new arrivals in return for letting them participate in our markets and culture. But something surprising is happening.

They have come to, for example, western pop culture in its penultimate chapter and see in it things we have forgotten or overlooked or so clothed in irony and post-modern self-referentialism that we lack all capacity to comprehend that someone else, coming from outside, might entirely fail to get the 'joke'.

For us, for example, heavy metal is no longer to be taken literally, but represents a raised eyebrow that speaks distantly of our own lost innocence. For our neighbours from the east, however, there is nothing lost about the innocence.

They may see, of course, a 'joke', but it is not the same joke we see. It is a joke about rebellion and liberation and physical release, but such things are, for them, too serious and too much fun to be treated ironically. Just as our rock 'n' roll culture was about to run out of steam, we find it colonised by a generation of newcomers who bring to it the hopes and demands we brought to it forty-odd years ago.

And, thanks to Ryanair and European integration, these innocents are living amongst us, reinvigorating our cultures and democracies, promising to bring their huge resources of energy, enthusiasm, resourcefulness and inspiration to bear on the way we live.

Their strength of numbers has significance beyond the capacity to influence the destination of the Eurovision trophy. They have the desire and the capacity to rewind the spool of Western society since the 1960s and play it again in a spirit of curiosity and expectation. Because we have become so bored with ourselves, our cultures now belong to them.

This, ultimately, is what the Irish song is about. 'They Can't Stop the Spring', meaning we can't stop the new pop revolution no matter how many times we tell ourselves that we've seen it all before.

12 May 2007

THE CRASH IS COMING

Mary Ellen Synon

I have said it before, but it still stands. All this about Brian Cowen's spending plans and Pat Rabbitte's corporation tax plans and everybody's stamp duty plans are just details; unimportant, unthreatening details.

They are only distractions from what is really going to shape our economic future. What we should be watching is what is happening in the European Union. That is what is going to shape us. Yet nobody here is taking much notice of events in the EU.

I had thought the collapse of the Spanish property market these last weeks might finally wake us up here to the damage the EU and its currency is doing across Euroland. But no. Beyond some fretting about the dangers to the value of holiday houses bought in Spain, the Irish just haven't grasped what is happening there. But what is happening there is exactly what might soon be happening here, and for exactly the same reason: euro interest rates were kept artificially low for years to suit the sclerotic German economy. That meant they were pitched too low for a growing economy such as Spain's (and ours). The result was, inevitably, a property price bubble in both countries.

So what is happening now in Spain is, for many reasons, what is likely to happen soon here. This is how the *Wall Street Journal* explained it ten days ago: 'The sudden steep drop of Spain's largest real-estate stocks spread fears that the country's decade-long building boom, which has propped up Europe's fastest growing major economy for years, could be about to crack as well. Five of the country's biggest real-estate stocks each fell more than 10 per cent, and the rest of the sector also posted sharp drops. The sell-off raises the spectre of a hard landing for the sector that has underpinned fourteen straight years of growth in Spain.'

The *Financial Times* then described the reason: 'The oversupply of new homes is a problem. For the first time in more than a decade, observers forecast insufficient demand from domestic and overseas buyers for the 800,000 residences [the population of Spain is 40.3 million] started last year.'

There are now too many empty houses in Spain. I will remind you of a statistic which came out of Davy Stockbrokers last year: in 2006 there were 230,000 vacant properties in Ireland.

The *Financial Times* continued, 'The steady rise in European interest rates is also starting to squeeze Spanish households. They have also been piling up consumer credits to furnish their homes and put a new car in the garage.' Meanwhile in Ireland in March, €2.5 billion was owed on credit cards, €350 million more than was owed at the end of February.

This will sound familiar, too: 'The Spanish government, however, has repeatedly downplayed risks to economic growth and even raised GDP forecasts earlier this month to 3.5 per cent for 2007. Spanish prime minister José Luis Zapatero told top businessmen and politicians earlier this month that the Spanish economy had never been stronger.' Meanwhile in Ireland, Mr Cowen is forecasting a continuation of 'strong economic growth' and, while most economists are forecasting that our economy will grow by just 3.5 per cent next year, the minister is insisting it will be 5.3 per cent.

Either Mr Zapatero has been writing Brian Cowen's speeches, or Mr Cowen has been writing his. They are both caught in the same political fiction that, whatever the problem is, the problem is never the euro. Yet the Spanish property price crash, like the coming Irish property price crash, can be traced to the decision by both countries to join the single European currency.

The correct medicine for an economy that has overheated its property market and distorted its economy by an overdependence on construction is to raise interest rates and maybe even devalue the currency. But membership of the euro makes both impossible. So since economic pressures are as inescapable as gravity, there is only one other release possible from the pressure of the bubble: deflation. Which is to say, a fall in the value of your house.

Of course, the European Central Bank is indeed about to raise interest rates again. But it is all too late for Spain, as for Ireland. The interest rates were so low – 2 per cent – for so long, the bubble grew to its present dangerous level. Just how low were those euro-inflicted interest rates, really? The economists at Lombard Street Research (LSR) in London have put the rates in historic perspective: 'That 2 per cent figure was the lowest since Emperor Trajan (98–117 AD).' So, our dangerous boom has been built, thanks to the European Union and its single currency, on the kind of freak interest rates that appear just once in 2,000 years. Of course, when the rates go up again next month, as they surely will, they will be at 4 per cent. Then, according to LSR, they will go higher again in autumn, to 4.25 per cent.

There is nothing the Minister for Finance can do about it. The ECB makes its decisions on 'aggregates'. That means that it cares about the German economy, which is one-third of the Euroland economy, in a way that it will never care about the Irish economy. We don't matter to the ECB. But that should come as no surprise. We don't actually matter to anyone in the EU.

An example: Mr Cowen has repeatedly said that this country will oppose any attempt by the European Commission to 'harmonise' the rate of corporation tax across Europe. In theory, tax policy remains within the power of each member state. But in practice the elites who run the EU intend to bring tax policy under the control of Brussels.

Charlie McCreevy, the Internal Market Commissioner, has warned the Commission repeatedly that they do not have the right to interfere in members' corporation tax rates. But he is just the Irish Commissioner, so nobody in Brussels much cares what he says. Despite his warnings, László Kovács, the European Tax Commissioner, has gone ahead and drawn up plans for consolidating the EU's corporate tax base, the first step towards forcing 'harmonisation' of the rate ('harmonising' only ever means one thing – raising the rate).

This week Mr Kovács launched his plans on consolidating the corporate tax base, but let it be known that he had been 'forced' to delete references to forming an EU-wide tax authority. Rubbish.

That is not the way it works. The EU deliberately goes too far with each step, just so it can be seen to 'compromise' and step back. Then, when the microphones are switched off and the journalists have left the press conference at Berlaymont, the elites go back to their desks and put every plan right back in place as it was before the 'compromise'.

That is the EU pattern. The most dangerous example of this refusal of the elites to take 'no' for an answer is their reaction to the defeat of the EU Constitution in the referendums in France and the Netherlands in 2005. The treaty was presented with the assurance that it must be agreed by all, or it would not be enacted. It was not agreed by all. But many of its provisions have already been enacted by the elite.

For example, the EU has set up an agency in Vienna to enforce the Charter of Fundamental Rights across the EU. But the power to set up such an agency was supposed to come only from the Constitution, if it were ratified.

The EU is going ahead with plans to establish a worldwide

diplomatic service and embassies, though the power to do that was to come only from the Constitution. The voters refused to ratify the Constitution, but the Eurocrat elites said, 'Who cares?' The leaders of the big European states also said, 'Who cares?' In these last months, the German chancellor, Angela Merkel, who holds the six-month presidency of the EU, has been manoeuvring in secret to advise the leaders of the member states how they can ratify a newly drafted version of the EU Constitution without having to put it to their voters in a referendum.

A letter from Mrs Merkel to certain EU heads of government has leaked out. In it, Mrs Merkel outlines her plan to bring back the Constitution under a new name, the point being, she wrote, 'to use different terminology without changing the legal substance'. She intends that the EU summit next month will come up with a constitutional text that can be disguised by 'presentational changes' as just a technocratic adjustment. Then it can be ratified by national parliaments without voters having a say in it.

Of course, by law the voters here must have a say in it. But an Irish referendum never worries the Euro-elites. They know the Irish will do as Brussels tells them, no matter what damage the Constitution – or the euro, or any other scheme to force 'an ever closer union' on once-sovereign states – will do. And there has been plenty of damage done already, and more to come. Just ask the Spanish.

5 May 2007

THE SUMMER OF THE BLACK FLAGS

Paul Drury

They were everywhere that summer. Black flags.

They hung from the lamp posts on inner-city streets and from telegraph poles on remote country roads. Not just north of the border but south of it too.

In hindsight, that omnipresence was, for those of us living in the south, the most remarkable thing about the hot, sticky summer of 1981 – and the sea change that it wrought in the collective conscience.

Years later, indeed, you could still turn a corner and come across a now tattered and faded black drape fluttering limply in the wind – mute reminder of an extraordinary chapter in our nation's history that most of us would have preferred to remain firmly closed.

And, if we are honest with ourselves, for more than a quarter of a century our wish has been granted.

Just like post-war Germany wiped its collective memory clean of the Holocaust and Austria of its support for the Anschluss, so we in the South chose to pretend that the hunger strikes never really happened.

There have been other films, other TV biopics, there have been countless books and maudlin ballads, Bobby Sands' iconic image still decorates scores of gable-ends in Belfast and Derry, streets have been named after him in European cities and as far away as Tehran.

But a visitor from Mars, landing in Foxrock, County Dublin, or Foxford, County Mayo, in the 1980s, 1990s and certainly in this decade, could have spent months on end without hearing or seeing Sands' name mentioned. Until, that is, this year – and Steve McQueen's award-winning movie, *Hunger*.

Maybe it is a sign of some new-found national maturity; maybe it is an unspoken acknowledgement that we have finally put armed conflict behind us. Who knows? What I do know is that, for me at least, these past few weeks have been an extraordinarily cathartic experience.

Quite frankly, I hadn't thought to any meaningful extent about the hunger strike and all that went with it in twenty-seven years. Then, all of a sudden, it all came flooding back – the black flags, the graffiti, the tension in the air that you could almost cut with a knife, the bitter arguments, the friendships shattered and never really repaired.

You see, 1981 was different – different to anything that went before and different to anything that came afterwards. I know because I was part of it – not in the North, where at least the issues were clear-cut, but working as a journalist here in the South, where the really painful soul-searching went on.

It is a shameful but inescapable reality that throughout the first decade of the Troubles – and, indeed, for most of the two decades that were to follow – we southerners cared very little about what was happening in the North.

Not since 1969, when refugees streamed south and Jack Lynch told the Dáil 'we shall not stand idly by' had most of us felt in any way emotionally involved in the bloody conflict taking place less than 100 miles away from our own homes.

There had been one or two atrocities, such as Bloody Sunday, that were so horrendous they simply could not be ignored. But as soon as we decently could, all but the most hardline republicans wiped their mental slates clean and got on with their own lives.

Belfast might be just ninety miles from Dublin, but for us it was another world; a nasty little world which, quite frankly, we didn't want to know about. We were, if truth be known, quite willing to stand idly by and let them kill one another.

Occasionally, and despite our own best efforts, the conflict forced itself into our cosy little lives – like when loyalist paramilitaries bombed Dublin and Monaghan in 1974, killing thirty-three people.

But even then, as soon as we decently could, the vast majority of us pulled the shutters down again and tried to pretend it had never happened. We had, after all, enough problems of our own to worry about, we reasoned.

In the summer of 1981, however, that option was snatched away from even the most self-centred of us. We had no choice. This was something we could not ignore.

There is an inevitable predictability about a hunger strike. A reasonably healthy person can last about thirty days without food and not suffer any long-term damage. After something between sixty and seventy days, however, a point of no return is reached.

The hunger striker becomes virtually blind and deaf and, after a period of tremendous pain, eventually lapses into a coma. Death quickly follows. As we watched and waited, we all knew as much.

It was not just the ten young men in the Maze who went through a long-drawn-out agony that summer. The entire Irish nation did – a painful process of polarisation and division which plumbed depths of bitterness that had not been experienced since the Civil War.

Our only reaction to the so-called 'dirty protest' which had been going on since 1976, in as much as we had any reaction, had been revulsion. Sympathy, for the vast majority of us, didn't come into it. After all, went the widely held belief, the IRA prisoners in the Maze were terrorists; they deserved whatever they got.

Those carefully contrived, Christ-like images of gaunt young men with long, bedraggled hair and unkempt beards in their stinking, excrement-smeared cells, wrapped only in their pitifully thin blankets, brought lumps to throats around the world; not, however, to ours.

But somehow the hunger strikes were different – especially the second one, when it became obvious that these young men really were prepared to starve themselves to death.

To a substantial majority of us, they and their cause remained fundamentally wrong. There was even a sneaking, although rarely publicly expressed, admiration for Maggie Thatcher for standing up to them. However awful their plight, it was hard to forget that between 1976 and 1981, the Provisional IRA had killed 472 innocent people.

But, as the days dragged on and their condition worsened, the hunger strikers gradually got under our collective skins – in a way nobody in the North had ever done before or since.

To some they were heroes, to others they were murderous hypocrites, to yet more the naive dupes for cynical Sinn Féin puppet masters. But as their lives ticked away like a metronome, the entire nation found itself emotionally involved.

The hunger strike is a form of protest that we in this country have made very much our own; from Terence McSwiney and Tomás Ashe to Michael Gaughan and Frank Stagg, it has sparked a visceral reaction in the Irish psyche unlike anything else. As McSwiney himself said, 'It is not to those who can inflict most, but to those who can endure most is the victory certain.'

And while we might not like these young men or what they stood for – Bobby Sands, for example, was serving fourteen years for bomb and weapons offences – and might not believe that their demands were justified, nobody could dispute their sincerity.

Whether they had been legitimately locked up for their part in a criminal conspiracy as I for one believed, or were, as they themselves saw it, prisoners of war, was irrelevant. Nobody had forced them to go on hunger strike; they had volunteered to starve themselves to death.

Whether they all believed from the outset that they would die remains unclear. Sands certainly did. But, somehow, it was hard not to admire them. Thousands of course did more than that, their emotions cynically whipped up by a Sinn Féin leadership that realised this was a weapon infinitely more valuable than any amount of Semtex or AK47s.

On his deathbed, 30,492 people in Fermanagh–South Tyrone made Bobby Sands their MP. More than 100,000 turned out for his funeral – the biggest this island had seen since Michael Collins's.

In the North itself, attitudes hardened rapidly – and predictably. Catholics, even those who had hated what the IRA had done for years, allied themselves with the hunger strikers. Protestants, even those who had found mainstream unionism distasteful in recent times, rallied behind Mrs Thatcher.

In the South, you were expected to take sides too. It was not an easy choice. Many of us, even those with a certain sympathy to the republican cause, felt that the hunger strikes were, to use an unfortunate image, being rammed down our throats and used to seek a wider endorsement for the 'armed struggle'.

Not surprisingly, support for the hunger strikers was most vocal in the border counties, in those parts of rural Ireland that had taken the anti-Treaty side in the Civil War – and, rather more intriguingly, in those poorer urban areas where Sinn Féin had quietly begun to build an electoral platform.

The middle and professional classes, for the most part, remained firmly behind Mrs Thatcher – even if they attempted to temper their feelings with moral scruples. But everybody had an opinion, whether they chose to voice it or not.

That was the real dilemma: It was next to impossible to find a middle ground. Families split down the middle, friendships foundered. I myself started that summer editing an Irish-language weekly newspaper in the West of Ireland; I ended it working for the *Irish Independent*.

I remember being called in by my boss at the weekly paper – the only occasion in two years on which this happened – and being asked why I had not taken an 'editorial line' on the hunger strikes. I replied, hypocritically, that it was because we were a local paper and this was not a local issue. In reality, he was sympathetic to the hunger strikers' cause and I was not. He knew that and I knew that, although neither of us said as much; our relationship never fully recovered.

Later, when I moved to the *Independent* – the national newspaper that had most trenchantly rejected calls for political recognition – I entered an institution still under siege, even though the actual hunger strikes had by now ended.

Bomb scares were, however, still routine; the paper's doughty editor, Vinnie Doyle, routinely received parcels of human excrement through his letter box at home, and staff members with known republican sympathies were treated with deepest suspicion.

There were, of course, other issues exercising our minds in 1981. It was just over eighteen months since Charles Haughey had replaced Jack Lynch as Taoiseach – and revealed that the economy was going down the toilet. Mr Haughey, who had already revealed his own unique ability to divide the Irish nation, had called a general election just as the hunger strikes erupted onto the public conscience.

Still hoping to do a political deal with Mrs Thatcher on the North, he was terrified to take an unequivocal stand. Liz O'Hara, the sister of hunger striker Patsy O'Hara, who met Haughey four times during that summer, asked him directly on one occasion if he believed the prisoners' five demands were justified. Mr Haughey replied that he wasn't 'willing to answer that question just then'.

The electorate, however, was. In the June general election, nine prisoner candidates polled 40,000 first-preference votes between them (15pc of the total vote) and two were elected. They cost Mr Haughey the election.

And, like it or not, the irreversible process by which Sinn Féin was transformed from a despised appendage to the IRA into the self-assured and influential political force that it is today, on both sides of the border, had begun.

Above all, however, we in the South had been forced, for once, to look into our own hearts and ask ourselves where we really stood on the Northern question.

Most of us, I suspect, did not particularly like what we saw there or what that answer was; and that is why we have tried so assiduously, until now, to forget.

31 May 2008

WHY NUALA WAS ALWAYS SOMEBODY

Dermot Bolger

Nuala O'Faolain was always somebody. Long before *Are You Somebody?* – her searing, honest mid-life memoir of love, loss and self-discovery – brought her international fame, she had already won scholarships to Trinity and Oxford, lectured in UCD, was a guest lecturer in universities like Indiana, reviewed for the London *Times*, was an innovative BBC television producer, was a confident, articulate and sometimes scalding commentator on political and literary affairs and wrote an outstanding *Irish Times* opinion column.

As an RTÉ producer she had won a Jacob's Award for a deeply affecting and deceptively simple series, *Plain Tales*, which allowed older Irish women to tell their own life stories in their own words and in their own way. This was an example of her gift to be on the one hand a brilliant academic and intellectual and yet on the other hand to be a person with whom ordinary women felt comfortable about opening up their hearts and their lives.

Her columns also possessed this duality to combine complex issues with a deeply human touch. Most weekly columns are like newspapers themselves, read and quickly forgotten. However, vivid images always remained with you from Nuala's column, tiny vignettes of life that made you realise that here was a writer with a special way of observing life.

I recall one description of an elderly woman queuing in a

Dublin butcher's to ask for one rasher for her dinner. Nuala described the tenderness with which the butcher selected and wrapped the single rasher as if it was the most expensive joint in his shop. While I recall nothing of the 'real' news of that day, I have never forgotten how Nuala conjured the dignity of the impoverished woman and the grace of the butcher.

Her column on adults learning to read late in life is actually entitled 'On Human Dignity'. Her column on the collected speeches of Charles J. Haughey, meanwhile, wryly remarks on how when he first began to serve the State – as a 15-year-old member of the Local Defence Force – he gained a worm's eye view of Ireland by crawling through wet fields, but now he mainly views the nation by helicopter.

When Paul McGrath was once asked how he felt about how Irish people identify with him and hold him in such esteem, he replied – with honest bewilderment – that he didn't really understand it and it slightly scared him. Similarly, it took Nuala a while to understand the extraordinary reaction of so many people to her memoir, *Are You Somebody?*.

In fact it took Nuala a while to even begin to call *Are You Somebody?* a memoir. The original volume had been planned by New Island simply as a compilation of her columns, and her memoir, which would bring international fame – and which caused her to receive over five thousand letters from across the world – started out as merely an introduction to the columns, on the premise that people might like to know something about the person who wrote them.

For somebody who was highly intelligent and articulate and yet also suffered from insecurity about the merit of everything that she wrote, this was actually a very clever ploy, a way to tell her life story almost by default. An autobiography sounds too grandiose, makes too many claims about its own importance. However slipping something out in the guise of an introduction to something else allowed a great deal of freedom for her to set down her story on her own terms.

From the start it was obvious that what she had written was incredibly courageous, remarkable and affecting. Yet when I first read it in manuscript form in the attic of her astute editor, Anthony Glavin, Nuala was still refusing to believe that readers would really be interested in this account of her life. Not only was she wrong, but nobody could ever have predicted how gloriously wrong she was.

Her memoir – raw and unflinching in its self-examination, unsparing in her description of loneliness, remarkable in its depiction of joy, utterly true in describing sexuality and the messy business of love, shot through with anger and compassion – touched people in ways that she could have never imagined.

In Ireland it proved impossible to keep the book in print after an astonishing *Late Late Show* appearance where Gay Byrne opened proceedings by remarking that she had slept with an awful lot of men, to which Nuala responded that only three of them had mattered, 'which is modest for a woman of my age'.

Soon some bookshops were not even bothering to stack the book by the shelves, but simply handing it to a scrum of customers from cardboard boxes as they were ripped open.

But if a curiosity to see the private person behind the public face might explain some of the initial Irish sales, there was no *Late Late Show* appearance in America or Australia or France or any other countries, where readers knew nothing about her previous careers or about her parents. In those countries all that mattered were the power of her words, their unrelenting honesty and her humanity which reached across all national boundaries.

For readers in both Ireland and abroad it was as if, by writing with such honestly about herself and about her parents, Nuala had given them permission to realise that their stories and lives had validation and were worthy of being written about, even if only by posting letters to this unassuming author.

The publication of *Are You Somebody?* was not without controversy. Under the name Terry O'Sullivan, Nuala's father had been Ireland's first social columnist, an impeccably dressed and glamorous man whose public life consisted of being chauffeured between receptions.

For some older people it seemed disloyal of a daughter to show the private chaos and irresponsibility behind that facade. But Nuala was claiming back her life for herself. She might be someone's daughter, but first and foremost she was herself.

This was her way of showing that we all own our own story and have the right to tell it as we remember it. Among those inspired by the book to tell their own stories was Nuala's younger sister Deirdre Brady, who wrote a very affecting memoir, *Thank You for the Days*, that is a wonderful record of her life.

One book that gave Nuala particular satisfaction was her debut novel, *My Dream of You*, published in 2001. If she could protest that she had become a memoirist almost by accident, then there is nothing accidental in a novel.

It was her long cherished dream to be a fiction writer and now in America she set about proving it. Her world had been transformed by that memoir. She had financial security at last and could divide her time between Ireland and New York. But previous success counts for nothing in the daily struggle by a novelist to fill each fresh page, where you need to overcome self-doubt and fear of failure. Many people dream of writing novels, but few succeed. Nuala succeeded wonderfully, seeing *My Dream of You* become a bestseller in German as well as English.

She went on to publish two more books, including a second volume of memoirs, *Almost There*, which charted the extraordinary changes in her life since she was catapulted to fame in middle-age. But it was a book that was equally honest about loneliness, about seeking a purpose and it was in no way self-congratulatory.

There are certain writers whose greatness is indisputable, but who speak to us and not for us. Then there are others like Nuala, uncertain, raw, edgy, painfully honest and utterly observant. These are the writers who touch people, writers whom people identify with and cherish.

People loved her brilliance, but they loved her flaws as well, her rashness in youth, her desire for love above all, the way that she rebuilt her life after disappointment, her anger at injustice, her love for her family and friends.

Even if Nuala O'Faolain had never written that introduction which became that book and had never become known to an international audience, her passing would still be marked in Ireland as that of a national figure who touched many lives. But her books mean that this sense of loss will be felt by readers across the world. Nuala O'Faolain touched so many lives. She laid bare her past, laid bare her loneliness and also her huge propensity for love, laid bare her utter humanity.

Thousands of people in thousands of different rooms opened her books and felt that in some way they were reading about themselves, that she was saying things which they had thought in their hearts but never articulated, that she was somebody and they were somebody too, with desires and regrets worthy of being addressed.

Few books change lives. Her books changed her life and changed the lives of others. It allowed people to examine their pasts and say that certain things were wrong. It allowed people to consider their present state and stake a mental claim to who they truly were.

If her memoirs showed people an honest way to live, then her remarkable interview with Marian Finucane showed them an honest way to face death.

There was no bravado in that interview, just a sense that, having given people a sense of permission to speak about their lives, she was also showing that you could speak about your death, that it did not have to be invisible and the dying do not have to hide themselves away.

A collective amnesia often exists in society and within families about uncomfortable truths. Once it was sex that was hidden away, back when Nuala O'Faolain was a young woman in a society fearful of sexuality. Now the great taboo is dying. In choosing to speak with clarity and candour, Nuala gave voice to a hidden world.

She spoke of her pain and then she made the most of every day that remained in those last weeks of her life when she travelled with family and friends. She was surrounded by people who loved her and who she loved. She will be mourned by more people than she could ever possibly imagine.

I last saw Nuala at the Ennis Bookclub Festival two months ago. She knew that she was dying but nobody else in the room did. As ever when addressing an audience, she was magical, casting a spell as she talked. She had to use a stick and had difficulty mounting the podium, but when we stopped to chat for a moment her smile was radiant.

This is how I will remember last seeing her. But the image that I will always retain of her comes in a story told to me by the New York-based novelist Colum McCann.

Some time ago he was showing a visiting Irish writer Brooklyn Bridge one Sunday morning when they were both almost knocked down by a lady on an old-fashioned black bone-shaker bicycle who looked like she had just pedalled out of an Irish village in the 1960s. They gripped the handlebars and laughed because it was Nuala: three friends meeting on Brooklyn Bridge like it was the bridge below some small Irish town.

I love the sense of collision that day between Nuala's America and her Ireland, how she cherished her past friends, yet was thoroughly immersed in the adventure of the present. And I can almost hear the warmth of her laugh, a warmth that made you feel special and made you walk away knowing that you had just encountered somebody who truly always was and always will be somebody.

17 May 2008

THE MOLLYCODDLED GENERATION

Mark Dooley

Soon all the anxiety shall subside as the long period of preparation for the Leaving Certificate will draw to a close. Next Wednesday, thousands of young adults will make their way to examination halls all across the country in pursuit of their dreams.

And there in the midst of them all will be our future politicians, judges, sport stars and scientists. Yes, the future of our little country will one day rest in the hands of those who are this morning furiously cramming for the most significant event of their lives.

Even now, when our universities have become an extension of secondary school, the Leaving Cert still casts a spell across Irish society. Even now, it is still regarded as a kind of national rite of initiation for those embarking on adulthood.

Like Baptism, First Communion and Confirmation, the Leaving Cert is considered a seminal event in a teenager's passage to maturity. It is, as it were, a secular version of those sacred events in which a young person becomes a fully fledged member of the community.

Of course, like every other stage of human development, the Leaving Cert is soon forgotten after the fact. But for those going through it, as well as for their parents, it is nothing short of a spiritual process in which the passions of tender youth are momentarily stilled and the burdens of reality weigh heavy. It represents a public purification of the adolescent as the fantasies of childhood are finally banished in favour of reason and responsibility.

I say 'public purification' because the whole event is played out before the steely gaze of television cameras and radio microphones. Every day, we hear 'experts' inform the students what they must eat, drink and study in order to succeed. And then, every night, we have the ritual TV confessions of those emerging from the examination centres, their tender faces scarred from stress and fatigue.

In no other country are final-year examinations subject to such unrelenting media scrutiny. But here things are different. Here, we pile on the pressure by placing our Leaving Certificate students beneath a powerful spotlight in which all their fears and frustrations are fully exposed.

Still, it would be silly to suggest that the media is the primary cause of their severe stress and strain. So why is it that, although the Leaving Cert has always figured prominently at the heart of Irish society, the pressure on students sitting the exam seems to be increasing? And what, in turn, does this tell us about the current state of our educational system? There is a strange paradox at the heart of Irish education. We want our students to compete with the best worldwide and yet, thanks to the egalitarian dogma that now infects the school curriculum, we believe that competition is morally corrupting. Consequently our schools, which were formerly centres of excellence, are now centres of child-centred mollycoddling.

This means that the time-honoured process of streaming students on the basis of intelligence and merit has been roundly rejected. What you have instead is a bizarre system where all students, irrespective of ability or lack thereof, are treated equally.

There is thus no attempt to distinguish the best from the rest for fear of discrimination or of calling down the wrath of aggrieved parents.

And so, in the place of a culture of competition, there now stands the ideology of 'all must have prizes', one in which failure is described as 'deferred success'.

Of course, it is obvious to most people that the purpose of education should not be social engineering. Its real purpose is to teach children the virtue of hard work, to show them that there are no free lunches and that success comes at a price. Most importantly, however, it bears witness to the fact that all are not equal.

Exams, by their very essence, are competitive exercises, the ultimate aim of which is to reveal distinctions between students on the basis of natural ability. But in this egalitarian age, such distinctions are considered the by-product of an outdated elitist system of education. The result is that by the time they reach Leaving Cert, students have no real idea of their abilities. The best, having been held back to accommodate the rest, don't excel at the rate they should, while the rest mistakenly believe they are equal to the best.

Things were quite different for people of my generation. By the time we reached Leaving Cert level, we had already discovered what we wanted to do and what it would take to do it. And that was simply because we had distinguished ourselves by virtue of the examination process. Streaming of students was just a fact of life that was accepted as the norm, and was certainly never regarded as a cruel system of discrimination by those of us subject to it.

Thanks, moreover, to an exacting curriculum that took no prisoners, we knew that the pursuit of knowledge was not something that could be dumbed down or made easy. If anything, it was something that had to be fought for and would only reward those who were prepared to weather the storm.

Yes, it is true that such a system rewarded the best. But in so doing, it did not discriminate against the rest. Its principal purpose was to enable students to find their niche in life, thereby resting easy with existence. Some, like me, chose the academic life, while others opted for a trade. Did I look down upon the latter? Not in the least, for I knew that they possessed vital skills that I could never master.

That is why, for us, the Leaving Cert was really no big deal. Yes, of course we knew it represented an important rite of passage. But because we also knew what we wanted from it, we entered the examination hall ready for the challenge.

We knew, in short, that some of us would emerge as plumbers and plasterers, others as professors and professionals. But that did not worry us, for we recognised that there is dignity and worth in every profession.

Nowadays, things are very different. The culture of child-centred mollycoddling has robbed students of their right to discover where their natural talents lie. Hence, the Leaving Certificate is considered by all and sundry as a passport to college. Forget the fact that there are many who simply won't be able for it. Forget also that there are many who will doss their way through university and still have no idea what they want to do by the end of it. What matters in the current climate is that every student progress to third level as a matter of course.

Now you can understand why Leaving Cert students look so troubled before the cameras on the nightly news. For it has suddenly dawned on them that, even after fourteen years of schooling, they still don't know what to do with their lives. And so they have no alternative but to endlessly defer that decision and stay in education.

What is worse, the universities have colluded in the experiment. Instead of raising the bar and forcing the schools to maintain educational standards, they have decided to follow suit by lowering their own standards. The result is what my late and great colleague Professor John Cleary called 'the numbers game', by which he meant the practice of abandoning rigorous university entry requirements in favour of an open-door policy.

The consequences of this have been nothing short of catastrophic. Many students enter university unable to write an essay. Many cannot follow a simple argument, while others can barely keep up with their basic reading assignments.

After a short while a good percentage of them drop out in total despair, while others suffer on and barely scrape by. And all for what? Is it not obvious that the current system, by proclaiming that all must have prizes, is damaging the long-term welfare of Irish students? Is it not obvious that some people are just not candidates for college, and that they would be better off pursuing a trade or some other career that doesn't demand a degree? And wouldn't that be a far better recipe for future success and happiness than steering them into a life for which they are ill-equipped and ill-suited?

Success comes in many forms and is by no means specific to the academic sphere. The Leaving Certificate used to reflect that fact. It pointed people in a direction best suited to their talents, and taught them that wisdom is not something confined to universities. In so doing, it showed that differences in ability are nothing to be ashamed of, but are the lifeblood of real existence.

Like most serious educationalists, I long for the day when the Leaving Cert will once again testify to those basic truths. In the meantime, let no one doubt the importance of the coming week in the lives of so many Irish students.

Sad, therefore, that many of them will one day glance back and judge the event as a meaningless exercise.

30 May 2009

PROTECTING THE VULNERABLE

Ger Philpott

I try to keep things real with my mother. At times this is difficult. She lives in a nursing home. She is fundamentally unhappy with her lot. Deeply religious, she prays daily that God will take her. But her God doesn't listen. She is doubly incontinent and wheelchair bound. In receipt of the best medical care and attention, she has no will to live.

I cannot say I blame her. My father is unhappy that he can no longer care for her at home. His love for her is undiminished.

And Mum frequently expresses her desire to be at home to care for him. Dad suffered a stroke over a year ago. He lost peripheral vision, some mobility and much independence. They are both on serious amounts of medication. Dad's daily mantra as he pops his pills is: 'This is a terrible way to live.' Mum has no quality of life.

On my weekly visits, I chat to Mum about everything and anything. I make a point of holding her hand, brushing her hair. I believe touch, human contact, is important for her, to ease her isolation and loneliness.

It makes me feel better. Sometimes, she looks into my eyes and I feel she can read my mind. Then she squeezes my hand, as if, I feel, to reassure me. I tell her about my garden, what's growing in my raised vegetable beds. Stuff that goes on at work. What's in the news. And what's happening with my friends.

My banter generally tends to pull her out of herself. She engages with it. Briefly. The effort tires her. She drifts off in catnaps. I often wonder what happened to my mother as I watch her doze. The person I grew up knowing seems far away in these moments. Yet her concern for my being tired on the drive back to Dublin is evidence of her enduring generosity. And kindness. We only get glimpses of this former self intermittently these days. Where is the vibrant woman who raised us?

We had a party for Mum's eighty-fifth birthday last month. We decorated the nursing home's conservatory. Her granddaughters prepared the food. It was a lovely day. And the warmth of Mum's smile, holding her youngest great-grandchild in her lap, in her wheelchair, struck a chord with all of us. When was the last time we saw her smile like that? It was the highlight of our day.

I spent several hours with Mum in advance of the party. And noticed the procession of residents heading for the restaurant. Lunch is served from 12.30 p.m.

From noon onwards, they made their way down corridors on Zimmer frames. Women first, then the men; self-propelling their wheelchairs, many using their feet to do so. Not their hands. And I debated with myself – were these the lucky ones? They have a routine. Despite being aged, infirm and vulnerable, there is still dignity to their lives. I thought of them when I watched this week's *Prime Time* special on Alzheimer's.

It was clear in that programme the depth of love and respect the carers had for their ill relatives. The extent of their isolation and frustration was palpable. Their plight was shocking.

The programme revealed a hidden Ireland. A deeply dissatisfying one. But there is a tendency to believe that once a problem is highlighted on TV, it is solved. Make no mistake about it. The reality we saw last Monday continues today. It will continue tomorrow. It is ongoing.

While our sense of outrage dissipates, nothing changes for the valiant people we saw on TV. And there is also a psychological dip experienced when one reveals personal stories in this way.

None of the programme's participants would have known this in advance. I imagine they do now. Their appearances on the programme were born out of their need for help, not to feel they are alone.

A friend involved in child protection told me she was in court the day the application for funding to send Daniel McAnaspie to Sweden was rejected. In Sweden, Daniel would have had the opportunity to get his life back on track. The State argued it didn't have the resources required to fund this exercise. My friend spoke of her frustration; wondering yet again why an obvious solution to a difficult situation was side-stepped. And what the real cost would be of the alleged financial saving in this context. She thought of that court decision the day she heard that Daniel's partially clothed body was found in a ditch in Rathfeigh, County Meath.

It would be interesting to compare the amount of money the Health Services Executive pays to protect its interests and that which it spends on the provision of care for the vulnerable in our society. I suspect the result of this exercise too would be shocking. What value does a human life have? When the State and its agencies are in clear dereliction of duty, it is all the more alarming when the courts equally seem to ignore the situation. The argument is that, due to the separation of powers, the courts will not meddle in State affairs.

If this is extraordinary, how bizarre is it that the government minister with responsibility for children has the power to develop policy but no control over its implementation?

More legislation is required to gain access to the information held by the HSE that can help us understand why at-risk children like Daniel McAnaspie can die while in State care. Some reports estimate that hundreds of children have died in State care in the past decade. Who will be held responsible for these atrocities?

I recently came across an alarming story. It is about a young child. He lives in a deprived Dublin suburb. His parents are chaotic drug-users. The child, now aged three, has no social skills. His communication skills are minimal. And the only food that passes his lips is from a jar.

The voluntary agency providing support to this child has had its funding slashed so family services are curtailed. If this was not bad enough, the child will soon be of school-going age. Funding has also been cut for special-needs teachers and special-needs assistants. What does the future hold for this child? He is already a statistic in the making. He is doomed for failure. Through no fault of his own, he has been dumped on the scrap heap of life. His is not a solitary story. His grandparents do the best they can for him. What are the prospects for this at-risk child should he end up in State care?

Ten years ago, I made the *Lowest Common Denominator* radio documentary about a northside primary school in Dublin. Located in the inner city, the area has a history of institutional deprivation and poverty. It was ravaged by unemployment. Then alcohol. And then drugs. And Aids. Manifestations of these problems still persist. Now they are exacerbated by crime, gang feuds and shootings.

In the documentary, the school principal and teachers spoke lovingly of the children. They explained how getting through the school gates each morning, even if late, was educational achievement for these children. Often some of them only came to school for respite from the horrors at home.

They also explained that within a relatively short period after finishing school, a certain cohort of the past pupils would become guests of the State. The costs of their incarceration, at the time, was in excess of €90,000 per person, per year. At that time, the average spend per annum on each child in the school – including teachers' salaries – ran at €5,500 per head. It does not take rocket science to work out the folly involved here. Does anyone do the math?

This week's bookend news stories of neglected youth, forgotten, ill elderly people and their carers in Ireland make it crystal clear that, right across the life cycle, government here turns a blind eye to society's most vulnerable people.

This is a sad indictment of our republic. Without joined-up thinking and connecting social policy with its implementation, those on the margins are cast further and further adrift.

How many tragic stories does it take to stem the flow of human carnage and indignity? There is little to recommend old age in Ireland. This is not how it should be. It is how it is. The efforts of advocates of the elderly are merely a testament to the 'otherness' of old age in official eyes.

I feel guilty about my mother's plight. Her predicament. While my overriding sentiment is of contentment and satisfaction when I drive back home to Dublin after visits, it's only part of the picture. The dutiful son has made an effort. As have my four siblings. While she is never far from my thoughts, it's easy for me, because I can get on with my life. Thankfully Mum has full-time care.

But the essence of my dilemma is that it's not easy to accept when the minder role flips.

I don't have an innings on Mum's internal life. I catch glimpses of it. In the final chapter, I sense her overriding sentiment is one of discontent and dissatisfaction. But I hope any inner turmoil is not too overbearing for her. Mum spent her life caring for us, then for her grandchildren. And now it is clear she still derives much pleasure from her great-grandchildren. I hope that she can draw sustenance from the love we surround her with. It may not be possible for the 3-year-old I spoke of earlier to do this. The odds are stacked against him.

Family is paramount. This was abundantly obvious on *Prime*

Time's Alzheimer's programme. In a small way I have a sense of the sheer helplessness those families experience. I am in awe of their forbearance. And I hope sharing their stories with us leads to ongoing support and recognition of their dilemma.

I sat with my Mum last Tuesday evening. I was struck by her level of interest in the photographs of her party.

Initially, she did not remember that she had a party. Or that I was there. Remembering how her smile had touched us, given us a glimpse of her former normality, I reminded her about placing her youngest great-grandson in her lap.

'He is a beautiful baby,' she said enthusiastically, her memory again crisp, sharply in focus. It was then I saw the packet of photos on her dresser. We spent a long time looking at them. Mum gazed at them, lingering over each image. I watched her closely, observing her journey, trying to read her mind. She was silent but I could see she was engaged.

The picture of her great-grandson on her lap roused her to speech. 'Isn't he lovely?' she said. 'Look at his rosy cheeks. I could do with some of that colour.' I laughed. She smiled. For a moment, she was back.

29 May 2010

JUNE

JOY OF EMIGRATION

Dave Hannigan

Eighteen summers have passed since I fetched up outside The Crown, a landmark pub in Cricklewood, and learned something about working for a living. One of those venues where the Irish traditionally went in search of casual labouring jobs in London, it was sometime after 6 a.m. when I took my place alongside dozens of my compatriots, hoping a subcontractor would give us the nod and end our waiting misery. And miserable enough it was too.

Even for a 19-year-old college student, just trying to make cash during the holidays, there was a terribly degrading air to this ritual. That much was etched in the leathery faces of the older Irish men in our midst, the lifers, with their salt-and-pepper beards and their eyes barely opened far enough to see in front of them. They weren't bushy-tailed either. They were beat-down, tired and humiliated from having to subject themselves to this daily routine.

For them, it wasn't a seasonal diversion from textbooks and tutorials. It was a way of life. They knew too well what it was like to be standing in that spot on a winter's morning when jobs were scarce and pickings were slim.

Even though I was aware that in another few weeks I'd be safely back on the UCC campus, dining out on tall tales about how hard I'd slogged, the memory of their hangdog expressions stayed with me long after that day.

Anybody who ever served time as an economic exile in England, Australia or America will have shuddered a little at the return of emigration to the national conversation this past week. The prospect of revisiting the days when Irish families waved off so many sons and daughters will fill many with dread. Whether talking about the diaspora of the 1850s or the 1980s, nobody ever remembers those goodbyes with any fondness.

Here's a revolutionary thought, though. A little taste of emigration might do some people the world of good.

There's an entire generation of Irish teenagers apparently consumed by MTV's *Sweet Sixteen* culture who might benefit from a few months waiting tables in Montauk or working the sites in London. It would teach the designer-label slaves lessons in humility which are unavailable on any modern campus and increasingly difficult to source in some Irish homes. They would also experience their own nationality in a way they will never be able to tap into on Grafton Street.

Me, I have carried a hod in Kensington, flogged timber from a yard in leafy Surrey, sold fashionably distressed 501s to Parisian women in a Rue de Rivoli boutique, and served Long Island iced teas to the super-rich stockbrokers of Greenwich, Connecticut.

Every single one of those gigs had its ups and downs but ultimately contributed to my growth, helped me figure out a career path, and made me appreciate my home place that little bit more.

I have friends who worked the tulip farms of Holland, the digging of the Channel Tunnel and, my own personal favourite, one of those insane crab-fishing expeditions that operate out of Alaska. They are all back in Ireland years now, yet every one of them will vouchsafe that those experiences stood to them, not only in short-term financial gains but in long-term character development.

Nothing fuels the desire to switch jobs or to gain more education better than the muscle memory of hard, physical labour.

Nothing makes you accept Mother Ireland, warts and all, more than an extended sojourn away from her. It's probably not a coincidence that the Celtic Tiger was driven by a generation most of whom had cut at least some of their working teeth in England, Europe, America and Australia.

They came from a time when the end of the Leaving Cert exams wasn't marked by a celebratory drunken fortnight in the Canaries with classmates, but a long, sobering bus and boat ride to London where the phrase 'Any chance of a start?' soon became lodged in their frontal lobes.

They got drunk and partied too. The only difference is they paid for it out of their own pockets and learned the true value of money along the way. That lesson stayed with them all their working lives, so when they were given a chance to do something in Ireland, they grasped it with both hands.

Factor in the additional knowledge gained about oneself from being truly isolated from home, the inevitable broadening of the mind, and suddenly there's a legitimate case to be made that a stint toiling abroad never hurt anybody.

If saying that is to be awfully glib about the Irish men and women who fell through the cracks of other societies and became stranded, those unfortunates are far outnumbered by those who blossomed once they left Ireland and never wanted to come back. Not to mention many of the more successful emigrants who needed to leave in order to find their way to the top, benefitting from the increased opportunity and more meritocratic circumstances of other countries.

Of course, all this is the inevitably biased opinion of somebody who swapped Dún Laoghaire for Long Island, New York in the summer of 2000. Unlike my previous foreign affairs, this was a more permanent move, motivated less by economics and more by my American wife wanting to be nearer her family.

When you choose to emigrate, it's much easier than when you

have to. There is longing still but none of the heartfelt pining that has spawned so many beautiful Irish ballads over the past century and a half.

Many of those songs now coexist handily in my iPod, byte-sized proof of the old adage that the moment you leave Ireland you awaken a previously dormant interest in the country's traditional music catalogue.

There are other strange side effects of the condition too. Once my son Abe turned 4 years old, I started teaching him basic Irish phrases to mangle in that accent which only ever sounds truly American to me when we are holidaying in Cork. Despite being one of those ignoramuses who denounced my native tongue after the Leaving Cert, I decided nothing would get my boy in touch with his roots better than learning how to say *'Dia Dhuit'* and *'Conas atá tú?'* Never mind that I have to go online to check some of the spellings beforehand – this is just further proof that exile brings a heightened appreciation of stuff taken for granted back home.

Absence enhances the relationship with where you come from and when you go back, you go to places and you do things. You bring the kids to historic sites and teach them about the unique story of the country in a proactive way you probably wouldn't be bothered doing if you actually lived there.

Perhaps the most wonderful perk for every emigrant is being able to cherry-pick the bits of Ireland you really like. You can explain the colourful history of the first Dáil while ignoring the cloud of corruption currently hanging over Leinster House. You can shake your head when hearing horror stories about the health service, knowing full well you won't ever die on a trolley in a New York hospital corridor. You can live it up during a week in Dublin then spend the flight home wondering how anybody actually affords to live there. That the cheapest part about going back is the flights captures how emigration has also changed since Ireland boomed.

Technology has shrunk the planet so Nana can now see her new grandson nestling on his father's lap 3,000 miles away simply by sitting in front of a webcam. There's no waiting for monthly letters from home when emails and text messages zip hither and yon every hour. Phone calls that once cost pounds per minute are so cheap, a daily check on the parents barely registers on the bill.

I'm aware of how much easier the communications revolution has made this life because every Sunday morning I meet men who departed Ireland in the 1950s and never knew if they'd ever get to see the place again. Now, unbelievably for them, they have to put up with relatives from Mayo dropping in for intensive shopping weekends in Manhattan.

We sit together watching the hurling and Gaelic football matches live by satellite in an Ancient Order of Hibernians Hall, still as crucial and authentic a part of the expatriate experience as occasional cravings for Tayto crisps.

Sometimes when those games are over, in an attempt to keep the vicarious high going, I drag Abe to the park with a pair of hurleys and a tennis ball.

What begins as a gentle puck around goes one of two ways. Either he repairs to the climbing frame and leaves me trundling around the handball alley alone or he changes the rules. He'll get into the baseball batter's stance, request that I put down my hurley, and ask me to start pitching to him like a major-leaguer. And each time he does it, I am reminded that every emigrant always has to pay a certain price.

28 June 2008

FATHERHOOD

Joseph O'Connor

My father Sean was born in Francis Street, in Dublin's oldest neigh-bourhood. The Liffey flowed adjacently, by Wood Quay and the Four Courts, and an oaten aroma drifted up from the brewery – all Dubliners will remember that evocative smell – as the barges plied the river, bringing barrels of Guinness to the world beyond a child's imagination.

An inner-city boy, he loved animals, especially birds, and he roamed the alleys of the Liberties exploring. The grid through which he moved had its lighthouses of familiarity – Saint Nicholas of Myra church, Francis Street School – but the map of my father's childhood had other landmarks too: the libraries of Dublin's inner city.

An email he sent me recently details some of those wonderful places:

> The one most used by yours truly was Kevin Street Library, and it may be still there. It was right beside the site where the Tech still stands. There was another one in Thomas Street, around the corner from Francis Street and up a bit. If you were in pursuit of something special, your chase would take you to Capel Street Library and sometimes to Inchicore Library or Pearse Street Library.

They were all run by Dublin Corporation and I visited all of them often, usually in pursuit of something exotic like *The Cult of the Budgerigar* by an author called Watmough, as I recall. The libraries were very much used by children after school, and I can vouch for the rush by a herd of them on the desk whenever the big book of the day arrived. The system was that the children had to have a guarantor of the return of the books, which were only lent for a few weeks.

It worked great for me, with my Uncle Joe as the guarantor until a certain day when I left a book behind me in a shop. I had to face the wrath of Uncle Joe when he got a letter from the Corpo looking for the cost. But all for art, I say!

Francis Street, nowadays, has antique shops and restaurants. Immigrants have come to the area, bringing colour, new commitment. The Vicar Street music venue is nearby. But in the years of Sean's infancy it was a district of almost Dickensian poverty. There were hungry children, parents beyond coping, large families in one-room flats. In my father's class at the school, there were fifty-three boys, all taught by a teenaged arts student, Thomas Devane, a Christian Brother.

He was a young man who loved poetry, storytelling and books, and in my father he found a child who was open to that world. And so I think of Thomas Devane as among those who changed the course of my father's life – who offered him chances, possibilities.

Sean, a bright boy, had a gift for English essays. It was an ability encouraged by his sisters, beautiful looking girls, keen singers, enthusiastic readers. They bought paperbacks when they could be afforded and shared them among themselves.

Indeed, such avidly hungry readers were those gorgeous young Dubliners that when one of them would become impatient for her turn with the paperback, another would tear out a page and pass it across the kitchen table, so that often you had five or six siblings all reading the same book, each of them on a different chapter. An early example of the Readers' Group, perhaps, from the days before Richard and Judy.

There were poetry magazines in the house; music was thought important. In that world of little material wealth but decent human values, my father came of age: the sort of kid who enters contests, learns definitions, tells yarns, gets sometimes into scraps, learns loyalties and promises, believes the answer to almost anything can be found in a book and is sometimes as impatient as a wasp.

I see him in my own sons, in my brothers and sisters. And I see him, as have others, in myself. As I age, I glimpse him in mirrors, in shop window reflections. I hear his voice coming out of my mouth.

What might be learned from books – this was always his interest, as he left school at the age of 13 and worked to help support his family. It was an inquisitiveness he would share with the girl he would marry, who was always, like my father, a great reader.

After their marriage he studied at night, did exams, worked by day, learned mathematics and draughtsmanship and trigonometry and physics, in time qualifying as a structural engineer. He opened a little practice in Dublin and in time it grew. He continued to study and read. I remember books by John McGahern and Edna O'Brien being in the house, Lee Dunne, James Joyce, Brendan Behan, James Plunkett, Sinéad de Valera, Frank O'Connor. Those paperbacks seemed to murmur to young imagination: 'Remember us. Give us a chance. Open us.'

Churches, schools, office blocks, libraries – they formed themselves on the drawing board he kept in a spare bedroom. Often, when I went to bed, he would be working at that board, in shirtsleeves, his tie flung over his shoulder. ('You can always tell an engineer,' he used to joke with us, 'from the soup-stains on the end of his tie.') And often in the mornings, as I got ready for school, he would be there again – his eyes raw with tiredness – so that it seemed to me, as it may have seemed to him, as though he had stood there working all night.

He sang as he shaved; little nonsenses or bits of arias. At night he would read to me before I slept.

He loved the Victorian writers, the old poets like Lord Tennyson, to whom he had been introduced by Brother Thomas Devane, in Francis Street School in the Liberties. And I can never read any poem without hearing my father's beautiful Dublin voice. Calming as a hearth on a rainy night, it was a voice that revealed whole worlds.

It was how I had learned to read, or certainly why I wanted to; his finger tracing capitals on the yellowed old pages of books that seemed to breathe wonder into life.

That I wanted to be a writer one day, I owe to my father – to his stories, but more to his voice. He is present in every book I have ever written, a part of their DNA.

He will be 70 next month. He reads every day. He retired in 2002 from a working life of more than half a century, during which he had been an engineer, then a barrister at law, then an arbitrator of building disputes. He reads poetry and the Old Testament; spends time with his grandchildren; has become, in some ways, like a child himself.

'I was so much older then,' sings Bob Dylan of his youthful years. 'I'm younger than that now.'

My eldest son, aged 7, has a look of my father as a child, and the same restless interest in stories. For some reason, he has developed an interest in the legends of the Greek gods and heroes, and when he said to me recently, 'Dad, you are my hero,' I found myself silenced, almost tearful. What a responsibility to be a father, to be anybody's hero, when the truth of my life now is that my children are my heroes and I can only hope I one day deserve them.

Last Christmas my son was in a children's production of

Dickens's *A Christmas Carol*, playing one of the famished urchins so detested by Scrooge, a role that required a costume of photogenic raggedness, as well as a certain suspension of disbelief. 'It's great fun being poor!' he chuckled to me after the final dress rehearsal.

The perfect innocence of a 7-year-old's laughter. 'Hey Dad, I wish we could be poor all the time!'

I thought about my father, at the age of my son, standing in Francis Street, perhaps with his mother, the gull-song and the reek of the river. I thought of the consolation brought to Sean's childhood by the world of the book, and of how he had wanted that for me. Of such small and great loyalties is fatherhood made.

For all a father can say is 'I will never leave you.' So I said that to my son. And he laughed.

Announcements were made. The lights went down. The taped music played, and the cameras clicked dutifully, and the teacher smiled warmly as she coaxingly beckoned, and her charges tottered out from backstage.

Dickens, the great sentimentalist, believed in the possibility of redemption, even to the most twisted of men. His story of crippled love turned to hatred of the world would touch the heart of a stone. Its meanings sounded quietly through that little church hall as my son and the other children pantomimed their starvation with the innocently fervent faces of those who will never know it.

The audience was small; there were rows of empty seats. But as he capered in his rags and took his final brave bow, the darkness around me seemed haunted, watchful; much closer than any of us imagines. Dickens's *A Christmas Carol* is a play about ghosts.

Perhaps all the ghosts of his Francis Street forefathers had come to support one of their own.

14 June 2008

SONG OF SUMMER

Peter Cunningham

In searching for one symbol that can sum up the essence of Irish seasons, the ash tree must be an Olympic contender. Many of the characteristics of the ash (*fraxinus excelsior*) are shared by Irish people. Both enjoy a protracted hibernation, followed by an exuberant but brief extroversion during the traditional summer months.

Both species are rooted in deep primal earth and dark primal winters respectively, and live lives of mostly intense introspection. In the case of the ash, I imagine it heeds only the stirring of the deep seedlings of its ancestry in mid-December; in the case of Irish people, mid-winter is a time for reflection and close gathering.

This connection between the ash, the seasons and the Irish is more than one of ancient myth or poetic fancy. In the long, damp Irish winters, ash is by far the handiest wood to burn; even when wet with sap, it crackles into heat-giving flame.

For summer, the first one and a half metres of a clean-boled ash trunk, including the upper section of its curved roots, is carefully sliced to make hurling sticks.

The clash of the ash is an integral sound of the Irish summer.

One ash tree I know, a broad-girthed, hundred-foot giant that was already an adult during the War of Independence, decided two weeks ago, with the utmost reluctance, to eventually come into leaf. It then did so with lush, theatrical profusion.

At ten that same evening, when the moon was visible through the upper fronds of the tree, the cries of play from our local football club were still riding on the warm air.

In the same week that this great ash suddenly leapt into leaf, a four-foot high plastic ice-cream cone suddenly appeared outside our local shop. Like the long-awaited appearance of the ash, the sudden emergence of this piece of cleaned-up, garish advertising was a telling event, just one of many tic-tac signs that confirmed that summer had at last arrived.

Later, in the shop of a nearby petrol station, people were gathered around a chest-freezer, frowning. This cabinet, which had earlier that week brimmed with twenty different types of frozen confectionery, was now empty and the perspiring store owner was phoning his supplier every half hour.

Sun cream, especially in the high factors, was also running low. On the main road out of town, a tiny caravan selling strawberries from Wexford had materialised, parked beneath a spreading ash tree. It was manned by two children who had not been seen for twelve months, or maybe it was their younger brother and sister.

In the explosions of senses that occur in summer, none are more uplifting than the visual. The backdrops to Irish summers are formed not only by rich deciduous woodland, such as ash, but by the apple blossom of Tipperary; the bright, musky-scented gorse of Clare and the sudden glow of fuchsia in Kerry.

And summer's colours are made up of the sports jerseys and flags of our counties that also appear at this time of year, displays of a county's pride.

Winter's sports colours, Munster red and Leinster blue, to name but two, are displayed against the background of the monochromatic Irish winter. The flash of a green jersey over the French try-line in Croke Park in February is nowadays observed under flood-lights. The colours of soccer on television have the appearance of a stage-managed illusion.

Yet Irish county colours, paraded in summer, manage somehow to be both heroic and within our grasp. Real. They also seem like an echo of an earlier, more innocent Ireland.

The most talented writer of the Great Blasket, Tomás Ó Criomhthain, described the great hurling match played each year on Trá Bhán, the White Strand, facing the mainland. 'The game was played on the White Strand without shoes or stockings, and we went in up to our necks whenever the ball went into the sea.'

And after the match.

'There wasn't a man able to drive his cow to the hill for the stiffness in his back and his bones; a pair or so would have a bruised foot, and another would be limping on one leg for a month.'

This account of the intense passion and team rivalry on a small island, the Great Blasket, published in 1929, is emblematic of the zeal that emerges during an Irish summer in pursuit of All-Ireland victory. In an age of unremitting professionalism, in which most sport is simply another branch of business, the symbiosis of the fleeting Irish summer and hurling and football is, like the ash tree, a seasonal phenomenon.

The sight of gulls, flowering escallonia and sea pinks in County Waterford for the next three months will be enhanced by the blue and white chequered flags hanging from houses, and from tree-shaded squares, and from the windows of hooting cars.

These bright favours will tell of a purpose beyond the saving of hay, or the footing of turf, or of trying to survive on one in-come where recently there were two.

The excitement of a summer campaign beyond the personal springs from the windows of these tiny villages, a focus that puts aside, for a few happily suspended months, the image of a nation on the verge of bankruptcy or the despair of decent men and women who worked all their lives just to see their pensions squandered by their employers.

In clubs like Mount Sion and Ballygunner, Tramore and Fourmilewater, teams have trained through the cold, dark evenings, many of them having done eight hours already in the day job. The boot of every car contains a stack of hurleys. The owner of every car wants a place on the team. A passion drives the commitments of these players, which, like that of their followers, is beyond the personal, but is driven by the same inner conviction that was there one hundred and twenty-five years ago, when these games were reinvented and when the term 'professional sport' was an oxymoron.

Meanwhile, just a few miles across the River Suir, a vivid reminder of how difficult it is to progress far in these championships is provided by the uncompromising vertical black and amber stripes of the jerseys and flags in County Kilkenny. For Kilkenny is the portal through which all hurling aspirations must pass.

Hurling and football are played in the knowledge that even if the pinnacle of these sports is achieved, the reward will be pride, not money.

This is a sustaining ethos in times of material stress. In lilywhite Kildare, or in suburban Dublin, dusty late summer evenings are invigorated by kids slapping a ball between them and by the rearing images of the green and yellow jerseys of County Meath, or those of County Down or Antrim or Tyrone.

There's a kind of ash-like primal sense of inheritance in adhering to an old, amateur code. It may be unfashionable and unmodern, but it comes with its own currency, its own values. In its insularity lies hurling and football's hope of remaining as they are, indigenous amateur sports, whose All-Ireland finals are attended by staggering numbers of faithful in the fall of every year.

Who knows how long an amateur code can survive in a world driven by financial quarters and the bottom line? But as long as it does, those ephemeral summer moments are vital, even as the leaves begin to turn, even as the great ash's thoughts turn inward again.

Irish summers are unpredictable and they end abruptly, in the same manner that an ash tree sheds its leaves. Unpredictable too is the manner in which some of today's hurling and football teams conduct themselves, where the almost unbearable pressures of modern professional sport and its expectations ride up against the traditional methods of some county boards and their appointees.

And yet, for the greater part of the months ahead, these differences will be put temporarily aside, just as the brooding financial calamities and the coming winter will be put temporarily out of mind and the business of county pride will take over.

The ash will be unfazed by the uncertain nature of the meteorology in the months ahead. The great tree presides in a woodland, where it droops over hundreds of its lesser relations and descendants, many of them saplings, mere whips, others planted in regimented rows and awaiting thinning when they reach a score of years.

These thinnings will be used mainly for fuel, although a few may find their ways into the workshops of furniture manufacturers. And still others, those of clean bole and swan-necked root, will be taken away and carefully fashioned into hurleys for our children.

6 June 2009

THE QUINTESSENTIAL DUB: LEOPOLD BLOOM

Declan Kiberd

When a devotee of James Joyce in Paris asked for permission to kiss the hand that wrote *Ulysses*, the author said: 'No – that hand has done a lot of other things as well.'

Joyce had little time for bohemians. Whenever he heard pretentious abstract terms being bandied about by intellectuals, he said: 'Don't you sometimes wish they'd talk about turnips?' His masterpiece *Ulysses* is set on 16 June 1904, to commemorate the day when a handsome Galway woman, Nora Barnacle, first walked out with him and 'made a man of me'. In effect she summoned a melancholy and introverted young artist back to the real world (she was a hotel chambermaid), and he remained forever grateful for that.

Ulysses has acquired a forbidding, intimidating reputation, partly because its opening episodes focus on Stephen Dedalus and on his convoluted thoughts. Many readers feel inadequate in the face of Stephen's learning, not realising that Joyce is mocking a mind which has been immobilised by the recent acquisition of an arts degree.

Stephen is a version of Joyce's younger self, so caught up in grief for his dead mother and in obsession with his own thought processes that he has lost connection to the everyday world. Many another graduate from college, before and since, has had difficulties in settling down to a workaday life. Joyce's foremost disciple, the young Samuel Beckett, told his dismayed mother, after he had taken a brilliant arts degree at Trinity, that all he wanted to do now was fart, lie on his back, and think about Dante.

It is such a state of nervous youthful pretension which is challenged in *Ulysses* by Leopold Bloom. Although a man of Jewish background in the gentile city of Dublin, he is quite at home in the world. He is shown as defecating on his garden jakes at Eccles Street early in the day, not so that Joyce can shock readers, but in order to depict a man devoid of pretensions about himself. He is utterly at home with the processes of his own body, unlike poor Stephen who would prefer to be a pure mind.

Joyce believed that how a man prepares food will tell you far more about his philosophy than how he goes to war. He celebrated the dailiest day, on which nothing much happens, to reassert the dignity of ordinary experience against the false heroics of World War I. Previous great writers – like Tolstoy whom he admired – reserved soliloquies for aristocrats about to risk death in battle. Joyce, however, gave long interior monologues to a Bloom making nothing more portentous than a cup of tea.

'The ordinary is the proper domain of the artist,' said Joyce, mischievously adding that 'the extraordinary can safely be left to journalists.' In his mind *Ulysses* was a healthy antidote to the shock-horror-outrage stories carried in most of the daily papers. It too tries to capture the events of a single day, but as lived experience, not mere sensation.

Which is not to say that Joyce dismisses newspapers. Far from it. In his youthful days in Dublin, he tried to raise the money to launch a continental-style afternoon paper called *The Goblin*. It failed to take off, only because nobody could put up the vast amount of backing money that he required. But it's no accident that the central character of his book works for the *Freeman's Journal* as a canvasser of small ads.

Like his author, Bloom is a shrewd analyst of the ways in which advertisements appeal to the subconscious. He combines artistic and business skills when he devises a logo of 'crossed keys' for the company of Alexander J. Keyes.

This image, he astutely considers, will play not only on the Irish Catholic awareness of the Vatican (keys to the kingdom) but also carry an innuendo of Home Rule. In Bloom's personality the ad man has blended subtly with that of the social anthropologist. When he watches old women approach the altar rail to receive communion at All Hallows Church, he listens to the words of the priest, which recall for him the techniques of an advertising jingle: 'Good idea the Latin. Stupefies them first.'

Yet soon afterward he himself is distributing bread to the birds that swoop over the Liffey; and at the book's climax he will rescue Stephen from a brothel, lift him out of his depression and offer him coffee and a bread roll in a clear, if unconscious, reenactment of that very sacrament of the Eucharist which he had earlier mocked.

That climax, when the poet and the businessman sit down together, is unique in the history of modern literature. Most of the other great modern authors, from Thomas Mann to Marcel Proust, believed in eternal enmity between bohemian and bourgeois – but not Joyce. He had, after all, helped to open one of the first commercial cinemas in Dublin and had tried to sell Irish tweed in Trieste. In his eyes the artist and businessman had much in common.

Both were brokers in risk who backed an initial creative hunch, often leading to years of hard graft in the attempt to bring the project to fruition. So he has Bloom explain all kinds of things to the awkward young poet – why chairs in cafés are piled on tables every night, why Stephen has as much right to earn a living by his brain as other men by their brawn, and so on.

Stephen's problem is that his education by Jesuits has not equipped him for what Bloom sees as the real university – 'the university of life'. But Bloom, by magnificently and arbitrarily offering help to someone who has no reason to expect it, lifts the young man's spirits by his blend of imagination and practicality, of theory and of experience. This was a role sought by Bloom. Although an ad canvasser, he would prefer a somewhat different job – as agony uncle on the newspaper. 'Dear Editor; What is a good cure for flatulence? I'd like that part. You'd learn a lot teaching others.' At the end of *Ulysses* that moment of blessedness comes, illustrating Joyce's belief that the best learners are teachers and the best teachers learners.

What can Bloom teach Stephen – and us? How to cope with death in an age of its denial; how to walk and think at the same time; how to eat food rather than gobble; how to purge sexual relations of the urge to possess or to dominate (he forgives his wife Molly her fling with Blazes Boylan); how to avoid conflict; how to tell a joke and how not to tell a joke; how to process the images and sounds of the city without being overwhelmed.

And he shows us how to make good use of public space. 'An Irishman's home is his coffin,' he muses sadly at one moment; but the corollary is that in the streets a person is free to encounter the unexpected. Bloom walks a lot and some American readers have wondered whether he is trying 'to walk something off'. But in the Dublin of 1904, everybody walked. They thought nothing of walking for more than an hour to play a short game of cards, and then walking for more than a further hour on the journey home.

For Joyce 'street people', far from constituting a problem, were the basis of civilisation. Although *Ulysses* is famous as a book of private, subjective thoughts, its main episodes are set in public space: beach, cemetery, library, restaurant, pub and, mainly, the street. The street is not just a neighbourhood, but also the zone of circulation; and such free movement is as vital to the life of a city as is the circulation of blood to the health of a human body.

I often ask young readers of *Ulysses* how they might respond if a 38-year-old gentleman met them in a late-night spot and invited them back to his house for the night. All say they would have to refuse. That is a measure of what we have lost.

At its best, the city used to teach good lessons – how to look out for people; how to respect difference; how to savour accidental meetings. When Bloom and Stephen encounter one another, each is transformed. In greeting the stranger without, each shows a capacity to make peace with the stranger within.

Not a bad lesson for multicultural Ireland. Today's immigrants often seem far more adept than those born here at making enthusiastic use of streets, beaches and parks. Perhaps they will in time also teach us how to reread *Ulysses*. The condescending, if well-intentioned, term 'new Irish' might once have been used of Bloom and of his family. But now he is fiction's ultimate Dub. The city is unimaginable without him.

Harsher critics of Joyce say that someone like Bloom could never read *Ulysses*, because it's too difficult. That isn't true. The author gave presentation copies to a favourite waiter in Fouquet's restaurant and to his beloved aunt Josephine. He intended it to be read and enjoyed by just the kind of people who are in it.

When a painter visited him in his Paris apartment, he pointed out the window at the concierge's son and said, 'Some day that boy will be a reader of *Ulysses*.' Young people look to art not just for beauty of form, but for advice on how to live. The works they admire in their teenage years – Harry Potter novels or, indeed, video games – deal with ideas of virtue.

The Potter books are in some cases almost as long as *Ulysses*;

the levels of difficulty in some video games seem (to me anyway) almost as challenging. Perhaps *Ulysses* is the logical next step. Until we return our focus to what Joyce had to say, that hopeful prophecy about the concierge's son will not be fully fulfilled.

13 June 2009

REVOLUTION BY TWITTER

Mark Little

The street running along the perimeter of the British Embassy in Tehran is named after the IRA hunger striker Bobby Sands. It's a calculated insult that speaks volumes about Iran's loathing of the UK. But Bobby Sands Street also tells you something about the Iranian psyche, an enigmatic state of mind suspended between an impossible past and an unknowable future.

Bobby Sands was a poster boy for the Islamic revolutionaries, but he also had a following among ordinary Iranians (there's even a fast-food restaurant in the Iranian capital named after him). Sands was a powerful symbol of the cult of martyrdom which has shaped Shia Islam for more than twelve centuries.

That strain of inspirational fatalism runs deep through all sections of Iranian society, even the courageous young people who have been beaten, gassed and shot on the streets of Iranian cities in the past fortnight.

The cult of the martyr frames the death of 26-year-old Neda Agha-Soltan, who died a heartbreaking death through the grainy lens of a cellphone camera. 'Neda' has become a one-word rallying cry threatening the bedrock of the Islamic theocracy: its moral authority to rule.

I can't get the bloody yet beatific face of that young woman out of my mind. In fact, I find it hard to get Iran out of my head these days. My visits there over the years have left me obsessed with the fate of Neda Soltan's generation: the 70 per cent of Iranians who are under thirty. They are a conflicted group: sophisticated yet repressed, idealistic but fatalistic. While I always recognised their potential, I have to confess I doubted their capacity for revolution.

On my last visit to Iran in 2007, I found myself in a smoky, chic café near Tehran University, where a portrait of Samuel Beckett looked down on the brightest of a lost generation. There was an air of resignation in the Godot Café that day. Change would come eventually, the young coffee drinkers told me, but not any time soon.

The world-weary students sounded as if they were channelling Beckett, waiting for their saviour. But they were also echoing a powerful article of faith among devout Iranians: the eventual return of the Hidden Imam, the Shia Messiah. He will return, they believe, some day. Just not today.

I came away from that last visit to Iran with a heavy heart. The smart, articulate kids who so impressed me on previous visits seemed to have given up. The most active among them had been let down by the last reformist president, Mohammed Khatemi, who had been overcome by a conservative backlash and succeeded by populist hardliner Mahmoud Ahmadinejad.

They still burned with indignation at harassment from the religious police and mourned the limits put on their public freedoms, but they had come to regard political activity as absurd.

And so Iran's youngsters retreated behind closed doors. If they couldn't change the world, they could still have fun. They shopped. They flirted. They partied with passion. I vividly remember surreal snatches of conversations with Iranian youngsters about acquiring illegal booze for their next party. I watched a rap band in an attic in Tehran recording music they would never sell.

In the streets, my eye was drawn to women pushing their

scarves further back on their heads in silent protest against the official dress code.

That last visit forced me to question my assumptions about Iran's rising generation. It reminded me that there was a lot more to the Islamic republic than those middle-class kids in the affluent northern suburbs of Tehran. It exposed the danger of simply replacing one cliché – the mullah in a turban – with another – the pretty young woman hiding behind Armani sunglasses.

It also drew my attention to a conservative impulse among the young in Iran. They were nationalistic to the point of prejudice. They talked with a superior air about being Persians. They looked down on Arabs. They were suspicious of Westerners. They mocked the Americans. And even as they talked about democracy, they rallied behind the regime's effort to develop nuclear technology.

This generation looked like a lost cause. But in hindsight, it only appeared that way. Beneath a layer of indifference, hidden forces were making young Iranians take control of their destiny. With the right spark, they were destined to ignite.

In one sense, these young people are the least revolutionary section of Iranian society, since they were born after the 1979 uprising against the Shah (part of a patriotic baby boom instigated by the mullahs).

They were also too young to remember the darkest days of the murderous war with Iraq. As a result, this so-called 'third generation' has a looser bond with the values of the Islamic regime than their parents. The state has offered them some tangible benefits.

Young women in particular have done very well out of the educational reform; in the universities, they now outnumber men by two to one. But more education brought higher expectations, expectations the Iranian economy can't deliver. Last year, one in four young people were unemployed, and the numbers were reportedly higher in the big cities.

The growing disillusionment among the young spread beyond

the wealthy suburbs of northern Tehran and began to erode support for President Ahmadinejad among the urban working class. By the time the presidential election rolled around, the level of discontent among the young had broadened and, in some very important ways, matured. At the outset of the campaign, few believed the leading moderate in the race, Mir-Hossein Mousavi, could harness that discontent.

But politics, like comedy, is all about timing. And this election would coincide with a profound shift in Iran's youth culture.

In hindsight, there are remarkable parallels between the movement that helped Barack Obama get elected in the US and the youthful surge which propelled Mousavi's campaign. Believe it or not, the common denominator is social media.

Platforms like Facebook and YouTube played a vital part in Obama's campaign, allowing him to reach more people and raise more money than any presidential contender in US history. I would argue that the current wave of dissent in Iran would have fizzled out were it not for the practical and spiritual potential of social media tools to bypass state repression.

The story here is not the technology, but the mindset of the generation that uses it. In the US, that means young people born after 1980. They are officially known as the Millennials, but they are also the Obama generation. They have internalised the ethos of Facebook which values creation, participation and sharing. When it comes to politics, they want to take part, not observe. They want to organise themselves rather than be led.

The parallel between the Obama generation and the Mousavi generation in Iran is striking. Born after 1979, Iranian youngsters are among the most computer literate in the world. There are 700,000 blogs in Iran and Farsi was the second most popular language on the internet before Chinese caught up. As the social media have taken root, so too has the self-starting, autonomous and interactive ethos that defines it.

It was this spirit which ignited the Mousavi campaign and guided the greatest outpouring of dissent in Iran since the overthrow of the Shah. Twitter did not turn a disillusioned generation into revolutionaries, but it reflected a profound change in the way young people relate to the institutions that dominate their lives, and not just political institutions. The role of social media in reporting events in Iran is a huge challenge to the institutions of the global media establishment.

Personally, I don't think things can ever be the same again for reporters like me. In the words of social media guru Clay Shirky, Iran was 'the big one'. But right now, the future of the media is of less concern to me than the fate of the young people I have grown close to in Iran.

After seeing images of stylish young women wearing the green ribbons of the Mousavi campaign stand up to a gang of militiamen, I emailed an old friend of mine in Tehran, an artist with an ambivalent wit. I thought she would appreciate the last lines from 'Easter 1916' by W. B. Yeats, which tell us that the places where the green is worn 'are changed, changed utterly'.

There was no ambivalence in my friend's response. She told me she was listening to the kids coming up Tehran's main drag, Vali Asr Street, and fearing for their safety. 'I am feeling overwhelmed by a mixture of hope and despair,' she wrote. 'I can't imagine this getting better before it gets worse.'

Old habits die hard for the young people of Iran. They still see hope and fear in equal measure. And yet they have also developed new instincts. They no longer wait for Godot. Or Bobby Sands. Or the hidden Imam. They have found each other.

27 June 2009

SAYING SORRY FOR BLOODY SUNDAY

Eamon Delaney

For almost forty years the tragedy of Bloody Sunday has cast a long shadow across our land, the images from that January afternoon in 1972 imprinted on our memories.

As the years rolled by, however, and the young boys who marched that day became men, and the grown men and women who took to those Derry streets that Sunday became parents, and then grandparents, a weariness set in, and many wondered was it better just to put it behind us, to let it go. But Bloody Sunday remained, on this island, a wound that wouldn't heal. And so there was no letting go.

And now, finally, this Tuesday, with the publication of the Saville Report, there's a chance, a hope even, that we can all move beyond the hurt and that the wound can finally be healed. It presents the opportunity for a new beginning, for catharsis even. It's been a long time coming.

First a number of things need to be said about Bloody Sunday. The atrocities came at the end of a sustained period of rioting and attacks on the police and army after what was an illegal march. This is not to excuse it, obviously, but the event needs to be put in context, just like anything else.

It is quite possible that the British decided to go 'over the top' in advance and make an example of the rioters. Although rioting was almost recreational in the North by this stage, it still represented serious disorder and the British authorities must have been sick of it, as they were of the IRA's by then three-year campaign of bombings and shootings.

These points were made by the British premier Edward Heath in an extraordinary telephone conversation on that January night in 1972 with the then Taoiseach Jack Lynch. A transcript of the call was dramatised on a radio show a few years back, and all of us on the panel found it very uncomfortable listening: Heath is defiant and unapologetic, repeating that the march was 'illegal'; Lynch tries to remonstrate but then relents and eventually waffles. 'All I'm saying is…', he keeps repeating, and by then you know that he has lost the argument.

And you sense that he knows it, and he's been here before, trying to tackle the British. Specifically, in 1971 and in 1969 at the outset of the Troubles, when the Irish government tried to raise the matter at the UN Security Council – and got nowhere. We can huff and puff but unfortunately they are still the British and they are a powerful adversary who, at that time, in a conflict situation, didn't brook questioning.

Whether pre-planned or not, it is quite clear the British army ran amok that day. We only have to look at the newsreels and pictures – most devastatingly the sequence of photographs taken by Colman Doyle. The notion that the British Army was seriously under attack from IRA snipers, or that they were responding to this, is ridiculous.

If this was the case, why did they then shoot the rioters in front of them, many of them fleeing? In some cases, prone victims were shot again on the ground, just to make sure. It was clear that the Parachute Regiment went in to teach the rioters a lesson, killing many, but not too many, so as to set an example.

It is not dissimilar, incidentally, to what the Israeli commandos did recently on the Gaza flotilla when they felt under attack. Both events resulted in carnage.

So why do we need a laborious and expensive tribunal about Bloody Sunday to tell us this? The main reason is because the British government at that time, like most European governments, could never, ever admit that they were wrong in such a situation and so the media official line, with an immediate Fleet Street spin after the event, smeared the rioters as being 'armed'.

It would be ever thus in the North. For example, no British soldier has ever been convicted for an atrocity or shooting in Northern Ireland – an amazing fact – despite widespread evidence of wrongdoing. This has only created further conflict and alienation, sending out a signal that soldiers are above the law.

It was the same with the Gibraltar killings when the SAS went to the Rock to take out a three-man IRA hit team intent on a bombing. The SAS team had no powers of arrest and the IRA squad were more or less summarily executed, but worse than that, the British government then tried to deny it, digging a bigger hole for themselves with the subsequent inquiries and allegations of a cover-up – not to mention an escalation in violence.

Better to come clean and say 'yes, we did it' because, in the case of tackling the IRA, 'these people are ruthless', or in the case of Bloody Sunday, 'we did it and it was a terrible mistake: we went too far, we didn't mean to kill civilians even if they were rioting.' To have made this admission would have had a huge impact. It would have reassured the nationalist community there that the army was not above the law and totally on the side of the dominant unionist community.

But, of course, they were on the unionist side and that was part of the problem, and still is, incidentally, with unionist politicians already lining up to criticise next week's anticipated Saville verdict. This is not surprising, for the British military is ingrained in

Northern unionism, from the very outset of the State to the fruitful relationship sustained through the Second World War. The British presumably felt that to admit liability for Bloody Sunday would be to question the whole ethos of Northern security policy.

This is unfortunate, but how unfortunate too that in the years and decades since, with a sense of normalisation restored to Northern society, the British still couldn't admit their guilt over Bloody Sunday. Indeed, the closest they ever came was when John Major, the Tory prime minister, who actually comes from that conservative military culture, admitted that the victims of Bloody Sunday were in fact 'innocent'.

He didn't go any further, and actually apologise to the victims' families, but it was at least a start. It was Major, after all, who began the process of healing and reconciliation that would lead to the ceasefires and the Good Friday Agreement.

Tony Blair, of course, during his time in office, apologised for the Great Famine which, although a catastrophe that was compounded by British negligence, was not actually an outright and unlawful killing, the way Bloody Sunday was.

For me, the real impact would have been for Prince Charles to admit that what happened on that fateful day in Derry was wrong and to say sorry for Bloody Sunday. He is the head of the Parachute Regiment, after all; a ceremonial role, but one he takes seriously nonetheless, often seen pictured wearing his red beret and Para army fatigues. If Charles had said it, it would have had a huge effect, coming from the heart of the British establishment, and illustrating a genuine feeling for people and their suffering.

But this has never happened. It has not even been suggested.

So, with no apology forthcoming, the events of that January afternoon became a running sore and the source of needless pedantry and argument, something which, incidentally, seems to appeal to the ever-politicised elements in the North, with their enquiries, their 'what aboutery', and their vexatious divisions.

The trajectory of the shots on Bloody Sunday is pored over, and the rights and wrongs debated. The day itself is memorialised with a hauntingly familiar iconography – the pools of blood, the gas-masked Paras and Bishop Edward Daly, waving his white handkerchief. And what an industry has been built around it all: the documentaries, the books, the TV dramas.

Likewise, there has been the effect on Derry itself, second city of Northern Ireland, which for a long time seemed to speak of little else and which now, almost forty years on, is remembered around the world for the tragic events of that January day. What's interesting is, of course, that while Derry suffered economically as a result of the Troubles, the Saville Inquiry has been a huge boon to the town in terms of official spending on lawyers and accommodation.

What bitter irony.

Few would also deny that in terms of other events of the Troubles, the intense preoccupation with Bloody Sunday does seem one-sided. There are no such tribunals, after all, for all the other atrocities in the Derry area, such as the Droppin' Well explosion by the INLA; or Patsy Gillespie, forced by the IRA to drive their bomb to an army checkpoint and blown to smithereens. But that is the way: the terrorists make no apologies for these atrocities. Consequently, how impressive it would have been if the British had quickly apologised for Bloody Sunday and so elevated themselves above the level of the common gunman.

Bloody Sunday commemorations have, of course, been hijacked by republican elements. I especially found this in New York, in the Irish American community, when I was there as a diplomat, dealing with Northern Ireland. But it is the same here at home.

It was, after all, following a Bloody Sunday commemoration in Derry a few years ago, and a subsequent long night's drinking, that a republican mob in Magennis's bar in Belfast set upon and savagely killed Robert McCartney – thereby insulting the Derry victims further. But this is beside the point. It is now up to the authorities to seize the initiative, to be bold and finally to take this divisive and traumatic event out of the still-rancorous present and assign it to the past as a cruel and terrible mistake by the British government.

Let the Saville Report give us the full truth and confirm what most of us know already so that the British government can at last issue an apology and take responsibility for the carnage of that day and for its terrible legacy on these two islands.

This way we can all move on, and the relationship between our two countries can be allowed to properly prosper. No relationship, be it one between friends or between countries, can ever truly work if one party refuses to acknowledge its wrongs – and to apologise for them.

That's why it is so important that, after all these years, it is vital that – at last – the truth is acknowledged. There is only one word that this country needs to hear from the British government next week – 'Sorry'.

12 June 2010

MY FATHER:
THE MAN WHO SMELLED OF ROSES

Colum McCann

Memory has a heavy backspin. Dublin in the mid-1970s. 9 years old. It was a school day, but I had been brought to work by my father, at his newspaper, the *Evening Press*. We climbed the stairs to his small third-floor office.

He was features editor and literary editor. There were more books than wallpaper. On the floor, magazines and papers lay open as if speaking to each other. I sat in his swivel chair and spun. He worked some articles, drew up some layouts, ran his red pencil through some sentences, his daily grind.

Outside, just barely visible through the window grime, ran the long grey sentence of the River Liffey.

Later in the morning we went to the library, the darkroom, the canteen. The further we went along, the more the building seemed to hum. We descended the stairs to the newsroom. A wash of noise – television chatter, telephones with their ringers set high, the hammer of typewriter keys. Copy boys scurried across the floor. Editors shouted into headsets. Photographers called out to one another. Pneumatic tubes ferried copy to the upstairs offices. Reporters jostled large rolls of paper into their Olympia typewriters, began their hunt and peck.

There was a raw sense in the air that anything that was ever important had happened exactly five minutes ago.

My father guided me under the fluorescent flicker, past the features desk, the news desk, the sports desk. He wore a grey suit, a white shirt, a red tie, the end of the tie crinkled where he chewed it. Messenger boys thrust envelopes in his hands. His fellow journalists looked up from their desks, nodded, winked, chatted.

There were handshakes all around. Men and women ruffled my hair. At the rear of the room he lifted me up and sat me on one of the long wooden desks.

'Listen to me now,' he said. 'Do yourself a favour...'

'Yeah ...?'

'See all this here?' I was swinging my legs off the side of the desk. He paused a moment. 'Listen here now. Don't become a journalist.' He put the tail end of his tie in his mouth and chewed. Even then I knew that he was good at his job, that he was liked around the offices, and that he brought home a good wage. And I liked the music of the place, the telex machine, the dictaphones, the carriage return bells on the typewriters, twenty or thirty of them going all at once.

'Why, Dad?'

'No reason,' he said, 'just try not to.' He patted the back of my head, looked away.

There was another noise in the background, a deep machine hum from the rear of the offices. My father lifted me down from the desk, took my hand, brought me back beyond the newsroom, along a stairway, through a series of swinging red doors.

The print room ran the length of a few football fields. A sort of darkness everywhere, the air soupy with ink.

We moved along the metal catwalks under giant compressors and whirling fans. Conveyor belts rolled overhead. Pistons jammed back and forth. Huge cylinders of metal turned in the air.

Down on the floor of the press, the pages were being laid out, the type turned backwards like some strange hieroglyphic. My father leaned close to me and shouted something in my ear, but I couldn't hear what he said. It was as if, by being close, he was drifting away.

He looked smaller now, in this enormous place. I held his hand as we walked through the presses.

A foreman sat in a cage in the centre of the room. A thin boy passed us carrying a tray of tea cups; he seemed not much older than me. Other men moved alongside us on the catwalks, shouting out to each other in the din. They looked like dark shadows, disappearing amongst the machinery.

It struck me suddenly how different these other men were to my father. A hardness about them. A rawness. And they dressed differently. They wore blue overalls. Their hands were dark with ink. They had tough Dublin accents. Their bodies took up another sort of space. My father moved softly amongst them in his well-tailored suit. Nobody laughed or joked or ruffled my hair. We went along the metal catwalk, following the line of a newspaper all the way back to the guillotine, where the papers were stacked and bundled and thrown into the rear of vans.

Outside, another hubbub. Motorcyclists. Delivery boys. Security men.

The news of the day to a boy 9 years old was how very big the world suddenly was, and how very different men could be, and how people seemed to have their own little corner, and every corner was a world. I glanced at my father, standing in the sunlight on Poolbeg Street, and it was something akin to growing older, something akin to moving away.

I grew up in the suburbs. My father had a rose garden. He loved it: one thousand roses so closely packed together that you could smell their fragrance fifty yards up the street.

He would put in his shift at the newspaper and then drive home, pour himself a glass of wine, and walk out the back door to go and talk with his roses. It was his moment of release: the necessity of a work beyond words. Later he would pull on his old fur-lined boots, his *Garden News* anorak, his old torn trousers, and he would dig, or he would mow the lawn, or cut the hedge, or fix the greenhouse windows, or cross-pollinate the seeds he had so carefully nurtured. He worked the soil as if he wanted it to tire him out.

Twice a year we would get a huge load of manure from a nearby farm, to fertilise the roses. It was dumped, stinking, in a heap in our front garden. It could be smelled all the way up the road. He liked nothing more than pulling on his wellington boots and taking out a pitchfork, loading wheelbarrow after wheelbarrow, letting the manure fly. My brothers and sisters tried to avoid the day when the shit would arrive, just so we wouldn't get called into service.

Once we found a tiny dead calf in the manure, no bigger than a shoebox. My father tossed it away and happily went back to work.

He trimmed the edges of the flowerbeds. He grew floribundas. He developed brand new breeds of miniatures. He labelled and bred. He pruned the stems back. He weeded. He squashed greenfly between his fingers. On summer nights he would stay out until the sky folded dark above him. On weekends he would spend his whole day in the garden or would take us down to Dún Laoghaire for a flower show.

There was one other passion too: football. He had been a professional footballer for Charlton Athletic when very young and although it pained him to watch us play football in the Dublin garden, he never stopped us, not once. I sellotaped the roses back together when the ball broke a stem. Once he clipped the broken rose and brought it in to my mother to put in a vase, the tape carefully removed.

I never really understood his desire for gardening, but while he was amongst his roses my father looked to me like the first man ever to whistle.

Thirteen years later, I got the chance to watch the printers at work again. I was a junior reporter then and still young enough to get a thrill from watching one of my stories roll off the presses. I walked down from the newsroom and stood on the metal catwalk.

I generally tried to avoid my father while I worked: not for any reason other than the simple fact that I wanted to avoid the talk of nepotism at the newspaper. I had gotten the job fairly and squarely – I had even won a Young Journalist of the Year Award – but I had no desire to hear the begrudgery. And there was always his admonition in my ear: don't become a journalist.

And the older I got the more I realised how important my father was in Dublin literary circles. He was known for taking on young writers. He had created a special page only for women journalists, something quite radical at the time. He paid everyone well. He encouraged people. He had even started, along with David Marcus, the New Irish Writing page that had published everyone from Edna O'Brien to Ben Kiely to John McGahern to Neil Jordan.

I stood one afternoon in the printing room and saw him coming down the stairs towards what was known as the 'stone', where the paper was laid out. He moved through the inky dark. He had a pencil behind his ear and a metal ruler in his hands. He seemed to wear the same grey suit he had years before. His tie was still damp where he still chewed it.

I had fallen in love with language by then and there was nowhere better than the printing room for words: the hellbox, the Devil's box, the slugbox. The widows, the orphans, the slugs. The galley, the stick, the guillotine. I recall thinking: there is my father down amongst the stonemen.

His pages were set and ready for printing. He read them for errors and style. He could read both upside-down and backwards.

Years of practice had made him fluent at reading any way he wanted. I watched as he finished his work, carefully and meticulously. He looked hurried. He stuffed some papers in his brown briefcase, and left; home, no doubt, towards his rose beds.

When their printers' shift ended, a group of them – compositors and proofreaders – trudged out the back door, onto Poolbeg Street. I fell in behind them. I don't know why I wanted to follow, I just went on instinct. There was a sort of melancholy in me – I was thinking of leaving Ireland at the time, giving up my job, going to America, maybe even going away to try to write a novel.

It was a short trip down to Mulligan's, a beautiful old pub that sat behind a 200-year-old facade. The printers knew the place well. They walked in through the haze of cigarette smoke and sawdust. The printers didn't know me – I was just another face in the crowd. I sat nearby and listened. Someone called out for a rozziner.

'Give us a rozziner there, will ya?' The word was repeated a couple of times, the hard Dublin music of it.

'What's a rozziner?' I asked one of the men.

'The first drink of the day,' he said. It took me years to figure out that they were talking about the rosin that goes on a violin bow before playing.

If play is the shadow of work, then maybe work stands in the shadow of play.

In early 2009, after finishing a new novel, I went back to Dublin from my home in New York. My father's garden was in good shape to an amateur eye, but for him it was a disaster. There was simply too much work to do. Some of the rose beds had been dug up and gravelled over. The soil was choked in weeds. The hedges were tatty. He looked out the kitchen window, his face drawn long by the fact that he couldn't nurture the place anymore.

He was long retired from the newspaper. In fact, the newspaper itself was long retired from the world – the whole *Irish Press* group had gone bankrupt in the 1990s.

I went outside and started to pull up the weeds. When a writer steps out from a novel there's often nothing better than hard physical labour to cure him of the failure. The work felt fresh to me.

My father stayed at the downstairs window most of the time, but by the end of the first day he was outside, standing on the doorstep. 'Would you stop doing that for crissake?' he said, looking at the deep cuts on my hands, my arms, my scalp.

The next day he stood out in the garden, leaning on a blue walker in a light rain, as I ferried in among the roses, getting thorned again. 'It's looking better,' he said, 'but jaysus you don't have to do it, we can hire someone in, you've got other things to do, just leave it.' The next day he had a glass of wine in his hands. On the fifth day, when the garden had begun to look fresh – and therefore ancient – my father literally got down on his hands and knees and started weeding in the flower bed alongside me.

An emigrant's guilt – weed your father's garden.

It may have stretched towards parody – by god the old man could handle a shovel, just like his old man – but there was something acute about it, the desire to come home, to push the body in a different direction to the mind, the need to be tired alongside him in whatever small way.

A month later, back in New York, I ended up with a case of osteomyllitis, a bone infection, which laid me up in hospital for a couple of weeks. The doctors said I had possibly gotten it from a cut on my hands.

No matter. Life deals its small dark ironies.

In the hospital – laid up on morphine – I got a chance to reread *Ulysses*. I stepped back into those pages. You pull back the words, you get the old skin. The novel returned me to Dublin, of course, my grandfather's Dublin, my father's Dublin, my own Dublin, even to Poolbeg Street, to the inkmen and the stone, and the shout-out for a rozziner.

I marked up passages and fell asleep at night under the ticking of an antibiotic drip and woke in the morning with the novel open on my chest.

My son came in one afternoon and asked me why I had written in the margins of the book. Six years old. There are always questions.

19 June 2010

JULY

AN ODYSSEY OF THE SPIRIT

Áine Ryan

Tomorrow, from dawn until dusk, around 30,000 people will climb a holy mountain that stands on the edge of the Atlantic in County Mayo.

Young and old, barefooted and booted, will replicate a ritual which has roots stretching back 5,000 years to the Neolithic festival of the Corn King. Hail, rain or scorching sunshine will not deter these trekkers. Sharp shale will cut their feet. Blackthorn sticks will balance aching limbs. Friendly faces will nod encouragement. Hunched shoulders will cradle exhausted children.

Among the motley hordes there will be Jesus lookalikes, bent over by crosses; reincarnated St Patricks in festive green and wielding staffs; flocks of African nuns in full habits; Tibetan monks, Presbyterian pastors, atheists, archaeologists, photographers, psychologists. Dozens of evangelists, mainly from the North, will line the lower track offering free tea, cordial, pamphlets. The only price: a sermon on true faith.

'This is not the true path to finding Christ,' they will chorus. 'It will not lead to redemption. You must read the Bible to be saved,' they will warn.

How come Mayo becomes Mecca each year on the last Sunday of July? Why do the progenies of the Celtic Tiger, whose religion of choice is materialism, flock to this pyramidal mountain? Surely the aisles of shopping malls are the new altars at which they genuflect? Or is it possible that all these Calvin Klein, Coco Chanel, Christian Dior and Ralph Lauren wannabes are feeling the pinch of emptiness, meaninglessness, soullessness?

The ancient holy mountain, Croagh Patrick, or simply 'the Reek', holds many secrets. It is a pervading bastion of thousands of years of Irish history. It is the keeper of the dark and distant recesses of the nation's culture and spirituality. Its stern contours and pyramidal peak have chronicled 5,000 years of human struggle, faith, hope and despair.

The story of Reek Sunday stretches across the millennia and reveals a fascinating tale of our pre-Christian origins. It illustrates an incredible historical assimilation, placing primal pagan ritual sacrifices, both human and animal, as direct precursors to the symbolic sacrifice of bread and wine, the body and blood of Christ, in the modern-day Mass.

This mountain's pilgrim pathways have been trod by Neolithic or Stone Age cultivators, Celtic cattlemen and Christian farmers. Long before the arrival of St Patrick in 432 AD, and his 40-day sojourn on the mountain in 441 AD, this dispassionate mountain was altar to the many deities worshipped by our distant forefathers.

At every harvest, from around 3000 BC to the arrival of the Celts, the gods of the Tuatha Dé Danann were appeased and pandered to during a nine-day ritual. Nature's elemental energies – wind, rain, sun, sea – were personified by a panoply of deities. These gods could infuriate the winds, stir up the seas, blind the sun. At a whim, they could destroy the harvest and inflict illness on herds of animals.

Nowadays, the first station that pilgrims reach on their torturous ascent is Leacht Benáin, a cairn (mound) of stones. They are instructed to walk around the cairn seven times, while reciting seven Our Fathers, seven Hail Marys and one Creed. This ritual has a poignant cross-millennial significance. It is thought that the Festival of the Corn King was held at Leacht Benáin 5,000 years ago.

Reputedly the Corn King was a person of noble birth who offered his life to the sun god on behalf of his community in thanksgiving for the harvest. After his interment, there was a wake and funeral games lasting seven days; thus the continued ritual of the above-mentioned seven prayers. During the ancient festivities, celebrants would place a stone on his tomb. Tomorrow many pilgrims, unknowingly, will replicate this ancient ritual by placing stones on Leacht Benáin. Four years ago in July 2003, a young woman in her early 30s dropped dead at this spot while undertaking the Reek Sunday pilgrimage.

There are three other such cairns on the west side of the mountain known as Roilig Mhuire or Virgin's Cemetery.

After the Celts arrived, around 600 BC, they incorporated this festival into their own seasonal rituals. The festival of Lughnasa (August) was held on the first day of that month. It honoured the European sun god, Lugh, and was held over nine days at 52 different sites around the country, including on the sides of Croagh Patrick, or Cruachán Aigle, as it was formerly called.

The elders of this pagan society would oversee this harvest féile. The druids, aosdána (wise ones), filí (poets), Brehons (lawmakers) and kings would coordinate the sophisticated religious ritual which also included aonachs (fairs), chariot-racing, hurling, storytelling and much music.

It is thought that both the Tailteann games and the Ould Lammas Fair, held annually at Ballycastle, County Antrim, originated at this ancient festival.

In later times when the symbolism of this primal festival was integrated into Christianity, the last sheaf of corn cut at the harvest was fashioned into a totem called the Cailleach or Corndolly and was used to ward off the evils brought by the darkness of winter; it was also used to make the bread for the Eucharist.

The dark spectre of the Great Famine has largely been consigned to the realms of history in modern Ireland. In recent years, a John Behan bronze sculpture of a replica coffin ship, its symbolic sails the skeletal bodies of famine victims, has been placed at the foot of the mountain. It is the national monument to the millions who died and fled the country. For the majority of tomorrow's pilgrims, the reality of this country's fragile dependence on agriculture is a remote memory.

However, even up to 50 years ago (less in some areas), small farmers from all over Connacht had a deep understanding of our intrinsic relationship with the earth.

At that time, for example, islanders from the Arans and Achill, Inishturk and Inishboffin, Clare Island and Inishbiggle would fast overnight. At dawn the following day, they would launch their currachs, loosen their hookers and yawls, and set sail for the little pier at Murrisk, at the foot of the Reek. They would climb the Reek barefooted like thousands of their mainland counterparts who had travelled by foot, bicycle, pony and trap, and car.

The pilgrims' story was a simple one. A good year was when the hay was reeked, the turf clamped and the praties (potatoes) pitted and free of blight. A good year was when the cattle and sheep had been sold at the May and November fairs held in every village and town in Ireland. These seasonal rituals of sowing and cultivating, reaping and harvesting weaved a colourful tapestry stretching back 5,000 years.

When our parents, grandparents and great-grandparents said their prayers and performed their penitential exercises, their faith was simple. When they bowed their heads or donned their mantillas, it was in thanks. Thanks for the small things.

When they finally reached that conical summit, walked 15 times around the tiny oratory and prayed for the Pope's intentions, as instructed in their prayer books, they were embracing a cross-millennial pageant. When they entered the church built by 12 local men in 1905 at a cost of £100, they genuflected, knelt down and lost themselves in the demands of their rosary beads.

Tomorrow, Mass will be celebrated half-hourly in this oratory. Young men in designer boots, girls in pink platform sandals and hooped earrings, teenagers with inflamed bleeding feet, the elderly with a palpable sense of familiarity, will crush into this historic house of prayer. They will come from all over the country. They will travel from all over the world, Texas and Taiwan, Hungary, Canada and Holland. The one thing they will have in common – their search for meaning. And where better to find it than at the top of a mountain.

Long-time curate of nearby Ballintubber Abbey, Fr Frank Fahey encapsulates it perfectly: 'There is an innate longing within us all to discover "the mystery", the meaning of life. And the decline in the number of churchgoers is irrelevant to this basic human need. When we climb to the top of a mountain, and especially a mountain with such a rich spiritual history, we can behold the edge of the world, the horizon. We can distinguish Hy Brazil, Tír na n'Óg, the elusive otherworld of metaphysics.' The Catholic Church may be in crisis in Ireland; recent clerical scandals may have wounded its institutional fabric; vocations may be at an all-time low, but that inviolable yearning continues.

Ironically, the pervasiveness of tomorrow's annual gig on the Reek – unlike Oxegen, Slane, or Marlay Park – needs no expensive marketing campaign. While it may have developed a certain commercial element with its 'I climbed Croagh Patrick' T-shirts and burger-and-chips stalls, commerciality is not at its core. Rather, it is testament to the persistent need for the transcendent, for community, for belonging.

Maybe one thing has changed for the better: it has become more a spiritual odyssey than a penitent pilgrimage.

28 July 2007

PRECIOUS HOLIDAY MEMORIES

Dermot Bolger

Memory is fickle and childhood memory the most fickle of all. While the parents of the recently departed Celtic Tiger may wish that the childhood memories their offspring retain will be of foreign beaches, tropical water slides and hard-paid-for happiness, often what children remember are seemingly random things – the drawn-out chaos of a Ryanair boarding queue, endless walks towards departure lounges or any tiny detail that lodges in a curious child's mind.

But when today's generation look back, no memory of a beach bar in Portugal or caves on the Canary Islands will seem as foreign to them as Courtown seemed to me as a Dublin boy in 1969. This was when working-class families rarely took holidays and when going abroad meant parents departing for parish pilgrimages to Lourdes or Fatima.

I can still smell the waxed lino from that magical summer, still feel the grains of sand between my bare toes on the bedroom floor and breathe in the summer air that came through the open window of Mrs Butler's guesthouse, situated a mile outside Courtown in County Wexford, where we stayed for a week during our last holiday as a family in the summer of 1969.

In my mind I see midges swarm beneath the trees in the field beside Mrs Butler's house and hear crickets chirp from the grassy roadside bank. I am 10 years of age as I sit alone on an iron bedstead in that long back room which will be occupied by my mother and father, my older sister and brother and me.

Wexford had a particular quality for my family because for generations we had been printers there, laying out the *Free Press* in letterpress before my father broke the mould by setting sail with the Wexford Steam Packet in the 1930s. He was still a sailor in the 1960s when nights home were rare for a seaman. That is what makes those few Wexford holidays seem special.

That summer of 1969 was not our first holiday in Mrs Butler's guesthouse, but it would be our last. By that Christmas my mother was dead and my childhood, as I knew it, was over.

However – as a 10-year-old during that magical week – there was no hint of such worries. It was a happy time, interrupted only by the small squabbles of any childhood family holiday. Mrs Butler's house seemed huge. Other families were also staying there. I remember a Ford Anglia with a Cork registration parked on the gravel.

In my mind I see the boy whose father owns it dance to the strains of 'Viva Bobby Joe' – a song played on the radio whose lyrics became impaled in my mind: 'I remember on his debut, all the town's people they boo-booed.'

But other music filled the night air in Courtown. At dusk in the swirling lights of a carnival – with the smell of salty chips everywhere and excited children racing around into the shadows, their faces bearded by wisps of candyfloss – the tinny sound of The Seekers blares out from loudspeakers: 'Say goodbye my own true lover, this will be our last farewell, for the carnival is over ...'

Each evening I move among booths where rifle sharp-shooters take aim and goldfish tremble in plastic bags, while overhead pubescent girls whirl, screaming and swinging back towards boys in the flailing swing chairs.

One memory is of the boy from Cork going to play golf with

his father. I tag along excitedly to the course. On the first tee his father asks me if I wish to try a shot. Golf is as foreign to me as the desserts served in Mrs Butler's house. The green with its flag shimmers in the distance like a mirage. I grip the club, nervous and excited, and am halfway through my downswing when the attendant runs across, shouting that I have not been paid for. I stop the club, inches from the ball, afraid to strike it, and hand the golf club back. For days afterwards my fingers ache to have struck a golf ball just once.

Courtown is where I also saw my first play in a makeshift parish hall. Years later I will hear those same words and recognise it as *Philadelphia, Here I Come!*

To the left of Mrs Butler's house is a field with a pond in one corner. I play alone there, exploring the vast plains and canyons of Wexford. A donkey watches with patient, suffering eyes while flies torture his face. Back at the house my brother and the Cork boy kick ball, while local children stand at the gate, silently staring in at the foreigners from the city like they were watching a film.

My mother calls us in for tapioca, rice pudding and custard. These semi-warm, curdled desserts look like the frogspawn in the pond. Over dinner the adults discuss reports of Hell's Angels riding in from Tramore and other dangerous far-flung locations while, a mile away in the gathering dark, Courtown throbs with all the sins I have yet to discover.

These are my summer memories, though I had no reason back then to know that they would become precious. But this is the trick that life plays on us.

We never know when loved ones will be taken away, when what seemed mundane will be suddenly precious.

This week my father-in-law died after an operation that everyone expected him to survive. Medical staff battled to save his life, but his time was simply up.

He was a charitable man who lived an unobtrusive life, devoting his last decades to quietly working behind the scenes for a succession of causes including Mother Teresa's nuns. I visited him in hospital recently and brought that day's *Irish Daily Mail*, in which I had an article. That was the paper that he read and it pleased him that his son-in-law had a piece in it.

The fact that I had nine novels published in a dozen languages was too abstract to mean anything, but a feature in the *Mail* was something tangible on his own terms.

We talked for an hour while outside his hospital window golfers made a mess of playing Elm Garden. It was an ordinary evening only made special in retrospect by the fact that – just like my summer in Courtown – it can never be repeated.

That is what makes holiday memories special – not where we bring our children or how much we spend on them, but how we need to realise that such moments can never be had again, that we need to grasp the present and savour it because none of us know what memory will be a last memory, what summer will forever stand frozen in time.

Some years ago I stopped off at Courtown, driving for miles around a maze of boreens and passing Mrs Butler's house several times before realising that I was back again outside it as an adult.

I stood at the rusted padlocked gate. The house seemed tiny. This could not be the front garden that I played in, the window behind which we ate our meals.

The narrow pitch-and-putt course could not be the Augusta where I had trembled on the tee.

I looked down the road and saw my family leave for another day on Courtown beach. I saw us walking back, telling ghost stories in the pitch dark.

The roadway was so small that my car blocked it. I did not climb over the wall. Instead I closed my eyes and, in my mind, walked up those stairs with sand between my toes and the long week ahead stretching for the length of eternity.

In my mind my family have gone downstairs and I am left alone. Later I will recognise this feeling as the moment when words come. But for now I am simply puzzled by an imperceptible yearning.

I am 10 years of age and I just know that I am trying to remember everything: the summer air blowing through the open window, crickets and the chamber-pot beneath the bed.

Tired and happy. I press my forehead against the cool window. Then my brother calls me from the stairs. Laughing, I turn and run towards him, with no idea – because none of us ever do – just what is to come.

19 July 2008

REJOICE IN DURTY NELLY'S

Philip Nolan

It's a Tuesday during the peak tourism season and all along the coast road from Galway to Lahinch, the rain is like an impenetrable wall, almost completely obscuring the Aran Islands. At this time of year, circles of light should be breaking through fluffy cloud and dappling the Atlantic like the footprints of halogen spots in a hotel lobby; instead, the sea is gunmetal, flecked with whitecaps and being driven offshore by a vicious east wind.

Holidaymakers expecting to see the harsh karst landscape of the Burren leavened by sunshine make do with the occasional break in the showers and dash from their tour buses to take as many pictures as possible before the downpour begins again.

All along the coast, the few who are out today look like refugees, their cagoules being lifted like Marilyn Monroe's skirt in *The Seven Year Itch*. On a drive from Galway to Lahinch, there are a few Northern-reg cars, a handful of Brits and one car each from Germany and the Netherlands. On a good day you would expect it to be virtually bumper to bumper but today, drivers have the road almost to themselves.

Back in Galway city things are little better. Though the western capital is more weatherproof than most holiday destinations, thanks to good shopping and a vibrant pub and restaurant scene, the numbers of foreign visitors, especially Americans, are giving cause for alarm, if not yet downright panic.

The West is caught in the middle of a perfect storm, literally and metaphorically. The Shannon stopover is consigned to history and most US visitors are flying straight to Dublin. Aer Lingus pulled the Shannon-to-Heathrow route last autumn to relocate to Belfast, leaving only Ryanair to service the biggest UK market from Luton and Stansted. The price of oil has seen the introduction of massive fuel surcharges. The depreciating dollar has left Ireland 20 per cent more expensive this year than it was in the middle of 2007, while the fall of sterling has led to a 17 per cent price rise for the British.

Even domestic visitors, the mainstay of the market, are leaving it until the last minute to book, keeping an anxious eye on the weather after last year's washout, a calamity repeating itself this year in the gloomiest way possible.

But even as accommodation prices are dropping, fuel prices have risen to record levels, especially for diesel. It is so bad that one hotelier, Paul Gill of the Claregalway Hotel, 10 kilometres from the city centre, has offered a €50 fuel voucher for use at a local garage to anyone staying three nights. The hotel is emblematic of many of the new three- and four-star hotels built in Ireland over the last decade, a boom facilitated by tax breaks. The rooms are large and comfortable. They have plasma televisions, tea- and coffee-making facilities, very comfortable beds and bathrooms with decent pressure in the showers.

The public areas are tastefully decorated and the food menu, in both the bistro and the bar, is extensive. The included breakfast is a buffet featuring every conceivable combination of cereals, fruit, fried food and pastries and there's no arguing the fact that an overnight stay is very good value for €79 B&B. Paul Gill says he launched his petrol offer in anticipation of a downturn rather than the arrival of one.

He believes that 'the confidence of the Irish consumer is gone, so they mightn't be going abroad and might instead restrict themselves to short breaks in Ireland. The problem is late booking. People believe that if they hold out, they'll get better deals but in the hotel industry, cash flow is king because wages are paid weekly and hoteliers need to get guests in.'

More and more places are competing for the same euro, though. There are now an astounding 51,322 hotel rooms in the Republic alone, with 4,429 guesthouse rooms, 11,871 farmhouse and town and country homes rooms, 9,985 self-catering units, 3,051 university rooms and 7,922 hostel rooms.

That's a total of 88,580 rooms that need filling every night of the summer and, based on double occupancy and not including visitors who stay on campsites or with friends, it means we need 177,160 tourists a night to fill them all.

In Galway city, the owner of one shop heavily dependent on tourist dollars was more forthright. On condition that she wasn't named, she told me, 'If the Americans pull out of here, we're finished. We need to stop building hotels on bypasses where the things that make Ireland different – the pubs and the people – are actually not even present.'

She said, 'Go to any bar in an out-of-town hotel and you could be anywhere in the world but if you stay at a city-centre hotel, you might be next door to a pub with live music and these are the memories we want people to take home with them rather than having a few forgettable drinks with piped music in the background.' There are other problems too. Businesses such as Moran's Oyster Cottage have formidable reputations for quality and there never is any shortage of people ordering delicious chowder, smoked salmon, oysters and mussels.

But across the mudflats of the estuary at Kilcolgan, what once was a rural panorama is now dominated by two newly built houses, and all over this area, Galway city is encroaching on rural land.

At Kinvara, historic Dunguaire Castle is faced by a row of huge homes, each maybe 300 square metres in area, and while it is hard to argue against people's right to enjoy the fruits of the disappearing boom, there is the feeling that this part of Ireland is becoming somehow less Irish.

Our unique selling point – the wildness and grandeur of the scenery, which is top of the attractions for the French and Germans – is under threat. This is especially worrying as an increase in continental visitors this year may soften the blow if the US market collapses.

Down in Durty Nelly's in Bunratty, one of the country's most famous pubs, the few Americans present had niggles as well as praise to share. Yes, they were having very enjoyable holidays and all agreed they had expected bad weather so weren't put out by it. But their complaints had a familiar ring: dangerous roads; poor service complaints up from 2 per cent to 9 per cent in five years; overpriced everything and, yes, the elephant in the room we're not supposed to talk about, the fact that so few Irish now work at the coalface in the hotels.

No one suggests for a moment that immigrant workers are bad at their jobs but the Americans confessed they didn't anticipate language problems when checking in or ordering food and missed the bit of wordplay they had been promised by friends who were here years ago.

This is especially important in this market, as Americans cite the friendliness of the people just below seeing the land of the ancestors, but above scenery, as reason to come here.

Diarmuid Lynch, assistant manager of Durty Nelly's, says numbers may be down this year but next year is causing more concern. He said, 'The US market tends to book early, up to a year in advance, and with the dollar low, prices might put them off.' And that's why we need to worry. In 2007, tourism revenues were

€4.9billion, up from €2.67billion just 10 years previously, but whereas 23 per cent thought Ireland very good value in 2000, that figure dropped to just 4 per cent by 2006.

Over the same period, those who thought that the country offered very poor value rose from just 1 per cent to 11 per cent, and these are seriously damning indictments that look a lot like a shotgun aimed at the heart of the goose that laid the golden egg.

A simple example. At €4.60, a pint cost an American $6.12 in June 2007 but this year, thanks to currency fluctuations, they are paying $7.21. That might not bring a bead of sweat to the forehead of a New Yorker, but the Minnesotans in Durty Nelly's agreed it was making them keep an eye on every cent they spent.

So what can be done? Well, very little about the worldwide crisis in the financial markets and rising fuel and energy costs, but we're not alone in that and they don't make Ireland any more expensive than competing destinations in Europe or even longer haul, which are facing the same agonies.

But what we do seriously need to address is the tourism product itself. We have to remember why Ireland was sufficiently attractive to convince almost 7.5million tourists to come here last year.

Travelling around the West, I had a very real sense of a different Ireland. We might very well like the new bypasses and dual carriageways, but they offer nothing more than the average foreign tourist is used to at home.

I saw endless soulless out-of-town retail parks, chain restaurants, glitzy car dealerships and hotels with giant atriums built in architectural styles that speak of everything but an Irish vernacular. Even the G in Galway, a much-hyped boutique hotel kitted out by milliner Philip Treacy, looks like little more than an afterthought to a shopping centre.

That's not what Ireland is about, even for the home market. If

I wanted to stay at a hotel like the G, I'd rather go to the Costes in Paris or the Delano in Miami, where style is more organic than grafted on.

We will look back in years to come and wonder why we made such a feeble effort to entice locals into the hospitality industry. We will wonder why we allowed so many pubs to close and so many of those still open to instead become cafes that must be revamped every five years because they are scarcely a citrus cushion ahead of the posse in the design zeitgeist.

Most of all, we shouldn't be ashamed of our past – romanticised or not, it still is what attracts a huge number of visitors to come here in the first place. Ireland, for most who venture beyond Dublin, is about sitting in the snug in bars like Durty Nelly's and singing along to everything from Leonard Cohen's 'Hallelujah' to that haunting (and, ironically, Scottish) folk song 'Will Ye Go, Lassie, Go' in the company of a people who, whether real or imagined, have a spiritual dimension that appeals to outsiders, a direct line to the soul.

If the price of a pint, no matter how much more it costs this year, is the price of admission to an experience that enthrals, excites and – yes – moves people, then we have a chance. But to play our part in providing that experience, we have to drop our recently acquired patina of sophistication and go back to being what we actually are. In a word, Irish.

5 July 2008

MUSIC FESTIVALS: CHANGING THEIR TUNE

Shay Healy

Lovers of music, freedom of expression and freedom of choice will celebrate the 40th anniversary of Woodstock this August. The three-day Aquarian Exposition in 1969 attracted half a million people to Max Yasgur's 600-acre farm in upstate New York for a counterculture blow-out that changed the face of America and served as a fitting coda to the Swinging Sixties.

Over three days, the cream of rock and folk musicians, including Jefferson Airplane, Richie Havens, Creedence Clearwater Revival, John Sebastian, Melanie, The Who and Jimi Hendrix played to 500,000 hippies, trippies, arties, farties, hicks, slicks, thieves, con men, liars, lovers, prophets and profiteers, who had miraculously blended their multifarious ways and wiles into a microcosm of a new America where everything could be achieved through drugs, loud music, bright clothes, peace and love.

And as if there was any doubt, Joan Baez led the counterculture army in their new anthem, 'We Shall Overcome'.

The first glimpse of the size of the counterculture had been seen two years previously at the 1967 Monterey Rock Festival. Predominantly a jazz festival until then, Monterey holds a special place in the memory for the guitar duel between Pete Townshend of The Who and Jimi Hendrix.

Both were eager to please and they tossed a coin to see who would go on first. Townshend lost the toss, but he wowed the crowd when he smashed up his guitar at the end of his set.

Hendrix was not to be outdone, especially in front of his fellow Americans, who were getting their first taste of his genius. Hendrix finished up on his knees, singing 'Wild Thing', while he simultaneously poured lighter fuel on his guitar, ignited it and then smashed the flaming instrument into smithereens. Game. Set. And matches to Jimi.

As well as being an arch back to Monterey, Hendrix, as one of the stars of Woodstock, was also the arch forward to the famous Isle of Wight Festival in 1970, where they say there were even more people than had been at Woodstock. Along with Emerson, Lake and Palmer; Joni Mitchell; Miles Davis; Jethro Tull; Donovan; Leonard Cohen and the ubiquitous Melanie, Jimi Hendrix was one of the brightest stars of the festival. Three weeks later, he choked on his own vomit and died, aged 27.

In the absence of rock festivals in holy, Catholic Ireland of the 1960s and 1970s, we had to fall back on our ever-reliable fleadh cheoils. Fortunately, there was an annual fleadh in every county, another four dedicated to the provinces, plus the daddy of them all – The All-Ireland Fleadh. We never went thirsty but the dizzying chance to mingle with 10,000 lovers of rock music didn't happen for us in Ireland until 1977 when Rory Gallagher played a stormer at our very first rock festival, The Macroom Mountain Dew Festival.

Niall Stokes, the editor of *Hot Press* magazine, painted a colourful picture at the time. 'The scene in the town of Macroom the night before the gig most closely resembled something out of Fellini's *Satyricon*. Not Woodstock, nor any other peace 'n' love charade out of a Coca-Cola ad. There were real people here, coming together in all their strangeness. No, these weren't all pampered kids from the United Methodist Church of the country coming down for a candy-floss-'n'-coke afternoon stroll.'

There was very little free love at Rory's gig, mostly because the majority of his audience were lads, a lot of them blue-collar youths on the dole.

Rory was their hero and if the birds so wanted, they could go looking for their own heroes amongst the supporting acts who included an English hard rock trio, Nutz, local band Sunset and Joe O'Donnell, once a member of The Woods Band.

In 1977, we also had No Nukes, our first counterculture festival held at Carnsore Point in County Wexford. Tie-dyed to the max, the few thousand of us held firm against the forces of Fianna Fáil who were endeavouring to build a nuclear power station on the spot. The festival ran for three years and across those years it attracted Jackson Browne and, predictably enough, the two Christys – Moore and de Burgh. When *Reeling In The Years* for 1978 comes on the telly, I have to remain sharp-eyed to spot myself with my two young sons, going through the discomfort of sleeping in a tent so that Ireland might be nuclear-free.

The Lisdoonvarna Festival in County Clare, which first ran in 1978, was our festival apotheosis, as good as Christy Moore describes it in his song.

> Ramble in for a pint of stout and you'd never know who'd be hangin' about!
> There's a Dutchman playing a mandolin, and a German looking for Liam Óg Ó Floinn,
> And there's Adam, Bono and Garret FitzGerald, gettin' their photo taken for the *Sunday World*.
> Finbar, Charlie and Jim Hand, and they drinkin' pints to bate the band …

Then in the 1990s came Féile, also known as The Trip to Tipp, which took place within the four sanctified walls of the GAA's Semple Stadium in Thurles. Parents were reassured and assumed their children would be safe at a festival that was under the aegis of such a paragon of propriety as the Gaelic Athletic Association. Féile was like a drinking version of the Munster Hurling Final – non-stop action, a few sore heads and, at the end, handshakes were exchanged and everybody went home happy.

The GAA was thrilled when Féile's four-year contract was finally up and after Tipperary, Féile moved, drifted and mutated to eventually become the very successful Oxegen which, this year, it seems to me, has 532 bands playing on 79 stages in 22 counties.

My heads hurts just reading the number of acts in this year's line-up. I come from a generation of dinosaurs for whom photographs of kids goofing around in mud was a kind of shorthand for festivals. It is not so in Ireland any more. And especially not at Electric Picnic, where amongst a cornucopia of delights you can enjoy playing paintball, which is mud-spattering for toffs.

There are also other terrifying headings on the Electric Picnic website:

'SLEEP?'

Who wants to know about sleep except that you hope you won't get any.

'TEAS AND TARTS'.

Sounds sexy and irresistible, but it comes under the heading of Arts and Theatrics, which probably means a bunch of dud actors ruining your weekend with their witless improv.

But by far the most threatening heading is the one that reads: 'NEED TO KNOW'.

We go there to forget, actually, not to find stuff out. We don't want to know that they have a healing area. We plan to cherish each day's hangover and aim to have another one on the morrow. That's all we need to know.

Maybe it's just as well that Jimi Hendrix is dead. He wouldn't have wanted a reiki session in place of a joint after his performance.

But then Jimi probably wouldn't have realised that Woodstock was far from being a spontaneous impulse by half a million people to descend on Yasgur's Farm.

Driving the impulse were four young men: John Roberts, Joel Rosenman, Artie Kornfeld and Michael Lang. They found each other at the right time in history.

As an heir to a toothpaste fortune, Roberts had the money and it was no big stretch for him to meet Rosenman, whose father was an orthodontist. Kornfeld had the entrée to the music world and Lang, as well as owning the first head shop in Florida, had produced the Miami Pop Festival in 1968 that drew a crowd of 40,000.

By early April that year, the enterprising promoters had appropriated the symbols, the signs and the language of the newly independent youth. They spread their gospel through underground publications such as *Rolling Stone* magazine and *The Village Voice* in New York and then as August approached, they intensified the campaign with ads in the august, mainstream, *New York Times*.

As the date drew nearer, everybody was growing a little tense. The cops and other services were ready to handle a crowd of 50,000. So were the promoters, until they heard that there was a 20-mile tailback on the New York State Thruway.

When the tide of punters continued to grow and grow, in the interest of safety, the promoters tore down the fences and created the enduring myth of Woodstock as a 'free' festival. Everything from toilet paper to drinking water was in short supply but, for three days, a crowd of potentially unruly punters embraced each other, shared food, drink, bodies and good humour, in a triumph for what had been billed as 'THREE DAYS OF PEACE AND MUSIC'.

We were a tougher breed of festival-goers back in the last

century. We took our licks and survived without Portaloos, trendy wellies or healthy snacks.

But the memory of those heady days of resisting the establishment and jousting with the forces of conservatism are cold comfort now, as we watch in dismay these latter-day, over-the-counter-culture festivals being staged by desperadoes who make sure that everybody gets home sober, 'greener', mud-free, healed and, of course, tax compliant.

4 July 2009

AUGUST

HOW ELVIS BROUGHT SEX TO IRELAND

Nell McCafferty

We were the first real teenagers. We breathed the same air as Elvis and Brando. We took part in the world's first rock and roll riots. It was the 1950s. If next week's anniversary of the death of Elvis brings the 1950s into proper focus, the fabled 1960s will look childish.

Which they were. Love and peace, man? Go take a bath in scented suds, wimps.

There were no bathrooms when Elvis roared 'Hound Dog' in 1956. We were using outdoor toilets in Derry and toilet paper was a page of the local newspaper cut into four squares. That was my job on a Friday night, putting holes in the squares, stringing a cord through them and hanging them off a nail.

For this, my parents gave me pocket money, pennies from heaven that marked the financial recovery from World War II.

The good times had begun. In 1956, when I was twelve, I got a shilling a week. All over Derry, as darkness fell on a Friday night, the young headed out to share a plate of chips (six forks) and play the jukebox (five records for a shilling).

'Hound Dog', 'Heartbreak Hotel', 'Don't be Cruel', Elvis moaned and jiggled and shook and ached. He was twenty-one. I had just received my first 'gift from the Virgin Mary' (Protestants eat your hearts out) and was 'All Shook Up' and I didn't know what was going on, but something was, and whatever it was, it was physically delicious.

There was only one cure for that young body of mine, which is nowadays described as sex, which it was and it wasn't.

Something, certainly, was stirring. My hormones, you might say now, were at me, though nobody knew then that hormones existed, never mind orgasms. 'I've got these feelings,' Warren Beatty attempted by way of a teenage explanation to the doctor in *Splendour in the Grass* – a movie which did not come out until 1960, which tells you where we were at.

Brando had just won his Oscar for *On the Waterfront*. However, the grown man he played had failed to become somebody and Brando, to us, was already old at thirty-two.

Elvis was an exuberant twenty-one, though respectful with it, to his elders. This was crucial in mild Derry. Elvis addressed them as 'ma'am' and 'sir', in the way we said 'missus' and 'mister'. Brando thumped them in the face and demanded a job, a pay rise and the right to join a trade union.

That might be what our fathers did (our mothers worked full time in the home and there was no divorce or separation), but we were entering our carefree teens and we were nothing but Hound Dogs, sniffing out the joint, hoping no adult would notice.

We noticed them, though – the American sailors who flooded Derry, a British naval port that was host to all the sailors who flooded through. You needed iron filings in your stomach to cope with the European men who had garlic breath. We hung on to every word coming out of American mouths.

They sounded like Elvis, had the same suntans and white teeth. They had dollars and called girls 'honey', just like he did. Luckily, they were looking for grown-up women and left us alone to adore the King who, just as luckily, couldn't lay a finger on our shy selves.

My aunt worked in the cinema and used to bring home movie magazines, which I was forbidden to read. So I did – and I read that Elvis had flipped the strap off a woman's off-the-shoulder frock and signed his name on her bare arm. This was portrayed as decadence.

Which it was. Teenage girls in Derry covered their bare shoulders in cardigans and our mothers wore cardigans all the way up their arms. Teenage boys wore grey flannels and greying white shirts and V-necked jumpers and our fathers wore jumpers under their suits.

You had to cover up to survive the cold. The day began with humping coal in a bucket from the backyard to the kitchen to make a fire in the range. That was often after we had scraped the frost off the inside of the window-panes in the bedroom, which was usually shared with at least three sisters (there were no radiators).

We had porridge for breakfast, minced stew for dinner in the middle of the day and a boiled egg for tea at six o'clock.

There was running water indoors, mind you, though it was cold.

On Friday night, our mother heated pots of water on the gas cooker, poured them into the tin bath on the floor in the scullery, and we had our weekly bath.

Escape from reality came in the shape of 'Heartbreak Hotel'. It was supposed to be a lonesome song but in Derry it reeked of luxury – imagine staying in a hotel; in a room of your own.

There was no TV then and only one radio per household so all we had was the raw sound of Elvis and the photographs of that lovely throat, that glossy hair, those sideboards, and that velvet flesh around his eyes.

Gimme strength.

And gimme home-made Italian ice cream which Mr Yannarelli laid onto the wafer with a trowel, the way brickies laid on cement.

He let schoolchildren stand around the juke box if we were quiet, but the booths were restricted to wage earners.

Perhaps he kept his fingers crossed behind his back – *Blackboard Jungle* had been screened in Derry in 1955 and it showed teenagers hitting the teacher in America.

As if. We were intent on getting through grammar school and into university, on scholarship, the first-ever working class generation to have a chance of escaping the factory.

And then the seminal movie came. *Rock Around the Clock* arrived in Derry in 1956 and jiving literally hit the streets. The cops baton charged what was formally termed a riot – the young had poured out of the picture house that first night, and were throwing themselves about in rhythm on the road.

We were puzzled, though. Bill Haley was plain and fat, Elvis wasn't in the movie and it was made in black and white.

Immediately afterwards came *The Girl Can't Help It*. In technicolour Jane Mansfield had an outsize bust. Little Richard and Fats Domino were from another planet and the cinema newsreels showed that desegregation in America was tearing the two planets apart. It was just too frightening for our little racist white hearts in Derry. Also, neither man was good looking.

When Elvis did appear, in *Love Me Tender*, dismay increased. They made him sing ballads, he didn't have the lead role and he got shot dead. We didn't know that in America, in television land, he had frightened adults who had more experience of sexual activity than Elvis, or us.

Talk show host Ed Sullivan averred that Elvis concealed a mechanical device in the crotch of his trousers. Adults were reading through his legs, which we certainly were not. Kissing was out. 1956 ended badly. Jerry Hall was born that year and Mel Gibson and – who cares? Elvis had been quashed. It was over.

The hell it was. In 1957, Elvis erupted in *Teddy Bear*, in technicolor. He stood there, legs wide apart, in a deliberately rigid stance. The music pumped, his legs trembled, then that pelvis and those legs did things no pelvis or legs had done before.

Sinatra said that rock and roll was 'the most brutal, ugly, degenerate, vicious form of expression'. Sinatra was forty-two years old. What would he know about us? His hit record then was 'Young at Heart'. Yeah, right. Try being young in the legs, Frank. I was thirteen and what was going on between mine, stirring beyond comprehension or expression, was delicious and Elvis was at the other end of the line.

Not that we had any telephones in the 1950s. Elvis came right back, again and again, in *Jailhouse Rock* (now that was pole-dancing) and *King Creole*.

His pristine shirt and proper trousers was a deliberate response to Marlon Brando's oul' torn T-shirts and jeans. Elvis Presley never, ever wore blue jeans, the garb of the class he was trying to escape. We were upwardly mobile ourselves in Derry and Elvis was our role model. Like him, we were also young animals at the start of a sexual mating game.

Our playmate died when Elvis was conscripted in 1958. Two years later, out of the army, he donned a tuxedo and did a duet with Frank Sinatra. He made Sinatra look cool.

It was 1960 and twenty-five-year-old Elvis was going out with a fourteen-year-old girl, Priscilla. I was a mature sixteen.

He went downhill in Hawaiian shirts and movies. They made him wear shirts.

He always had a complex about his bare, skinny legs. He should have kept his trousers on.

Mystery is potent.

11 August 2007

THE MESSAGE OF OMAGH

Mark Dooley

It was Ireland's 9/11. It was the moment when 500 lbs of explosives killed 29 people and wrenched the heart from this country. It was, said Tony Blair, an 'appalling act of savagery and evil'. As always in times of great crises, the former prime minister's messianic vernacular was entirely apposite.

Yes, I speak of the Omagh bombing. I speak of that terrible day ten years ago when Northern Ireland's orgy of violence reached its shocking crescendo. I speak of an event that traumatised this nation like no other in its deeply troubled past. I speak of a quiet market town reduced to ash on a sunny Saturday afternoon. I speak of mass murder, mayhem and mourning.

Who can forget those scenes of carnage and devastation? Who can forget the shattered and bloodied bodies strewn around Market Street, some barely alive, others having been completely consumed by the conflagration? And who will ever forget that awful silence, punctuated only by the odd sob and the distant sound of sirens?

We had seen something similar before, of course. Think of Enniskillen on Remembrance Day in 1987 when eleven souls were sacrificed at the murderous hands of the Provisional IRA.

Once again, we witnessed horror on an unimaginable scale.

Once again, we looked on helplessly as corpses were hauled from the rubble and the stench of death pervaded the morning air. In that awful instant, evil appeared triumphant, its wicked fist raised high in victory.

As the cliché goes, however, appearances are deceptive. It is true that Enniskillen did nothing to stop the cycle of violence and retribution that had characterised daily life in Northern Ireland for nearly two decades. But something startling emerged from the embers that day, something which showed that evil would not ultimately endure in Northern Ireland. It was the gentle and saintly voice of Gordon Wilson.

You may recall that Gordon Wilson's daughter, Marie, perished beneath six foot of rubble on that fateful November morning. But what few of us will forget is what Mr Wilson subsequently said in a radio interview shortly after Marie's demise: 'I have lost my daughter and we shall miss her. But I bear no ill will. I bear no grudge. Dirty sort of talk is not going to bring her back to life.' He then forgave her killers, saying, 'I shall pray for those people tonight and every night.'

Those beautiful words stand out like jewels in the tormented history of the so-called 'Troubles'. They gave hope and solace to those who had none and they proved that nothing is impossible for a human heart steeped in the love of Christ.

Gordon Wilson's Christian courage was the beginning of the end of evil's dominance in the province of death.

'Father, forgive them, for they know not what they do.' He said it in agony from the Cross. He said it in the midst of misery and carnage, when the light of humanity was on the verge of extinction. In the darkest hour, He asked that his tormentors be granted His Father's mercy. He pleaded that they be given a place in paradise. And then He went to his death, having absolved mankind of its transgressions.

The triumph of Christianity is that its founder did not demand submission, but forgiveness. He demonstrated that the cycle of violence which characterises all human societies can only be stemmed when the other is forgiven his faults and failings. As such, the Christian religion is unique amongst its counterparts in that it is not a cause of violence but its cure.

Now, there will be those who will argue that Christianity has not always lived up to Christ's commands. That is certainly true. Still, that reality does nothing to take from the heroic majesty of that moment on Calvary when the God-man showed the price that must be paid for earthly peace.

Gordon Wilson did not manage to disarm his daughter's murderers. But by emulating Christ on the day of his own Calvary, he demonstrated what was needed to bring Northern Ireland from Golgotha to the empty tomb. In his noble words and actions, he dramatically illustrated that the blood of the Cross can cleanse a community, no matter how traumatised or afflicted.

Omagh brought to fruition the promise of peace that lies latent in all acts of true forgiveness. By the time of the atrocity in 1998, Gordon Wilson was already in the tender arms of his maker.

But the seeds that he planted some ten years prior were about to shoot, thus signalling a new dawn for a broken people.

No one has ever formally atoned for the crimes committed in Omagh. And yet from the horror sprang a precarious yet precious peace that still persists to this day. Yes, the victims' families have been treated appallingly. Yes, the violence and intimidation endures. Yes, the names of Robert McCartney and Paul Quinn should forever remind us that evil still lurks in our midst. But were it not for Omagh, the North's murder machine would still be churning out its hapless victims by the dozen.

Return to Calvary for a moment. What Christ taught was that real forgiveness is a phenomenon of hopeless situations. In other words, it is relatively easy to forgive minor transgressions. But it is not so easy to forgive your persecutors, or those who slaughter your family. It is in those moments of unparalleled devastation, however, that forgiveness is most necessary.

As Christ's example showed, forgiveness really counts when even the Son of Man believed that his divine Father had abandoned him.

I don't say that Omagh produced forgiveness of that extreme kind. But once the rubble had been cleared, the people of Northern Ireland entered a period of what Nietzsche once called 'active forgetting'. Gordon Wilson did not actively forget. He truly forgave. But active forgetting is the next best thing and is sometimes more effective for societies in search of salvation.

To actively forget means to make accommodation with your opponent while not totally forgetting his crimes.

It is, as it were, a prelude to full forgiveness. And it is an emotion that took hold of Northern Ireland in the wake of its worst outrage.

If Enniskillen produced Gordon Wilson, Omagh produced courageous politicians such as David Trimble and Seamus Mallon, men who ushered the province into its first phase of tentative tranquility. It was as if the Real IRA had bombed the North into peace, thus perpetually consigning itself to the lunatic fringe of terror outfits.

True, the walls dividing loyalist and nationalist did not fall. Trust between Catholic and Protestant remained at a minimum. And the bigotry that had personified the Northern psyche for so long was still very much in evidence.

Something, however, had tangibly changed. When I visited the heartland of nationalist West Belfast some years ago, I found a society slowly creeping from the shadows of its shady past. Sinn Féin was still dominant and the old republican murals still projected their frightening message from every wall. And yet no one that I met spoke about 'the war' in the way that they had done on my previous visits there prior to Omagh. Indeed, I met a number of hard-line nationalists who told me that after Omagh there could be no going back to bloodshed.

On the Protestant side, things were no different. A few years ago, some friends and I arranged a small gathering in honour of David Trimble. He had just resigned as leader of the Ulster Unionist Party. During our discussions, it soon became clear that Lord Trimble believed the violence was, for the most part, over, and that democracy, imperfect as it then was, had taken hold of the North.

Their families have every right to disagree, but I believe there is truth in the assertion that the victims of Omagh were not sacrificed in vain. On 15 August 1998, those poor souls climbed Calvary and were hoisted upon the cross.

In so doing, however, they broke the catastrophic cycle of destruction that had for so long purged Northern Ireland of its soul. It could even be argued that the Northern Assembly, fraught and fragile as it may be, is their true legacy. For it is there that the process of active forgetting, and even at times real forgiveness, is acted out on a continuing basis.

Ten years ago today, Omagh resembled Golgotha. Today, in its dignified serenity, it is more like the open tomb, the resurrected spirit of which hovers over the entire landscape of Northern Ireland. Some have forgiven, others have forgotten.

Most are simply savouring a relatively normal life without a daily diet of death.

On the day Marie Wilson died, her father said through his tears, 'Don't ask me, please, for a purpose. I don't have a purpose. I don't have an answer but I know there has to be a plan. If I didn't think that, I would commit suicide. It's part of a greater plan, and God is good.'

It could be said that God finally revealed his greater plan in the aftermath of Omagh's dreadful day. And just as the Christ-like Gordon Wilson had promised, it was indeed good.

16 August 2008

THE JOY OF COUNTRY LIFE

Roslyn Dee

Every day they excused themselves from class ten minutes before the final bell of the day rang for the rest of us. The 'early bus' girls. A gaggle of them who lived out of town, either on the fringes of rural life or at its very heart – on the farms that dotted the rolling landscape of County Derry in the late 1960s.

Kilrea, Garvagh, Swatragh, Macosquin, Moneydig, Maghera – all names that evoked an alien world, one where fathers didn't go to work in a collar and tie, where mothers wore aprons and baked buns and where boys drove tractors years before they first shaved.

The girls of this world, like those in my school, had already milked the cows or collected the eggs of a morning, hours before us townies had struggled out of our beds and sat down to our toast and cornflakes.

They even got a 'potato-gathering' day off school every year, spending it with family and friends in the fields, in the wide open spaces, while we sat cooped up indoors poring over our books in a soulless building that stood in the centre of the large, bustling town of Coleraine.

The country girls – a community within a wider community, and a tight-knit clan at that. They talked of barn dances, basket teas and church socials, of the Young Farmers' Club and a host of other gatherings.

Always there was a gathering and everyone, it seemed, knew everybody else. So-and-so's sister was going out with someone else's brother who was best friends with so-and-so's cousin. Their sense of loyalty was strong – to each other and to their community.

Occasionally though, a townie breached the ranks and I was privileged for five or six years to spend many happy, carefree holidays on a friend's family farm in Moneydig, just outside Garvagh. When I think of childhood summers, I think of Torrens's farm.

But as a townie, you are always an outsider, always the person who doesn't quite get the nuances of life beyond the commercial hub. And yes, of course, you laugh from time to time at the country folk, taking pleasure in their 'hickey' ways, in their different accents, in their alien way of life. The sniggering put-down is always the easiest option when ignorance – your own ignorance – is rife.

And yet that line that distinguishes that rural/town divide can be a very thin one at times. After all, even those who feel more sophisticated, more worldly than those from the countryside, are not always themselves such city slickers.

When I was growing up, Belfast, just fifty-odd miles away, was another country. Coleraine was still, in the mid-1960s, only shaking off its market-town roots and had yet to become a fledgling university town; Harry Bedi, a respected, local businessman who had arrived from India a couple of decades before with only a suitcase to his name, was the only Asian face I ever saw when I was a child.

Maybe I didn't understand what a heifer or a hogget was; maybe I laughed at my Moneydig friend because she loved the music of Charley Pride, but I knew nothing of Belfast city life and when a neighbour's son went to work in New York we thought we'd never see him again. Ever.

Kilrea and Garvagh represented rural life to me, but to my contemporaries in the 'big smoke' of Belfast, Coleraine itself was culchie-land. Being a country girl was – and still is – a relative thing.

But, come early summer every year of my childhood, that dividing line blurred even more when country came to town in the form of Coleraine Show, and Railway Road, where the showgrounds were located, became a rural jamboree of farm machinery, livestock, women in best dresses and ruddy-faced men in Sunday suits – and wellies.

Somewhere in my mother's treasure trove of family photographs is one of me, aged about nine, holding my little dog Skippy on a lead, a yellow rosette attached to the front of my blue pinafore as I grin delightedly at the camera: Skippy and I the proud, third-place prizewinners in the dog show at the showgrounds on that sunny Saturday in June.

Show time. Back then and now, four decades later, it's still a phenomenon. It's the colour, the sound and the smell of the rural Irish summer as, the length and breadth of this island, the agricultural shows which are all now in full swing illustrate with pride and passion that despite all the current negativity, this is what we still do well – this is still the real soul of our country.

'It's show time' may well have been the mantra of PJ Mara – Charlie Haughey's representative on earth – but what a world of difference there is between the grasping greed and political backstabbing of Ireland's tiger pups and the genuine sense of sharing and striving for excellence that is so potently displayed in our country shows.

Last weekend Tullamore, the daddy of them all, returned with a bang having been abandoned for the past two years because appalling weather had wiped it off the show map.

Today in Roscommon town and in Swinford, you'll find the best of country life on display. Tomorrow it's the turn of Mohill and Mullagh, Ballyshannon and Tullow.

And so the names and the dates stretch on and on, points of local pride on the calendar, right up until the days are noticeably shorter and the smell of home fires burning permeates the evening air at the end of September.

I have long crossed over that blurred identity line of my youth. For thirty-odd years I have lived a predominantly city life, all tentative nods to being a 'relative' country girl well and truly laid to rest.

From Liverpool to Oxford to Dublin, I have prided myself in leaving behind that townie who flirted with rural mores. Not quite in the league of a Belfast-born friend who swears that she starts to hyperventilate if ever she finds herself setting up home more than a fifteen-minute walk from a Marks & Spencer outlet, nonetheless, I have embraced city life with gusto.

Yet two weeks ago, over in Mayo to visit treasured friends who'd moved west a year ago after a lifetime in Dublin, and lured by the signs all over the town, Sunday afternoon found me making a snap decision to visit the agricultural show on the outskirts of Claremorris.

Sure it would be a bit of craic. Cows and chickens and all that guff. People talking funny and making eejits of themselves. So along I went, in the rain, with the wrong clothes and the wrong attitude.

There were cattle and sheep and goats and chickens and dogs. There were children and parents and grandparents. There were aunties and uncles and cousins. There were competitions to beat the band.

Apart from the competing livestock, there was an array of farm machinery, there was a daredevil biker, a best-dressed lady – and farmer, and child.

There were floral displays – some simple, some spectacular – there were champion onions and carrots and all manner of vegetables, there were prizewinning jams and cosmetics and some superb local craftsmanship.

Here was competitive excellence on view among people who knew each other well, as their fathers had known their fathers before them.

This was for-the-people stuff. By the people. Yet it wasn't all cosy camaraderie, for there was a competitive edge on display here that was actually quite inspiring.

If you'd poured time and energy into producing the very best carrots that you could, then, by God, you wanted to examine the ones that beat yours – and shake the hand of the man or woman responsible for such excellence. For make no mistake about it, the achievement of excellence is what these shows are all about.

It might not be cutting-edge high finance or multi-million euro property dealing (and look where all that got us) but there is a spirit afoot in the Irish countryside that is captured, tableaux-like, in an afternoon spent at an agricultural show.

Farmers are suffering – we all know that – but somehow that can-do spirit that country people have allows them to rise above the gloom and doom. If you've only ever heard the roar of the tiger economy way off in the distance, then the silence, when it comes, is not nearly as deafening. There was, of course, banter and joking and craic that afternoon in Claremorris. But there was seriousness too.

In the dog show ring, and with the heavens now cascading, the judge was showing an attention to detail that you'd usually witness only in national competitions. Feeling limbs, making owners run with their dogs, then stop, then run again. Points awarded, rosettes distributed, pride displayed.

There were two youngsters engrossed in watching the proceedings, each one holding a lead with a sheep on the end of it. *Father Ted* characters? No; if anyone was fit for a walk-on part in *Father Ted* on that bank holiday Sunday, it was me.

For the 'lovely girl' who won the best-dressed accolade was

indeed a lovely girl. The sheep were on leads because they were being led back to their trailer, via the dog show.

By 5.30pm there was no sign of drunkenness or obnoxious behaviour and throughout the afternoon people were welcoming and polite and courteous.

If only our foreign visitors could experience a bit more of this, the true spirit of the nation, and less of the false, Temple Bar phenomenon of our capital city, maybe we could truly, once again, stand proudly over our Céad Míle Fáilte reputation.

Nobody wants to turn the clock back. Nor should we regard our country heritage through JM Synge-style, rose-tinted glasses. The world, after all, has changed utterly. But the soul of our country, the part that embraces excellence and cherishes community, that remains steadfastly – and inspiringly – the same.

You'll see it in Swinford today, and in Roscommon. Tomorrow it'll be there again, writ large, in Mohill and in Tullow.

This is the best of what we are. We should celebrate that.

15 August 2009

WHY THE CHURCH IS FINISHED

Tom Inglis

The announcement earlier this week that the number of new seminarians has increased this year must be a cause of some joy for the Catholic Church. Thirty-six men have started training for the priesthood. This is twelve more than last year and the highest since 1999.

But the Church has been in deep recession for the past fifty years. In 1966, there were 254 new seminarians. The number of priests, nuns and brothers is dwindling rapidly. Most of those who are left are retired and elderly. In this respect, the Church is literally dying.

So while the increase this year may be seen as a green shoot, the reality is that the strength and influence of the Catholic Church in Irish society is in decline and will continue to decline in the years to come.

The main reason for this is that it has lost touch with the people. It no longer responds to their needs and interests. Irish Catholics have found new sources of meaning, new ways of living a good life.

While the decline in the institutional Church was inevitable, it was quickened by its attitude to sex. Ever since 'Humanae Vitae' in 1968 and the declaration that the use of 'artificial' contraceptives was immoral, the laity began to move down a different path.

Most no longer accept the Church's teachings on sex. They no longer believe that it is wrong to have sex outside of marriage, that people have to be married to have children, or that homosexual behaviour is immoral. They increasingly see sex as something to celebrate, as a central part of a normal, healthy, fulfilling life. In my view it was this new attitude to sex which made the findings of the Ryan Commission all the more horrific. It revealed what happens when sex is repressed.

Despite moving away from Church teaching, if Irish Catholics follow their European counterparts, they will still continue to see and understand themselves as Catholics. They will continue to believe in God. But God, the Church and salvation will not have the same influence over people's lives.

The majority of Irish Catholics no longer believe in hell or the devil. While the large majority – close to 80 per cent – still believe in heaven and life after death, there is increasing uncertainty about what happens when people die, about who gets into heaven and, more importantly, whether getting into heaven depends on following the teachings of the Church.

Irish Catholics are not only becoming similar to other European Catholics, they are also becoming more Protestant-like.

Salvation is achieved less through the Church and its sacraments and more through the individual. Increasingly, Catholics make up their own minds about what is right and wrong, good and bad. They follow their own consciences.

But Catholic Ireland is also becoming secular. This is happening at two levels.

In everyday life, God, Jesus and the saints no longer have the same influence. They are no longer on people's lips or in their hearts and minds. People no longer live in Catholic time and space. Their lives do not revolve around feast days, holy days, Lent, Advent. They no longer troop into Church for May and October devotions.

Meanwhile at another level, the Church has lost much of the

influence and control it had in Irish society, particularly in education, health and social welfare. These were crucial instruments in maintaining the faith.

Similarly, it is no longer able to influence and control the State and the media as it once did. The voice and influence of the Church has weakened. It is no longer, as it might like to think, the moral conscience of Irish society. The media has taken over this role.

But many of the messages of the media are very different from those of the Church. The media accentuate desires, pleasures and the importance of the individual's satisfaction. The failure of the Church to adapt to the media was central to its failure to adapt to the modern world. People no longer talk and relate to each other through the language, beliefs and practices of the Church. They communicate and create meaning with each other through the internet and what they see, hear and read in the media. They realise themselves as individuals by tastes, preferences and lifestyles created through the media.

At the same time, religion has become private and personal. Irish people used to become shy, awkward and embarrassed when they spoke about sex. But now it is increasingly difficult for people to talk about their belief in God. The main difference between the Church and the media is the attitude to the body, sex and self-fulfilment.

The Church is still rooted in a theology which sees the self as something to be denied. It is still rooted in a view of sex as a potentially dangerous disorder.

But the Catholics of Ireland have moved on. They see the self as something which has to be discovered, explored, expressed and fulfilled. And they see sex as a major part of this voyage of self-discovery and realisation.

Earlier this year, the gap between the Church and the people grew larger with the publication of the Ryan Commission Report into clerical child sex abuse. For the first time, Irish people began to realise that it was not just a case of there being some rotten apples in the Church barrel. There was something rotten about the barrel itself.

And I believe that it all had to do with sex.

Back in the 1990s, the laity were scandalised by the revelation that priests like Bishop Casey and Fr Cleary had sex and fathered children. The very people who preached and regaled against the evils of sex were indulging themselves. But as time passed, people began to realise that their sins were mild compared to sins of other members of the clergy.

The Ryan Report findings presented a new, horrific side to the Church's attitude to sex.

Significant numbers of priests, nuns and brothers who were supposed to be paragons of virtue were shown to be deeply troubled sexually. How did this happen? How was it that ordinary young boys and girls who fervently believed in God, who had dedicated their lives to the Church, were turned into brutal, sadistic creatures?

The answer, in my view, lies in the Church's attitude to sex and, in particular, to celibacy.

What these young boys and girls learned when they were being trained for the religious life was that whatever else they might say and do, they could never mention or talk about sex, let alone do anything that could be deemed sexual.

But it went deeper than this – they could not confess the truth about themselves. And so they buried it deep inside. But it may well be that the more they buried it, the more it became their focus. This regime of silence and denial was a recipe for disaster.

Many were able to deal with it but for many others this repressed sex became a volcano of anger and frustration that, given the right circumstances, could explode.

We now know that industrial and reformatory schools were the circumstances in which these volcanoes exploded. The stories of what took place in these schools reveal the enormous gap that has emerged between the Church and the laity. The laity has shaken off the shackles of sexual repression. They have learned to talk openly and honestly about their sexual feelings and emotions, their pleasures and desires.

The idea of being lectured to about sex by celibates has become strange. Indeed, the notion of celibates supervising and controlling the education of children may also be becoming strange.

It would be wrong to think that the Catholic Church will disappear altogether. The vast majority of people in the world today and throughout history have been religious. Atheism and agnosticism may be growing in Ireland, but so too are new, alternative religions, new ways of being spiritual and moral. And yet the Catholic Church still holds a monopoly position in the religious field.

Irish Catholics may be becoming more Protestant in terms of their beliefs and practices, but they are not actually switching over to Protestant denominations.

They may be trying alternative ways of being spiritual, anything from yoga to reiki, but they still look to the Church when it comes to major life transitions such as christenings, marriages and funerals. The Church will, of course, continue to be the main source of comfort and consolation when it comes to illness, tragedy, and death.

It is important, however, to remember that many people in Ireland are still deeply committed to the Church. It remains a powerful influence in their lives. If the Church can reach out to the young and into the cities then it may well be able to survive.

But will it survive without embracing the media and sex? Can it survive without allowing priests to marry and women to become priests? Changing circumstances – world wars, diseases, disasters – could change Church fortunes. It should know. It has been around for more than 2,000 years.

29 August 2009

SEPTEMBER

PIUS XII:
THE POPE WHO TOOK ON HITLER

Mark Dooley

Pope John Paul II will soon be a saint. So too will Blessed John XXIII. But what of that towering figure whose presence in St Peter's during World War II saved Christendom from the Antichrist?

On 2 March 1939 Eugenio Pacelli was elected Supreme Pontiff of the Catholic Church, a position he held until his death in October 1958. He chose the name Pius XII. It was one of the most controversial pontificates in history.

Pope Pius XII was the last great papal prince. He looked and sounded like a monarch. He was a theological conservative who despised communism. And yet despite his mystical aloofness, he was universally revered.

Here is what Albert Einstein said of Pius in 1940: 'Only the Church stood squarely across the path of Hitler's campaign for suppressing the truth. I never had any special interest in the Church before, but now I feel a great affection and admiration because the Church alone has had the courage and persistence to stand for intellectual truth and moral freedom.

'I am forced thus to confess that what I once despised, I now praise unreservedly.' Einstein was, of course, a Jew. And it was because of Pius's courage in the face of Nazism that he paid tribute to the Church.

So too did the Chief Rabbi of Israel, Isaac Herzog. 'The people of Israel,' he wrote in 1944, 'will never forget what His Holiness [did] for our unfortunate brothers and sisters in the most tragic hour of our history.' In 1945, the World Jewish Congress gave $20,000 to Church charities. It did so to acknowledge 'the work of the Holy See in rescuing Jews from Fascist and Nazi persecutions'. According to one Israeli diplomat, the Pope saved 'at least 700,000 Jews, but probably as many as 860,000, from certain death at Nazi hands'. When Rome was occupied by the Germans in 1943, Pope Pius ordered his clergy to do everything they could to protect Italian Jews.

The Jewish scholar and author of *The Myth of Hitler's Pope*, Professor David Dalin, estimates that 'in Rome, 155 convents and monasteries sheltered some 5,000 Jews. At least 3,000 found refuge at the Pope's summer residence at Castle Gandolfo.

'Sixty Jews lived for nine months at the Gregorian University, and many were sheltered in the cellar of the pontifical biblical institute. Hundreds found sanctuary within the Vatican itself.' Put simply, 'while 80 per cent of European Jews perished during World War II, 80 per cent of Italian Jews were saved', thanks largely to Pope Pius XII.

Moreover, when Rome was bombed on 19 July 1943, Pius summoned his Assistant Secretary of State, Giovanni Battista Montini, the future Pope Paul VI. The Pope asked how much cash was stored in the Vatican bank. 'About two million lire, Your Holiness,' replied Montini. 'Draw it immediately and take the first car you find in San Damaso courtyard. We will join you,' the Pope declared.

Without protection, the two men then headed towards the flames. The journalist Dan Kurzman describes what then transpired: 'As the Pope plodded through the smoking rubble of charred houses where more than 500 dead victims were strewn, survivors struggled to touch his white cassock.

'Then a labourer spread his jacket on the cobblestones and the Pope knelt upon it to pray. Before departing, he cradled a dead infant in his arms and ordered Montini to distribute alms from his bag.' On 13 August, more bombs fell on Rome. According to Kurzman, 'Pius again rushed to the scene to comfort the injured, pray for the dead and distribute alms to the homeless, and returned to the Vatican with his cassock bloodstained.' Another account describes how, during the bombings, 'when Jews and other refugees were hidden in the Vatican, the Pope provided for their needs. Whenever possible, kosher foods for the Jews were supplied'.

Why then has Pope Pius XII been branded 'Hitler's Pope'? Why did the journalist and author John Cornwell label him as 'arguably the most dangerous churchman of modern times'? Why, in other words, has such a courageous pontiff become the subject of a ruthless campaign of vilification?

His detractors say it is because 'he continually refused to condemn the Nazis – even though he was one of the first European leaders to be made aware of the Final Solution'.

In his international bestseller, *Hitler's Pope: The Secret History of Pope Pius XII*, Cornwell makes the following observation: 'Pacelli was no monster; his case is far more complex, more tragic than that.

'The interest of his story depends on a fatal combination of high spiritual aspirations in conflict with soaring ambition for power and control. His is not a portrait of evil but of fatal moral dislocation – a separation of authority from Christian love. The consequences of that rupture were collusion with tyranny and, ultimately, violence.' Such outrageous caricatures of Pius XII are not new. In 1963, five years after Pius's death, a German communist named Rolf Hochhuth staged a seven-hour play entitled *The Deputy*.

In it, he portrayed Pius as a scheming and cynical cleric, for whom the Vatican's fiscal fortunes mattered more than the extinction of the Jews.

Since then, dozens of books have peddled similar propaganda against Pius. Most of them, as Dalin points out, have been penned by 'lapsed or angry' Catholics. Cornwell, for instance, is an ex-seminarian.

Consequently, argues Dalin, 'their real topic proves to be an intra-Catholic argument about the direction of the Church today, with the Holocaust simply the biggest club available for liberal Catholics to use against traditionalists'. David Dalin is no cheerleading apologist for the canonisation of Pius XII. He is a leading Jewish scholar and author of nine highly acclaimed books.

That is why he is a more credible witness to Pius's courage than a controversialist like Cornwell.

Dalin believes that 'to make Pius XII a target of our moral outrage against the Nazis, and to count Catholicism among the institutions delegitimised by the horror of the Holocaust, reveals a failure of historical understanding'. Why? Because Pius hated Hitler just as much as Hitler hated Pius.

And no, the Pope certainly was not silent on the Holocaust.

Between 1917 and 1929 Pius was papal nuncio to Bavaria in Germany. He saw first hand the rise of the Nazis. In 1935 he denounced them in an open letter as 'false prophets with the pride of Lucifer'.

On the eve of war in 1939 the new pope issued his first encyclical, in which he openly criticised racial ideology. In response, Allied planes dropped thousands of copies all across Germany in an attempt to isolate the Nazis.

That same year the Pope agreed to a proposal hatched by Nazi rebels and the British government to remove Hitler.

He even promised to convey classified information to the British and, according to Dan Kurzman, 'to support a decision to kill Hitler if the plan to take him prisoner failed'. In 1942 Pius denounced the Vichy government in France for 'the inhuman arrests and deportations of Jews from the French-occupied zone to Silesia and parts of Russia'.

Joseph Goebbels responded by producing ten million copies of a pamphlet in which he described Pius as the 'pro-Jewish pope'.

But by far the best evidence of how much Hitler despised Pius is provided by Dan Kurzman in his intriguing thriller, *A Special Mission: Hitler's Secret Plot to Seize the Vatican and Kidnap Pope Pius XII*.

When Mussolini was overthrown in July 1943 Hitler was convinced that Pius had planned Il Duce's downfall.

In reaction, the Fuhrer summoned the leader of the SS in Italy, General Karl Wolff, and ordered him to undertake the following 'special mission': 'I want you and your troops to occupy Vatican City as soon as possible, secure its files and art treasures, and take the Pope and Curia to the North.

'I do not want him to fall into the hands of the Allies or to be under their political spell and influence. The Vatican is already a nest of spies and a centre of anti-National Socialist propaganda.' Hitler's plan was never executed as Wolff and other diplomats sought to persuade Pius to act as an intermediary for a negotiated peace.

But the Pope was made aware of the kidnap plot and became obsessed with the prospect that he and the Vatican would be destroyed by the Nazis.

Pius's fears were not unfounded. Official documents published in 1998 and cited by Kurzman reveal that Hitler actually planned to murder the Pope in January 1944.

Code-named 'Operation Rabat', the plot involved storming the Vatican, killing all the members of the Curia and arresting the Pope. If Pius resisted or tried to escape, he too was to be shot.

In short, the Antichrist intended to slaughter the Vicar of Christ.

What this sensational story reveals is that Pope Pius XII was not an anti-Semite. Neither was he Hitler's Pope. If anything, he heroically saved more Jews from slaughter than 'all other churches, religious institutions and rescue organisations combined'. That is why the Fuhrer desperately wanted him sacrificed. Yes, Jewish elders like David Dalin wish 'that more explicit excommunications had been announced'. But, as Dalin himself admits, such a papal declaration of excommunication could have been disastrous.

If the Pope had acted so, the Chief Rabbi of Denmark declared after the war, 'Hitler would probably have massacred more than six million Jews, and perhaps ten times ten million Catholics'.

It is time to rehabilitate the reputation of Pope Pius XII. It is time to proclaim that no other pope in history has shown such saintly stamina in the face of pure evil. And yes, that includes Blessed John Paul II.

After the War, the Chief Rabbi of Rome, Israel Anton Zolli, converted to Catholicism. He chose as his baptismal name 'Eugenio', in honour of Pius.

In his diary, Zolli wrote: 'No hero in all of history was more militant, more fought against, none more heroic than Pope Pius XII in pursuing the work of true charity!'

It is shameful that Eugenio Pacelli is not already a saint.

As David Dalin asserts, he was a 'righteous gentile' who saved the world's soul as tyranny sought to slay it.

Let there be no more excuses: canonise him now.

16 August 2007

CLASH OF THE CASH

Dave Hannigan

Tomorrow afternoon, Croke Park will thrum to the noise of 87,000 people when the ball is thrown in for the All-Ireland hurling final. In every corner of the world, Irish people will gather before TVs to witness the clash between Kilkenny and Tipperary.

Where else would thirty amateurs fill a stadium, generate millions of euro in revenue, and all in the name of representing the county where they were born and grew up and learned the game?

For seventy minutes, everything will be right with the sporting world.

This week, of all weeks, we need a dose of something Corinthian and pure because the sports pages have been hijacked by a cautionary tale of what professionalism can do to a sport. Towards the end of last season's Heineken Cup quarter-final against Leinster, Harlequins ordered Tom Williams to fake a blood injury, using capsules purchased from a joke shop, so he would have to be replaced by fly-half Nick Evans. Trailing 6-5, the hope was that Evans could come on and kick the winning drop goal against Leinster. So far, so bad.

In trying, in this dastardly fashion, to win a game and to halt Leinster's historic march to the trophy, Harlequins ended up exposing a culture of cheating, demonstrating how rugby has been changed since turning pro in 1995.

It is, as it was always destined to be once players were paid, a win-at-all-costs environment now. Never mind the rules. Disregard the history and traditions. Needs must when the result and the cash is on the line. Forget the offensive old adage about this being a game for ruffians played by gentlemen.

The new standard appears to be the American locker-room motto: 'If you ain't cheatin', you ain't tryin''.

It wasn't always like this. In the years BC (Before Cash), things were different. The record book states that Jack Daly scored the second-half try that beat Wales and won Ireland their first ever Grand Slam at Ravenhill on March 13, 1948. Photographic evidence proves that at the final whistle, the supporters who invaded the field in Belfast ripped his shirt from his back and carried him shoulder-high from the fray.

When the train carrying the Irish team pulled into Dublin the following day, Daly was met by a glamorous woman in a sports car, carrying a precious fragment of his jersey. They drove off together and he stayed so long in her company that by the time he got back to work, he'd been sacked.

With no job and no money, he rang up Huddersfield rugby league club, who had been on his trail for a while, and turned professional for a signing bonus of £1,000, a basic weekly wage of £6 and double that for every win.

A less salacious version of his biography involves Daly ringing his mother down in Cobh the night of the triumph over Wales, discovering that she required £500 for an urgent operation and contacting Huddersfield within the hour. Either edition more or less conforms to the writer Ulick O'Connor's contention that the amateur Daly ended his Irish career prematurely by being forced to take the league shilling 'through sheer penury and noble rage'.

That was then. When the current Irish team clinched the country's second Grand Slam earlier this year, the victory was worth well over two million euro in prize money alone to the IRFU.

It was worth a fair few bob to the players too in performance-related bonuses and in amplifying their value as endorsement vehicles for corporations.

Whether it's Brian O'Driscoll putting his name and profile to the selling of cars, razors and mobile phones or Ronan O'Gara selling silver cufflinks, this is the best paid and best looked-after generation of Irish rugby footballers ever.

No worries now about the superstars being lured to rival codes by money. And yet, fourteen years after finally turning professional, the sport is in a state of disgrace. Much like when first dealing with the spectre of steroids, it would be naive to believe Dean Richards of Harlequins was the only coach (his official title was the more all-powerful 'director of rugby') to pull a stunt involving a fake injury.

Already, rugby writers are making subtle and legally circumspect references to previous abuses of the blood substitute rule and the apparently widespread circumventing of the regulations regarding uncontested scrums too.

How did it come to this?

'The IRFU will oppose the payment of players to play the game and payment to others such as coaches, referees, touch judges and members of committees for taking part in the game because the game is a leisure activity played on a voluntary basis,' declared the powers that be in Dublin in May, 1995. That almost quaint testament of faith was Irish rugby's last stand, the moment the blazers clung one more time to the rock of amateurism as the tide of professionalism was rising all around and about to sweep them away. It's fashionable to mock those men as hoary dinosaurs, especially when turning pro has seen the sport in Ireland transformed in terms of success, profile, and popularity. Yet there was a method to their madness.

The old-stagers knew the game they grew up with and loved would never be the same again once money started changing hands. And so it has spectacularly proved.

Every aspect of rugby has changed. Physically the players are unrecognisable. The once-beloved easter-egg shaped prop forward is now almost svelte and fleet of foot. Centres look more like second rows, weighing in 20 to 30 lbs heavier than in the early 1990s. Most of that added girth is muscle too, meaning the tackles are harder and more jarring and, consequently, the injuries are more plentiful and severe.

The need to be bigger, faster and stronger filters right down to the schoolboy game where kids must now bulk up, and parents shudder every time they collide with opponents.

Professionalism has brought other unseemly baggage too. The rugby players from the southern hemisphere are the equivalent of the badge-kissing soccer players of the Premiership, charlatans in love with a club until more money is available elsewhere.

The Aussies, New Zealanders, and South Africans parachute into Ireland and proclaim their sudden passion for all things Munster/Leinster/Ulster and talk about the Heineken Cup as if it was the stuff of their boyhood dreams back home. Which it wasn't, for many reasons, but mainly because it didn't exist when most of these fellows were kids.

If the Harlequins shenanigans have shone a welcome light on the darker corners of pro rugby, the whole debacle should frighten those denizens of the GAA who want the players to be recompensed.

Whether it's the Gaelic Players' Association agitating for 5 per cent of the association's annual revenue for its members or the odd individual footballer or hurler who'll brazenly admit to wanting to be paid to play, all need to realise the games would never be the same again.

Imagine the impact on Gaelic football, a sport already veering towards worrisome violence at inter-county level, if money was at stake. Is it a huge stretch to imagine counties going out to seriously hurt star opponents in order to increase their own chances? Kerry would have to put a protective force field around Colm Cooper.

How long before the blood sub rule is being abused and a free-taker is being brought onto the field at a vital juncture while somebody more expendable feigns injury? As rugby is learning the hard way, once jobs and money are at stake, anything goes.

There is already plenty of evidence inside the GAA that a little money goes a long way to causing trouble. What better time than the eve of hurling's showpiece to remember that over the past two decades several victorious teams have run into difficulties afterwards.

Why? Certain players were, rightly or wrongly, accused of milking the Sam Maguire or the Liam McCarthy success for a few extra quid behind the backs of their colleagues.

At grass-roots level, money divides too. Almost every hurling and football club in the country has experienced infighting about importing high-profile coaches and paying them €200 a training session. At county level, the sums tend to be significantly larger and payment better disguised, but they still breed bitterness amid the rank and file.

Croke Park's large willingness to ignore the paying of huge salaries to a few inter-county coaches also lends weight to the players' complaints that they deserve a few grand too. See what money does.

There is also the matter of loyalty. The entire cornerstone of the GAA, what still makes it different and special, is the players playing all their lives for their native places. With some form of compensation available, the counties with the richest benefactors would suddenly become attractive destinations for gifted individuals in search of some extra income.

One or two people will allege that this has happened already but in a professional era, the pride of the parish aspect, the most fundamental quality of the association, would be shattered forever.

To understand how quickly the world has changed, we must recall a Monday night after an All-Ireland football final in the early 1990s. A journalist and a player were sitting together on the bus ferrying the new champions through their home county.

Amid the standard issue bonfires and mayhem, one more tumultuous crowd checked the vehicle's progress and the player turned to the journalist with a manic look on his face.

'Look at how much they love us,' said the wide-eyed footballer, pointing towards the people swarming around the windows. 'We'd be fools not to cash in on this.'

'You'll have to be careful how you do that, though; the GAA are still very strict about amateurism,' the journalist replied.

'Money? Who's talking about money?' asked the footballer. 'I'm talking about the women.'

5 September 2009

THE ARCHITECTS
OF POLITICAL DECAY

Richard Waghorne

Several days after Rody Molloy resigned in disgrace from FÁS, I walked into Town Bar and Grill on Kildare Street. The subterranean restaurant is the lunchtime haunt of the political class and was busy despite the recession. In the circumstances, you might have expected Mr Molloy to be maintaining a deservedly low profile, holed up at home with the curtains drawn perhaps.

Instead, he was sitting in the middle of the not inexpensive restaurant with a seemingly smug smile on his ruddy face, eyes beaming. I remember it perfectly precisely because I could not understand why a man recently ushered out of his job under the darkest of proverbial clouds was looking so evidently pleased with himself. Well, we know the answer to that now.

It is becoming clear as the story of those days and his seven-figure pay-off has started to seep out, that the case of Rody Molloy embodies much that is grossly wrong with our self-serving and utterly contemptuous political class.

Here we have a man who was running a billion-euro-a-year State firm with a sclerotic performance record and rampant irregularities that have already seen two files sent to the Director of Public Prosecutions. These irregularities defy parody, from the bizarre tale of the $400 worth of wash-and-blow-dries for Mary Harney through to a car bought for a raffle that never happened and which later disappeared.

There are few clearer cases of outright failure than the long lamentable story of that agency. Indeed, Rody Molloy's FÁS was a good deal worse than merely incompetent. It was run as a slush fund for first-class travel and dining for the self-selecting circle of Social Partners and government ministers, with tens of thousands of euro run up in restaurants on credit cards funded by taxpayers.

To remember that all this was done by an agency set up to help people without work get into employment is to remember just how badly the people who were meant to be getting the benefit of that money were betrayed.

To say that this man should simply have been sacked is to state the obvious. This, though, was no mere accident and not even ministers as incompetent as Mary Coughlan make such colossal payouts by mistake. It is not an isolated example of failure being rewarded. The vast pay-off Mary Coughlan authorised without even bothering with the pretence of legal advice, saying it was not needed, is simply one of the more shocking examples of a rotten political class that treats taxpayers with undisguised contempt.

When these years of decline are remembered in the future, the sheer disdain the political elite demonstrated towards the public is what will stand out all the more starkly with the benefit of hindsight. Repeatedly since the recession arrived the people entrusted with the destiny of the country have looked after their own interests first.

We are a long way from the political standards of old. De Valera died not quite in poverty but sufficiently worried about money that civil servants at Áras an Uachtaráin were concerned for his old age. Seán Lemass believed that the dignity and probity of the Taoiseach's office required him to forsake even his enthusiasm for attending race meets. There was no past golden age of public standards in this country, far from it. But there was once an understanding that the powerful hold their offices in trust for their voters.

The culture of our ruling class today has decayed so far that not even traces of this decorum remain. The roll call of recent dishonour demonstrates that much beyond doubt.

Ministers do not think of themselves as being on our side any longer. The Rody Molloy story proves that conclusively. There is no possible rationale for Mary Coughlan's decision to transfer a seven-figure sum from taxpayers to her disgraced FÁS chief that does not involve a deliberate decision to put the political class before the public.

The revelation that this truly revolting pay-out was made ought to crystallise permanently the true instincts and intentions of a government that runs its own affairs strictly for its own benefit.

The same is true of all those ministers who abused public money through their participation in pointless and expensive FÁS junkets. Mary Coughlan will forever be the Tánaiste who decided to hand Rody Molloy this money and it ought to go without saying that her resignation is necessary but Mary Harney is another particularly discreditable case in point. She is a woman whose party notionally once stood for high standards in public office.

Yet she was slurping at the trough along with the worst of them in FÁS, running up meal bills on the public account that would be excessive whatever the circumstances. To do this while being the minister responsible for explaining cuts to front-line medical services is more shaming still. This is, however, a woman who has no compunction about billing Michelin-starred meals to the State while HSE cuts compound the suffering of those children at Crumlin Hospital whose vital operations have been postponed indefinitely. She ought to have sided with the public and lobbied for these abuses to be ended and those responsible sacked. Instead, her allegiance was not to the public but to the semi-anonymous cabal of insiders who have been milking the public purse at FÁS and elsewhere.

Only with this endemic contempt for taxpayers was it possible for John O'Donoghue to behave as he has. This is not simply a matter of billing the public for €900-a-night hotel rooms and the full, almost endless list of largess and, at times, sheer waste.

The utter refusal even to comment on the revelations of his spending until finally ambushed by a microphone looks to be the deed of a man who believes the public purse is there not only for ministers to rifle at their whim but to do so without even accounting for it afterwards.

It seems that only a lingering instinct for self-preservation produced his eventual non-apology. He has shown no remorse, offered to pay back no money, admitted no specific wrong and continues to bet that his constituents and the rest of us are sufficiently supine that we will put up with being treated that way. It is the same calculation Martin Cullen made when notoriously billing the taxpayer a four-figure sum for a few extra inches of leg-room while travelling to America to attend a St Patrick's Day celebration.

That is the central calculation in all of these political decisions. Repeatedly in recent months, people in positions of trust have gambled that the public will tolerate being treated with complete and utter contempt by people supposed to be guarding their interests.

When Patrick Neary quit as Financial Regulator with his own enormous pay-off – after his gross failure to prevent a banking meltdown, which will stand in Irish history as one of the most abysmal records of any public servant – he and the ministers who authorised his package simply gambled that they would get away with it. The same is true of Michael Fingleton's million euro bonus, awarded around the time of the bank guarantee scheme.

He promised to pay it back, has not done so, and Brian Lenihan has not lifted a finger to force him. Nor has Seán FitzPatrick, at this point, been so much as asked to answer a few questions by gardaí.

All countries tell themselves pious myths about their national character. We like to pretend that the Irish are a rebellious lot of plain talkers who will not put up with being exploited. Actually, the capacity of voters to allow their representatives to abuse their trust and their energy is remarkable. The public has been kicked in the teeth again and again in the last two years, starting with the government's attempt to award itself a pay rise in late 2007 under Bertie Ahern, long after recession was becoming apparent, through to invariably vast rewards for people whose failures are the reason a quarter of a million have emigrated and half a million will soon be out of work.

It is no hyperbole to say that in plenty of democracies people would be rioting in the streets if treated this way. It is not entirely to our credit that we are so placid as a country when treated so abominably.

The revelation that this government voluntarily handed Rody Molloy more money than most people earn in a lifetime, on his exit in shame, ought to dispel any illusions about the nature of politics in Ireland.

The decision is so inexplicable, the award so disgustingly opposed to natural justice that the scales should finally fall even for those whose healthy first instincts are to give people the benefit of the doubt.

Mary Coughlan's resignation should, if there is any hope of ending this culture of contempt for voters, now be unavoidable. That Brian Cowen has given her his full backing regardless only demonstrates anew that that rot goes all the way up to the Taoiseach's office.

But her departure should not simply be a convenient opportunity for the government to get rid of a minister who has long proved herself a profound embarrassment. It should happen swiftly and for the right reasons, namely because she has become the embodiment of all that is sick and rotten with political standards here.

We will know that we truly live in a country that has been hijacked by a circle of plunderers if she somehow does not, displaying to all again the unapologetic refusal to behave decently that has seeped so far through our public life.

26 September 2009

OCTOBER

HOW THE SISTERHOOD SOLD OUT

Áine Ryan

Feminism has failed. Abysmally. Thirty years ago women burned their bras. Nowadays they turn their boobs into silicone weapons. They bow at the altar of Botox and botched facelifts. They hobble on the heels of Prada and Marc Jacobs while whimsically manipulating the spoils of their forebears' revolution.

Imagine Victoria Beckham in a head-to-head debate with suffragist Charlotte Despard or even Katie Price on a panel with former President Mary Robinson. The subject: the role of women in the twentieth century.

Groan. Admittedly, Despard and Robinson may have inadvertently sprouted some metaphorical follicles on their mammaries while on their epic quest for women's liberation, the only thing the other two – Posh and Jordan, Barbie and Bratz – have sprouted is hair extensions.

But can such female icons of modern feminine fatuity such as Posh and Jordan be blamed for a former generation's failure to bring an ideology to its ideal fruition, its most sophisticated culmination? Equal but different. Equality with distinctions. Fraternity for the sorority.

Ironically, the fatal flaw of the women's liberation movement was the exclusion of men. That glaring error was further compounded by the suppression of the feminine in favour of the expression of the masculine – 'Don't you dare hold that door open or I'll knee you in the balls,' for example.

As a young philosophy student at St Patrick's College, Maynooth, in the late 1970s, my Socratean logic fell on deaf ears when I argued, at the newly-founded Feminist Society, that real progress would not be made if men were excluded from the group. (What a daft irony making such an argument in a – back then – flourishing bastion of religious patriarchy.) Feminist scholars divide feminism into three distinctive 'waves'.

The first was during the late nineteenth and early twentieth centuries when the main impetus was the drive for suffrage, or the right of women to vote. It also manifested itself in a number of industrial protests and strikes for better working conditions. The genesis of International Women's Day, held each year on March 8, can be traced to these protests, one of which occurred in New York in 1907 when women, working in extremely unsafe conditions in a clothes industry sweatshop, went on a hunger march and called for better wages and a ten-hour day. A ten-hour-day – and that was undoubtedly before they fed and washed their children. While the march was quelled by police, it provided a symbolic impetus for future protests.

The second wave started during the 1960s and was defined by the inextricable links between cultural and political inequalities. Through the arts and political lobbying, the spotlight was brought on insidious strands of discrimination inhabiting the most mundane aspects of women's lives. The movement encouraged women to become reflective, critical, and militant about the sexist structure of power.

The ongoing third or last wave is patently a more academic construct than a mass movement. It was effectively born out of the failure of the previous movement which, in some circles, is viewed to have been dominated by white middle-class women. It has a focus on race-related gender issues and is not confined to any socio-economic class. It even eschews the term feminist in some cases as some believe it is associated with an exclusive man-hating elite.

Recently anointed Nobel Literature Laureate, octogenarian Doris Lessing once inspired a whole generation of feminists. Her 1962 autobiographical tome *The Golden Notebook* told the story of the life, loves and mental breakdown of a contemporary 'free woman'. In real life Lessing abandoned her two children from her first marriage, comparing her actions to eighteenth-century Enlightenment philosopher Jean-Jacques Rousseau's justification for putting his offspring into a foundling home: 'They are going to be much better brought up because, look at me, I'm so rackety.'

However, nowadays, Lessing views her inspirational book as her 'albatross', the sisterhood as horrible people and, moreover, as 'some of the smuggest, most unself-critical people the world has ever seen'.

She argues that after an initial burst of energy feminists became political, turned on each other and failed to achieve their aims.

However, being fair, the many achievements of the women's liberation movement were mammoth. Take that historic institution of cassocked misogyny in Maynooth as a microcosm of these revolutionary changes, implemented during quite a short period in Irish society. In fact the national seminary provides a perfect laboratory for examining the impact of the feminist movement of the 1970s.

For example, it was through the conviction and activism of feminist and writer Evelyn Conlon that a crèche was established on its sanctified grounds in County Kildare. Conlon, a mature student at the time with two small children, thus – to the shock and displeasure of the traditionalists – opened the doors of the hallowed halls to married women and mothers.

It was furthermore the very presence of these early female students in the fledgling secular university that forced open formal debates on such distasteful subjects as contraception, divorce and, after much lobbying, abortion. The day-to-day casual canteen interactions between young clerical students – committed to a lifetime of celibacy – and young female students – committed to the exact opposite – proved healthy and enlightening.

Of course there were lots of sexual sorties and minor scandals, the majority of which were repressed, thus avoiding public scrutiny or questioning. In a way this seething undercurrent of heterosexuality that suddenly suffused the college and challenged the tacit blind-eyedness to rampant homosexuality – typical of any male institution – was also liberating on other levels, especially for the men. It undoubtedly also led to many's the dark night of the soul for the sincere clerical students faced, for the first time, with young revolutionary women whose appetite for carnal pleasure was not quelled by deans of discipline or morning prayer in the so-called Gun Chapel.

There is no question about the fact that the women's movement has scored many points, has won a number of battles. It hasn't won the war though. The statistics tell the story.

The relatively well-off and highly educated women of Europe still earn just 74 per cent of male earnings, still perform more than 80 per cent of household chores, only represent 18 per cent of decision-makers in EU institutions, and number 27 per cent of members of the EU parliament.

It is also an uncomfortable reality that a woman working in a Chinese sweatshop would have to work fifteen hours a day, seven days a week for 700 years to earn what the chief executive of Nike, Phil Knight, earns in one year.

Moreover, it is horrific to contemplate that, despite a global commitment following a 2002 UN convention, there are still an estimated three million sub-Saharan African and the Middle-Eastern women being subjugated to the barbaric practice of female genital mutilation.

Feminism has failed and continues to fail because of its gender exclusivity. There's been too much heckling, too much shouting; not enough inclusiveness and not enough listening.

Doris Lessing is also right, albeit for some of the wrong reasons, about the sisterhood's inability to be self-critical. Nowhere has this manifested itself more than in its dismal humourlessness – ritualistically sacrificed on the altar of political correctness. It has left its ideology strangled and hysterical.

Examples abound: a party in a Dublin suburb in the late 1980s where a female academic almost starts a riot because another female reveller sings Maria Muldaur's hit, 'Midnight At The Oasis'. Check out the lyrics. Sweet Jesus! Ok, it's about polygamy but, in the circumstances, so what! – 'I know your daddy's a sultan/A nomad known to all/ With fifty girls to attend him, they all send him/ Jump at his beck and call.' Luckily, we sane members of the gathering were already stunned by copious amounts of alcohol. The poor, unsuspecting chanteuse, though, had to be consoled in the ladies room.

In recent years, men's groups have sprung up all over the country. Their aim is to afford men – big boys – a safe forum to express their anxieties, fears, worries. The groups are also effectively the fallout from the botched female revolution.

Clearly some of these men have been emasculated during the intensity of the socio-cultural upheaval of the revolution.

Last week at a conference in Westport, entitled Turas na mBan (the journey of women), author and Glenstal monk, Mark Patrick Hederman introduced the little-known word called 'gynecide'. while addressing the subject of Creativity and the Feminine. Gynecide, he said, is the universal attempt to purge ourselves and the planet of the feminine principle.

'This seemingly almost innate tendency in our species has led not just to worldwide sexism, which we are beginning to redress slowly but surely, but it has also meant the violent and sometimes maniacal hatred for, and extirpation of, any manifestation of the feminine inside the male variety itself.' He cited the Rugby World Cup matches as a 'blatant celebration of macho masculinity in its most undisguised and inane form'.

Hederman argued that what was important in today's society was to recognise the 'infinite and complicated permutations of both the male and female' within each one of us.

He also observed that it is sometimes 'a question of a few chromosomes here or there' as to whether you are born Bernard or Bernadette, David or Goliath, Joseph or Josephine.

However, whether Posh could have been a Becks, or Jordan a Peter Andre, the widespread cosmetic carving of the female body shatters every feminist principle. Nips and tucks are nothing more than basic butchery.

They are the new blood sport of the nouveau-riche female slave.

21 October 2007

THE NEW AMERICA

Mark Little

At the end of this rollercoaster week we are reminded why American politics packs such a visceral punch. Part of it is fear: the initial collapse of that banking bailout makes us realise how desperate we all are for credible leadership in Washington. Part of it is fascination: those election debates are car-crash television, part soap-opera, and part reality show, as much *American Idol* as *The West Wing*.

But what if there was something more dramatic lurking behind the freak show and the financial meltdown? What if the Obama/McCain bout is just a warm-up for the main event: the birth of a New America.

The United States is a moving target. If you become fixated on its eye-catching detail you can't see the landscape changing in the background. That's exactly the danger we face right now; the travelling circus of the election campaign has obscured something more important: a profound transformation of American life.

The first transformational force is the exodus of a new generation of American pioneers away from the old, established cities – particularly in the east and Midwest – towards a 21st century frontier way out west. The last US census found that America's population centre is moving south and west at a rate of three feet an hour, five miles a year. The current predictions are that by 2030 two out of three Americans will live in what is commonly known as the Sunbelt.

This new frontier, stretching from California to Texas, is the scene of an unprecedented collision of all the forces that have shaped US history. It is as if this vast stretch of parched earth had become a particle accelerator propelling the American dream towards a chain reaction with a million contradictory fragments of the past and present.

The New America is at its most dynamic in the exploding suburbs – or Boomburbs – springing up around the expanding cities of the desert. They are places like the Phoenix suburb of Mesa, which is now bigger than Miami, Minneapolis, Cleveland or Atlanta. These communities of 300,000 or 400,000 people were little more than desert outposts a generation ago but now they are America's centre of gravity.

The Boomburbs have produced a rebellion against the tired old clichés of a suburban life. They are built around an elemental craving for community, the promise of a better life and a more sophisticated lifestyle. They are a thoroughly modern version of the legendary 'shining city', offering all-comers their own personal version of the American dream.

The politics of the Boomburbs are optimistic but cautious. Their citizens retreat from extremism. They want politics to talk about issues like jobs, energy and water, and not gay marriage and abortion. They have had enough of the 'culture war' which has paralysed American politics for decades.

Most Boomburbs are located in swing counties which go Republican or Democrat by small margins. As they have grown, they have transformed Sunbelt states like New Mexico, Nevada and Arizona into swing states, dramatically increasing their importance at election time. Increasingly, the Boomburbs instincts are setting the tone of politics in the New America.

The Sunbelt is the New America at its best but also at its worst.

Take a trip to Las Vegas and the desert suburbs around it and you see a turbo-charged version of the American dream that just can't be sustained. In 2006, a new resident was arriving here every six minutes and a new house was being built every nineteen. Las Vegas now has the highest rate of water consumption of any big US city but it is also the driest urban area in the United States.

The contradictions at work in the Boomburbs are forcing a growing number of Americans to confront their nation's environmental delusions. In the past year there has been a marked shift away from those petrol-guzzling mega-cars. Sales of the Hummer plummeted by 30 per cent in the first three months of 2008, while sales of the fuel-efficient hybrid, the Toyota Prius, rose by 54 per cent in 2007.

There is also a shift in consciousness among Sunbelt politicians like Governor Arnold Schwarzenegger who has committed California to cut carbon emissions by 25 per cent before 2020. In Boomburbs, planners are embracing the 'smart growth' credo of the 'New Urbanist': less driving, less sprawl; more town squares, more walking and cycling.

For now, the 'greening' of Boomburbs has taken a backseat to the meltdown of the financial system. But you can also trace the source of this global economic crisis to Sunbelt, and the property boom and bust which overwhelmed places like Orange County, California. Almost half of the twenty biggest sub-prime lenders in the United States were based in Orange County and in 2006 sub-prime mortgage funding there was rife. There was a nasty edge to the sub-prime boom in the working-class neighbourhoods of OC where lenders targeted poor Latino neighbourhoods that had been shunned by the mainstream financial institutions. The easy money had a name in these neighbourhoods: *la droga*.

The web of sub-prime insanity began to unravel in early 2007 and consumer watchdogs estimated that almost one in four sub-prime mortgages agreed in Orange County in 2007 were doomed to end in foreclosure. The unfolding crisis spread across the Sunbelt and helped topple the giants of Wall Street, sending a tidal wave through the global financial system and on to Irish shores.

Back in the US, the economic tsunami of recent weeks has created an awakening of sorts. The collapse of those giant financial institutions coincides with profound concern about growing inequality and declining social mobility and it has reinforced a shift in attitudes towards government and private enterprise. Even before the drama of recent weeks, a CBS News/*New York Times* poll found a majority of Americans support government intervention in the housing market and higher taxes on richer Americans.

More than 40 per cent said they would prefer a larger government that provided more services; more than at any time on record. In the emerging New America, there is a definite move away from the unregulated individualism of recent decades towards a more civic, collective ethos. That trend is being hastened by another great transformational force, the rise of the Millennial generation, those Americans born between 1980 and 2000.

Some observers talk of the Millennials as a 'hero' generation that marks the beginning of a new era in American history. It is too early to say, but this generation is certainly very different. Millennials are nothing if not socially responsible; they use fewer drugs, commit fewer crimes and have less pre-marital sex than previous generations. They are more politically active than ever; youth turnout in this year's primaries was higher than at any time since 1972. And perhaps just as important, the Millenials are the first generation of Americans to be raised with the altered consciousness of social technology like My Space and YouTube and their spirit of collective innovation. They will also be the most diverse generation in American history; 40 per cent of them are from racial minorities.

That youthful diversity is a clue to the final transformational force in the New America: another historic wave of immigration. The United States is expected to grow by another hundred million people in the coming decades and a growing share of the new citizens will have been born somewhere else. By 2025, if trends continue, a record proportion of Americans will be foreign-born.

The New America looks set to be a breathtakingly diverse place. It's expected that by 2050, roughly a third of Americans will be Latino. One in five will fall into the multi-racial category. According to the most recent forecasts, white Americans will be a minority by 2042.

All of this might lead you to believe that a young, post-racial leader like Barack Obama is a perfect fit for the New America. But the transformation of the United States is an uneven process, marked by insecurity and conflict as much as by optimism and confidence.

Obama has a problem connecting with Americans who want change but don't want to lose their values in the process. Older, whiter, poorer Americans in particular seem to feel less comfortable with him, and not just because of his race. By contrast, John McCain does what Ronald Reagan once did: he speaks about the future with the accent of the past.

In a strange way, the outcome of the battle between McCain and Obama will be a snapshot, freezing a moment in time. It is an eye-catching image which will live with us for generations to come. But America is not a snapshot, it is a movie. And the plot is about to change. No matter what happens on 4 November.

4 October 2008

COMING OUT

Ger Philpott

I wish I had never had to come out. And I'd wager Dónal Óg Cusack feels the same. In our less-than-perfect world, however, to avoid the implied imperative wasn't an option. Like many of us, Cusack has been forced, again and again, to explain something to family, friends and others, that really is none of their business. To come out is to take back ownership of power.

Cusack now walks tall, as indeed he should. But when the dust settles on the Cork hurling superstar's precedent-setting revelation about his sexuality in his recently published autobiography, *Come What May*, it remains to be seen if it makes one iota of difference to young Irish boys and girls who are coming to terms with their homosexuality. For the record, I doubt that any gay helpline will recommend joining the local GAA club as part of a coping strategy to deal with homosexuality.

Mr Pussy's appearance in the 1970s on RTÉ's *Tangents* – the *Nationwide* of its day – was also groundbreaking. My fascination and fear existed in equal measure as I watched the programme *en famille*. My concern then was that someone would recognise, in my interest, some of the turmoil in my mind. I now have similar concern for the young male and female GAA players – and in other sports, countrywide – who may be negotiating the miasma that is coming to terms with gayness. Cusack wields a hurley stick, not a magic wand.

The challenges these youngsters face haven't diminished. Conversely, now cast under a glaring spotlight, potentially they have actually increased. Chants of 'Brokeback' may run easily off Cusack's broad shoulders. Younger frames, however, will continue to struggle. The fruit of Cusack's symbolic stance is still a far-off harvest.

Long before the social and sexual networking site Gaydar took its name, gay men and lesbian women, self-identified or not, operated their own gaydar. This was, and is, a form of self-protection.

A quick scanning of environments to gauge levels of safety or, more critically, levels of threat. When homosexuals are murdered, the level of violence used generally far exceeds that involved in other forms of homicide.

Sociologically, this is known as 'overkill'. Irish research indicates that the defence offered, in most of these cases, cited 'uninvited sexual advances'. Surprisingly, it appears to have worked. In the majority of instances, on conviction, short sentences were handed down. What does this say about us as a society? And spare a thought for Irish demographics if women were to resort to the same solution in similar – so-called – situations.

Little wonder then the licence taken by the neanderthals who texted their homophobic comments to RTÉ's *Tubridy Show* this week. The former GAA president, Sean Kelly MEP, stated on air that Cusack would be judged as a sportsman and not as a gay sportsman. Nice aspiration, Mr Kelly. Can you also ensure the sun always shines on Sunday? The national public service broadcaster respected its responsibility not to incite hatred by refusing to broadcast the offensive texts.

This contrasts with the GAA's deafening silence last summer following the wholly unacceptable assault on Cusack as he prepared to take a free at Semple Stadium, when some lout with a megaphone launched a sustained anti-gay attack on the player. And where were the objections of the rest of the GAA community present on the day? I love the ribald tribalism that lies at the heart of GAA. And can't think of anywhere else I'd care to be on September Sundays other than Croker. But tolerance of the Semple Stadium behaviour condones it. None of us can, or should, be proud of this. Somebody must know the identity of the idiot with the megaphone.

Out him. Offer his name up to the powers that be and let the GAA bestow a ban on his attendance at any future fixtures. That would send out a strong message that the GAA will not tolerate unacceptable behaviour.

I read in dispatches this week that the GAA has proudly led the way with multiculturalism, integration and tolerance.

Really? The sporting organisation could learn a lot from the community which hosts the jewel in its crown, Croke Park. The people of Sheriff Street and its surrounds last week welcomed with open arms Stephen Gately's remains. The talented local was done proud by his community.

Gately's sexuality wasn't an issue at his funeral. Neither was the presence of his husband. And hats off to the local church and parish priest for the manner in which proceedings were facilitated.

It is this humanity the GAA needs to emulate. For the record, gay people shouldn't be tolerated. We are to be accepted.

For a period, I ran the gauntlet of taunts of 'sissy' on a daily basis when I was at primary school – as it happens, a renowned Cork GAA factory.

One bully followed me home one day, his chant unrelenting. I struggled to understand why this was happening. It seems I 'talked posh' for a working-class lad. Nearing my home I stopped, not wanting to bring the scenario to my doorstep. A classmate urged me to stand up to the bully.

He explained that otherwise, the torment wouldn't stop. That

I had to do something. Suffice it to say, being thrashed by his victim didn't do much for the bully's self-esteem or his ranking in the pecking order of the crucible of the schoolyard.

On another occasion while at primary school, a Christian Brother teacher called me a sissy in front of my class. This was too much for me to deal with. I called in the troops. My father drove me to school that afternoon and spoke to the teacher. The Brother apologised in front of the class. What motivates this type of behaviour? Dónal Óg writes in his book of the Semple Stadium incident: 'That's what gets to you. Other people. I leaned over the free and took it and struck it well. I have trained for this but my father is in the back of my mind.' The player's sister has, on a number of occasions, also been upset by what she has heard. His mother has stopped attending games because of the stress of hearing homophobic abuse shouted at her son from the terraces. The heckling bigots ruined match days for her and now she stays away.

'I hate what it does to those around me, especially when it doesn't hurt me at all,' Cusack writes. I can only imagine his armour was hard-earned. But where was the GAA in all of this? The dogs on the street knew of the rumours about Cusack's private life. Those who were important to him – family, friends and teammates – already knew he was gay.

Cusack's concern for those he loves lies at the core of this issue. Coming out is also about protecting our nearest and dearest. The maverick GAA star is to be commended for wresting back power. His public declaration has thrown down a gauntlet. In fact, he has lobbed a huge challenge at the GAA's feet.

A perusal of various forums streaming the Cusack story provides interesting reading. For example, the man who claims it would be truly sensational had Cusack come out about the reasons behind his penchant for the 'short puck' rather than being gay, brings welcome humour to the debate.

The jaded comments of homo-apathetic gay men – I'll scream

if I read another thing about being gay – bring no levity to matters. They reek of the self-loathing 'straight-acting' descriptors often found in gaydar profiles.

What are worthy of concern, however, are the homophobic ones. It is against this backdrop that closeted individuals struggle.

Clearly, the journey to the place where you are sufficiently buoyed to weather the storm of disclosure can be an epic one. Spare a thought for the individuals who don't make it. I defy anyone to tell me the suicide statistics for young men have nothing to do with gay youngsters who, through no fault of their own, succumbed to despair.

And what of those who continue to live in fear; leading compromised, frightened lives, constantly looking over shoulders.

Often, though not always, these people live in rural and isolated situations. How refreshing, if backbench TDs' voices were heard on this issue rather than on the alleged plight of some folk who can't have two pints and drive home of an evening.

You only come out once. Then those you come out to must follow suit.

Cusack's debut, so public, puts it up to the GAA and, by extension, to Irish society. How each responds will reveal a lot about who and what we are.

The measure of success in GAA circles will not be judged on how many young people come out. Justin Fashanu didn't forge the way for an influx of openly gay footballers. Neither did Olympic gold medal-winning US diver Greg Louganis open the floodgates for other gay divers.

No young person again should ever have to endure what Dónal Óg Cusack went through. The goal shouldn't be that more young people should come out. The point is that they shouldn't have to do so in the first place.

24 October 2009

DEATH'S SWEET GIFT

Kate Kerrigan

My son chose his Hallowe'en outfit last week from the vast collection of ghoul masks and pound-shop ensembles he has collected over his eight years. He came downstairs wearing (aside from a scraggy Elvis wig) what seemed like an everyday outfit of sweatshirt and jeans.

'That's not much of a costume,' I said. 'Da-daa', he announced, lifting up his top to reveal a black vest with skeleton bones on it. 'Look,' he said, laughing delightedly, 'I'm really dead.'

My eight-year-old knows all about death. This year he lost two uncles, and when he was four his friend, Alana, lost her battle with cancer.

When Alana died, her family waked her at home. She was embalmed and laid out on her regular spot on the sofa in her favourite outfit for two days. It seemed like she was sleeping, plump and pretty, while the network of neighbours and friends who had shared the extraordinary journey of her short, stolen life, milled about eating and drinking and crying.

I didn't know what to do with Leo around it all. He was very upset when I told him she had died and when I asked if he wanted to go and see her to say goodbye he said no, he didn't.

The day before the funeral Alana's mother asked if Leo would bring gifts up to the altar. I confessed I was thinking of not bringing him to either the wake or the funeral.

'I'm worried he'll get too emotional,' I said. I was not so much worried at his grief, but that his displaying it might upset other mourners.

Una, with her extraordinary strength, reassured me. Death is upsetting, she said, let him come and say goodbye. So I brought him into the house and he saw her and it was fine. Leo was completely composed throughout the funeral mass while I sobbed horribly and he stroked my face and comforted me.

We got to the graveyard early. I wanted to prepare Leo for the reality of a burial. He ran towards the open grave then came straight back to me full of wonder. 'Look, look,' he said. 'Come and see.'

The grave was lined with wild flowers, a thick mattress of soft, colourful foliage that the men who had been up the night before digging had prepared for their neighbour's child. All of the local children were given a flower to throw in on top of their friend. One of them played a traditional air as she was lowered into her new home of flowers.

The day of Alana's funeral was one of the most emotional but uplifting days I have ever experienced. I will never forget it and I keep it fresh in my son's mind by talking of her often. We light candles for her after mass, along with our neighbour's dog Yoda and now for Leo's two uncles.

The honest, generous way we traditionally handle death is one of the things I most appreciate about being Irish. My reputation as being one of the first on the scene of a recent bereavement is something I get teased about among friends who have lost someone close. If you see me unloading trays of sandwiches and fruit cake out of my jeep, you'll know somebody has died.

We say that a good funeral is as enjoyable as a wedding, and while I have yet to attend one that hired a DJ and involved dancing until dawn, there is little doubt that our system for dealing with the emotions that surround the loss of a human life is a good one – it works.

Our traditional culture around death embraces the realities and the strong emotions of early grief. Our fearlessness about displaying our dead loved ones in open coffins, remembering them with laughter one moment, tears the next – is something we should fight to preserve. I feel saddened when it is increasingly announced in the death notices, 'house private'.

While it is every person's choice to grieve as they feel they need to, I am always impressed by the snaking lines of mourners outside my local funeral home. And when my brother died in London earlier this year, although few people here had met him, I nonetheless felt supported and strengthened by the good wishes and condolences that came flooding in from my wider community.

Growing up as I did in England, death was an essentially private affair. Funerals were small and closed and when somebody lost a loved one, we were culturally discouraged from mentioning it.

But I have found when one does take the courage to call and sympathise with an English friend, however reserved they are, there is a palpable sense of relief and a deep gratitude for my having made the move. Bluntly, unless you are a member of the royal family, the stiff-upper-lip attitude towards death in England simply doesn't work.

All Souls' Day, following tomorrow's All Saints' Day, has nowadays become so thoroughly entwined with the children's party atmosphere of Hallowe'en that precedes it that it is easy to forget that these few days are essentially a time for remembering our dead.

Perhaps we have embraced the gaudy commercialism so thoroughly because it acts as a distraction to that act of remembering. Remembering a lost loved one is painful – and it would be sad to think that we are somehow losing the tradition of thoroughly celebrating a person's life through the process of their death.

Grief is best experienced as a long and thorough journey. It is emotionally and physically debilitating, and grief gobbles up modern life's most precious commodity – time.

My brother died in February and by late spring I was wondering when I would have the wherewithal to start working properly again. Life goes on – but being intimately acquainted with death alters life's perspective.

It puts mortality at the top of one's list – altering completely those previous everyday worries like decorating the house, and pursuing a fulfilling career, and wondering about what you are going to wear to a wedding. It causes an adjustment of priorities so that having your hair blow-dried for a night out or checking whether your child brushes their teeth or not before they go to bed suddenly seems unimportant.

Yet these things are essential to keep our lives, and the lives of our families, ticking over – and so we must try to put behind us the anguish of bereavement.

Forgetting is a necessary way of getting one's own life back. It loosens the painful grip of remembering that the person you loved isn't around any more. Which is why ritual, religious or otherwise, is so important to help ensure that we do remember.

Keening and waking, the month's mind, anniversary masses and All Souls' Day – these are all the rituals that show us how to stay honest around not just death but life. Talking about who and what we have lost is an important reminder of what we still have. Crucially, honouring our dead on All Souls' is not just a reminder of what we lost when the person passed but what we got from them when they were alive.

After the first shock of losing someone has passed, going back and remembering who they were and what they stood for can offer us a valuable opportunity in living our lives to the full.

Every time I sit down to write, I remember my brother – a gifted musician – and the way he always encouraged me to be creative. It's still painful but it's not paralysing like it was eight months ago and pain is not a good enough excuse not still to hear Tom's voice in my head.

My brother-in-law died very recently in Vietnam. A lively, vivacious character, his death was sudden and shocking. Nonetheless emails came flooding into my husband's laptop, full of warmth and memories of his laughter and easygoing charm. The wound is still raw but in years to come we will sit around and wonder, 'What would Fintan have made of this?'

2009 has been a year that has brought my family two new babies as well as lost us two of our precious sons. We will be glad to put it behind us but we will never forget the two men whose deaths dovetailed into two new lives. Their individuality and the unique gifts that their lives brought while they were in this world will never be allowed to slide into infinity.

I remember the day little Alana was diagnosed as terminal. Shaken after the news, I was lifting my son out of the bath. Sensing something was wrong, he chose that moment to throw a rare tantrum.

'I hate you,' he screamed. 'You're the worst mother in the world!'

I held him tight as he wriggled and kicked against my hold – for the first time feeling how strong he was. 'He's alive,' was all I could think. The words kept repeating themselves back and over like a reel in my head, 'He's alive, he's alive, he's alive.' The grip on gratitude I felt in that moment has never left me. Alana's gift will stay with me for as long as I have my son. And for that reason, I will always remember her – and so will he.

31 October 2009

THE POWER OF FORGIVENESS

Melanie Verwoerd

Two years ago I was driven around a township in Cape Town by an elderly white American called Linda Biehl and a young African man, Ntobeko Peni, who was her driver and security.

I was sitting in the back, listening to the animated discussion between the two of them. At one point Ntobeko became a bit upset and Linda put her hand, in a calming gesture, on top of his. For a moment I froze, for I realised that Linda's white hand was holding the dark hand of the man who had killed her daughter.

I met Amy Biehl shortly before her death in 2002. She was a Fulbright Scholar who came to South Africa to contribute to the peace process. She had worked in the ANC and was bright and charming. Everyone loved her.

The night before her final departure back to the US, she drove to Gugulethu Township in Cape Town to drop off an African colleague. As they drove into the township, they ran into a large group of excited young men who had just come back from a radical political rally.

Chanting a famous slogan, 'Kill a farmer, kill a boer [kill the whites]', they spotted her in her car. The car was overturned and Amy pulled from the vehicle. The pleas from her colleague fell on deaf ears and Amy was stabbed and stoned to death in front of the petrol garage where she hoped to get some safety.

I will never forget the shock we all felt when we saw the pictures in the newspapers the next day of Amy lying in a pool of blood on a cold cement floor in the nearby police station with her beautiful, long blonde hair protruding from under the sheet covering her body.

The young men who stabbed and stoned her were caught and, after a difficult trial, they were convicted of her murder and received life sentences.

However, a few years later they applied for amnesty to the Truth and Reconciliation Commission. Linda and Peter Biehl (Amy's parents) were present at the hearings and made it clear that they would not oppose their request for amnesty. They had set up a charity in Amy's name in order to continue her work in the township and felt that it did not serve any purpose for Amy's killers to stay in jail.

A year after amnesty was granted, Peter and Linda were stunned when they received a request through an intermediary to meet with two of the young men.

An extraordinary process of forgiveness and reconciliation began. Today, the two young men work for the Amy Biehl Foundation and Ntobeko, one of her daughter's killers, has become Linda's driver and security. He calls her Gogo (grandmother) and she was a guest at his wedding.

Linda has told me how she worries about him and that she sees both of the young men as her sons. Ntobeko said that he became concerned for Linda because she did not take her security seriously enough when going into the townships.

When I tell people the story of Amy, Linda and Ntobeko, they usually doubt Linda's sanity. They find it difficult to believe that anyone in their right mind could forgive such a senseless and hideous deed.

Indeed, when I look at my 19-year-old daughter with her long blonde hair, just like Amy's, and I listen to all her dreams of changing the world and contributing to a solution for Africa's many problems, I find it hard to imagine what inside yourself would allow you to forgive someone who would, in cold blood and with such cruelty, kill your child.

And yet over the years I have met so many people who have forgiven those who did exactly that.

In Kigali, in Rwanda, the Genocide Museum has a special section for children. This is one of the most heartbreaking places I have ever visited. The information boards detail stories of children bludgeoned to death – often by their own neighbours.

They also record the children's fears and even their last words, like those of 8-year-old Fabrice, who shouted out in panic, 'Mommy, where shall I run to? Please help me!' And yet today, the women from both sides of the Rwandan horror make peace baskets together and have become friends.

Why do some people forgive when all natural instinct would drive you to seek revenge and retribution? Maybe a part of the answer lies in the words of Father Michael Lapsley, an Anglican priest who joined the ANC in South Africa in the 1970s. While in exile in Zimbabwe in 1990 he lost both his hands and an eye in a letter bomb sent in religious literature to him by the South African government.

Talking about this experience he said, 'Quite early on after the bomb I realised that if I was filled with hatred and desire for revenge I'd be a victim forever. If we have something done to us, we are victims. If we physically survive, we are survivors. Sadly, many people never travel any further than this. I did travel further, going from victim to survivor to victor.'

For Linda Biehl the journey to forgiveness was also motivated by her determination not to become a victim. Forgiveness therefore is a crucial part of the journey for victims to regain some sense of power over their lives and circumstances.

Archbishop Tutu echoed this when he said, 'To forgive is indeed the best form of self-interest since anger, resentment, and revenge are corrosive of that *summum bonum*, the greatest good.' I believe that the Christian tradition helps with its imperative to 'forgive those who trespass against us'. But for the majority of people I have met over the years, it seems that their own survival, the regaining of their own sense of centre and balance, is what drives them on this long and painful journey of forgiveness.

Jo Berry, whose father was killed in 1984 in the IRA's Brighton bombing, went through this harrowing process when she decided to meet with Patrick Magee, the man who planted the bomb. This Tuesday, a day after the 25th anniversary of the Brighton bombing, Patrick Magee will enter Westminster and, accompanied by Jo Berry, he will address an all-party parliamentary group on the issue of conflict and forgiveness. Jo makes the point that she regained some of her humanity during this process, which she felt she lost with the bomb.

Of course, Patrick Magee also regained some of his humanity during the process of engaging and forming a strong bond with Jo. However, Patrick has made it quite clear that he was not seeking forgiveness, that he only wanted Jo to understand what led him, as a republican, to these actions.

This is echoed by Alistair Little whose life story was recently portrayed in the film *Five Minutes of Heaven*.

Alistair joined the UVF when he was 14 – and when he was 17 he killed a man he did not know as revenge for the death of a friend's father. His journey to renouncing violence happened during the twelve years he spent in Maze Prison.

Even though he continues to spend his life working towards reconciliation and peace, he is clear that he cannot ask for forgiveness.

He says, 'I don't think I have a right to ask for forgiveness. It only adds insult to injury and places yet another burden upon relatives and family members.' Herein lies the core of the issue – forgiveness is something that can only be offered, it can never be demanded. It is not something that can be asked for or expected – even if a heartfelt apology has been made by the perpetrator. Only the victims can decide if they are willing and ready to forgive.

Some might never choose to do so and it is important to remember that those who choose not to forgive are neither morally suspect nor bad individuals. They are just not ready or willing to look those who changed their lives forever in the eyes. However, for any form of forgiveness to have any chance both sides need to be able to tell their stories and be listened to.

In particular, it seems that it is important for the victims to understand why perpetrators did what they did. This understanding is crucial before any individual or collective forgiveness can be possible.

In the words of Jo Berry, 'Perhaps if we all lived the others' lives, we could all have done what the other did.'

This of course raises the following big question for me: If I had grown up in an African township, constantly humiliated by the whites and then told by charismatic political leaders to kill those whites, could I have killed Amy Biehl? I really hope the answer would be a categorical 'no'.

But I think that if I and, indeed, all of us are honest, we must say that the answer is 'perhaps'. If we recognise this unsettling and disturbing possibility we come closer to understanding those who forgive and the nature of forgiveness.

It is in this recognition of our human weakness that the human strength is also revealed. Because whatever drives people to torture and kill, it is blatantly clear that if it was not for the extraordinary human capacity for people to forgive, there would not be a peaceful South Africa, Rwanda, Bosnia or Northern Ireland today.

10 October 2009

NOVEMBER

WHY FAITH WILL FOREVER FLOURISH

Theo Dorgan

I have been thinking lately about one of the most spectacular failures of the late USSR; its failure to eliminate religion. Over a span of seventy years the authorities bulldozed churches by the thousand, forbade all but the most distorted religious texts to be published, eliminated religion from the curricula, persecuted and murdered believers, made it next to impossible for a professed Jew, Muslim or Christian to secure advancement in work or society, and yet the instant the CPSU lost its grip there was a wild and sometimes bewildering explosion of religious (and superstitious) practice.

I was in Moscow and Leningrad on a number of occasions during the Gorbachev years, and I was particularly struck on the one hand by the speed with which churches were re-consecrated and monasteries refurbished, and on the other by the large number of people, many of them State functionaries, who took to wearing silver crosses as a badge of – what? Defiance? I was struck, as I say, by the speed with which Orthodox Christianity in particular re-emerged, and struck also, though not surprised, by the reactionary political formations which this sudden revival embraced.

Despite the expenditure of vast resources and the deployment of an immense number of repressive measures, this most totalitarian of states had failed entirely to achieve a major 'progressive' objective – to rip religion out by the roots. It's difficult to say 'where' religion was during the seventy years after Lenin seized power, difficult to explain how those roots, frozen in permafrost, were able to send up such spectacular new growth in such a short time, but we who live in a world menaced on all sides by religious fundamentalism on the march would do well, I think, to reflect on this strange phenomenon.

When organised religion in the former USSR re-emerged from the silence into which it had been thrust, it proved inflexible in its theology, deeply conservative in its politics, and all too ready to align itself to a new Greater Russian Tsarism. It is, in one sense, easy to see this as a perfectly predictable response to repression, one dogmatic simplicity replacing its antithesis. I see a similar response in the emergence of a somewhat virulent and reactionary Catholicism in Poland, although one can also see, in that instance, the mischief-making of the previous Pope still at work.

It may not matter, in the long perspective, that on first re-emergence into the light, these churches should take up reactionary positions; it may not matter because there is at least a chance that this is a temporary corrective, just as a ship knocked to one side will roll exaggeratedly to the other before, in time, coming into equilibrium.

It may be that in time these churches will address individual responsibility, the vindication of women as persons and the rights of the poor, questions which are exercising other Christian denominations – we'll have to wait and see. But what I was witnessing all those years ago was an element in the rise of a new fundamentalism even though I didn't recognise that at the time.

I have also been thinking a lot lately about the rise of fundamentalist Christianity and politics in the USA, the rise of a hybrid religious/political zealotry in the Islamic world, the religious/historical ethos of the Israeli State.

Everywhere we look now we see the saved and the damned, 'we' being the saved, of course, and 'they' being the damned. I know very well that, as an ex-Catholic, I am damned in the eyes of some kinds of believer, just as I know that as an agnostic who tries to be respectful of believers, I will be damned by doctrinaire atheists.

Fundamentalism isn't confined to religious people, by any means; there's a kind of hysteria in the air these days, a rush to fixed positions on everything from the serious to the trivial. As if there could be no virtue in doubt or an open mind.

I have been a non-believer for forty years of my life and I see no prospect of that changing. Simply put, I do not believe, but I make no argument for non-belief. I have done my imperfect best to live my life well, to consider the moral context of my life, to do no harm. I have tried, always, to do some modest good. I share with most people a profound sense that there is more to human life than passive consumerism; I am appalled by the cancer of ruthless capitalism and equally unnerved by the paralysis of imagination of the secular left. I share these views with believers as well as with non-believers, but those of us with a lively sense of what I might call the non-materialist dimensions to life seem everywhere at a loss right now.

The unfettered pursuit of wealth as an end in itself is more and more the dominant ideology in the world; it seems to me that this is bringing catastrophe to the poor and the powerless even as it concentrates undreamed-of wealth in the hands of a few.

I also believe that the elevation of greed as the highest good corrupts and undermines the innate humanity even of those who appear, for the moment, to be beneficiaries of its operations. I know very well that, in the world today, not everyone agrees. I walked around Moscow and Leningrad in those turbulent days feeling disturbed by the rise of religious passions and the political expression of those passions, but like many other people, it seems to me now, I was not really paying attention. I was failing to understand what was at stake.

The rise of fundamentalist versions of Islam, for instance,

might have been foreseen if we had paid more attention to the nature of organised religion and to the sophisticated elements that have both cultivated and fed on organised belief. We might, had we been paying attention, have better understood the appeal to the poor and the powerless of a belief system that counterpoises the revealed word of Allah the Merciful to the widespread cruelty and perceived inhumanity of those who wield actual power in the material world.

The rise of fundamentalist Christianity might have been countered in the US if more people had been paying attention to the power available to those prepared to use organised religion for political ends. It's as if it had escaped notice, that so many ambitious people believe God wants them personally to prevail; and that far too many of these people are far too powerful, that they do indeed consider themselves crusaders for righteousness.

It seems obvious that religions cannot be simply wished out of existence; I have seen myself that even a ruthless and all-powerful state cannot eliminate religion.

The obvious conclusion, therefore, is that religions must be transformed from the inside, by believers. I remember the remark attributed to Gandhi, to the effect that Christianity would be a very good thing if only someone would try it.

We non-believers need to understand why ordinary people will not easily be shaken from their beliefs, why people need to believe, and then we need to make common cause with those who alone can transform religions from within, the compassionate believers with whom we have so much in common. But unconscious and lazy heirs of the highly-conscious and energetic Voltaire, we have discounted religion as a meaningful presence in the world and now we are paying the price.

Worse, we have forgotten that at the root of every religion, no matter how (and perhaps inevitably) it is corrupted by its hierarchs and clerisy, there is a profound and ineradicable sense that life is mystery, and that there is more to human life than the material world.

The idea that we have somehow 'advanced beyond' religion is both dangerous and, very likely, premature. We have ignored the metaphorical and imaginative power of religious ideas, preferring to shoot down simplifications and absurdities of our own making, preferring indeed to damn all believers as paranoid and deluded zealots.

We have made the profound mistake, we non-believers, of conflating the diktats of the Inquisition with the Sermon on the Mount.

We have ignored our common human power to imagine the good into existence, and thereby make it real even in imperfect conditions.

I have spent much of the past two years – in reseaching a book – sifting through innumerable collections of prayers from all times, places and religions. I have been searching for texts where the language itself dares us out beyond ourselves into imagining a cosmos shimmering with depths of meaning. I sought these prayers out as neglected instances of speech pushed beyond light and shadow, of the urge to express a fullness of meaning in our common life on earth.

I was looking for, and found, places where a non-believer might share common ground with a believer. Here and there, in half-forgotten places and sometimes right under my nose, I found words that deepened and steadied my sense of being more fully human. I am still a non-believer, after all that, but a somewhat more thoughtful one.

3 November 2007

OBAMA: WILL HOPE VANQUISH FEAR?

Colum McCann

The Russian writer Maxim Gorky once wrote that 'life will always be bad enough that the desire for something better will never be extinguished in man'. Of course it was another century, another political system, another set of desires, but what Gorky's words might eerily prefigure is that which currently lies at the heart of perhaps the most pivotal election of our time.

America lies in tatters. The housing market. The stock crash. The tumbling dollar. The unemployment lines. The coffins still being laid out at the end of runways. The angry graffiti that's seen increasingly on the streets and in the subways: No Iraq, Smash the Bankers, Bush W Terrorist. There is a sense of being trapped, by the news, by the markets, by the future.

It seems that each corner turns into a series of other corners, until all is corners. There is no doubt that the country is in its worst financial – indeed moral – predicament since the Great Depression of the 1930s when Franklin Delano Roosevelt finally stood up and said that there was nothing to fear but fear itself.

Barack Obama has been compared to FDR, and in a speech last Wednesday the Illinois senator invoked the sense of fear currently filtering through the country.

But talking about fear is rather un-American these days, and his point was that hope had to trump fear. Why not be in the habit of hoping? he said. Why not believe in the possibility of change, the audacity of it, the necessity of it?

If his lexicon sounds slightly borrowed from an infomercial, he has to be forgiven. If he's playing the lowest common denominator, forgive him. If he cuts a cheap corner, forgive him. Because if Barack Obama's not forgiven for clawing at hope, the consequences for the United States seem dire.

Perhaps it is not even Obama himself that's important for America next week – it's the dream of Obama, what he represents, signifies. It's what he stands for rather than what he stands on.

When Barack Obama is put under a microscope, maybe he's just another politician in an ill-fitting white shirt. He gives a good speech, but he more or less keeps himself to the middle road.

He works hard, perhaps too hard, on his gravitas. He minds his manners at all the tables, even the Republican ones. He sometimes seems a little stiff, as if he's pushing against the air around him. His speeches can swerve towards the saccharine.

But the dream of Obama – the thing that wakes nine-year-old kids in the morning to put on their Obama T-shirts and run to school – is a dream of something approaching forgiveness.

Rightly or wrongly, Obama represents a step towards an act of contrition, not just for the obvious things – history, race, the perversity of war – but for the smaller things too, like those horrific images of old women waving at helicopters in New Orleans, or the roll of fat falling over the waistband down on Wall Street, or even the way an American accent gets sniggered at in the streets of Dublin, London, Paris.

If Obama gets in, America changes and shifts – even if just in our imaginations.

In travelling around the United States, I've come across a lot of contradictions, but none stranger than the white sheriff in southern Georgia, near the Okefenokee Swamp, who was running on a segregationist ticket. He was just another bigot in a straw hat. He hated the niggers. He hated the queers. He hated the camel jockeys. He even had a little corner of hatred for the Micks.

I was chatting with him on the porch of his house one evening when there was a car crash down the road. A young black family had smashed their car into a tree. The father was slightly hurt. The mother and kids were fine.

The sheriff drove the father to the hospital and later returned to his house with the mother and children. He had his wife make up beds for the family and cook a meal.

The following morning the sheriff made sure the young black family's car was fixed. He even helped pay the hospital bill. When the family was gone, down the long road of cypress trees, I asked him why he had helped. He was stunned by the question, even deeply insulted. 'They're human,' he said.

This is the gulf between the private and public American: you can hate a man and fix his car and make a bed for his family and still not know why you want to call him a nigger.

The same mentality operates across much of the rural United States, the difference between how you outwardly act and inwardly feel. It is the crux of the election and still a point of deep confusion in the American psyche.

Despite the polls massively weighted for Obama, there is still a feeling that a shock could come about when that curtain is pulled across the voting booth and decades of institutionalised hatred make themselves manifest.

This is Tuesday's test – which sheriff steps out from the Okefenokee?

There is talk of an assassination attempt if the election goes Obama's way. Perhaps there will always be this sort of talk. Every culture kills its prophets, after all.

But perhaps the good thing about Barack Obama is that he is not a prophet – nowhere near it – and he has the humility to understand this. He is simply the symptom of decades of misrule, a culture that isolated itself, a nation that finally has to look in the mirror. And every mirror always holds a surprise.

The real looking-glass moment is if Obama has the power to turn things around. If he gets elected, his first 100 days' charge will be vital. It will shape not only the economy but a great deal of the moral texture of the American future.

This is often ridiculed as an overblown construction – many commentators believe that it will simply be more of the same, no matter who gets elected – but the fact is that the country is at its most acute crisis point in almost a century.

The most analogous historical time is when Roosevelt was inaugurated in March 1933.

The unemployment lines went around the block. Farmers saw their prices fall by 60 per cent. Two million people were homeless. Banks were closing down. A rising tide of European fascism was approaching. FDR's administration stepped in with his New Deal programme – comprising relief, recovery and reform.

Much of his agenda was ushered in during his first 100 days, when presidents traditionally get a blank cheque.

The New Deal was a radical shift, not only for America but for the world at large.

Along with the Second World War, the New Deal changed America's idea of itself more than ever. The idealism, the humanitarian instinct and the social conscience of the policies were remarkable, and these tendencies only began to dim with the advent of the Vietnam War.

More recently, the Bush years have been brutal, indifferent, hateful, selfish and ruthless. The administration has tried to assure peace by waging war. They have turned justice into revenge.

The American people are finally aware that they have been defended by lies. They are fed up with apologising for the smugness of those who represent them. A lot of ordinary people feel they have been paraded out mercilessly in front of a laughing world.

Ralph Waldo Emerson once famously said that 'all history resolves itself easily in the biography of a few stout and earnest people'. Certain voices come along and make sense of a time, an era, a culture. Obama is the current personification of that moment.

One might even say that a sense of humility has come about, accompanying the simple necessity of change – and some of that humility is embodied in Obama, with his head down, questions flickering behind his eyelids: Who has invented our isolation? Who has decided that we should not like another? Who has said that the voices of other lands are strange to me? Who has destroyed the house that Lincoln built?

It's all very dangerous of course to talk of Obama in the elevated terms of dreams and heroes – especially given the economy that confronts him if he's elected – but if not him, whom?

No matter what happens, the next president inherits decades to come: the economy, the wars, the mire. But the general feeling is that Obama is the only one who is fresh enough and new enough and smart enough to give impetus to change.

He is a man with strong social convictions and a calm international vision. He may end up serving a series of cracked glasses but the feeling is that he's the man behind the counter in the Last Chance Saloon. It may be a bitter drink for some in Europe or Asia or Africa to swallow, but Tuesday's election also closely coincides with the fate of the world's prosperity.

This is quite flattering for a withering empire but it's historically true. As America goes, so goes the rest of the world. It just may be that this new president will be the last to oversee this sort of American power, or it just might be that Obama can help bring us all back from the brink.

Still, this has more to do with psychology than actuality. It has more to do with hope than law. It is, in fact, the dream of change that institutes change. Nothing matters quite so much as what we desire or hope for or want.

On Wednesday morning the sun will rise. Just where it rises, and how bright it shines, is the question.

1 November 2008

WEARING THE POPPY WITH PRIDE

Paul Drury

For fifty years or so, the small brown cardboard box sat at the back of the drawer where my mother kept her sewing kit, her knitting needles and her spare set of spectacles – for all the world like one of those little containers in which chunks of wedding cake used to be sent to faraway relatives who couldn't make it to the ceremony.

But this brown cardboard box – addressed in immaculate copperplate writing to 'Dr Maurice O'Connor Drury, c/o St Patrick's Hospital, James Street, Dublin' and emblazoned not with a conventional stamp but the words 'On His Majesty's Service' – did not contain a stale square of fruit cake and stale icing.

Inside instead, wrapped in flimsy tissue paper and accompanied by a compliments slip from Buckingham Palace, were three medals – one for service in the 1939–1945 war, one for service in the North Africa campaign of 1942–1943 and finally the France and Germany Star, for service in continental Europe from D-Day to VE Day.

You see, my father – who, by the time I came along in 1957, was a bespectacled, mild-mannered psychiatrist in charge of a private nursing home outside Dublin that catered mainly for wealthy dipsomaniacs and members of the landed gentry who had fallen prey to their nerves – had also served in the British army during World War II.

Like the estimated 90,000 other Irish men and women who joined that army as volunteers, he did not need to. Although born in England, my father always thought of himself as Irish and rightly so: both his parents were born here, he had spent all his summers at home in Ireland ever since he was a boy and on the outbreak of war had just qualified as a doctor from Trinity.

But in 1939 as the storm clouds gathered and as his own career began, he signed up as a member of the RAMC – a decision made all the more remarkable in his case because my father was a pacifist who hated violence of any kind. However, like those other Irish volunteers, he felt a moral imperative to play his role – whatever the possible cost – in ridding the world of the Nazi monster.

And so, in due course, that gangling, bespectacled tyro medic bravely followed in the wake of another Anglo-Irishman, Montgomery, through the deserts of North Africa, tending to the wounded and the dying as best he could.

And later, on 6 June 1944, armed with nothing more than a first-aid kit and a white armband emblazoned with a red cross, he was one of the first to wade ashore on the beaches of Normandy on D-Day.

Typically, for he was a genuinely modest and unassuming man, one of the few war stories my father ever told me was how he had spent most of that glorious June day sunbathing on the beach – because the stretch of shoreline they had invaded was virtually undefended – and listening to what he described as 'the glorious sound' of the big guns.

For his sake, I hope the story was true; although in my heart I doubt it.

But by the time I was old enough to question him properly he was dead – felled while I was still in my late teens by a premature heart attack brought on, I have little doubt, by a lifelong addiction to tobacco that can only have been reinforced by the free cigarettes he was issued in the army to quell pre-battle nerves.

Later, and again he never spoke about this, I was told that he was present at the liberation of one of the Nazi concentration camps – an experience that must have burned its way deep into his sensitive soul.

But what I do know for sure is that he voluntarily sacrificed six years of his life – the very prime of that life – in the cause of freedom.

It is a choice that I very much doubt whether I would have the courage to make myself. Yet not only did my father never talk about his war record, it was – to all intents and purposes – written out of both our family history and, most shamefully of all, our national history. On Remembrance Sunday my father never wore a poppy, let alone his medals. Until the day he died they remained unseen, tucked away at the back of that drawer in their tissue paper wrapping.

I do not retell his story here out of boastfulness; I do not do so because I feel my father deserves a special place in the history books that he would never have wanted for himself.

No, I do so for the very simple reason that he was not alone; there were another 90,000 Irish men and women – and a further 200,000 in World War I – who do deserve that place. It is a place that, for the fifty years those medals lay at the back of my mother's drawer, was denied them.

Year after year Remembrance Sunday came and went almost unnoticed in the southern half of this country – except for the handful of stalwarts who organised a low-key annual wreath-laying ceremony in their local Church of Ireland parish church.

The route into Dublin city from the nursing home in Lucan that my father looked after ran past the Garden of Remembrance on the banks of the River Liffey – designed by Sir Edward Lutyens at enormous expense just after World War I.

Throughout my childhood and early adulthood, I can still see in my mind's eye how it lay tragically abandoned – weed-infested and unkempt, its cut-stone pavilions cruelly vandalised.

Then in 1966, the entire nation was declared *en fête* to commemorate another set of volunteers – those equally brave men who went out fifty years earlier, at Easter 1916, to confront, in cruel irony, the self-same army in which those commemorated at Islandbridge (and indeed, years later, my own father) had served so selflessly. Now the medals were definitely going to stay in hiding.

Even in my little two-teacher, Church of Ireland village national school, we learned the words of the Proclamation by rote.

I was as guilty as anyone. For that summer at least, every child in the country – Catholic, Protestant and dissenter – stopped playing cowboys and Indians and instead became insurgents and Auxies. No prizes for guessing who the baddies were. And, rare as poppies had been on Irish lapels before 11 November 1966, they became even rarer afterwards.

As a teenager in the early 1970s – the outbreak of the Troubles – it was infinitely more tempting, even for a Protestant like myself, to dabble in Republicanism of one hue or another than to pay homage to the sacrifices of my father's generation. I certainly yielded.

Unlike our Iar-Thaoiseach, I was not present on the night the British Embassy was burned – but I vividly remember feeling a surge of glee as I watched the flames flicker skywards on the television screen.

Later, of course, Republicanism itself became a dirty word as the Provos unleashed their unspeakable reign of terror in the North and we realised that there were no black and white answers.

The framed copies of the Proclamation that had been distributed in 1966 were quietly removed from the walls, not just of Protestant schools, but of most classrooms and public buildings.

I, like many of my contemporaries, became as virulently anti-Provo as any unionist.

But revisionism, inevitably, only went so far.

The heroes of 1916 became anti-heroes; there was, however, no corresponding attempt to rehabilitate the heroes of the trenches – who, let us not forget, had been encouraged by Irish politicians to sign up and fight 'for the freedom of small nations' – or of World War II . They remained untouchables.

And yet, I slowly realised as I moved through adulthood, I was by no means alone.

When I went to work on the *Irish Independent*, I discovered that my editor and mentor, Vincent Doyle, was himself the son of a former soldier in the Royal Dublin Fusiliers – invalided home after a German gas attack that robbed him of good health for the rest of his life. Once again, it was a story rarely told.

There were thousands like us – and like our fathers. Over a beer one night, I found out that Paddy Gillen, the genial Galwegian who worked in the public relations department of Ford in Cork when I became motoring correspondent of the *Independent* in the 1980s, had landed on the Normandy beaches with my own father. But it was an unspoken brotherhood.

Change, when it did come, came slowly. By the mid-1990s, however, it finally began to be acknowledged that if the two sides of the sectarian divide in the North could live in peace and mutual respect then it was about time that we in the South shook some of the historic chips off our shoulders. The process has, if anything, accelerated in recent years; the pilgrimage by President McAleese to Messines in 1998 was a watershed.

The Garden of Remembrance has been restored magnificently – even if it is still little visited. We now have a national day of com-memoration, marked diplomatically, if tellingly, in July, at which all those Irish men and women who died in past wars or while serving with the UN are remembered. The men of 1916 are again properly remembered at Eastertide – and rightly so!

But Poppy Day is still acknowledged, if at all, only begrudg-ingly. And that is simply wrong.

As a nation, we can never hope to lay the ghosts of our past until we learn to truly embrace all traditions – and to properly honour all those who died, or who risked their lives, in the cause of freedom from tyranny of all kinds.

And that is why I, for one, will be wearing a poppy tomorrow – with pride in my own father, of course, but above all pride in what he, and thousands of others, risked for all our sakes.

I may not have my father's courage; but I am, I comfort myself, brave enough to do that much in his memory.

8 November 2008

THE RISE OF HIV

Ger Philpott

The man I had planned to spend the rest of my life with died in 1983. Paul had Aids. He became ill in the early days of the epidemic and was one of the first to die of the disease in this country. I was twenty-six years old at the time and his death has had a lasting impact on my life.

When Paul died, very little was known about Aids. The term 'safer sex' had yet to be coined. And as far as officialdom worldwide was concerned, this was a cut and dried issue – Aids was a 'gay plague'.

So it was left to gay people to mobilise and fight back. Act Up, the predominantly gay community group in the US, was born, with the phrase 'Silence = Death' becoming their mantra. New York's Cooper Union building hosted its weekly meetings, where complex strategies of advocacy and direct actions were democratically decided.

That was the 1980s. And it seems like a lifetime ago. We've moved on – Aids is no longer the bogeyman disease it was back then, we've learned how to deal with HIV infection, how to live with it, and how to avoid having to live with it. Or have we?

The number of reported Irish cases of HIV is 5,243, according to the Health Protection Surveillance Centre. And annual costs for

Aids medications (combination therapy) and treatment is €30,000 per head – at conservative estimates.

HSE boss Brendan Drumm has claimed that 'health services will be bankrupt unless they do more on health promotion'. Clearly, someone somewhere in that 'they'-land needs to do the math. And soon. Latest figures from the HPSC, up to the end of December 2008, showed that there were 405 fresh cases of the virus in Ireland.

This was a 3.6 per cent increase on the year before. This Monday, on the eve of World Aids Day, the HPSC will publish further figures, covering until the end of June. But, alarmingly, this time last year, The National Virus Reference Laboratory claimed that 15 per cent of confirmed HIV infection cases were not included in the surveillance centre figures from 2003 to 2007.

'I think there is certainly enough evidence to suggest that the current system is not working as well as it could or should,' claimed the NVRL's Dr Cillian De Gascun.

There is still a voluntary system in place for the notification of HIV cases to the HPSC. Clearly, a mandatory system is required to overcome the problem of under-reporting. Without this, we aren't even on the first steps to properly managing the challenges we still face from HIV infection in Ireland.

Before Paul died, before Aids appeared on the global radar, I had previous experience of gay activism in Ireland – setting up UCC's Gay Soc, for example. Initially banned by the authorities, the group had more straight than gay members. However, I properly cut my teeth in Aids activism in New York's East Village at the end of the 1980s.

On my return to Ireland a few years later, my self-imposed remit in setting up the AIDSWISE organisation was to establish a comprehensive HIV prevention agenda in this country. Aspects of this work included promoting a significant media discourse on issues around Aids and HIV prevention. Interestingly, official figures for reported HIV infections at this time showed a marked decrease.

In 1992, there were just under 200 such new cases and this fell to less than 100 in 1995.

It's not rocket science to work out that keeping the issue of Aids and HIV prevention in the public eye helped to reduce the spread of the disease. Given the absence of any significant debate in Ireland on the issue over the past decade, it is little wonder that the rise of HIV infections has escalated.

And worryingly so.

The only discourse around HIV in recent times has been concerning the storyline around the character of Lorcan in RTÉ's acclaimed medical series, *The Clinic*. We can only hope that the departed show will have had some impact on matters. Last year's 405 newly reported cases – the largest annual increase since records began in 1990 – is a damning indictment of those charged with our public health.

Officialdom needs to really start working if it is to reverse the tide of rising infections. Clearly, the figures alone aren't doing the trick. And the work of the NGO sector, better funded centrally now than before, is also off beam.

For example, the gay lobby has, of late, been preoccupied with the issue of civil unions. In the effort to present a homogenised, squeaky-clean image to the world, sex has been driven off the agenda.

Issues surrounding living with HIV and Aids are complex. So, while some important attention has been given to some related issues, prevention work has suffered. Not least because the hoary issue of gay sex has been swept under the carpet.

International research shows, for example, that the best practice for successful intervention in the global increase in HIV infections amongst men who have sex with men (MSM in official speak) is at an intersection.

The cause of the HIV infection increase in homosexuals and heterosexuals is down to unprotected sex. Clear and simple.

What is not clear, however, is how to motivate change in this behaviour. The evolved HIV prevention message – gay and straight – must kick in when people are about to engage in risky sexual behaviour. This calls for (very) sophisticated – and doubtless expensive – safer-sex campaigns. But this makes fiscal sense in the long run. The proper use of a condom still offers the best protection against HIV (and other) infections.

The challenge in the first instance is to get those in 'they'-land to recognise this, to join up their thinking on these two straightforward facts. And then engage the proper professional know-how to come up with the most effective ways to sell that message.

David Norris, when asked if he was a practising homosexual, was famous for replying, 'No, I've been proficient for years.' Gay men of my generation, generally speaking, though not exclusively, are adept safer-sexers. Anything else is just not an option. Safer sex may no longer equate so specifically to death protection, due to scientific and drug developments in the fight against Aids.

But our first-hand experience of the early onslaught and devastation among our peers caused by Aids helps, all these years later, to keep us aware.

Younger gay men don't have this motivation. They account for around 75 per cent of sixty-six newly notified infections in 2008 – the biggest increase being among 20- to 39-year-olds.

Heterosexuals of the same age – also devoid of knowledge of the devastating impact of Aids – account for 64 per cent of the increased infections among the straight community.

And, again, those between 20 and 39 years old saw the highest level of infection increase, with seventy-nine women reporting the virus compared with forty-four men.

The sustained spread of infection has been consistent in these groups of young people for the past number of years. Ironically, against the backdrop of paltry public health HIV and Aids campaigns, it appears that effective combination therapy for both has worked to kill off the practice of safer sex.

Now that Aids is a chronic long-term manageable syndrome, the belief is that a magic-bullet cure exists. And ill-informed generations gamble with folly. Meanwhile, the virus seemingly continues to spread unhampered.

The World Health Organisation said that 2006 saw the biggest increase in new HIV infections among gay men since the start of data collection in 1986.

The rate has continued to increase annually, as it has for heterosexuals. HIV prevention is not prioritised in this country – and I defy anyone to show me evidence to the contrary.

Consequently, the budgets of Brendan Drumm (and his successors) will continue to sustain ongoing assaults down the line. HIV infection has not gone away. The fear of funding loss and perhaps inappropriate political strategies can often combine to silence disquiet.

At an Aids conference in Croke Park earlier this month, it was refreshing to hear the President call for a renewal of our commitment, vocation, discipline and politics to get this illness truly on the agenda. Silence may no longer equate to death.

But I agreed with Mary McAleese when she said that 'the rising diagnosis rates here in Ireland raise concerns about the effectiveness of the prevention message. They point up the need for that message to be preached relentlessly, without let-up'.

Will somebody ring the alarm bells out there in 'they'-land? And in 'us'-land too. Loudly, please. And right now. There's not a moment to waste.

28 November 2009

GOLF'S MASTER RACE

Patricia Davies

Let's get the adjectives out of the way first. Antediluvian. Incandescent. Insulting. Laughable. Will that do for a start? They may be long-ish but this being a family newspaper they're polite-ish. What I really want to say is that the judgment allowing Portmarnock Golf Club to continue to bar women from full membership is a load of ******** but I'm afraid that that will appear as a load of asterisks and that's not nearly as satisfying.

This is an emotive topic and, whatever about the long, convoluted, erudite legal discussions on the matter, the fact is that this week's Supreme Court decision finding in favour of Portmarnock stinks. It's outdated, mealy-mouthed and plain wrong.

Well, that's the initial reaction out of the way, the Sir Alex Ferguson jumping up and down in a temper tantrum on the sidelines bit before switching to suave, reasoned assessment mode in front of the cameras (depending on who the broadcaster is) and concluding that, on reflection, yes, all referees are unfit for purpose, ill-suited to the demands of modern football. Sounds as though they have quite a lot in common with some golf clubs.

Now for the confessions. I grew up in County Derry in a family so steeped in golf that I didn't realise until much, much later that this was a game that a lot of people thought I, as a female, wasn't really supposed to play. I'm a golfer of the traditional kind, brought up in the game so that its more arcane mores, like 'attending the pin' or 'addressing the ball' seem perfectly normal. The response is automatic, unquestioning, seeing nothing odd in the oddities because they're ingrained.

It used to be the same way with all the other stuff that golf got itself stuck with too, the endless list of petty don'ts, the never-ending stream of negatives that stops the game welcoming people as it should, the nonsense of no denims, no trainers, no shorts, no collars (no, that's wrong; golf, for some reason, is obsessed with collars, you have to have collars, don't get me started on collars), no blacks, no Jews, no Prods, no Papes, no dogs, no women. Shocking isn't it? Written down like that.

Just because something works perfectly well – if you're one of the master race – and that's the way that it has always been, it doesn't mean that's the way it's got to stay, or should stay.

Injustice, big and small, thrives on inertia, on people accepting the status quo and that's how places like Portmarnock get to remain Portmarnock when they should, now, in this day and age, be different. Not least for the simple reason that we know better although that's not the same as behaving better.

Portmarnock's problem is that it is, as one of the learned judges this week said, a national institution. It is a victim of its own success as keeper of one of the best golf courses in the world, not just in Ireland. It has become a national treasure, known and renowned throughout the world, a place of pilgrimage for golfers of every stripe. It matters how Portmarnock conducts its affairs. It should be setting a good example.

It is no longer just a golf club or a club for men – sorry, gentlemen – who wish to engage in the athletic activity of golf and want to drink in the sanctuary of a bar where the person behind it is the only member of the other monstrous regiment to darken its doors, or whatever it is we women do in such establishments.

It'll be something dark and menacing, that's for sure, nothing as prosaic as having a bit of a laugh at a bad joke or a ridiculous ruling over a pint of Guinness or a glass of wine.

This supposed national institution allows women to play the course; it even allows us to be associate members or members of the ladies' section or whatever the current gender-related designation is. That was probably designed to keep us quiet and lull us into a sense of false equality but it may in the end prove to be a crucial error of judgement because it means we're halfway in already, acknowledged at least as golfing beings of a sort.

Some clubs are firmer and use different tactics, often keeping women at bay by the simple expedient of not letting them through the front door, literally.

Royal Troon, on the Ayrshire coast of Scotland, for instance, has a nice revolving door and not so long ago the then editor of *Golf Monthly* magazine and the then golf correspondent of the *Daily Telegraph* swirled in through it and swiftly swirled out again, ejected because, although invited to play, they were women and unworthy and had to use a special entrance, a tatty, undistinguished, unwelcoming bog standard door, complete with security buttons, down a dark alley.

No wonder Vivien Saunders, a tireless campaigner for golfing equality, wanted the Queen to make the place plain old 'Troon' again.

Saunders, incidentally, got so tired of beating her admittedly hard head against the bastions that she bought herself her own club for her fortieth birthday. That is not an option open to many of us but what really upsets me about this whole kerfuffle is that it gives golf, at base the most inclusive of sports, suitable for everyone from toddlers to totterers, such a bad name.

It is naturally woman friendly: there's no heavy lifting, no bone-crunching tackling, and brute strength, while no disadvantage, is not a prerequisite for launching the ball a reasonable distance.

The fairways should be swarming with women of all shapes and stages swinging away with a will, revelling in one of the world's timeless sports.

Instead, in practice, it's the men who dominate, inside and outside the clubhouse and in too many places the game is still seen as a stubborn citadel of male chauvinism. Whatever the rights and wrongs of the Supreme Court decision over Portmarnock, it has helped underwrite that sorry state of affairs. It is a bit depressing that we golfing women seem to have made so little progress in the last hundred years or more that so many men seem to be surprised that we exist at all, that we have to expend so much energy fighting our corner and justifying our existence.

Still, the price of freedom is eternal vigilance and the Portmarnock Pronouncement is a salutary reminder that it's too early to be lolling around in our dressing gown and slippers assuming that the battle is won, that equality of opportunity and association is, for women, a given.

The encouraging news is that the case has thrown up some wonderful images, with Portmarnock's athletic gentlemen – and given that it's quite hard to find a good man these days, let alone a gentleman, isn't it great to know that there are 600-odd of them in a little corner of north Dublin? – aligning themselves with the likes of gay rugby clubs, strange bedfellows perhaps but there you are, life's like that. Weird and wonderful.

The full frontal assault of a court case may not be the best way to change old attitudes – people dig in behind their preconceived prejudices or principles and chunter about not being bullied, threatened or intimidated and freedom of this, that and the other – but trials are good for broadening the mind, especially when they create more questions than answers.

At some stage in the recent case, I believe that Bulgarian-only bridge clubs were also thrown into the legal mix. Why stop there? It's not specific enough, surely.

There could, in these days of the EU, adoption and IVF, be all sorts of odd Bulgars, some of them vulgar, some of them, perhaps, women, maybe even some men, some of them might have been adopted and not even speak Bulgarian.

Just what sort of Bulgar is allowed to play bridge? Do they have to be black, white, married, gay, miserable or merely like-minded? What if they're just downright unpleasant? So many questions, so many possible answers, so much manure. That's why lawyers love legislation, especially legislation that tries too hard to be all things to all people, to cover every nook and cranny of the human condition. It leads inevitably to litigation and litigation leads to lucre and, with luck, more litigation, and appeals – lots of appeals.

So the lawyers are happy and, so, in the end, I must confess, am I. Because when it comes down to it, this isn't about golf at all, it's about the battle of the sexes, a battle that is as old as mankind, a battle that will never end and a battle in which there will be, ultimately, only one winner.

So the next time I get a chance to play at the male-only bastions of Troon, Portmarnock, Muirfield or Augusta with Mr Justice Whoever, will I turn it down? You bet I won't. Having grown up playing Portstewart, Portrush and Castlerock, I'm a sucker for a great course and if the devil has all the best ones, I'll trust my soul to take its chances. Besides, you don't win many battles sulking in your tent.

7 November 2009

MEDIOCRITY RULES: *X FACTOR* OR *STRICTLY COME DANCING*?

Mark Dooley

I do not want to suggest that everything we witness on *X Factor* is devoid of talent. It isn't. Indeed, over the years, viewers have been treated to flashes of brilliance which flickered brightly for a while before losing their flame.

Today, however, the spectacle revolves around Irish twins John and Edward Grimes, or Jedward as they have been christened by their fans. I cannot add anything more to all that has been written about the Grimes brothers.

What I can say, however, is that this frenzy at their so-called 'success' proves that *X Factor* now finds itself mired in mediocrity. It also signals that we have drifted into a cultural stupor from which it will be difficult to escape.

I know some will say that I am wildly exaggerating and that *X Factor* is just harmless entertainment. There are others who will feel that such shows have brought equality to the arts, thus bridging the 'elitist' gap between high and low culture. Art, they will say, is a matter of personal taste, a sphere from which judgement should be absent.

Swallowing those criticisms would be less difficult if I did not believe that human beings were capable of far more than is dreamt of by Simon Cowell.

The real problem, as I see it, is that in the absence of real culture, this and other shows are polluting young minds with fake culture. Fake because it ignores the great artistic precedents of the past against which genuine talent and achievement must be judged.

This means that culture relies upon judgement and criticism, for without it we could not distinguish the mediocre from the masterpiece. Now there is, of course, plenty of criticism on *X Factor*. It is, however, of a callous kind, in which the looks and personality of the contestant are subject to withering disparagement. But what else can you expect from a show that is a product of the pop age? I say pop age rather than pop culture because I don't believe there can be such a thing as popular culture.

Yes, we are saturated with pop music and pop art, but to brand them as culture is simply a corruption.

The word 'culture' stems from the word 'cult'. In so doing, it refers to that original act of settlement when people first gathered on a spot of land and made it their own. They 'cultivated' it, as it were, and they did so through signs and artefacts that symbolised their eternal yearnings.

Culture is, therefore, intrinsically bound up with the religious aspirations of a tribe. More than that, it gives a community its political and social identity. Communities are formed and sustained, in other words, by virtue of their symbols, songs, totems and traditions.

The great anthropologist Claude Lévi-Strauss who died last week aged 100, suggested that our contemporary totems are but more advanced versions of their primitive counterparts.

There was a time when we worshipped totem poles as an expression of our common identity. We still do, of course. Only now such worship takes the form of pledging allegiance to the flag, the constitution or the motherland.

When observed thus, we see that national and political identity is less defined by boundaries and borders, for these are not the things that fundamentally tie a people together. Rather, it is their common culture, in the form of their literature, music and art, which serves to consolidate a community or a country.

Think, for example, of the way in which people of all ages and social classes used to recite reams of poetry, sing traditional folk songs, play an instrument and dance in formation.

For them, this was not merely a means of entertainment in the absence of satellite TV. It was nothing less than a ceremonial endorsement of who they were as a people.

That is why those old cultural rituals usually concluded with a rendition of the national anthem. No matter how intoxicated, people spontaneously rose to their feet and sung every word with conviction. For them, this was a moment of collective thanksgiving for their land, their primal loves and sacred longings.

Put simply, culture is the means by which a person is inducted into a community.

By teaching children how to recite, sing and dance, we are not only teaching them invaluable skills. We are also, and much more importantly, giving them a sense of who they are and where they come from.

Now compare that to the so-called pop culture. The very essence of pop is to defy the common culture in favour of adolescent self-indulgence. It is a gesture of disobedience against home, settlement and communal belonging. Or, to paraphrase Bob Dylan, the devotee of pop has no direction home, is a complete unknown, a rolling stone.

Pop, in other words, promotes alienation and isolation. Hence it is more appropriate to label it a cult of personality.

The pop star stands before the fan as a God-like icon, his music a summons to sever all those ancient bonds of family and fraternity. For the lover of the classics, on the other hand, the performer must always be a slave to the music. That is why, within the hallowed precincts of the concert hall, the music eclipses those from whose instruments it soars. And it is a sacred sound listened to with awe and appreciation, not only for the talent that it reveals but also because it fosters harmony and social cohesion.

Imagine now that you had the choice of standing outside a rock venue or a classical concert hall at the end of an evening's performance. Where would you rather be? I would opt for the concert hall. Why? Because, despite the cultural nihilism we are currently experiencing, I still yearn for what real culture can give us socially, spiritually and morally. That is one reason for the resounding success of shows like *Strictly Come Dancing*, and why I suspect it will survive long after the likes of *X Factor*.

Formation dancing is a genuine skill that demands order, harmony and civility. Unlike the pop variant, which usually takes the form of a solitary hedonistic gyration, real dance invites us to move with others to music that must be listened to and understood. Such dancing is, in effect, a moral gesture in that it relies upon respect for shared customs and common values.

But it also expects its participants to be polished and polite, as evidenced in their cordial behaviour.

Strictly Come Dancing owes its popularity to the fact that it has fulfilled this deep cultural need. In their hearts, people sense that with the loss of real culture comes the loss of a social and spiritual legacy, without which we cannot truly function as human beings. And so they look at *Strictly*, not simply as a Saturday night spectacle, but as a reminder of the wonderful resources which culture contains for self-improvement.

This also helps explain why there is such renewed interest in the works of Jane Austen, Charles Dickens and C. S. Lewis. It explains the success of period dramas such as *Cranford* and *The Tudors*. It is the reason why classical performers such as Katherine

Jenkins, Nicola Benedetti and the sublime boy group, Libera, are causing such a sensation.

Recently, I sat a couple of feet from Benedetti as she performed Tchaikovsky's *Violin Concerto in D Major* on her beloved Stradivarius. She is only twenty-two and yet she did so without a score or without once looking in the direction of her conductor.

Benedetti is a child of the pop age and yet she still chose to take the path less worn. Amid all the frenzy of *X Factor* and *American Idol*, people like her demonstrate that we need not forsake our cultural roots in order to fit in. Indeed, we need only tap the great artistic touchstones to find that they are timeless, and that with a bit of effort they too can be ours.

All this is by way of trying to convince you that should you feel the need to watch TV tonight, please opt for *Strictly Come Dancing* over *X Factor*.

Better still, unplug the TV, gently caress some nice claret, and listen to Benedetti as she takes you to heaven with Vaughan Williams's *The Lark Ascending*. Believe me, you won't ever want to come back.

14 November 2009

DECEMBER

TIME TO MAKE SACRIFICES

Maryalicia Post

There was a news item in *The New York Times* the other day.

'To buy children's gifts, mothers do without.' And what's new about that? I asked myself. But then I'm from a generation where that would have gone without saying.

As for which generation is that, I'm sure there have been more than a couple. But in my case, it's the one where I was a child in Brooklyn during the 'Great Depression' as it's being called now. (Soon, maybe, like the 'Great War' which later became WWI, it will become GDI.)

So far, the only thing that seems familiar this time around is the delay in calling this a recession. Then, too, it was a long while before they put a name on it. Years later, leafing through a collection of *Time* magazines I found in the attic, I chased in vain through 1930 and 1931 for the word 'depression'. It wasn't there. It was just a time of things changing, like leaves falling off a tree.

But back to the mother who told the *New York Times* reporter that she was going without a pair of designer jeans she 'would have loved' in order to buy a mini walk-in kitchen for her daughter plus a pile of other gifts. And that's because she wants the child to look back and see that 'even though they were bad times, my mom was still able to give me stuff'.

Were we worse off back when a single modest Christmas

present was all we expected (and our mothers did without something to make even that possible)? I'd like to say 'yes' but have to admit that we didn't expect so much. We had no TV adverts driving our desires on. That's one problem parents didn't face in the good old Depression days.

Of course, we knew the children of film stars got miniature automobiles to drive and giant plush giraffes and dolls with real fur coats. FAO Schwarz, near Central Park, was one place they bought them. My mother sometimes took my sister and me there, as if it were a toy museum, just to look at the cabinets of dolls, the zoos of cuddly toys.

She thought we'd enjoy this but it wasn't fun at all and I can't recommend it as an outing. We couldn't help but notice the price tags and the attendant salespeople, or avoid knowing these wondrous things were for sale.

But we also knew we couldn't have them. Any more than our mother could move in to one of the vacant houses she and her friend visited on Saturdays, with us in tow.

That was called 'house hunting'. Many empty houses had signs outside saying 'Viewing Today' and we'd trail from one to the other, with my mother and her friend saying things like, 'No cross ventilation!' Or, 'Where would you even PUT a couch? No wall space.' Actually we didn't even own a couch. We had a table and chairs in the kitchen and the sitting room was totally empty except at Christmas when the tree, which arrived as if by magic on Christmas Eve after we were in bed, stood in the middle of it. In the early morning we found it glowing in lonely splendour on our gifts – one gift each from our parents (a doll, a big pencil case or a book) and a few parcels from Santa, who seemed obsessed with cold weather as he tended to leave a knitted hat, a scarf and matching gloves, or warm pyjamas.

We did learn something from the hands-off toy shop and the

house hunt though; it was the difference between wanting something and needing it. We might want a great plush lion and mother might want a sunny house with cross ventilation and good wall space for a couch, but we knew we didn't need them, just wanted them. We could – and did – live with that.

Were we happy? In fact, were we happier? There was a pleasant kind of solidarity in being part of the family – mucking in, feeling important, helping it stay afloat. Those were the summers of the lemonade stands and the years of the paper rounds and turning in much-read books at the second-hand shop for more books.

There's a lot to be said for being part of the solution instead of being the problem. There's a lot to be said for being positively involved. When I heard my mother remark to my father that she'd had only one new dress in the past seven years (and that was a fact) I didn't have a stab of guilt about having a wardrobe full of clothes. I had my school uniform and some hand-me-downs for playing in. My father said our family motto was 'one for all and all for one' and we knew that what the family had, we shared, including being 'hard up'.

We didn't even feel particularly poor. Though many lost their jobs and were on relief, my father kept his job (he was a skilled mechanic) and although it changed from a day job to night job in 1931, we could still sometimes treat ourselves to sandwiches at Horn and Hardharts.

The way it worked was this: there was a wall full of little glass cages with food inside and you chose the product you wanted and put nickels in the slot until the door flew open and you claimed your purchase. I do remember feeling bad, though, for the people sitting at little tables making soup from free ketchup and the hot water that came out of a little spigot and was meant for making tea (for those who'd purchased a teabag).

But we were happy. Because we hadn't had PlayStations, we

never missed them. We played card games and board games on a 'bridge table' that collapsed if you kicked a leg of it by mistake. You think kids would have to be lured like wild creatures out of a tree before they'd sit down at a table and play Monopoly with their parents? You'd be surprised.

We didn't have many clothes. Never mattered to us kids anyway, as no one else had, either. One thing that did matter was your shoes. When the soles wore they were either 'half-soled' or you made cardboard layers to use as an insole. The cardboard soon got damp and you could always feel the shape of the hole on the ball of your foot. Far better for you if the money was available for 'half soles'. Then you would sit in one of those little booths in the shoemaker's shop, where a half-door shielded you from the view of other customers while the shoemaker went to work cutting away the half of the sole with the hole in it and replacing that with new leather. These were the days of 'while you wait' – shoes, hats, suits repaired, spectacles mended. Because, of course, you only had one of each.

Men who had to have their suits cleaned sat in little cubicles like a shower stall while the work was being done. The procedure was called having the suit 'sponged and pressed'. They would take off their trousers and jacket and pass them out to a person who stretched the garments out on an ironing board, pounced on each spot with a sponge, and scrubbed it clean. Then they would press the suit and great bursts of steam hissed out of the damp patches. We often took Daddy's suit in to be sponged and pressed while he slept, once he was on the night shift. I don't know what kind of a catastrophe would have required dry cleaning.

We had other pleasures. Perhaps the oddest was skating in a vacant apartment under the benign eye of the building watchman who'd let us in. I loved the satisfying click of the ball-bearing wheels on the parquet floors. And Saturday afternoons at the movies, in the company of all the kids in the neighbourhood, was a collective excitement worlds away from the isolation of a DVD watched alone in a bedroom.

Pleasures for us, yes, but what would the sophisticated children of today make of them? And anyway, where could they go? The world is now a smaller, scarier place with less freedom in it for all of us.

Now that the good times may be out of reach for a while we are all like the mother in *The New York Times*, wanting to shield the ones we love from a change in 'lifestyle'. But we have to cope with it just as generations ago coped in the Great Depression. Is it simplistic to think we can make up for the lack of a Wii with what is now called 'quality time'? (The time a parent spends with a child doing something they both enjoy. So rare now it is carefully labelled, like a specimen.) We could try it before saying it won't work. And we could be truthful with them: 'We have a lot less money this year. We have to plan together to make it go round,' and see if that doesn't feel better.

Could we put off both the mini walk-in kitchen extravaganza AND the designer jeans? Santa has a lot less money this year.

Could we explain to the kids, and to ourselves, the difference between 'want' and 'need'? Would they get it? Would we? It's worth a try. Recognising that there is simply no such thing as shoes 'to die for' or a 'must-have' handbag gives us a clearer view about what to worry about and what we can safely let go.

Being fully aware of the difference between 'needing something' and 'wanting something' makes you feel better, whatever your age. It's like finally going on a diet to lose that half stone you've always meant to shift – hard at first, but becoming easier and then finally, satisfying. And it can even make you happier.

6 December 2008

CHRISTMAS:
A TIME TO REJOICE IN THE FAMILY

Dermot Bolger

In January twenty years ago I asked a friend of mine in a flat in Dublin how Christmas had gone back home with his family in the country.

Each previous Christmas had been marred by a simmering feud between his two older brothers, but he assured me that this year had, 'in the main', passed off peacefully.

'What does "in the main" mean?' I asked. 'It means,' he replied, 'that my brothers were perfectly civil when they met, civil during the opening of presents, civil throughout the pre-dinner drinks and so civil that when they both inadvertently went to occupy the same chair at the dinner table each one stepped back and repeatedly insisted on the other one having the good chair until my eldest brother got so exhausted from so much civility that he picked up the chair and smashed it over my other brother's skull.'

People to whom I tell this story often find it oddly comforting, perhaps because it makes whatever stresses occur during their own family Christmases pale by comparison. I have lost touch with my friend but I suspect that his two older brothers still grumpily sit down together every year and that their children – and at this stage maybe even their grandchildren – all look towards the one good chair and hold their breath.

They sit down together because generally this is what families do at Christmas. Sometimes they argue, always they catch up, they reminisce, they remember absent relations, they evoke previous Christmases, they relive – through the wonder in their children's or grandchildren's eyes – the wonder of their own childhood Christmas mornings. They become aware of how time is passing, of how they have grown up or aged since last Christmas. They become aware, amid their diverse and busy lives, of the chain of familial memory that still binds them.

This is not true of all families or of all Christmases. For some it can be a time of fear: recalling Christmas Eve in County Limerick, the poet Michael Hartnett once wrote, 'In the pubs the men filled up with porter and in the homes the women filled up with apprehension.'

For others it can be a time of loneliness or else an occasion of chosen isolation, a declaration of their own independence. Some people who feel no wish to go home will stake their claim to be different by spending Christmas alone – not being lonely or obstinate or difficult but merely as an expression of the right to be themselves.

While many friends would have gladly hosted her, the great independent thinker and inspirer of others, Sheila Fitzgerald, regarded it as pure heaven to be outdoors birdwatching on the Wexford slobs on Christmas Day, even after she entered her ninetieth year, a tiny old woman in yellow oilskins that reflected in the winter sun like a burnished flame. Christmas is different for every family, because every family is linked by different Christmas memories. My main childhood Christmas memory is sad because four days before Christmas in 1969 I lost my mother. Yet such a tragedy only served to bring my family closer together and make Christmas more special for us because I had two older sisters and an older brother who went out of their way to look out for me and who look out for me still.

You always remain a kid brother. Last week my eldest sister phoned amid her Christmas shopping to ask what size I took in a golf shirt. I had to confess that I hadn't a clue but it is whatever size my big brother takes because I find that generally I still wind up wearing his.

Any sad memories of Christmas were transformed by those Christmases since I married, by the Christmas when my eldest son was just four weeks old, by Christmas mornings of waking to the excitement of children, by the magic each year conjured not out of thin air but – as is the case in so many households – conjured by my wife's hard work and careful planning.

My Christmas is also made to seem magical and privileged by the fact that for decades now my sister and brother-in-law have hosted a Christmas singsong that will not begin until after midnight and will not end until dawn. Their daughter will sing the same song that her grandmother sang every Christmas night when she was a central presence at those parties, the song that she sang when that annual Christmas family party was held in a different house, the song that she sang when she herself was a girl.

This never-ending party has serenaded new arrivals over the decades as new generations find their voice and take their place on the floor. There will be absences felt there this year, absences that will leave deep voids, absences that are irreplaceable, but the songs and the singing will go on – with new songs always being blended amid the old songs that have been carried from generation to generation.

This Christmas night my sons will produce their guitars (and a cheese grater and whisk) to sing songs that they themselves have written. Then there will be a call for silence as my father, now in his ninety-first year, will be coaxed to sing the songs that were his party pieces when he was a youth in Wexford town, the songs he sang before he ever took to sea. And while he sings 'Bantry Bay' his great-grandchildren will wander through that crowded living-room in their pyjamas, interested and disinterested, exhausted and exhilarated by the wonder of Christmas.

Beyond the walls of that house, across Dublin, across Ireland and in other countries where Irish people are gathered, there will be other songs and other parties, there will be long-distance phone calls and emails and text messages and cards from relations people have not seen in decades.

There will also be silences. This year in Donegal the playing of the great traditional fiddler James Byrne will not be heard. In America and Wexford the poet James Liddy will be missed. In Ireland the poet and raconteur Sydney Bernard Smith will be silent.

The memoirist and novelist Nuala O'Faolain will be mourned by her family, her friends and by people she never knew to whom she meant so much. People reading this will add their own names to the list of the recently departed as many families will have one less place setting at the table, one less card on the mantelpiece.

Yet there will be new arrivals too, new babies passed from hand to hand, new infants with their first awareness of Christmas, children who, for the first time in their lives, could not sleep on Christmas Eve with the excitement.

This will be the first Christmas that my sons will spend without sitting down with their other grandfather – my late father-in-law – but the sadness of his absence will be tempered by the arrival this Christmas for the first time of a new aunt home from Australia and two new cousins: all part of the continual absences and arrivals that form part of the story of any family.

People are born and die throughout the year but the rush of life is so fast that it is often only at Christmas we find time to reflect on what we have lost and gained, at how we have aged or our children have grown. At how precious and fleeting the gift of a childhood Christmas morning is and at how exhausting it can be for those grown-ups who work around the clock to make the magic of this day happen.

This Christmas thousands of families will sit together – those who regularly do so and those who rarely do so. They may sit in easy friendship or uncomfortable proximity. But they will sit, held by a necklace of Christmas memories.

Elsewhere snooker halls will be full of migrant workers, men gathered around poker machines, exploited waiters from some ethnic restaurants to whom Christmas Day and Stephen's Day are just days when they are not paid, when they earn no money to send home.

In Dublin's Mansion House there will be a babble of accents and tongues. In Tallaght and Clondalkin and Letterkenny and Clonmel parents will be telling tales of past Christmases in Latvia and Poland. There will be people settling down alone with meals for one and people setting out for walks on Howth Head and Rosslare Strand and Hook Head and Rosses Point.

There will be old couples alone and young couples dying to be alone. There will be toasts to absent friends and love expressed or old animosities set aside. There will be jokes about Irish ham and uneaten piles of Brussels sprouts and hopefully no chairs broken over people's skulls. There will be tears shed for absent friends.

There will be misgivings and rows but also rows made up or suspended for one day. There will be forgotten memories recounted, photo albums taken down from attics, children seeing their parents in a new light through stories about long distant Christmases, previous gatherings in those same rooms.

There will be a sense that this is who we are and this is how far we have come on our journey of life and that these people we sit down with – regularly or irregularly – are the people who know us inside out and, while nothing else is certain any longer in this very uncertain world, it is certain that if we survive another year then we will sit down together again to the same meal, the same stories and the same sense of being part of an ever-changing and yet forever constant family.

20 December 2008

HOW WE FED THE FOOD CRISIS

Richard Corrigan

Let's just pause a minute while the food industry frantically scrambles to get pig meat products back on the shelves and the State agencies congratulate themselves on their response to the contaminated pork crisis.

Let's just take a few moments to look at how we got here, how we have reached a stage where food is no longer food but a commodity; a debased, denatured, sometimes downright dangerous commodity.

We pay a very high price, so to speak, for cheap food. Factory farming is all about producing as much meat as possible, as quickly as possible and as inexpensively as possible. And such are the pressures that come with this industrialisation of farming that agriculture, despite EU support, is just another business. It's a business that finds it increasingly difficult to compete with products, especially chicken and pork, produced in low-cost economies and shipped thousands of miles to us.

The next time you see an unbelievable special offer – buy one and get one free – for supermarket chicken, for example, you can be sure it's the producer and not the retailer who is paying for it.

This is a race to the bottom. I would sooner turn vegetarian than eat pork or chicken from the factory farming system. Factory farming doesn't care about anything other than the bottom line. And real food, proper food with genuine flavour comes from people, from individuals, who care about a hell of a lot more than that.

It's very simple. If animals are happy and well looked-after, the meat is good. If the farmer is driven by a passion for quality and can take real pride in what he produces, the result has to be great food.

There are plenty of demoralised farmers out there. Despite the fact that agriculture still enjoys the kind of artificial supports that the rest of us in business can only dream of, it's getting harder and harder to make a living on the land. The emergence of the part-time farmer is truly a sign of the times. As is the way in which small farms are being absorbed into larger ones.

You can sense a kind of despair among farmers and in many ways it's easy to see what ails them.

They know that the current situation can't go on. Industrial agriculture will end up eating itself as the illogical conclusion is reached where food becomes so cheap it's almost free. And, of course, complete rubbish. Is it any wonder that so few children of farmers have any intention of working on the land?

And is it any wonder that there seems to be less and less pride in farming? Wouldn't it be wonderful if farmers could take even half as much pride in what they produce as they do in their local GAA clubs? Of course the GAA, at local level, is all about a sense of place. But despite all the talk of traceability, there's precious little sense of place about agricultural produce. Support your local farmer? How do you do that?

Even supporting Irish farmers in general is made very difficult by the EU labelling laws. Take chicken meat from Brazil, process it here in Ireland and it can be called Irish. This is a fine example of labelling serving the needs of the retailers while completely ignoring one of the prime concerns for consumers: where was this meat produced?

Times have changed. Myrtle Allen, one of the great heroes of Irish food, tells a story that underlines what has been lost.

When she opened Ballymaloe House in County Cork in the early 1960s as a restaurant, her first concern was to serve local food. She was particularly impressed with some farmhouse butter from just down the road and one day she met the brother of the woman who made it. She complimented him on the quality. 'Oh yes,' he said. 'That field always gave great butter.'

What I witnessed growing up in Ballivor, County Meath was, in effect, the last gasp of the real rural Ireland where people were self-reliant and where self-sufficiency, or something close to it, was a necessity, not an aspiration for people who are tired of the consumer society and want to go and start a new life on a smallholding in West Cork.

We had our own milk and my mother churned the butter. She made bread every day, brown and white. And some days there would be curranty bread too. There was never any question of buying bread from a shop. We didn't have the luxury of waste.

We grew all of our own vegetables and herbs and fruit; we kept geese and ducks, chickens and hens. In an old perforated zinc bath suspended in the river we kept live eels. And just like in rural France or Italy, the annual killing of the pig was a kind of festival for family and neighbours. All of this happened less than an hour's drive from central Dublin – and until comparatively recently. I'm middle-aged now and it formed a huge part of my early life.

We weren't educated about food but we knew a hell of a lot. That whole country cycle of farming, shooting, fishing, cooking, eating is what teaches you. It was a way of life that was going out of date even then. Our neighbours would have been eating Angel Delight and white sliced pan and rashers from plastic packets. That was the way forward.

But in some ways, the wheel comes full circle. Every time I head into the countryside, either here or in Britain, I keep meeting people with a whole new attitude of care and attention and sheer bloody determination to fight uphill battles that is a million miles away from factory production.

What is so happy and inspiring about the situation in Ireland is that it is not only us natives, but also immigrants who have settled here and brought their skills and their ethos of quality, who are laying down the DNA for a new generation of food producers. And I'm meeting more and more people who are rediscovering what attracted them to farming in the first place.

It's extraordinary how many high-flyers are swapping their stressed-out lifestyles for raising rare-breed pigs, hand-making chocolates, making cheese or baking artisan bread. What a change from making million-dollar deals to putting sourdough into a paper bag at the farmers' market down in Schull on a Sunday morning.

I can rant away with the best of them about the onward march of the supermarkets and the religious-like zeal of massive companies taking over everywhere. But all those cellophane alleys with so much wrapped food, no smells, no excitement, have really screwed things up and corrupted the way we think about food. We're all governed by shelf life and sell-by dates – which means that we are often buying old food, pushed to the end of its natural life with preservatives and technological packaging. This is why, when you open your bags and packets your salad leaves will wither and your meat will go off quickly. Fresh food doesn't do that. There is a great deal of sense in people saying to themselves that they don't want to spend €200 in the supermarket each week and instead of a trolley they take a basket and spend €100. Then they use the rest to spend on buying good meat from a local butcher or vegetables from the farmers' market. And maybe instead of buying chicken breasts wrapped in plastic they will buy a whole free-range organic chicken and make two or even three meals from it.

This is not an idealistic world that I'm talking about. I'm just saying that you can save yourself a lot of money and eat better by doing things properly in the old-fashioned way. Seek out good ingredients and learn to cook simply again. That's it.

I go to a huge amount of trouble to find artisan ham and bacon and when I cook it, it's like it comes from another planet. It's a totally different experience because it has been produced with respect. Respect for the consumer, for the animals, for the planet.

The crisis in the Irish pork industry is very telling. For a start, it makes a mockery of 'traceability' and it gives everyone pause for thought in terms of what goes into animal feed. And remember that we are what we eat.

Isn't it simply crazy that, thanks to food-safety regulations, you can't buy scallops in the shell any more? Or a dressed crab? And while we are being 'protected' by daft measures like these, we end up with toxins in our pig meat.

Food processing – that vast industry that adds so-called 'value', but in reality adds mainly water – made a bad situation worse. The minority of Irish pork that was contaminated was processed with a whole lot of pork that was not contaminated, which made the whole lot inedible.

This is what happens when the distance between producer and consumer is allowed to get too big. And there is plenty of room in that gap for middle-men who make inferior and frighteningly cheap food into inferior and vastly overpriced food.

Factory farming and the food processing industry has let us down. They have put us at risk. We need to reclaim our food, take control.

It's about respect for food. Pay the extra few shillings for organic and taste the difference. If we support local, artisan producers – forget about the politics and the elitism – we are regaining a sense of security about what we eat. The price of cheap food is simply too high.

13 December 2008

THE LEGACY OF CLERICAL ABUSE

Nell McCafferty

One night last May, when I was out campaigning for the election of Mannix Flynn to Dublin City Council, I had an experience that lasted just ten minutes but it is seared in the memory.

Two winos came racing across the road, waving newspapers at me. The Ryan Report into the institutional abuse of children had been published that morning.

'Now you know what happened to us,' one of the winos said to me. 'Now you know why we are the way we are.' They were laughing and joyful, exonerated at last. They waltzed with me on the footpath – a thing no wino had ever done before.

His mother had died thinking him a failure, one of them said, succumbing to remorse. She had never known he was abused. He could tell his father now at least, I foolishly suggested. The wino looked at me in astonishment.

'I can't wave this newspaper at him and say, "You know now Da, why I am this way." That would be saying, "You failed me, father. You failed my mother, you failed our family." I won't do that to him. Let him end his days in peace, blaming me. He's suffered enough. He blamed himself all his life, thinking he had reared us wrong.'

The wino had descended into drink, depression, madness, and

the gutter because of what had been done to him. He descended with his secret into agony and silence. 'I couldn't tell my mother. That would have been a nail in her holy hands, on top of what I had done to her and my father and the rest of them, disgracing the family on the street where they tried to rear me.'

There are similar examples of destroyed families throughout the Murphy Report. One file on a priest refers to the inability of the girl he raped to cope with sex during her subsequent marriage.

A victim of Ivan Payne talks of how upset his mother became when he reminded her, after Payne's conviction, that he had told her as a boy and she refused to believe that a Holy Man could do that. Holy, or reverend, is the title which the Catholic Church confers on priests.

They were robbed of their childhood, Diarmuid Martin said last week about the children who were raped by priests. He was wrong. The Murphy Report declared that entire families were robbed. 'He destroyed a family and destroyed the children of that family and every child since,' one mother is quoted.

There are many such comments, but to find them you'd have to read hundreds of pages to the very end. Meantime, suffice to quote the Limerick woman who recently asked that Bishop Murray be allowed to remain in office, in order to understand the cataclysmic effects on a family of the abuse of a child by a priest.

The woman's husband, Peter McCloskey, was raped as an altar boy. He killed himself after seeking and failing to get justice.

He was treated worse than a criminal, said the man's father and mother and sister and brother. The man's daughters and wife back Bishop Murray. There you have it again – a family destroyed and now riven.

What you do not have, and did not get from Bishop Murray in Limerick last weekend, was a reading in Mass of those sections of the Murphy Report which referred to him.

What parishioners got was a general apology from the bishop which did not refer specifically, not once, to what he had done wrong.

His failure of imagination about the extent of his abject wrong-doing is not far behind that of Dr Martin, who did not mention, in his nationally televised apology, the effect on family of rape by priests. One has to wonder how much and how deeply these 'Princes of the Church' talked to and listened to the people who were abused.

The reverend fathers did not just rob the crib and rape the child. They robbed mothers and fathers of their families. The abuse cascaded down from child to siblings to parents to subsequent partners.

And when they weren't abusing children, the Holy Men, abetted by the Vatican, banished unmarried pregnant women to Magdalen homes, and banished their babies to the institutions and orphanages where they faced physical, mental and sexual abuse.

Added together, the numbers of women and men, boys and girls, mothers and fathers thus destroyed amounts to several thousand since the foundation of this Republic. Whole generations became 'poor banished children of Eve', as the doleful prayer has it.

The prayers due to be said on Tuesday 8 December, the Feast of the Immaculate Conception, will be difficult to enunciate. The import of 'Hail Mary, full of grace' is freighted with agony. Archbishop Martin, for instance, is called 'His Grace'.

The Virgin Mary, he will be obliged to tell his parishioners, conceived a child without sin. That is to say, she did not have sexual intercourse. This gives an exact measure of the attitude of the Catholic Church to women who conceive in the traditional way. How many of the parishioners in the Pro-Cathedral were forced to conceive by priestly rape?

We will never know exactly, but we can use our imaginations. The Murphy Report referred only to a 'sample of abusive priests' and to only one section of Ireland. A trawl of files in Ireland would take at least a decade.

It is savagely ironic that the cribs due to be placed in Catholic churches next week will not feature a baby. The birth of Christ will be celebrated on 25 December by then placing a plastic baby in the crib. The empty space in the doleful days leading up to that date will be filled by the imagination in the wake of the Murphy Report, and its continuing reverberations.

Will any Holy Man place the Murphy Report in the empty space in the crib? Many parishioners will not have accessed that report on their computers and few will be able to make the trek to government buildings where the printed report is not even actually available.

The Murphy and Ryan reports would make salutary reading material in churches. Do priests dare face up to what they have done and what they have colluded in covering up?

Let nobody say that such reading material would spoil the spirit of Christmas. It was desecrated long ago. The Vatican files on abusive priests go back thousands of years, since Christian time began. The files are folders of horror. Oh come all ye faithful, in the name of Christ and His mother, and spend one hour with them reading of what was done in their name.

What was done was arguably blasphemous. Middlemen abolished an inconvenient God during the cover-up. In the words of the government last week, 'The Report leaves us in no doubt that clerical child sex abuse was covered up by the Archdiocese of Dublin and other Church authorities. The focus of those authorities was on the avoidance of scandal for the Church and the preservation of the good name, status and assets of the institution, rather than on the welfare of children.'

Or, one might add, on the welfare of their mothers and fathers and sisters and brothers.

It is worth noting here that the first person to take out insurance on priests was Archbishop Kevin MacNamara, who was promoted up from Kerry after leading successful campaigns against abortion during the referendum years of the 1980s. His worship of the fertilised egg did not lead to protection of the fruit of the womb. MacNamara kicked off his campaign in Kerry by saying Mass, at their invitation, for the Irish Medical Organisation at the start of their annual meeting.

MacNamara did not arrive in Dublin in a bubble. A prior visit to America, where the priestly rape of children was costing a fortune in damages, became a steep learning curve for him. He learned, above all, how to cover up priestly crime.

Other priests were similarly up to speed in excusing themselves. One Holy Man who seduced children in the swimming pool dismissed the accusations against him as mass hysteria, by referring to Len Bradshaw, an actor in *Coronation Street*, who had just been convicted of indecently assaulting the children to whom he had been giving swimming lessons.

One rapist priest targeted a boy and cultivated his parents by turning up at their home every night for tea and telly, then assaulted the child during a goodnight prayer session in his bedroom.

Most of the accused priests fought successfully to keep the right to say Mass. They must say Mass in private or when standing in for priests who have gone on holiday. The Dublin Archdiocese defends this practice. The Mass is a central sacrament of the Catholic faith. It beggars belief that on Christmas Day these guys will say, 'Hail Mary, full of grace … soul of Christ, sanctify me.'

Dr Martin will wear his big gold bishop's ring on that day, and a gold crucifix on a gold chain round his neck – he wore that jewellery last week when apologising to the children.

He will ask for prayers for 'His Holiness, the Pope', who also defends the right of abusive Holy Men to say Mass. 'Silent Night, Holy Night' promises to be a nightmare.

The government's contribution to this festering quagmire in

next week's Budget will be a cut in child benefit. Yet again, women are not to be trusted with money to spend on children.

'The most dangerous place in the world is in a woman's womb,' as one Bishop Cassidy said during MacNamara's campaign. Blighted will be the fruit of their wombs next week. Holy Mary, mother of God, pray for women on welfare, now and at the hour of baptism in the hands of a Holy Father.

Murphy reports that many of the known vile reverends were given relatively golden handshakes when leaving public ministry.

Funded still by the diocese, not one squalid priest or religious has been forced onto welfare or down among the winos in the streets – these damaged men and women to whom the reverend fathers denied a life of familial love and understanding.

And there's another dispensation that these abusers got – convicted priests are allowed to administer the last rites in an emergency. They are needed to supplement a shortfall in vocations. That last rite could well be a last grisly waltz in the street with a dead wino, a man that now, years later, they probably won't even recognise.

The angelic features of innocent youth were warped decades ago by the priests.

5 December 2009

FAIRYTALE OF NEW YORK

Dave Hannigan

A couple of weeks back, I happened to be in the downtown New York neighbourhood of Soho for a meeting. When it was over, my next appointment was two hours later on the Upper West Side.

With time to spare, I did the only logical thing. Eschewing the convenience of the subway, the expense of the yellow taxi, and the mystery of the bus service, I started walking.

I'd worked up a bit of a sweat from the journey through the city and when I arrived at my destination, I was asked how come I was so flushed in the cheeks. When I explained the nature of my stroll, there were gasps in the room.

If these people have grown too blasé about the wonders in their midst, I certainly haven't.

For me, the opportunity to walk this town is still a chance to trip back through evenings in the 1980s spent watching *Mickey Spillane's Mike Hammer* with my late father in Cork.

There is still something hypnotic about the streets of Manhattan, striding between the canyons of skyscrapers, inhaling the distinctive sights, sounds and smells. The cacophony of car horns, the fragrances of the city smorgasbord and the great ocean of people as oblivious to your presence as you are to theirs.

Given the season that was in it, there were even a few Salvation

Army Santas on the sidewalks, ringing their bells, their bright red suits a festive delight under a piercing blue winter sky.

How could this stuff ever get old? How many times do you have to do this before you stop picturing yourself in a movie? Soon it will be almost a decade since I moved to New York. Abe, the four-month-old boy we wheeled through JFK in a buggy that clammy July afternoon in the summer of 2000, will turn ten in a few weeks and speaks with a pronounced American accent.

Of course, he never sounds American to me until I'm home in Ireland. Then I'll be standing in a shop wondering who that loud kid with the New York twang is and, even more obviously, the New York attitude.

He has a swagger and a confidence that embarrasses and thrills me at the same time. He's a product of his environment, as much shaped by this place as I once was by Cork.

As a teenager back then, I remember reading newspaper reports of U2 playing Madison Square Garden and catching a glimpse of the live footage on the RTÉ News one evening. It all seemed impossibly glamorous and so far away. Four boys from Dublin selling out the most famous arena in the world, the hallowed venue where Muhammad Ali fought Joe Frazier.

The first time I walked through its doors I was a wide-eyed twenty-seven-year-old journalist trying to conceal my childish glee. Now I'm rearing a son who is so nonchalant he merely thinks of 'the garden' (his name for it) as a place where he goes to watch New York Knicks games a few times a year. No biggie.

The funny thing is, I was never one of those Irish kids who grew up nursing great ambitions to pursue the American dream.

Even when so many of my university friends entered lotteries for green cards and nervously prepped for awkward interviews at the US Embassy in Ballsbridge, the thought of actually moving here never seriously entered my head.

Then I met, fell in love with and married a New Yorker named Cathy Frost.

There was the usual clause in the pre-nup about us always having to live in Ireland but this was later declared null and void. Following lengthy deliberations, it was decreed that six years in Dublin was penance enough for any woman. Not much has happened since we got here – just the birth of another son, Charlie, a highly disputed election, the worst terrorist attack in the nation's history, two major wars, and the first black president.

An unforeseen consequence of all the tumult is that I have found myself becoming more and defensive about my adopted home. One day you think yourself a stranger in a strange land, marvelling at all the peculiarities of the natives, the next you are in heated arguments with Irish people where you find yourself justifying every American foreign policy initiative of the past fifty years.

I'm not sure exactly how that happens. I guess a fondness for the place seeps into your bones and you realise, for all its flaws, this ongoing, giant experiment in democracy is truly a sight to behold.

A nation of racists? How do you explain Barack Obama sweeping into office then? A nation of Christian fundamentalists? My kids attend state schools where all mention of religion is so strictly prohibited that even Hallowe'en parties must be described as harvest festivals. Not to mention the linguistic dexterity that has to surround everything to do with Christmas.

There are so many clichés about America and the longer you live here, the more you come to understand there's a smidgen of truth in all of them.

The one about New Yorkers being straight-talkers was at first unnerving but quickly became a refreshing antidote to the celebrated Irish tendency to cling to euphemisms.

In conversation here, nothing is off-limits, no subject too embarrassing to discuss frankly and life is far more entertaining as a result.

I've been at a dinner party where a sober woman offered a lengthy and a little too graphic description of the circumstances in which she and her husband conceived their children.

I've sat at a barbecue and listened to a patient recently released from a mental institution joke about the orderlies removing the ribbons off his flowers lest he commit suicide.

Just the other week, I met one of my son's friend's fathers at the deli. Somewhere after ordering roast chicken, he started telling me about the problems he caused earlier in his marriage by his relentless cheating.

That's New Yorkers for you. This sort of compulsive candour is linked to another trait that becomes more obvious over time.

Beneath the brash exterior, there is a sincerity to Americans that, though initially almost suspect, is one of their most endearing qualities. They really mean what they say.

When they ask how you are doing, it's a genuine enquiry, not merely the requirement of social ritual. When they offer to help, they do so hopeful that you will ask them to provide some assistance.

All the clichés about New York itself ring true too. Everybody has their own favourite places, the bagel store they swear by, that undiscovered gem of a restaurant they don't want to share with anybody but would still like to boast about and, of course, their own very special corner of Central Park, that perfect spot where they like to sit in quiet contemplation or just people-watch. Personally, I'll take a seat in Riverside Park on the banks of the broad, majestic Hudson.

Around about 70th Street, there's a promenade jutting out into the water, the perfect location for watching the world sail by. A modern successor to those historic piers downriver where generations of European settlers once docked. That those people stayed and made this country their home is evidenced by the most amazing soccer pitch just yards from this same walkway.

The field is tucked neatly into a parcel of land, partially beneath the highway, abutting the water and backdropped by gleaming skyscrapers. Old and new. America in microcosm.

These are only a few of the reasons why it has been so easy to fall in love with America in general – and New York in particular.

There are so many others that contribute to the fairytale of this amazing city.

Having four seasons to the year is a wonderful boon, made even better by the fact that between May and September flip-flops and shorts are the standard uniform.

When you are brought up shivering on the strands of West Cork, you never think you'll end up spending your summers baking on the beach, watching your boys cavorting on boogie boards, throwing surfer dude shapes like naturals. If I was in the water for the rest of my life, I wouldn't look as comfortable as they do every day. To the manner born.

Then again, I'm Irish and, even if Abe did take his first breath in Holles Street, my children are American. No matter how many decades I'm here, that won't change.

I won't take up my option of changing citizenship and I do live in morbid fear that the lads will eventually morph into the sort of crass Irish-Americans who tattoo 'Fightin' Irish' leprechauns on their arms.

To try to avoid this apocalyptic scenario, I've taken the difficult step of no longer trying to force feed them Irish history and culture, resisting the urge to drive them an hour to play Gaelic football with other children of the diaspora once a week. Best to let that stuff happen organically if it happens at all.

Nobody is saying New York is perfect. I could do without having to pay $1,200 a month in health insurance even if the calibre of care is always commensurate with the cost.

The rigorously-enforced legal drinking age of twenty-one means, scarily enough, that my kids are more likely to try pot than pilsner when they reach high school.

It freaks me out that the local supermarket has a freezer full of doggie ice cream (Frosty Paws!) right next to the Häagen-Dazs.

And of course, St Patrick's Day needs to be abolished before I end up doing something I regret to the drunken yahoos at the annual parade.

These are small enough crosses to bear and the latter is just one more reminder that I will always be a man with a foot in two countries. Neither quite here nor there.

This was brought home again just the other day. A sales rep from a local cemetery phoned, wondering if we were interested in buying a plot.

It's apparently never too soon to plan. We weren't in the market but it did force an uncomfortable kitchen table conversation about where, when the time comes, I want to be buried.

The country of my birth or the country of my death? It's not an easy question but one that will someday require an answer. Eventually. Many, many magical New York Christmases from now.

19 December 2009

WE WON'T BE FOOLED AGAIN

Dermot Bolger

The two great dangers preoccupying people on the eve of the millennium, if I correctly recall it a decade ago, were that the sky might fall on our heads and that the champagne might run out. The reason why the sky might fall on our heads, with all technological life grinding to a sudden halt, was because of the dreaded Millennium Bug.

Rumour had it that this malaise would cause all computers – originally programmed with space for just two digits to represent the year – to crash at midnight on New Year's Eve 1999, when two noughts would pop up, literally heralding the advent of year zero.

Civilised life, however, didn't end at midnight on 31 December 1999 when the dreaded noughts arrived. And yet, how appropriate that the Noughties began with a battle against the perceived danger of a pair of noughts appearing alone on a computer, because as the decade advanced, noughts were rarely let out in single pairs again. They appeared in public only in long sets of threes, spaced out by commas, especially when house prices and bankers' bonuses were involved.

It also seems appropriate that the decade began with a small group, working in a mysterious high-tech field that nobody else understood, making a fortune by panicking the public with a threat that didn't exist. Between alleged weapons of mass destruction in

Iraq, global investment managers playing pass-the-parcel with worthless bundles of sub-prime US mortgages and an alleged shortage of building land in Ireland, we spent most of the decade coerced into believing a succession of lies.

We were led to believe that unless our children got onto the property ladder as soon as possible, they would be left behind. As house prices soared by a ridiculously inflated 300 per cent in six years, we were led to believe that such a fantasy was sustainable, or that it would at least come with the softest of landings.

In retrospect, it was a complete fantasy, a scam like every other pyramid price bubble since a mania for tulips in Holland in the 1630s saw people panicked into buying bulbs that cost the price of a canal-side Amsterdam house.

We were never, of course, led to believe that negative equity would become the name of a townland of half-finished houses somewhere beyond Kinnegad. Perhaps the most negative thing we are left with as the decade closes, however, is a complete absence of trust. We had been coerced for years into believing in the power and the caring of the Church.

Gradually we came to understand that conservative forces within that Church still saw themselves as beyond the remit of ordinary law, more preoccupied with the preservation of what people once viewed as the most trusted institution in Ireland than with truth or justice or healing for its victims.

Of those, many could never have been harmed if indisputable evidence of past crimes had not been concealed.

There is little to be said in favour of Irish banks, but at least if they found that a branch manager was robbing customers in Clontarf they did not solve the problem by simply transferring him to Fairview.

Unfortunately, for every public apology, there was private foot-dragging and hard-nosed business haggling.

The sad consequence – and it is sad, because with the drift of all political parties to the centre in search of the middle-class swing vote, very often it is individual priests and nuns who wind up in part carrying the fight for marginalised communities – is that as the decade ends, the Church faces an almost impossible battle for credibility.

The endless revelations have left victims betrayed, along with dwindling congregations and decent priests and nuns who do tireless work.

And the lies didn't stop with the Church.

We also learned that many other once-esteemed professions such as hospital consultants and bankers could also not be trusted to regulate themselves, having at their core the primary instinct of self-preservation and an abhorrence of outside regulation.

One of my abiding memories of the past decade is of a minor banking official breaking down in sudden tears, talking to me about the pressure she was being put under to meet targets. We could say that we learned to understand the nature of corruption, but maybe the real lesson we learned was about human nature and how most people caught up in any system or institution have a natural propensity towards being cowed into conformity, generally being too focused on individual survival to see the bigger picture.

It may have been a decade of plenty, but it was also a decade of pressure and lack of personal responsibility.

Ireland remains a cold country for whistle-blowers. We like to think that we would have been the banker who blew the whistle, the priest who shouted stop, the medical consultant who risked odium and professional ostracism by saying that what another doctor did was wrong.

But in reality, most of the time, most of the people don't want to know.

Indeed, cases like the one in Listowel last week show that the cost of standing up can still remain as high now as at the start of the decade, that still, in this country, we don't want to be confronted by uncomfortable truths.

We learned in the Noughties that every Irish town would be changed by the uncertainties and difficulties of dealing with an influx of new faces, by tax-incentive holiday homes springing up like a form of acne, by the fact that three dozen languages can be spoken in a primary school playground without any plan on how such integration might work.

The end of this decade has been so catastrophic for breadwinners who have lost their jobs and pensioners who have seen their nest-eggs wiped out, that we tend now not to see the complete decade in perspective.

There were positives.

Who would have believed twenty years ago that it would have been possible for a working class suburb such as Dublin's Ballymun to possess a brilliant, state-of-the-art theatre like the one it now has in Axis?

The regeneration of Ballymun is far from complete and is still behind schedule. Christmas lights have been strung this year from the balconies of the one remaining isolated high-rise tower but the Noughties saw a genuine attempt by planners there to engage with an existing community in order to make life better.

Who also would have imagined back then, in this cynical age where professional sport is primarily a cutthroat business, the two-fold miracle of Croke Park?

Firstly, that it could construct Europe's fourth biggest stadium from an amateur sport essentially confined to one small country. And secondly, that it would open its doors to soccer and rugby in a way that increased the GAA's prestige and stature both here and abroad.

It was, of course, financially astute but it also displayed a new, confident maturity.

And the positives extend further. People mention Jedward as a symbol of our time, as if the hollowness of an obsession with celebrity culture could be laid at the door of two teenage boys. In reality, however, the past decade was a good era for Irish music, with acts from Jape to Lisa Hannigan and Duke Special to Oppenheimer opening up interesting territory.

We may not have turned out to be the sharp global investors that we purported to be, but in those areas where we do things well in this country – like literature – we continued to excel.

Who would have thought that one generation of writers would come of age so brilliantly with their award-winning and internationally acclaimed works of fiction – with Anne Enright's *The Gathering*, Colum McCann's *Let The Great World Spin*, Colm Tóibín's *Brooklyn*, Joseph O'Connor's *Star Of The Sea*, Sebastian Barry's *A Long, Long Way* and Hugo Hamilton's *The Speckled People*.

The hardest part of writing is to learn to believe in yourself. Maybe the hardest thing we need to do as we start this new decade is to start believing in ourselves again. We leave this decade angrier and poorer than a few years ago but we leave it open-eyed, wiser than we were before.

We have learned to be less trusting. Our challenge now is to open ourselves up to new ways of thinking and reinvention, new ways of planning our way out of crisis.

Have we lost our national character? No, I don't think so. A nation cannot 'lose' its character because such character is never fixed, never perfectly definable but rather a fluid, evolving force.

Let's not box ourselves in. Ireland's character has changed, certainly, but that's no betrayal. The world has changed. We need to move on, but we must not forget and so we need to apportion blame. It is only by being angry and by understanding exactly how we were coerced by all those lies that we will learn.

Only then will we not be fooled again.

26 December 2009

CONTRIBUTORS' BIOGRAPHIES

DERMOT BOLGER was born in Dublin in 1959 and is one of Ireland's best-known writers. His ten novels include *The Journey Home*, *The Family on Paradise Pier* and *New Town Soul*, his recent debut for young adults. His award-winning plays have been staged in many countries. He is a poet, and he has edited many anthologies, including *The Picador Book of Contemporary Irish Fiction*. (See pp. 141, 208, 340, 363)

RICHARD CORRIGAN grew up on a small farm in County Meath and went on to become one of our most celebrated chefs. He owns and runs Corrigan's of Mayfair and Bentley's Oyster Bar, both in London's West End. He is the author of *The Clatter of Forks and Spoons*. (See p. 346)

PETER CUNNINGHAM is best known as the author of the Monument novels. Set in the fictional landscape of Waterford, these stories are about Irish people and their lives and loves from the late nineteenth century to the present day. His most recent novel, *Capital Sins*, is set during the last year of the Celtic Tiger. (See pp. 3, 69, 171)

PATRICIA DAVIES was born in Belfast, raised in Portstewart, and now lives in landlocked Birmingham. She has been writing about golf for more than thirty years and has co-authored *Beyond the Fairways* and *Teach Yourself Golf* with her late husband, Dai. (See p. 323)

ROSLYN DEE is Associate Editor of the *Irish Daily Mail* and the *Irish Mail on Sunday*, and is the commissioning editor of The Saturday Essay. An award-winning travel writer and broadcaster, she is joint author with her photographer husband, Gerry Sandford, of *A Sense of Place: Irish Lives, Irish Landscapes*. (See pp. 24, 238)

EAMON DELANEY is a Dublin-based writer. He is the author of *An Accidental Diplomat, The Casting of Mr O'Shaughnessy*, and, most recently, *Breaking the Mould: a Story of Art and Ireland*. (See p. 187)

MARK DOOLEY is a philosopher who has lectured at University College Dublin and NUI Maynooth. In 2003 he began writing for the *Sunday Independent*, before moving to the *Irish Daily Mail* in 2006. His books include an acclaimed biography of conservative philosopher Roger Scruton, and the forthcoming *Why Be A Catholic?* (See pp. 45, 148, 232, 253, 328)

TOM DOORLEY is a food and wine writer and broadcaster based in County Cork, and restaurant critic with the *Irish Daily Mail*. He started his media career as newsreader on a Dublin pirate radio station while a student at Trinity College Dublin. His latest book, *Eating for Ireland*, is published by Liberties Press. (See p. 105)

THEO DORGAN is a poet, prose writer and editor. His most recent publications are *Greek*, a collection of poems from Dedalus Press, and, from New Island, *Time on The Ocean: A Voyage from Cape Horn to Cape Town*, both published in 2010. (See p. 301)

PAUL DRURY is Managing Editor of the *Irish Daily Mail* and the *Irish Mail on Sunday*. A Dublin native, he has worked as a newspaper journalist for more than thirty years and has edited the *Irish Daily Star*, the *Evening Herald* and *Ireland on Sunday*. (See pp. 134, 312)

DAVE HANNIGAN is a Cork-born journalist who now lives in Rocky Point, New York, from where he contributes to several Irish publications, including the *Irish Daily Mail*. Author of four non-fiction books, his first children's novel, *Kicking On*, has just been published. (See pp. 33, 161, 259, 357)

SHAY HEALY is a broadcaster, writer and musician. His song, 'What's Another Year', won the 1980 Eurovision Song Contest. His musical, *The Wiremen*, was staged at Dublin's Gaiety Theatre in 2006. He is the author of two novels, *The Stunt* and *Green Card Blue*. His favourite occupation is writing his 'Cat Among the Pigeons' column every Saturday in the *Irish Daily Mail*. (See pp. 19, 219)

TOM INGLIS is a professor of sociology in UCD. He writes mostly about the influence of the Catholic Church, the media, sexuality and globalisation on Irish culture and society. His most recent book was *Global Ireland: Same Difference*. (See p. 244)

KATE KERRIGAN is author of three novels, *Recipes for a Perfect Marriage*, *The Miracle of Grace* and *Ellis Island*, which was selected as a TV Bookclub Summer Read 2010. She lives in the fishing village of Killala, County Mayo with her husband and two sons. (See pp. 98, 289)

DECLAN KIBERD is Professor of Anglo-Irish Literature at UCD. Among his books are *Inventing Ireland*, *Irish Classics* and *Ulysses and Us: The Art of Everyday Living*. (See p. 176)

MARK LITTLE is the founder of the social media news agency, Storyful.com. He is a former presenter of RTÉ's *Prime Time* and an award-winning foreign correspondent. He has written several books about global affairs and presented documentary series on

Islam and US politics. His latest book, *The New America and the Rise of the Obama Generation*, examines the changes which led to the election of Barack Obama. He lives in Dublin with his wife and two children. (See pp. 63, 182, 279)

FIONA LOONEY is a writer and broadcaster. As well as weekly columns in the *Irish Daily Mail* and the *Irish Mail on Sunday*, she has written two hit plays, *Dandelions* and *October*, and is currently working on two more. (See pp. 55, 86)

NELL McCAFFERTY is an award-winning journalist, television and radio commentator from Derry. She is a founder member of the Irishwomen's Liberation Movement, and was involved in the civil rights campaign in Northern Ireland. Her nine books include four collections of newspaper columns and the story of the Kerry babies case, *A Woman to Blame*. She has appeared in the *Vagina Monologues*, written two plays, and been conferred with an honorary Doctor of Literature by the UK's Stafford University. Her bestselling autobiography, *Nell*, was published by Penguin in 2004. (See pp. 227, 351)

COLUM McCANN was born in Dublin and lives in New York. He is the author of five novels and two collections of stories. His short film, *Everything in This Country Must*, was nominated for an Oscar in 2005, and his bestselling novel, *Let the Great World Spin*, won the National Book Award in 2009–10. (See pp. 193, 306)

SUSAN McKAY is an award-winning journalist from Derry whose books include *Sophia's Story*, *Northern Protestants: An Unsettled People* and *Bear in Mind These Dead*, a study of the legacy of the Northern conflict for those bereaved. She is currently the chief executive of the National Women's Council of Ireland. (See p. 80)